The
SPICE
MAKER'S
SECRET

BOOKS BY RENITA D'SILVA

Monsoon Memories
The Forgotten Daughter
The Stolen Girl
A Sister's Promise
A Mother's Secret
A Daughter's Courage
Beneath an Indian Sky
The Girl in the Painting
The Orphan's Gift
The War Child

The
SPICE
MAKER'S
SECRET

RENITA D'SILVA

bookouture

Published by Bookouture in 2024

An imprint of Storyfire Ltd.
Carmelite House
50 Victoria Embankment
London EC4Y 0DZ

www.bookouture.com

ISBN: 978-1-80019-803-6
eBook ISBN: 978-1-80019-802-9

For Louise Swain.
Spirited. Kind. Generous. Warm. Forgiving.
A brilliant storyteller.
Who on a cold and wet day gave a very pregnant colleague a lift, thus instigating a friendship that has changed my life.
Who took me under her wing and guided me when I needed guidance the most.
Without whose encouragement I wouldn't be where I am now.
I thank you, wonderful friend, from the bottom of my heart.

PROLOGUE

Gently kissing her child, Bindu picks up the kajal pot and draws a round tikka (black dot) on the babe's forehead, behind each ear and on each cherubic cheek.

'This will protect you, even when I'm not there,' she whispers, trying and failing to hold back the tears that smudge the sooty kajal on her child's cheeks.

And then, Bindu hugs her little one to her heart, whispering endearments and her wishes for her child.

She commits her baby's face, which is already stamped in her heart, to memory, the feel of her child in her arms.

The kajal will keep you safe, it will keep you from harm. I love you, my heart, now and always.

CHAPTER 1

BINDU

1924

SURYANAGAR, INDIA

Bindu loved to hear the story of her birth, even though she knew she should feel sad that her mother had died while she was being born. But her mother was an abstract, sainted figure whom Bindu had never met, and she had Ajji, who held her close, kissing the top of her head with its lucky double crown. Ajji smelling of onions and spices and sweat and love; Ajji who was her world.

At four years old, Bindu was absolutely convinced that Ajji would protect her from danger, would guard her with her life, that Ajji would live forever. These tragedies she spoke of seemed far removed from Bindu's daily life, here in the village, sitting snug in her grandmother's lap in their little courtyard, birds singing in the trees above them, the humid air that caressed Bindu's cheeks flavoured with the scent of Chinnakka's bubbling congee. No harm would come to her when Ajji held her like this, Ajji's rapt audience, looking at Bindu, miracle child, with awe.

No matter how often she heard this story, Bindu never tired of it. Yes, Ajji would be tearful at times during its narration, but it had a happy ending. *Bindu* was the happy ending, sitting right there with a tumbler of warm milk sweetened with jaggery – the milk from Chinnakka's goat, freshly squeezed that morning (obtained in exchange for Ajji's special *sheera* semolina pudding, which Chinnakka, who had a sweet tooth, could never resist).

'Well,' Ajji would declare, winking fondly at Bindu, when she proudly boasted about her beloved grandchild to all and sundry, 'I don't know what I'd do without this little one after...' Her voice would tremble ominously at this point and she would pause, seemingly unable to continue. Bindu would lay her soft cheek against Ajji's weathered one, offering comfort, knowing she was talking about Bindu's parents, whom Bindu never knew.

Her father, Bindu was told – not only by Ajji but by everyone in the village – a coconut picker, had died in an unfortunate accident while his wife was pregnant with Bindu.

'A freak storm came out of nowhere,' they would cry, the women clucking sadly and wiping their eyes, the men looking up to the heavens, shaking their heads at the gods for their incomprehensible, whimsical games, played at the cost of human lives, 'winds like you'd never seen. Whipped nature into a whirling frenzy. Lightning struck the tree your father was on. A sitting target, poor soul. Dead before he touched the ground...'

'And your mother,' the village women would sob, slapping their bosoms with their fists, 'breathed her last giving birth to you. The wise woman helping with the labour tried her best. But what to do? Your bad—'

And at this, Ajji would swoop in, gathering Bindu tight into the protective circle of her arms, barking at whoever was speaking, interrupting them rudely, 'My Bindu is *lucky*, you hear? To have survived. She could have died too and where would I be then? What fate to outlive my family! The gods saw fit to bless me with only one child, my beloved son. And then, oh Shiva, both my husband and son, cruelly snatched in their prime. Daughter-in-law as well. But this one' – planting kisses on each of Bindu's cheeks – 'She's lucky. Look...'

And Ajji would gently bend Bindu's head, to show the two whorls of hair sprouting from a double crown. '*So* lucky,' Ajji would intone. Then, her gaze far away, looking beyond the fields to something only she could see: 'The wise woman was sure this little one was dead after that difficult birth. No crying, nothing, when pulled out of her poor dead mother's womb. Blue all over.' Ajji would shudder and Bindu, snug in her grandmother's embrace, would feel her upset all down her own body. She would look at her arms, the burnished brown of cumin seeds, and try to imagine them blue. She could not picture it, even when she scrunched up her face in concentration, eyes shut tight against distractions. 'Oh, I thought she was gone all right,' Ajji would cry, voice wobbling, all the while cradling Bindu tight.

'So,' the listeners would prompt, 'you thought this babe here was dead too.'

'I did. I was hitting my head, my chest and lamenting my fate. And then...'

'And then?' The audience would inch closer to Ajji and Bindu and Dumdee would come bounding up, his nose tickling Bindu's side, making her laugh.

Bindu's mirth made Ajji chuckle and caused her chest to rumble in warning.

Ajji cleared her throat, turned to the listeners, her face serious, all hint of laughter gone. 'So, there was this infant, floppy and blue, no sign of life, mother lying dead – sorry, Bindu, my heart.'

Bindu buried her face in her grandmother's chest, feeling all weepy, not because of her mother – death was a concept she couldn't quite fathom and she didn't miss her mother, for she had never known her – but because her grandmother's voice shook dangerously.

She felt Ajji take a deep, bolstering breath.

'And the wise woman,' Ajji said, her voice all outrage, 'suddenly grabs the child by its tiny feet and dangles it upside down!'

The audience gasped.

Bindu, huddled in Ajji's spice-scented embrace, shivered, despite the hot, grit-flavoured breeze stroking her face.

'"What are you *doing?*" I cried.'

'Rightly so,' an old lady, all her teeth missing, mumbled from the agog group surrounding them. Everyone else nodded assent.

'But the wise woman didn't reply, just shook the child vigorously.'

Ajji's grasp on Bindu tightened.

'Oh, the poor dear,' cried the rapidly swelling crowd – as by now several people, neighbours and passers-by, had gathered under the banana trees to hear the tale.

'I was beside myself with shock and upset,' Ajji was saying, 'as you can well imagine. I was just gathering up my wits when...' She paused dramatically.

Bindu looked at Ajji, breathless with anticipation, despite having heard this story many times. The audience all did the same. Even Chinnakka's hens, forever pecking in the mud hoping for a stray seed or two, were quiet. The eavesdropping air was still and waiting, impatiently, for Ajji's reveal.

'When?' nudged the toothless old woman.

'There was a cry. A little kittenish mewl.'

Everyone's attention fixed upon Ajji.

'The baby was no longer blue. She was red and thrashing, protesting angrily.'

And now Ajji laughed, even as her chest growled, provoking a coughing fit. When she regained her breath, she beamed at the crowd as she stroked her granddaughter, perched on her lap, triumphantly delivering her coda. 'This here, my lucky, blessed, double-crowned Bindu.'

Now, in their courtyard, the air flavoured with dust and spiced with chillies and tamarind laid out to dry on coconut-frond mats in full glare of the blistering sun, four-year-old Bindu clamps her lips and shakes her head as Ajji tries to feed her watery gruel that tastes of nothing at all.

'*Aiyyo*, what are you making that face for? Too bland, is it?' Ajji clucks, shaking her head, her chest, against which Bindu rests, moving up and down, even as it rattles with that phlegmy growl that accompanies Ajji's every utterance.

Ajji, with Bindu on her lap, sits in the shade of the mango, guava, banana and coconut trees in their courtyard. But even from here, the potency of the chilli seeds and the tart sweetness of the tamarind tickles Bindu's nose, inciting a sneeze even as it makes her mouth water, intensifying the disappointment of the zestless congee porridge Ajji is feeding her.

Ajji chuckles at her expression and both Bindu and Dumdee watch her anxiously.

'You were the one to name him, you know,' Ajji says, smiling fondly at the tableau of Bindu and Dumdee in front of her. 'He arrived in the courtyard, an emaciated stray puppy howling piteously, just as you were learning to speak. I was going to shoo him away, but you toddled up to him, threw your arms round him and said, clear as anything, "Dumdee". And that was that. He stopped howling instantly and was your shadow from then on, only answering to Dumdee, so Dumdee he became. You would manhandle him, climb on him, pull at his ears and he meekly accepted everything you inflicted upon him. What a pair!' Ajji tutting, her gaze full of love.

Dumdee's usually wagging tail is tucked floppily between his hind legs, his liquid eyes soft with worry, for, sure enough, Ajji's chuckling morphs into hacking coughs that rock her fragile body, like their neighbour Rajanna shakes Chinnakka, his poor wife, when he's had too much to drink.

Bindu has yelled, 'Stop,' and tried to intervene, Dumdee whining beside her, picking up on her pain, but Ajji always holds her back.

'You're a kind girl, my heart, but you must be careful. If we intervene, he might do that to us too and neither of us is strong enough to withstand it.'

'But...'

'He's senseless when he's drunk.'

'I drink too, but I'm not senseless,' Bindu offered with her innocent four-year-old logic.

Ajji smiled gently, bent down to kiss her. She smelled of love and comfort, glazed onions and sweat. 'You drink goat's milk, which is good for you. Rajanna drinks toddy, which is very bad indeed.'

'How?'

'It turns people mad if they drink too much of it. It's potent liquor. It's brewed from palm trees...'

'Oh!' Bindu gazed at the coconut tree they were sitting under in wonder. It looked harmless, but...

'You've seen those mud pots attached to the tree trunks, haven't you?'

Bindu nodded. Yes, she had.

'The sap from the tree is collected in those pots and toddy brewed from it,' Ajji explained patiently. Ajji always took the time to answer Bindu's every question. She never talked down to her or dismissed her queries, not once, no matter how busy she was. 'Girijamma served it when we visited that time, remember, and you were curious?'

And Bindu recalled then the bubbling brew, which had smelled of fruits gone bad, sickeningly sweet and pungent, flies buzzing madly around it. Girijamma had distributed a tumbler each to Ajji and her other friends, dipping each tumbler right into the brew and handing the frothy liquid out: 'Drink up while the men are away. What they don't know won't hurt them.'

Bindu had been intrigued by this strange concoction. She had hoped Ajji would give her a sip to taste, like she did her tea. But...

'Not this, my heart. This is for adults only.'

Bindu had sulked. She had whined, but Ajji had remained firm.

The memory fresh in her mind, Bindu ruminated on Ajji's words, *It turns people mad if they drink too much of it.* She realised, in hindsight, that all of the women had been overly giggly and Ajji had swayed like a banana tree in the wind when they had walked home after. In fact, Ajji had been floppy all evening – Dumdee had regarded her suspiciously, emitting little barks of concern – and Ajji had fallen asleep in the courtyard when she was meant to be shelling coconuts.

'I will never drink toddy,' Bindu vowed, shaking her head vigorously, so her pigtails that her grandmother had carefully plaited after oiling her hair that morning danced crazily, as if *they* were drunk.

'Good girl,' Ajji beamed, gently pinching Bindu's cheeks.

. . .

Now, Bindu and Dumdee watch with deepening concern as Ajji's hunched body is tormented by coughs, frightening the cackling crows and chittering bulbuls off the trees.

'Ajji, are you OK?' Bindu asks, needing reassurance.

When her coughing fit has subsided somewhat, Ajji takes several gasping breaths, smiling at Bindu and nodding between each one. 'I'm all right,' she finally manages.

And it is only then that Dumdee's tail starts wagging again and he resumes duties as guard dog, eyeing the parrot that has tentatively dared alight near the drying chillies and tamarind. He emits a low, snarling growl and the parrot startles, flying away in a dust-spattered green gust of wings. The cat opens one eye from where she's snoozing on the mossy well surround and proceeds to lick her paws.

'My heart, I think it's time for your first cooking lesson,' Ajji says, clearing her throat and preparing to stand, hands on her knees as she gently eases Bindu off her lap. 'It's our livelihood, after all.'

'Livelihood?' Bindu scrunches up her nose.

'It is how we make money, live from day to day,' Ajji explains, cupping Bindu's face and kissing her nose. 'By selling, or most often bartering, the food I cook for things we need.'

'Bartering?'

'Exchanging. So, I cook something Chinnakka wants, say...'

'She likes your *sheera*.'

'Exactly, and she gives me the goat's milk that makes you grow big and strong. Similarly, when they have guests, the villagers bring me their vegetables and chickens and I make delicious curries so their guests are happy. In return, they give us things we need – the shopkeeper Dujanna gives us oil and flour and rice and lentils, for example... Do you understand?'

Bindu nods, her plaits dizzily cavorting about her head.

'Even the landlord who lives in that great big house atop the hill asks your old Ajji to cook when he hosts parties, which is often, thank the gods...'

'Why thank the gods?'

'Because the landlord actually pays money. The villagers are like us; they don't have money to spare, so they give in kind.'

'But the landlord does have money to spare?'

'Yes.'

'And even he wants your food, Ajji, for you are the best cook in the entire *world*,' Bindu declares. And, after a thoughtful minute, 'But the gruel wasn't tasty.'

Ajji laughs and coughs, and once again Dumdee bounds up, looking worried.

'You're right,' Ajji wheezes. 'I must have forgotten to temper it with spices. But no harm done, as now you'll season it to your taste, all right?'

Bindu nods again.

'Come.' Ajji holds out her hand and Bindu takes it, liking the feel of Ajji's wrinkly, puckered skin – to her, it spells comfort and security.

Ajji leads her into their hut, the one room doubling up as living space and kitchen – they wash in the lean-to outside (fashioned from coconut mats held aloft by coconut tree branches), using a great big mud pot, in which they boil water drawn from the well.

Ajji places the bowl of gruel in front of Bindu. 'Now, salt first. Salt adds flavour even to the blandest of foods. And it's free! If you've the means and the time to collect it from the seabed when the tide is out, that is. Krishnanna collects it for us in return for my spicy deep-fried frogs' legs.' Ajji takes a pinch of salt, shows it to Bindu. 'Now, shall we add, say, this much?'

Bindu nods.

Ajji adds and stirs the gruel. 'Here, have a taste.'

Bindu does, smacking her lips.

'It's OK?'

Bindu considers. 'More salt, I think.'

'Hmmm...' Ajji rocks on her haunches.

Dumdee, who knows not to come inside, watches them from where he's sprawled upon the threshold.

'You add it,' Ajji says, nudging the mud bowl containing the salt towards Bindu.

Bindu carefully adds a pinch of salt, stirs as she watched Ajji do.

'Taste it, go on,' Ajji prompts.

'Too salty.' Bindu makes a face.

'You have to be very careful with salt,' Ajji says. 'That's the first lesson. Too little and it ruins the taste. Too much and it also ruins the taste.'

Bindu puts her hands on her hips. 'Now what do we do? We've ruined it,' she sighs.

Ajji smiles. 'Here, let me add some congee water.' She uses the ladle she has fashioned from a scooped-out coconut shell to do just that. 'Now taste.'

'Ah, that's just right. How did you know how much congee water to add?'

'That takes practice, my heart.'

'I'll practise every day,' Bindu vows.

'That's my girl.' Ajji beams. Then, 'Is the gruel like the one I usually make, now?'

'Not quite,' Bindu says.

'What's missing, do you think?'

Bindu points to the pepper powder. She's seen Ajji add it to the dishes she prepares.

'Good girl.' Ajji is approving. 'Pepper gives a nice kick and this too is free.'

Bindu nods. 'It grows in our courtyard. I've helped you pick the green and red peppercorns and dry them until they become black, then pound them into a paste.'

'That's right.'

'I tasted the green ones and the red ones and even the black ones.'

'And what did you think?'

'They made my mouth burn, but each one did so differently.'

'Yes, there are degrees to the spice, aren't there?'

'The black ones were the most spicy. I had to drink a lot of water to make my tongue stop burning. Like Dumdee when he drinks from the stream.'

Upon hearing his name, Dumdee pricks up his ears and lets out a happy bark.

'You're a natural, my heart.' Ajji beams and pinches Bindu's cheek fondly. 'So, shall I add this much pepper?' She holds up a generous pinch.

'Perhaps a little less,' Bindu says and Ajji beams some more.

'How's that?' she asks, offering Bindu a taste, after adding and stirring.

'It's OK, but still not like the one you usually make.'

Ajji nods, hands on hips, regarding her granddaughter. 'What do you think I should add next?'

Bindu thinks of the chillies drying outside, how their heat has tickled her nostrils, making her mouth water. She points to the crushed chilli flakes in the mud bowl next to the pepper.

'Yes, you're exactly right,' Ajji says happily. 'This much?'

Bindu nods.

'Now taste.'

Bindu closes her eyes, the better to savour the explosion of flavours in her mouth. 'Exactly right, Ajji,' she says.

She feels Ajji's arms round her, her wrinkled cheek upon hers. 'You definitely have the gift,' Ajji whispers in her ear and there is such pride in her grandmother's voice that it makes Bindu's heart swell. 'Did you enjoy that?' Ajji asks.

Bindu nods, her mouth too full of gruel to speak.

Ajji smiles. 'So, you'll help me cook supper?'

'Yes, I like cooking with you, Ajji,' Bindu says and Ajji laughs and she coughs, and from the threshold of their one-roomed hut, Dumdee wails a warning and parrots screech among the chikoo branches outside and Sirsi the cat mewls.

Once Ajji's coughing fit has subsided, she and Bindu cook together, tart sweet perfume of spices, flavoured smoke rising from the hearth; Sirsi, who has climbed in through the rafters holding up the hay roof to avoid the dog, circling in the hope of handouts. Dumdee watches from the threshold, huge eyes tracking their every move, jumping up to accompany Bindu when she runs into the courtyard to pluck coriander and mint and curry leaves, and collect wood for kindling.

Following Ajji's instruction, Bindu pounds chillies and cumin, peppercorns and coriander seeds and the herbs she has collected into a paste. Then, she helps Ajji to season coconut oil with mustard seeds and curry leaves and add the triumvirate of chopped onions and ginger and garlic, frying until they are honey-coloured and release a sweet aroma. At Ajji's prompting, Bindu adds the spice paste – delighting in the bubbling hiss it emits like a spitting snake – and cinnamon bark and cardamom pods and turmeric. Bindu watches in awe as the fragrant spice mixture turns vermilion gold.

'Now,' Ajji says, 'add the vegetables.'

Bindu does – they only have potatoes and spinach – and uses the coconut shell ladle to coat them in the sizzling curry paste. Once the potatoes are coated and the spinach has wilted, she and Ajji add grated coconut and coconut milk, and then they cover the pot and watch the lid dance a rat-a-tat rhythm as the curry bubbles inside.

'It's from the steam produced in the pot as the curry cooks,' Ajji explains.

'It's as if a ghost is trapped inside, knocking desperately and hoping for escape,' Bindu observes, and Ajji laughs and coughs.

And in their one-roomed hut, as the sun sets beyond the fields, dusting the green ears of paddy in a saffron rose glow, Bindu and Ajji (and Dumdee, with Sirsi mewling plaintively from a safe distance away) watch as all the disparate ingredients they've picked and chopped and fried and pounded mingle to create deliciously mouth-watering magic.

CHAPTER 2

EVE

1980

LONDON, ENGLAND

'Knock, knock! Deliveries!' Sue calls through the letter box, rattling it for good measure.

'Coming.' Eve wipes her hands on her apron and goes to the door.

A brief flash of relief in Sue's eyes, which she quickly hides when Eve opens the door. There then gone, like the tantalising glimpse of the dimple on Joe's cheek, which would appear when he smiled, or felt like smiling – a gift to the observer. Disappearing in a flickering instant. Like he did that sunny Saturday. There, then gone...

'Finally,' Sue says, setting down the bags she's carrying, enveloping Eve in a hug.

Her friend smells of outdoors, wet grass and blossom and cigarettes and peppermint overlaid with the jasmine perfume she favours.

'I wasn't long,' Eve protests.

'Long enough.' Sue affects a suffering sigh.

'You're just impatient,' Eve says.

'I'm a busy girl, no time to waste.' Sue shrugs.

But Eve knows what she's not saying, the worry she tries to

make light of behind her good-natured blustering, both of them remembering that time just after the accident when Eve did not – could not – come to the door.

'Have you been cooking?' Sue asks, bright eyes taking in Eve's apron.

The apron, busy with sunny daffodils – both Eve and Izzy's favourite flower – that Eve hasn't worn since the last time...

When Eve put it on earlier today – deciding to make an effort, bake something for her friend, who trekked across town to see her each week, no matter how pressed for time she was – memories had ambushed her. Her daughter's matching apron, which Eve had tied round her child's small body that fateful morning. Izzy's arms round Eve, her little girl smelling of chocolate and innocence. 'Mama, I love cooking with you.'

'I tried,' Eve says to Sue.

She'd laid out the ingredients, hearing her daughter's chatter in her head. 'You're making a banana cake, Mama? Why not something from Nana's recipe book?'

That book – worn pages bearing the imprint of gluey fingers, turmeric stains, chilli powder, rose essence and memories. So many vivid hours spent poring over it with her daughter, selecting recipes, shopping for ingredients, measuring them out, chopping, peeling, stirring, tasting.

She hasn't touched it since. And despite her daughter's phantom voice urging her to cook from Nana's book, she hadn't been able to this morning either. Instead, she'd made herself a cup of tea and stared out of the kitchen window at their patch of garden. The grass so overgrown, it was nearly Izzy's height.

A pang then as she realised, afresh, that Izzy would never grow taller, that there would be no more marks notched onto the chart in Izzy's room, where Eve and Joe would record her height each summer before school resumed, all of them thrilled to note how much higher the mark was compared to the previous year.

In the flower borders at the edges of the lawn, daffodils danced in the frisky spring breeze, sunny beacons of hope. Izzy had helped her plant the bulbs, wearing her favourite cream dress – unsuitable for gardening, but she would not be dissuaded – and her green wellies with pink polka dots, digging into the mulchy earth with the child's gardening set they'd picked at the supermarket, screaming in thrilled excitement when she encountered a squiggly earthworm.

When spring came and the bulbs they'd planted together pushed through the earth, wearing buttery smiles, Izzy had declared daffodils, 'my favourite flower, and yours, Mama.' She had helped Eve pluck and arrange them in jars in every room of the house.

That fateful afternoon when Eve's life had changed forever and her husband's and daughter's had stopped, Izzy was wearing a sundress with daffodils splashed onto cream linen. It was stained afterwards with her daughter's blood.

Eve was the one with the weak constitution, forever falling ill, always down with some ailment or another. Her daughter and husband were robust, Izzy taking after Joe healthwise, for which Eve had rejoiced. And now, irony of ironies, she was the one who lived, while her daughter and husband were gone. Why?

As Eve stood in the kitchen, failing to bake a cake for her friend, from the road at the front of the house wafted the happy chatter of children as they walked to the primary school on the main road, the same one Izzy had attended.

Eve was trying very hard to move forward, move on, even without her family to give meaning, purpose to her life. She pulled herself out of bed each morning – unlike in that nightmare time just after the tragedy when she had lain in bed for days at a time, nibbling on stale bread when her stomach cramped with hunger, her body moving on while her mind could not, getting up only to use the loo and make endless cups of tea that would go cold and look like she did – wan, listless, lifeless. These days, she got dressed, brushed her hair, even put on make-up. She ate sandwiches and fruit.

And she tried to write.

Each morning, she sat at her desk, opened her notebook. Flicked through the pages and pages of ideas and notes jotted in her cramped handwriting before...

Before.

She turned the leaves of the notebook, found an empty page. Picked up her pencil. She always wrote in pencil, so it was easy to rub out, begin again.

Oh, if only in life it were as easy.

She would stare at the pristine page until it blurred before her eyes, clutching her pencil so hard that there were indentations of her fingers upon it.

But nothing came. No words. No ideas. Nothing.

Once upon a time, she had wanted this, wished for this, a few hours of silence, precious minutes of peace in which to write. Now she had all the silence in the world – endless, undisturbed time to write. She had exactly what she had wished for once, in surplus. But she could not write.

She couldn't cook either.

Not even for Sue. Not even a recipe unconnected with the book whose every recipe she had cooked with her child.

But Eve was trying. That was something, wasn't it?

CHAPTER 3

BINDU

1926

Bindu is dancing along the path between the fields, Dumdee loping behind her, so close his muzzle tickles her back. There's only space for one pair of (six-year-old) feet on the narrow path – adults have to walk with one foot in front of the other – so Dumdee is forced to tail Bindu. He had tried a couple of times to walk by her side, but his paws squelched and sank in the wet mud of the paddy fields and Bindu couldn't help but giggle at his expression of mournful disgust. Mynahs sing and parrots screech in the fruit trees bordering the fields. Cows moo and buffaloes low. Emerald ears of paddy bejewelled with monsoon tears sway languidly to a tune only they can hear. Every so often, the breeze rippling through the branches overhead sprays guava- and mud-flavoured droplets on Bindu – it rained this morning, although now the sky is cloudless, sun beading sweat on Bindu's face and body.

Dumdee skids to a stop so suddenly that he bumps into Bindu, making her nearly lose her grip on the bag containing the oil and flour she had been sent to collect from Dujanna, in exchange for Ajji's famous chitranna – spiced rice flavoured with lime and studded with peanuts.

'What is it, Dumdee?' she mouths, turning to look at him.

Dumdee is whining in a low fearful tone she hasn't heard

before, his gaze fixed ahead, and Bindu is aware of a strange tension in the air, everything, all of a sudden, menacingly still – even the yellow and turquoise butterflies, which were flitting about showing off their sun-spangled wings, are nowhere in evidence.

And then she hears it – an ominous hiss.

She turns slowly, Dumdee nuzzling into her, his fur standing to attention, growling softly.

A cobra coiled majestically on the path in front of her, hooded neck arching forward, forked tongue poised to strike.

Bindu's heart seizes in fear. She has been warned about cobras, heard tales of people dying a horrible death from their lethal bites, how not the wise men, not even English medicine, could save them.

She is all alone among the fields. Ajji is too far away to help, even if Bindu was brave enough to call for her. And, in any case, Bindu seems to have lost her voice, which is well and good as she doesn't dare startle the cobra.

The snake hisses, beady eyes flashing onyx sparks, regal neck arcing, poisonous tongue descending on Bindu with malicious intent.

Dumdee cries the dirge Bindu cannot as she shuts her eyes tight, hands sweaty on her paper bag of provisions, which is disintegrating from the pressure she's applying, mind blank as her six-year-old self waits for the toxic bite that will flood death into her body.

A cry, a hiss, a squeal, a scuffle.

Bindu's eyes fly open. *I'm not dead.* She is looking at a spectacle.

For, in front of her, a small grey animal wrestles with the cobra, which is three times its size, unafraid, the two animals locked in a fierce fight.

She watches, stupefied with fearful amazement, as, at the top of the hill, Ajji comes running, as fast as her painful knees will allow, her hands upon her heart, her eyes, bright with the terror Bindu is feeling, never leaving her granddaughter's face, as if by sheer willpower she can keep her safe.

Chinnakka and other neighbours collect around Ajji and

Bindu hears stunned whispers behind her, more villagers arriving among the fields, summoned by the noise.

Ajji gestures urgently to someone behind Bindu and, presently, Bindu hears footsteps approaching, feels hands on her shoulders, gently leading her away, Dumdee following, to safety.

Ajji throws her arms round Bindu, her body trembling, anointing her head with its lucky double crown, her face, her body, with her tears, her kisses tasting of fear and love as the mongoose that came to Bindu's rescue triumphantly drags its limp, unresisting prey away.

'My lucky girl, my heart,' Ajji cries. 'What did I tell you, this child is so lucky even cobras cannot harm her!'

The assembled villagers nod assent, their voices, like Bindu's, stolen by what they've just witnessed.

The story of Bindu's near miss with the cobra, and rescue by a mongoose at just the right moment, is the talk of the village for the next few days and Bindu revels in her notoriety.

She hears her name as she is walking back home with Dumdee after delivering rice cakes to Ratnakka in exchange for sugarcane, imagining the sweet dishes Ajji might make with it – payasam definitely, ginger halva perhaps. She's taking the long route along the mud road, eschewing the fields for now: 'You're lucky, but it's best not to tempt fate too much,' Ajji had said when she'd asked Bindu to avoid the shortcut through the fields.

'Bindu…' she hears as she passes Girijamma's house and it gives her pause.

Instead of walking on to take the turning that leads to the hut she shares with Ajji, Bindu silently leans against one of the walls of Girijamma's hut, peering round it. Dumdee is by her side, understanding, when Bindu puts her finger to her lips, that he needs to be quiet.

Girijamma is sitting in her courtyard with some of Ajji's friends – the usual suspects who gather at Ajji's for *paan*, spiced betel and gossip. But today Ajji is not present.

Why? Bindu wonders.

But all conjecture flies away when she hears her name again.

'Bindu is lucky, my foot,' Girijamma is saying vehemently and Bindu experiences stunned shock, hot tears pricking her eyes.

Has she heard right?

'That girl is nothing but bad luck. She killed both parents – father when in the womb, mother coming out of it. And even holy cobras are not exempt. Her grandmother has aged a hundred years looking after her. She's in league with the devil, she is.'

Bindu is incensed. These women – her grandmother's friends – agreeing that she is lucky in her grandmother's presence and saying this in secret. How dare they!

Trembling with anger, she scrabbles around the ground where she is standing, grabs a handful of pebbly mud and with all her might throws it at the women gathered in a circle in Girijamma's courtyard.

'Ow!' They startle as dirt spatters their faces, turning to look in her direction.

Bindu picks up another handful, flings it at them, yelling, 'I am *lucky*. I've a double crown.'

Then she picks up the bag containing sugarcane and runs as fast as she can, Dumdee at her heels, her mouth bitter with salty bile, trying and failing to outrun their wounding words, flung at her, 'Your Ajji'll have sore trouble with you. You bring bad luck, on top of which, you're a handful, you are.'

CHAPTER 4

BINDU

1927

Bindu is washing the pots and pans she and Ajji used to cook their orders for the day beside the well in the shade of the coconut trees, Dumdee running circles around her, bees humming in the jackfruit-flavoured breeze and alighting on the bright crimson hibiscus. Ajji is taking a nap – she hasn't been feeling well today, her cough worse than usual.

Abruptly, and with no warning, Dumdee stops running and Bindu almost trips over him – he has a tendency to stay very close to her – nearly dropping the mud pot in her hand. She manages to retain hold of it, despite her slippery palms, thank goodness – it is the biggest one they own.

'Dumdee, what's got into you?' she admonishes.

In response, he lets out a sharp howl of warning and bounds to the tamarind tree, where, from repeated use, is hewn a rough path down the hill to the stream and the fields beyond. Dumdee stands guard, barking furiously now, flustering the crows nattering in the branches above into flight and sending Sirsi the cat, who was, as usual, snoozing on the mossy well surround, for cover.

Bindu follows Dumdee's gaze, one hand clutching the pot, the other the coconut coir puff she was using as a scrubber, and sees two birdlike beings emerging through the heat haze, their black and white habits dancing in the frisky, chilli- and grit-flavoured air, looking incongruous as they walk single file along the narrow path between the fields. Bindu blinks at these visions in entranced awe. It takes her a minute to identify them as the nuns from the new missionary convent that has recently set up in the village. They hold their pristine skirts up above their feet, but even so, Bindu wonders how the garments are as dazzlingly white as the cloudless sky when everything here is always coated in a mist of red dust no matter how much care you take.

'Come here, Dumdee, and stop barking. They're just nuns and probably heading to Chinnakka's hut – they must have some business there,' she tells the dog.

It does occur to her that perhaps they want to place a food order with Ajji. But no sooner does the thought hover than she dismisses it.

'I don't have much to do, really. They're a self-sufficient lot, but they've the most peculiar eating habits,' Bhanuakka had reported the week before, following her first day working at the newly established convent. Bhanuakka did odd jobs for the priests at the seminary in town and had been asked to help when the nuns moved into the village.

'Do tell.' Ajji and her friends, gathered under the giant peepal tree with its gnarled and sprawling network of interconnected trunks against which to rest in blessed relief from the unrelenting sun – their favoured meeting spot despite the monkeys that colonised the tree being a nuisance and stealing any food left unattended – were agog.

'Bland and tasteless.' Bhanuakka sniffed, her paan-stained mouth making it appear as if she had messily drunk a goblet of blood. 'No spice, no chilli, no onion or garlic, *nothing*. Just plain boiled vegetables, fish, even meat, can you believe it?' Her voice was dripping with disdain.

'Must be penance they've to do for their god,' Ajji mused, noisily spitting out her paan and picking up one of the sweet, spiced tamarind balls she and Bindu had spent the morning concocting.

. . .

Now, the two nuns, when they've climbed the hill, panting and stopping a minute to gather breath – habitual for visitors unused to the ascent – instead of turning left for Chinnakka, head towards the one-roomed mud hut Bindu shares with Ajji.

Galvanised, Bindu rushes inside, wanting direction from Ajji, blinking as her vision adjusts to the shadowy gloom after the bright gold sunlight outdoors.

Dumdee has stopped barking and followed her. He waits at the threshold, his face poking through Ajji's old sari that passes for a door. Ajji is fast asleep, small snores escaping from her partly open mouth, her chest wheezing with each rumbling exhale, and Bindu is loath to wake her.

As she stands beside her grandmother, undecided whether to disturb her, Bindu wrings her hands, becoming aware of how wet they are. Then, noticing the water she has trailed in, she sighs – quietly. The floor is pooled in patches and will need to be mopped again, never mind that Ajji had swept it just that morning with the fresh cow dung Bindu had collected from the meadow where the neighbourhood cows graze. But she has no time to do anything about it right now, for she hears a musical voice call in a strange, clipped accent, 'Anyone there?'

And Bindu, with one last look at her snoring grandmother, goes outside, pushing aside the sari door decisively, Dumdee loping protectively at her heels, a low growl emanating from his chest.

The nuns are the first white people Bindu has seen. Their faces gleam pink and cream – a different, more characterful white than the pale monochrome of their habits. Their eyes are exotic marbles, reflecting light in iridescent combinations: one nun's blue with twinkling silver depths like the water in the well holding the rising sun; the other has eyes the palest grey of the predawn sky, secretively nursing rumours of the day to come. Their lips are red – not with paan, but naturally so! – the translucent crimson of ripe pomegranate seeds.

Bindu is starstruck. Even the dog seems awed, for he has

stopped growling and is now shamelessly licking their feet – a sure sign of affection and allegiance – even though they, unlike Bindu's and other villagers', aren't bare but clad in sandals. The nuns leave Dumdee be, rather than brushing him away, clucking in annoyance, like Ajji's friends do.

They smile at Bindu, their faces creasing in kindly pink folds, their cheeks glowing bright like the sun. 'Now, who have we here?'

They speak Kannada in such a way as to make it sound foreign. They truly are magical beings, Bindu decides.

Completely entranced, she cannot find her voice; it is hiding naughtily, stubbornly in her throat. She wills Ajji to wake and come to her rescue.

They nudge her, gently: 'What is your name, child?'

Dumdee pauses in his obsequious sniffing of the nuns' feet to look at her, as if to say, *Aren't you going to answer?*

Bindu looks to the hut again – no Ajji coming at just the right moment.

She clears her throat, manages to coax her voice from its hiding place, croak out, 'Bindu.'

Dumdee barks assent: *That's my girl.*

'Ah, a beautiful name,' the blue-eyed nun says and the other nods, beaming at her.

Bindu blushes. Their gentle approval makes her bold. 'My Ajji named me. My parents are dead.'

As soon as she says the words, she regrets them, biting her lower lip in annoyance. Why has she told them about her parents being dead, spoiling the mood? *Big mouth.*

But their eyes, if anything, turn even kinder. The grey-eyed nun reaches out to her with a very white hand, clean nails like rain-washed shells, and pats her cheek. It feels so soft, different from Ajji's gnarled hand, crêpe skin, fingers permanently stained by spices.

'We are so sorry, child,' they say in unison, eyes shining.

'Don't worry, I'm lucky, I've a double crown on my head,' she was going to say. But perhaps it's the empathy in their eyes, for the words evaporate on her tongue and suddenly, irrationally, she bursts into tears that she cannot explain.

Dumdee bounds up to her, whining in sympathy, jumping up on his hind legs to lick the moisture from her face.

The nuns look around and, upon spying the washing stone by the well where her pans are lying abandoned mid-wash, gently lead Bindu there, sit her down.

The blue-eyed nun digs in her pocket, finds a handkerchief. 'Here, my dear, blow your nose.'

Bindu's tears dry up as she gingerly takes the pristine handkerchief that smells of exotic flowers, her fingers looking grubby in comparison.

'Now, child, is your grandmother around?'

'She's sleeping indoors.'

'Ah. Well, the reason we're here is to inform you and your Ajji that we're starting a free girls' school at the convent. It will run every weekday from eight a.m. to three p.m. We'll also provide a midday meal.'

Bindu ponders this. It sounds tempting to be with these kind nuns all day. Except for the meal – now, if it's bland like Bhanu-akka said... Maybe she can smuggle in Ajji's fiery spice paste made by pounding dry chillies with peppercorns and sea salt and cumin and coriander seeds. Ajji prepares rasam with this paste and offers it to anyone who's ill in the village – she says germs and disease bugs shrivel and die in the face of her potent soup.

The spice mixes were Bindu's idea. Saradamma had come to Ajji one afternoon asking for food to take to her daughter-in-law in the next town, who was about to give birth to Saradamma's first grandchild. 'I'm going to stay with her for a few days. I'd like something that'll keep, provide sustenance during those exhausting weeks just after birth.'

'I'll prepare strength-giving curries, fortified with medicinal herbs. They'll be ready for when you leave for your visit,' Ajji had promised.

But afterwards, Ajji had sat under the guava tree, munching paan, looking troubled.

'What's the matter?' Bindu had asked.

'It's Saradamma's order. I've several recipes I can make to build up her daughter-in-law's strength. The problem is how to make them last. Everything will spoil in this heat in a couple of hours, let alone a few days.'

Bindu too had pondered the problem while playing with Dumdee in the fields as she had collected the raw mangoes that had fallen down before they ripened so she and Ajji could chop them up and preserve them in brine, to be pickled later, or to be fried in mustard-seasoned oil with chilli flakes and crushed peppercorns – a tart, piquant side dish, wonderful with boiled rice.

And that was when she had the idea.

'Ajji,' she had said on her return. 'You know for every one of our dishes, we first crush all the spices together, make a spice mix or masala to add to the tempered oil with the vegetables or fish or meat?'

'Yes?' Ajji had looked at Bindu, turning from the hearth, where she was mixing green chilli and ginger with curds made from the goat milk she obtained from Chinnakka in exchange for whatever dish Chinnakka wanted that particular day.

'Why don't we make spice mixes and pastes and give them to Saradamma – they will keep, won't they? It's only when we add coconut milk and vegetables that the curries then need to be eaten quickly, isn't it?'

And Ajji had set down the curds and squatted on her haunches to pinch Bindu's cheeks with beaming affection, eyes shining with love. 'Now why didn't I think of that? Yes, my heart, this way they'll last longer *and* they're versatile – people can cook different curries with the same spice mix at their convenience, adding vegetables, eggs, meat – whatever they can afford or is available. Bindu, my love, you surpass me in the kitchen. If I say it once, I'll say it a thousand times, I don't know what I'd do without you.'

'But the villagers complain to you that I'm a firecracker,' Bindu had said, thinking back to when she'd lost her temper with them, that time she'd caught Girijamma and her friends gossiping about Bindu bringing bad luck; the time when Dujanna had refused to give her the pulses and coconut oil he'd promised in exchange for

Ajji's vegetable rice with lentils for he'd said it had gone off; another time when...

Ajji had planted soft kisses on Bindu's cheeks, interrupting her train of thought, the litany of her transgressions. 'A little bit of fire is necessary, my heart. When we're cooking, fire is what you need to mingle all the disparate ingredients together, spark magic. A touch of fiery heat enhances a dish.'

Bindu's heart had lifted with exalted relief.

'But...' Ajji had winked at Bindu, 'too much fire ruins a dish, remember that.'

Now, Bindu considers the nuns' declaration. School. She doesn't really understand what that entails. The meal on the other hand, that too free... That *would* be good, given how sometimes, when orders are scarce, she and Ajji have to make do with watery gruel, day after day. She could smuggle Ajji's lethal rasam spice mix into the convent and sprinkle it over the nuns' tasteless offering, to make it palatable. It is *really* kind of them to give all the children a meal.

Bindu's heart sinks as a thought occurs. 'Do I have to be there *every* day from eight in the morning to three in the afternoon?'

'Yes, you do, we're afraid.'

Why are they afraid? Bindu wonders briefly, but she has more pressing concerns. 'I'd love to, but I can't. I've to help Ajji cook. That's how we earn our living. And Ajji's hands have recently started to tremble, so she needs me to add the spices – they have to be just right, and when her hands shake, she ends up adding too much or too little, and that's a disaster when cooking.'

'Hmmm...' The nuns appear to be thinking.

'Does your Ajji need help all day every day?' The sky-eyed nun asks.

'No, she doesn't,' says a familiar, weathered voice.

Bindu and the nuns turn as one to where Ajji is stooped by the entrance to the hut, blinking in the sunshine. Although Ajji is only slightly taller than Bindu – 'You'll be catching up with me soon,' she likes to tell Bindu fondly, proudly patting her head – she has to stoop to enter and exit their hut.

Dumdee bounds up to Ajji, tail wagging, and starts lapping at her feet.

'You *will* go to school, my Bindu. Book knowledge'll give you better prospects. And it's free?' Ajji squints at the nuns.

'Completely free,' the blue-eyed nun concurs.

Bindu's heart lifts. She has a feeling she'll enjoy school. But...

'Ajji, you still do need help when there're orders from the land-lord. If we don't get those right, we'll lose our livelihood.' Bindu's voice is high-pitched with anxiety.

'Look, my dear, you come to school, and on those days when you need to help your Ajji, we'll let you skip lessons, as long as you catch up on the work you've missed. How's that?' The blue-eyed nun twinkles at Bindu.

Bindu grins, nodding her head vigorously. Ajji beams and Dumdee dances around them, jubilantly wagging his tail.

'That's settled then,' the blue-eyed nun says, smiling. 'We'll see you on Monday at the convent, at eight o'clock sharp.' A keen glance at her. 'We're very strict on punctuality – you must come on time. Doors close at eight a.m., you understand.'

Bindu nods even more vigorously.

'No need to bring anything.' The blue-eyed nun again. 'We'll provide you with slate and chalk with which to write and do your sums. Keep the handkerchief, my dear.' And, patting her head, they leave, trailing the scent of clean flowers and kindly love in their wake.

CHAPTER 5

BINDU

Just a few more paces, Bindu tells herself, but she is seriously flagging.

Her arm aches from holding the pot on her head securely, so as not to spill a single precious drop of the water that she has collected from the lake. Her hip aches from where the other pot is digging into it. And her other arm aches from holding it in place. Her legs ache from the long walk back from the lake to the hut. Her head aches from the pot pressing down on it and from the unrelenting glare and dazzle of sun. The mud road feels endless, dust rising off it, an orange-gold mirage, gritty red smog stinging her eyes.

Just a few more paces up the road, then down through the path among the fields, which are dry and parched in the drought that has gone on and on, to the farmers' despair, their gaunt faces as yellow and arid as the fields they cannot work on, as they lay offerings they cannot spare at the shrine by the lake, pleading with the gods for rain – precious drops of milk squeezed from their emaciated cows' udders, last year's grains, the worms picked off, stones thrown away.

The drought has dried up the wells in the village, which is why Bindu has made the trek up to the lake. It, too, was almost dry, but thank goodness there was *some* water – such a welcome sight, despite being stagnant and stale with a muddy, fly-spattered film. She had greedily filled her pots – she would boil the water to sterilise it once home.

But her aching, hoarse and thirsty throat could not resist the temptation. She had scooped up handfuls and drunk straight from her palms, lapping up the gritty treasure like Dumdee used to at the stream at the bottom of the hill, back when it was bursting at the seams with monsoon abundance – a distant memory now.

Dumdee, who had accompanied her to the lake – he still never left her side and she was grateful for it – also drank from the muddy dregs, but with none of his usual gusto. Like the villagers, and their animals, he too was skin and bone, the enthusiasm, the zest for life sapped out of them with each relentless, arid day with no hint or rumour of rain.

'The landlord is inviting a renowned guru to conduct a puja in praise of the gods at his mansion – he wants my brinjal bhath, puri bhaji and drumstick sambar, with shyavige payasam for afters. One of his chauffeurs dropped off vegetables and flour and basmati rice, milk and nuts and dried fruit for the payasam this morning. He's returning this afternoon to collect the order. But how will we cook when there's no water?' Ajji had looked at her wits' end that morning, her hands shaking even more than usual and her voice the most upset Bindu had heard it.

Bindu had been possessed by a great rage towards the landlord. 'I've heard they've several wells in their huge compound with plenty of water in them. Will it kill him to provide us with water with which to cook, especially considering we're providing food for the occasion of holy worship?'

The farmers had talked of nothing else since the drought had started. They had plenty of time on their hands while they waited for the monsoon and they'd taken to congregating under the peepal tree – Ajji and her friends' prize gathering place – much to the women's chagrin, with tumblers of toddy they'd brewed themselves to slake their thirst and share their woes.

The farmers' main pastime, as reported by Muthakka, the fisherwoman who hawked the day's catch from under the tree, was fantasising about the many springs and bodies of water in the landlord's gated compound, news of which had been brought back by those fortunate enough to work there and have access to the clean water.

This sparked a tangential, hearty debate as to whether those in the landlord's employ were really lucky when the landlord was a strict and remorseless taskmaster, paying the bare minimum but expecting too much. He got rid of staff for the silliest of offences, and even sometimes just because he was in a bad mood. And his only son and heir – whose birth, after two daughters, had been heralded with much fanfare – was even worse. Only twelve years old – two years older than Bindu – but thoroughly spoilt and naughtier than the monkeys when they'd illicitly quaffed unattended toddy.

Bindu eavesdropped, in shocked awe, even though she didn't fully grasp much of it, as Muthakka relayed the farmers' gossip to Ajji and her friends in painstaking detail. What she *did* understand was that the landlord was famously miserly to the point of sadism, delighting in keeping what the villagers most wanted from them.

'There is abundant water within the landlord's great compound, but the servants are only allowed rationed amounts and they cannot take any water with them when they go home,' Muthakka breathed.

The farmers had gone en masse to ask him if he could divert some water from inside his compound to the fields. They were unceremoniously kicked out.

'I've barely enough for my own needs,' the landlord had shouted, adding, 'Oh, and I'm increasing the rent on the land you lease from me.'

'But why?' the farmers had cried.

'Well, you're complaining of drought, so the crops will be late this year – and not only that, they'll be substandard as the delayed monsoon will mess with the yield.'

'How're we supposed to pay you when we can barely get by?' the farmers had lamented.

The landlord had merely shrugged. 'I need your rent to get by myself. This drought is causing problems for me too.'

The farmers had returned to the village defeated, raging at the injustice of the landlord claiming that he was suffering from the drought while sitting beside a fountain spewing water *just for decorative purposes.*

'It was all we could do not to drink from it,' the farmers had ranted.

So, instead, they'd got drunk on toddy and taken out their misery, their frustration, their angst on their wives, who came to Ajji the next day, barely able to walk, emaciated children clinging to their threadbare sari skirts, looking drained and gaunt and old beyond their years. For, alongside her spice mixes, Ajji was skilled at concocting medicinal pastes too, knowledgeable in the healing properties of herbs.

Along with potions to apply on their bruises and their black eyes, Ajji and Bindu fed the battered women rice with pickle concocted from lime rind and mango skins that they had made when limes and mangoes were in abundance, even though they were scraping the barrel of both their rice and pickle jars.

It was tempting to squirrel away some of the landlord's ingredients – the pristine grains of basmati rice (not a stone anywhere in sight), the flour so milky white (not mixed with grit and crawling with maggots – plucking them out was Bindu's least favourite job), and milk and nuts and exotic fruit, some of which Bindu had not set eyes on before, but...

'He keeps count,' Ajji had warned, when she saw Bindu eyeing the abundance of provisions from the landlord. 'He gets the servants to weigh the rice and flour. Knows exactly how much of each ingredient he's sent. We can't, my heart.'

It was sheer torture, to cook these feasts, this lavish plenty for the landlord, and then eat a few grains of stony rice, dry chapatis made from maggot-infested flour that Ajji had plumped up with herbs and cumin seeds, and pickle made from dried and brined vegetable skins flavoured with mustard and vinegar and chillies and peppercorns and Ajji's eye-watering spice mix to give it a kick.

Even knowing how miserly the landlord was, that morning, clocking Ajji's despair, Bindu couldn't help saying, 'Can't he give us a pot of water to cook with? He knows there's a drought.'

'Ah, my heart, that's the privilege of being rich and owning the entire village – you don't have to share, you can do what you want.' Ajji sighed.

'But you're cooking for him,' Bindu insisted.

'He's forgiving us our rent on this hut for this month.'

'Why do we have to pay rent on this hut – a single room fashioned from mud with a hay roof? It leaks in the monsoons and dries up and cracks in the drought. He has a huge house, so much land and more water than he needs, why does he want this too?'

Her grandmother laughed, but it was sad, mirthless. 'He owns all the land in the village, my heart, and he has kindly allowed us to live on it in return for the farmers working on his land and those of us who don't farm doing jobs for him.'

'But he still charges rent.'

'He pardons the rent when we cook for him and if he has a lot of parties, he pays us some money on top, which is very welcome.'

'Not nearly enough. And he won't allow us to eat a morsel of what we cook. He even deducts money if we taste the food to check if the seasoning is right!' Bindu took a breath, tasting indignation, chilli-hot. 'I think he's selfish. He should not be charging the villagers rent when we're so poor and he's so rich.'

'Well, we owe him our livelihood.'

Bindu heard the wobble that Ajji couldn't hide in her voice. Bindu knew that although she and Ajji cooked for the villagers, they didn't make money from them. Ajji was the best cook in the village, so when the villagers had important visitors, relatives they wanted to impress, when their daughters were of marriageable age and prospective suitors were coming to see them, when a longed-for son was born and celebrations were in order, they asked Ajji to cook and in return gave her something in kind – whatever they could afford.

Ajji always said, 'I don't expect anything when cooking for the villagers and they know it. But when I need help, a favour, I can turn to them. Or when they've a good crop of mangoes, or chikoos, or guavas, they share with us. But for our livelihood, we depend on the landlord.'

'Chinnakka said that the lake in the forest has water,' she said now. 'If I go—'

'Ajji, you can't. How'll you carry the pots?'

Ajji's hands were now shaking all the time and recently her head had started shaking too.

'I'm all right,' she protested.

'You're not. It's because you give me all the food and go hungry yourself.'

'Not true. In any case, you're a growing girl. I'm OK, I can manage.'

'Ajji, you won't be able to carry the water back. It'll spill. I'll go.'

'But you're only young.'

'I'm strong.'

And it was a measure of how desperate Ajji was; she cupped Bindu's cheek, and, eyes shining, said gently, 'You're a kind and wonderful soul, my heart. Don't overexert yourself. One pot will do.'

Now, Dumdee, who is walking beside Bindu, giving her company, tongue hanging out, already parched, although he too had helped himself to the water at the lake, suddenly growls, long and low. Barely enough warning before the red haze delineates to reveal a smirking boy standing in the middle of the mud road, blocking Bindu's path.

He reaches out before she can react, pushing her veil from her face.

'You're so pretty. I'm going to kiss you.'

Bindu sighs, annoyed. She has no time for this. She wants to get home and set the pots down.

'Out of my way,' she bites out, while Dumdee barks angrily at him.

The boy's smirk is kidnapped by a scowl. 'You don't speak that way to me. Don't you know who I am?'

'No, and I don't care. Out of my way,' she demands.

He bends forward and suddenly his face is inches from hers, his lips bearing upon hers.

Startled, she jumps aside and some of the precious water from her pots, that she so carefully carried, spills, the dry dust greedily lapping it up, turning a bright and happy red.

She is incensed.

But the boy is not to be deterred and bears down upon her again.

Dumdee jumps at the boy and he bats the dog aside. Poor Dumdee whines miserably.

'How dare you!' Bindu is raging now. Her hands are occupied holding the pots to prevent more spillage, so she lashes out with her legs and one of her kicks connects with the boy's shins.

'You'll pay for this,' the boy shouts, but his voice is breaking, tears in it. Her kick must have hurt him. Good.

She steadies the pot on her head and, keeping a firm hold of the one at her hip, she squats down and asks, gently, 'Dumdee, are you all right?'

The dog looks at her with huge, wounded eyes but manages to wag his tail in reassurance before turning to bare his teeth at the boy.

He's shaking his fists at them both. 'My father will hear of this. He's the landlord. He'll punish you.'

Oh no, this is the landlord's son! And Bindu has kicked him! Does this mean the landlord will sack Ajji? Not ask her to cook for him any more? Then what will they do?

'With this cough and now the shakes, not to mention having you, my heart, to bring up, I can't work as a servant, so isn't it lucky that I'm a good cook with the best helper in the world and can provide for us this way?' Ajji has often said, smiling fondly at Bindu, 'Generations of our women have woven magic with food. And you, my heart, have the gift too.'

'Ajji, I can help you with the cooking *and* work as a servant,' Bindu had declared.

Ajji had lovingly patted Bindu's head with its lucky double crown. 'My heart, you're very good at your studies, so the nuns say...'

Bindu had beamed. She loved her lessons under the mango and coconut and jackfruit trees in the nuns' compound while bees buzzed, drunk on nectar, and the sun shone and the nuns read them stories of faraway lands where it was so cold that rain became ice and covered the land in glittering white even more pristine than the nuns' habits.

On warm days when there was no threat of rain – most of the school year in fact, what with the drought – Bindu and her classmates would sit under the fruit trees in the convent courtyard, butterflies twinkling sapphire and iridescent saffron, balmy air tasting of fruit caressing their cheeks as they recited times tables and read Bible stories. Lunch was rice and vegetable curry, with a dab of lime pickle – spiced to their taste, although not as good as Ajji's: the nuns had employed Bhanuakka to cook the children's meals in addition to her cleaning chores. Served on banana leaves, it was often the only proper meal of the day for most of them, Bindu included. For, while Ajji went without to ensure Bindu had a full meal, Bindu did the same, saving her food even though she was starving, hiding it away, making congee with the rice in the morning, leaving it for Ajji's lunch while she ate at school.

Sometimes, especially during the drought, and when she and Ajji were short on orders, Bindu felt bad because she looked forward to school – not so much for the lessons as for the meal and tumbler of water the girls were supplied. Then she didn't have to worry about Ajji going without, so she could eat and drink; for this meal was just for her and clean water during the drought was sheer heaven.

Bindu was good at studies, but mostly she enjoyed school for the fun she and her best friend Sunitha got up to during break times – chatting, gossiping, running wild in the nuns' compound. Carefree times without worrying about helping Ajji. For Bindu fretted, secretly, if perhaps there was some truth in what she'd overheard the villagers say out of Ajji's earshot, that she might be bad luck for her. Was Ajji's health deteriorating? Would she die too, like her parents had? Not her beloved Ajji. *Please.*

At school, she could leave these worries behind, improve her English, work on her sums – she picked up things quickly, to the nuns' continued astonishment: 'You really are good, Bindu, the best we've taught.' Sounding surprised every time, as though they couldn't quite believe a mere village girl, a native at that, was blessed with such talent.

'You go to school, study hard and you'll secure a job in an office in the city.' Ajji's eyes glittering with dreams.

'I'll build us a brick and mortar house and dig a well so deep that we never want for water,' Bindu vowed fiercely and Ajji laughed with delight and coughed.

And now she has sabotaged their livelihood, Bindu thinks, heart sinking, and she'll have to give up her studies and work as a servant in town, as the landlord will not employ her.

The boy is bearing down on her again.

She looks at Dumdee, hoping he'll understand her non-verbal cue, then, gathering the pots to her, she grits her teeth and charges at the boy.

He jumps aside, startled, like she was when he accosted her, and Bindu takes advantage of this and runs, deliberately kicking up even more dust so he is momentarily blinded.

She runs even though she is so tired, she could lie down right there on the dusty road and sleep for days. Even though her whole body aches, her heart aching most of all with worry, wondering what this daredevil spurning of the landlord's son is going to cost her and Ajji.

Dumdee, who thankfully did comprehend her unspoken message, keeps pace with her, tongue hanging out.

'I'll give you a drink as soon as we get home, Dumdee,' Bindu pants, even as, from the distance, the boy's voice wafts on the grit-laden saffron and adrenaline air: 'I'll get you for this.'

'You're quiet,' Ajji says as they cook in tandem, preparing the landlord's order.

Bindu, as she sautées the aubergine in the brinjal bhath spice mix she has prepared to Ajji's specifications, as she roasts the nuts and fruit in ghee that the landlord has supplied (they'll have to return every ingredient they don't use or that's left over, with the prepared order), as she peels and boils potatoes, as she kneads the dough for puris, is waiting for the landlord's emissary to arrive and say, mouth pursed and bitter like a mango seed with all the juice sucked out, 'The landlord doesn't need your services any more.'

'It's carrying all that water,' Ajji says.

Bindu shudders, remembering what happened. *Please,* she prays, *let it not have repercussions on our livelihood. Let a miracle happen and the landlord's son doesn't go bearing tales to his father. Please, gods.*

'I'm so grateful, but you must be exhausted.' Ajji sighs. 'I wish I was younger, my heart—'

'No, Ajji,' Bindu cries. 'I'm fine. Honestly.' She manages a smile for Ajji's benefit, hoping it doesn't waver, hoping her grand-mother doesn't see right through her to her desperate fear.

But Ajji is busy stirring the payasam, concentrating on trying not to spill it because of her trembling hands. 'Nevertheless, after the order is collected, we'll have an early night, eh? You're a godsend, my lucky girl.'

Will you still be saying this when we're sacked because of me, Ajji? Bindu worries.

She goes outside and buries her face in Dumdee's flank. He smells of comfort and earth. When she lets go, he gently licks her nose, communicating, with his huge expressive eyes: *It will be all right.*

CHAPTER 6

BINDU

Amazingly, the miracle Bindu was hoping for does occur.

The landlord, far from sacking Ajji and Bindu, is so pleased with the food they supplied for the puja that he asks them to cook for the Maharaja of Jabalpur's cousin and his family, whom he has invited to stay at the weekend.

'And he will pay us for our efforts too, as our labour is above and beyond the cost of rent – even the increased version!' Ajji is jubilant.

It is a marathon task and Bindu has to make the trip to the lake and back several times. Each time, she prays that she won't be intercepted by the landlord's son. But, thankfully, the visits pass without incident.

Bindu is relieved, but also puzzled and more than a little scared – the boy vowed to take revenge. What is he planning? But everything becomes clear when, after Ajji and Bindu have finally dispatched all of the landlord's orders (for he wanted them to cook every meal during the royal visit), Ajji and her friends meet – in Beeramma's courtyard, as the men are still congregating under the peepal tree – to catch up on gossip.

'Word is that you're in favour with the landlord,' Beeramma says, mouth full of paan.

'Exhausted,' Ajji breathes. 'Not that I'm not grateful, mind you. If it wasn't for my wonderful Bindu, the poor child going back and forth to the lake hefting pots of water and doing more than her fair share of cooking too, I wouldn't have managed his recent deluge of orders.'

Bindu, who is hiding behind a cashew tree at the edge of Beer-amma's courtyard where it dips into the fields, Dumdee sprawled in the grass beside her, his head on her lap, the air honeyed with the scent of ripening fruit, glows.

'He usually gives notice when he has visitors and would like us to cook, but this came out of the blue.' Ajji spits her paan into the hibiscus bush near where Bindu is crouched, a plague of flies descending on the red flowers now festooned with frothy, half-chewed betel.

'Ah, well there's a story behind it,' Muthakka pipes up, her voice bright and breathless with the pleasure of imparting news nobody else knows.

Even from where she's crouched, far enough away so she won't be caught eavesdropping but near enough to hear every word, Bindu gets a faint whiff of the fishy stink that never quite leaves Muthakka.

'Do tell,' the women urge.

Although she can't see them, Bindu can picture Ajji and her friends leaning forward, agog and eager, the better to catch every last morsel of gossip.

'It appears the landlord's son messed with the wrong girl.'

Bindu feels a frisson of terror rock through her. *Oh dear.*

'None other than the King of Jabalpur's niece.'

Oh, thank you, gods.

'One of the family invited at the weekend?'

Bindu imagines that Muthakka nods assent.

'Damage control.' Muthakka's voice is puffed up with self-importance as she regales her audience. 'The landlord's son's been packed away to boarding school abroad.'

'Oh!' Ajji and her friends gasp.

Bindu hugs Dumdee in exalted relief. That explains why he

wasn't there to accost her during her subsequent trips to the lake, why there has been no retaliation from the landlord.

Bindu throws her head to the dazzling heavens and smiles, the cashew-scented air, gritty and humid, caressing her face.

CHAPTER 7

EVE

1980

'How's the book going?' Sue asks.

'It's not.' Eve sighs.

'Now, now, Evie, what's all this, eh? I thought you were turning over a new leaf with spring in the air and all that.' Sue lets out a guffaw. 'See what I did there?'

Eve smiles. You can't help but love Sue. Short, stout and loud with it, from her voice to her dress sense, and fiercely loyal to boot. One of the few who has stuck by Eve through it all; Jenny from next door, mum to Maya, Izzy's best friend, is another.

Every week, Sue brings groceries and gossip, filling Eve's silent house with noise and life. And for this, Eve is deeply grateful, even as a small, cynical part of her pipes up: *She has to. You are her livelihood.*

Not necessarily. At the beginning perhaps – Sue's reputation grew in direct proportion to Eve's success. But now, Sue has more authors than she can handle – 'And you will not believe the size of my slush pile.'

Sue was Eve's parents' friend. Eve's father – journalist, editor and small-time publisher – had been her mentor. When Sue had decided to start her own literary agency, Eve's father had said, 'My daughter's written a book and it's really rather good.'

Sue had read it and loved it. Eve was the first client she signed and also her most successful.

But Eve hasn't written a word for a while now.

After the tragedy, she had floundered, refusing to let anyone in, and while nearly everyone else fell away, Sue persisted, refusing to take Eve's put-downs personally. She just kept on coming, week after week, delivering groceries and news, keeping on at Eve to eat, to wash, to write, and not taking no for an answer.

One thing she hasn't been able to cajole Eve into attempting, and not for lack of trying, is stepping foot outside the house. Every time Sue comes round, she sets her bags down, surveys Eve, hands on hips, and says, 'This is the last time I'm bringing groceries. Next time, you're coming with me to get your own.' Her constant refrain, but still it is Sue bringing Eve her groceries.

Now, 'Keep at it, darling. The words will come.' Sue puts her arm round Eve and Eve rests her head on her friend's shoulder.

'Do you say this to all your authors when they're behind on their deadlines and don't even try to come up with an excuse as to why this is so?'

'Only very special ones,' Sue says, smiling. Then, 'Have you been shopping?'

'Not yet.'

'You must...'

'I know.'

'Come with me?'

'Next time, I promise.'

Sue sighs. 'I'll hold you to it. I mean it this time. And try to write, anything at all. One thousand words by the time I'm here next?'

'I'll try, but what's the point, Sue?'

'The point is that you've the rest of your life ahead of you. You need to find a way to navigate it.'

'I know. I'm lucky. I've a roof over my head. I've an understanding agent who has my back...'

'She can be too understanding at times, can't she?'

Eve smiles, nudging Sue gently. 'I like that she is.'

'Perhaps she should be tougher. That might work.'

'I'm functioning.'

'You're not enjoying life.' Sue tuts.

'I... How can I, when they're not?'

'They want this for you. You said so yourself that night...' Sue shudders, eyes shimmering.

Eve rubs at the scars on her wrists. If Sue hadn't found her, Eve would be with them – her family. She resents Sue for rescuing her almost as much as she loves her for doing so.

For after Eve had slashed her wrists, just as she was losing consciousness, she had heard her daughter's voice, clear as anything, sobbing in acute distress, 'Mama, what're you doing? Why're you doing this? Please don't. Please stop. It's not your time yet. Please, Mama, call Aunty Sue.'

And Eve, faint with blood loss, unable to say no to her daughter, even now she was dead, had somehow dragged herself to the phone and managed to dial Sue's number.

The last thing she'd heard before she lost consciousness was her daughter's voice, crying, 'Please, Mama, promise you won't do this again. Please? Promise, Mama.'

'I promise,' she'd whispered, and then fainted right away, waking up in hospital, Sue keeping vigil beside her.

And, hard though it's been, she's stuck to her promise. She's tried to move on, getting herself out of bed, getting dressed. Eating. Living. Although why her daughter wants her to live in this colourless world, why she wants her to go on when Eve doesn't want to, she doesn't know.

But...

'You can never refuse her,' Joe would say with that twinkle in his eyes. 'But you always refuse me.'

'Always?' She'd lift an eyebrow. 'How come we're married then?'

'Often,' he'd concede with that dimpled, infectious chuckle that always started her off. 'But you *never* say no to our daughter.'

'Kettle calling pot,' she'd tease back.

And Joe would laugh, drawing her into his embrace, fondly kissing her nose, her lips: 'Pot calling kettle, silly. Call yourself an author!'

Oh, how she misses her husband's laughter, his hugs, his love. Her daughter's smile, her voice, the feel of her in Eve's arms.

. . .

'And I said to him, "I know your lifelong dream is to win the Booker, my dear, but for this book, please stick to the terms of your contract with the publisher. They want a thriller. That's what you promised..."' Talking all the while, Sue puts away the groceries she's brought, popping the milk and cheese in the fridge, the vegetable basket overflowing with fresh vegetables and fruit.

Sue was Izzy's godmother and they'd shared a special bond, Sue never talking down to her, which Izzy loved. And she'd been just as good a friend to Joe as she was to Eve. She had spent many a happy evening with Eve, Izzy and Joe, regaling her godchild with a story or two before bed and then sitting on this very sofa with Eve and Joe, sharing a bottle of wine and setting the world to rights.

'Promise me you'll come shopping with me next time?' Sue says now.

'I promise.' Eve means to, but as soon as Sue leaves, she guesses that, just as with her previous visits, all her good intentions will evaporate along with the last lingering traces of Sue's perfume.

Sue reads her mind, clicks her teeth. 'You have to walk past where it happened, Eve. You can't postpone it forever.'

Why can't I? Eve thinks.

'Now, I've to get going. You're not the only client I babysit, you know.'

Eve smiles. 'I'm your best one.'

'That you are,' Sue concedes.

She leans in for a hug, the scent of busyness mixed in with jasmine.

And then she's gone.

Through the thin walls of the semi-detached home Eve had once shared with her family wafts the laughter of the little girl next door, her daughter's best friend, as jarring in the quiet here as a swear word in church, the silence reverberating with a thousand reminiscences of jollier times, making all the more potent everything that Eve has lost.

CHAPTER 8

BINDU

1935

Bindu is walking to the lake for water – another year, another drought – when she hears her name spoken and it gives her pause.

Usually anklets give one away, but, much to Ajji's chagrin, they've not been able to afford anklets or any form of jewellery for Bindu – not that Bindu minds.

'I wouldn't wear necklaces or anklets even if you were to buy them, Ajji. They'd be itchy, uncomfortable, especially in this heat. As it is, I only wear these glass bangles because you want me to. Same with the paste earrings – I don't need them.'

'No, you really don't. You've grown into such a beauty. The most beautiful girl in all the villages and towns around here, even prettier than the Maharaja of Jabalpur's daughters, people say, and they've had poets composing odes to their loveliness.' Ajji beams.

'Ah, Ajji, stop,' Bindu grumbles.

Her beauty is a curse, attracting unwanted attention, even, shockingly, from married men who've watched her grow from an infant. She can't walk out of the hut without being subjected to wolf whistles, catcalls, and recently, horribly, as she was queuing at Dujanna's for oil and rice, someone pressing into her, their scent of unwashed skin, their sour breath hot against her cheek. At first, she thought it was a mistake, but she stepped away and they just stepped right along with her. Upset and near to tears, she had run off without looking to see who it was, her face ablaze, coming up with some excuse – she couldn't remember what – to placate Ajji about returning home empty-handed. She'd washed as best she could with the water they were rationing, but couldn't rid herself of the smell of that man who had pressed into her. She felt violated. And angry with herself for having run away instead of standing up to him. She vowed it would never happen again. But how to prevent it happening?

She'd lain awake all night, Ajji softly snoring beside her, Dumdee softly snoring sprawled across the door to their hut, their loyal guard dog, and had finally, as dawn was heralded by creamy jasmine-scented breezes, come up with a plan.

When she was little, Ajji had religiously applied kajal, which she made from fragrant sandalwood paste and castor oil, to Bindu's cheeks, behind her ears and on her forehead to ward off the evil eye. Well, Bindu would use her own version of this.

That afternoon, when Ajji was having her siesta, Bindu pounded chillies – both fresh and dry and the more fiery, the better – with red, green and black peppercorns, until her eyes watered. She carefully transferred the paste into a pouch and tucked it into her sari blouse. Armed with this, she went into Duja's shop again at the same time as she had done the previous afternoon.

Sure enough, in a matter of minutes she was assailed by that unwashed sour male scent that she hadn't been able to get rid of. Just as the man was going to press into her, she dipped her hand in the spice paste – it stung, but after years of cooking with spices she was immune to the pain, unlike, she hoped this man behind her – and whipped round, slapping it onto the man's face.

It was, she realised with stunned shock, Madanajja – Beeramma's husband, father and grandfather many times over.

He let out an agonised yelp, and, as he blindly teetered into the bags of rice and flour and lentils, the wheels of jaggery and the vats of oil, crying, 'I've been blinded. It hurts. It stings. Help!' she slipped out, but not before hissing in the dirty old man's ear, 'Don't you dare come near me again or you'll suffer worse.'

Since then, Bindu has taken to carrying the paste everywhere, but she hasn't had to use it again, for although catcalls and whistles still follow her, they do so from afar. Men now give her a wide berth, no doubt having learned from Madanajja's fate – he was bedridden for a week, his face and eyes swollen and beset by rashes – to leave her alone.

Bindu has not shared her troubles with Ajji, not wanting to worry her, especially since she's dealing with them well enough herself, so Ajji waxes lyrical, proud as punch of her granddaughter's beauty. 'Look at you! You make the moon jealous. So fair and blemish-free, such perfect features. You'll catch the eye of a prince among men.'

Bindu shudders, her recent experiences having turned her right off men. 'I'd rather study and get a job in the city and take you there with me.'

Ajji beams even more. 'Beautiful *and* clever, and not only that but kind-hearted too,' she enthuses, cupping Bindu's cheeks. 'How did I get so lucky!' Then, tenderly, 'You can have a job and also get married, you know, my heart. As it is, I've had proposals for your hand already.'

'Ajji, I'm fifteen!'

'Old enough, many would say.'

'I want to focus on my education.'

Ajji nods, smiling placidly. 'There's no hurry. Your beauty's not going to disappear.'

Bindu wishes, sometimes, that it would. The village women have taken to regarding her with suspicion and distrust.

And now, they are congregated at the lake, gathering water, washing clothes, their children and grandchildren playing beside them, monkeys chittering in the trees above while they gossip about Bindu.

Bindu hides behind a wide-trunked banyan tree, dry leaves and parched dust beneath her feet, blessedly free of anklets that would give her away, motioning to Dumdee to be quiet.

'She's a witch, weaving black magic with her looks.'

'Have you seen the way she walks? Swaying her hips in that obscene way?'

Behind the banyan, a shocked Bindu feels hot tears sting her face. She hasn't once given a thought to her walk – it's just a means of getting from one place to another. It hurts that these women, whom she has grown up among, cooked for alongside Ajji, would talk of her this way, their voices bitter as lime pips, coated with malice.

'The gods have blessed her with an abundance of beauty to make up for the fact that she's so unlucky, killing her parents and sentencing her poor grandmother to steadily worsening ill health. Pity the man who, entranced by her looks, marries her. He's condemned to a much-abbreviated lifetime of very bad luck,' Sudhamma hisses.

'She has the kind of beauty that drives men senseless. Even grown men, married men aren't immune, behaving like besotted teenagers in her presence.' Kavyamma tuts.

'But they stay well away from her, have you noticed? She's poison and they know it. At least the men from our village do.'

'She's a demon with a goddess's face.'

'Forget grown men, even little boys flock to her.'

Bindu has heard enough. Hoisting her pots, she comes out of her hiding place and walks boldly, thrusting her hips out for good measure, up to the huddle of women, all of whom she has known her whole life and has cooked for at one time or another.

They fall silent at her approach, only their little ones calling, 'Binduakka!' and running up to her, boys and girls, asking, 'D'you have anything for us?'

'No,' she says with a sigh, shaking her head.

'Are you sure?' they query, their eager little mud-streaked faces hopeful.

She looks at them, these children whose births had been celebrated with Ajji and Bindu's festive payasam, on whose cheeks and foreheads their mothers had applied the kajal prepared and distributed by Ajji and Bindu to ward off the evil eye. The same mothers who're gossiping so venomously about her now.

She makes a show of digging about in her sari skirt. 'Hmmm... let's see. No, nothing.'

'Oh!' Their faces fall.

And then, from her blouse, she takes out the pouch of

tamarind and jaggery balls she makes and carries for just this purpose. 'Ah, but what do I have here?'

The kids cheer as she distributes the sweets, one little boy kissing her hand, saying, 'You're the best, Binduakka.'

Bindu feels the women's eyes boring into her, guesses what they're thinking: *See, she entrances little boys too. None of our menfolk are safe.*

Once the sweets are distributed, the kids scatter and Bindu turns to their mothers and grandmothers. Sweetly, she asks, 'Who were you talking about just now as I approached?'

Their smiles flee, their gazes flustering away from her. 'Oh... um... someone from another village.'

'Also called Bindu! What a coincidence,' she says.

Their faces shrivel like rotten guavas.

She turns away, fills her pots. Then, with a jaunty wave good-bye, she begins the trek back home, making sure to sway her hips, thrust her breasts out.

The women look away, red-faced.

But if she thought the worst was behind her, just as Bindu is nearing the turning into the fields that will take her home, Dumdee barks sharply, and *he* emerges from the dust haze – a ghoul haunting this dreadful day. The landlord's son, Guru, she now knows, reaching out and flicking her veil from her face as if he owns her.

She jerks away from his touch, but with her hands full she cannot pull her veil back down.

'Well, well, they did say you're the prettiest girl in the city, but the rumours don't do you justice. You're by far the prettiest in the country, I'd say. And, believe me, I know.' He winks.

This is true, she thinks sourly. She's heard from eavesdropping on Muthakka when she visits with Ajji that the landlord's son is a ladies' man.

'Good job he's at boarding school for most of the year. He creates enough havoc during the holidays. The landlord issues warning after warning and his son ignores them all. No pretty woman or girl is spared, they say. You better keep Bindu away from him.' Muthakka to Ajji, caution in her voice.

'Ah, my Bindu is very good at taking care of herself,' Ajji replied, pride in her voice, and Bindu, crouched in her hiding place that was perfect for eavesdropping, wondered if, even though she'd not told Ajji what she'd done to protect herself from unwanted attention, Ajji knew anyway.

Guru has left her alone since their previous encounter but she knew this day was coming and she is prepared.

'They say you're beautiful but untouchable. Well, I've yet to meet a woman who hasn't succumbed to my charms,' Guru is saying.

'Charms? I don't see any,' Bindu mocks, even as she sets her pots down, gently, so as not to spill a drop, and, delving into her sari skirt pocket, grabs handfuls of the spice paste, all the while thinking, *Time you got what was coming to you.*

'Well, you haven't given me a chance, have you? When I approached you the last time, you weren't ready. Perhaps you are now?' He is smiling, eyebrows raised in question.

In response, she quickly smears the spice paste – this one even more lethal than the one she'd made for Madanajja, with twice the amount of chilli – liberally, on his face, onto his hands, anywhere she can, before he can get at her.

Then, while he weaves and cries out, groping blindly, 'What've you done, woman?' she wipes her stinging hands on her sari, pulls her veil back down and picks up her pots and, as she leaves, whispers in his ear as he sobs, eyes shut tight against the pain, 'Listen carefully. I'm a good girl. I'll only allow the man I marry to touch me, kiss me, you understand? Do not try this again, for, next time, it'll be ten times worse.'

'Please,' he entreats. 'I'm dying here. Help me.'

'A lotion made from crushed aloe will ease the pain and swelling. Ask one of the maids you've not offended to make and apply it to your skin. Goodbye.'

'Are you just going to walk off and leave me here? I cannot open my eyes to see where I'm going.' He's whimpering like a wounded little boy now, the coward.

She sighs. 'Where's your chauffeur?' She knows he wouldn't have walked here – he's used to being valeted everywhere.

'Parked under the peepal tree,' Guru says, through hiccups.

'I'll get him. Remember, aloe paste helps. And remember another thing: do not come near me again. I will not be one of your conquests.'

She lugs the pots in the sweltering heat to the peepal tree, where the car sits, too big for the mud road. The stray dogs and cows that usually sleep on the road in the shade cast by over-hanging peepal branches, and the monkeys that have colonised the tree, eye the car, like the farmers as they sip their toddy, with disdain. Muthakka is idly shooing flies away from the rank, sorry-looking pile of fish in her woven palm basket, wilting in the sun, with a banana leaf.

They all perk up as Bindu approaches, a thrum of energy infusing their otherwise lackadaisical day, the lethargic, humid air vibrating with the buzz of fresh activity, lending a gold-tinted slant to the interminable sameness.

The chauffeur is fast asleep, window down, flies dancing around his open mouth with each snort of expelled air.

Bindu raps on the door and he startles awake.

'Your sahib needs you. He's down there.' She points.

The men ogle her, silently. She knows they'll be speculating about her the moment her back is turned, knowing she's somehow involved in whatever's going on with the landlord's son – they best their women at tittle-tattle any day, especially with a few tumblers of toddy down them.

Muthakka beckons Bindu, wide-eyed with urgent curiosity, her intuition, honed for gossip, sniffing out a story. 'Bindu, what happened, do tell?'

The chauffeur starts the car, its roaring throttle and thrum splintering the dozy afternoon languor into screeching shreds, releasing great diesel-scented gusts, enveloping them in a gritty orange haze, the monkeys in uproar, cows lowing, dogs barking, flies buzzing in protest.

Bindu uses the noise as cover to nod and wave at Muthakka and escape, walking briskly down the road, Dumdee at her heels, watching as, up ahead, the chauffeur leads a sobbing, swollen-faced Guru into the car.

She is no longer afraid of Guru. If he has any sway, it is that he's the landlord's son. But he's not in his father's good books – he hasn't been for a long time. And, on top of that, he is a coward, all bluster; Bindu realised this when he burst out crying just now, asking her for help like a lost babe. She knows as surely as she knows her name that he won't go complaining to his father, nor will he tell anyone about this incident, for he'll be ashamed of being bested by a mere girl – his father's tenant at that.

She smiles, even though her hands are stinging from the spice paste, her body aching from carrying the pots the extra distance to the peepal tree and back, and Dumdee, sensing her triumph, licks her feet.

But as Bindu turns into the narrow path between the fields that leads to the hut she shares with Ajji, she recalls the gossiping women, their hard voices, their hurtful words, and her smile droops. Since she grew up and grew pretty, it's as if they've forgotten the person they've watched develop into adulthood from an orphaned babe – she is only judged by her looks and their effect on their men and *she* is blamed for it and that *hurts*. It hurts that they no longer see *her*, that they condemn her, not only for their men's lechery but also for protecting herself by using her lethal spice mixes on anyone who dares come too close. It hurts that they persist in assuming she's inviting this attention when she hates it and is doing all she can to repel it.

I'll show them, she thinks, tasting anger, chilli paste hot and burning, *just like I showed the landlord's son. If they think they can get away with gossiping about me, they can think again.*

CHAPTER 9

EVE

1980

'But, Mama, the recipe in Nana's cookbook says we must add coriander leaves and cashew nuts,' Izzy says, hands on hips.

'It's all right, love, she also says that we can substitute different herbs and nuts. Won't make that much of a difference.' Eve smiles at her daughter.

'It'll make *all* the difference to the flavour,' Izzy declares, nose scrunched up in indignation. 'We've tried it before with parsley, remember, and it wasn't as good. You said so yourself, Mama.'

She looks so sweet that Eve, overcome by love, bends down and drops a kiss on her daughter's upturned nose. Izzy smells of chocolate and cinnamon, from the biscuits they've just made, which are baking in the oven. It is Izzy's job to lick the bowl clean – she has taken this upon herself. She's just learned the saying *Waste not, want not* at school and she's applying it with vigour to the foods she loves; carrots, which for some reason she dislikes, not so much.

'*And* we've run out of saffron. Turmeric just won't taste right, even if Nana says we can use it instead,' Izzy asserts, as Eve, who loves it when her little one speaks like a grand old know-it-all, gathers her sweet-smelling girl in her arms and kisses her cheeks. 'Mama, are you listening?' Izzy asks, turning round in Eve's arms and cupping her face so they are eye to eye.

'I am, love.'

'We can't make the biryani unless we've all the *right* ingredients.'

'Can't we?'

'No. We *have* to go to the Asian shop again.'

Eve loves the way her daughter emphasises certain words, the way she speaks as though everything is a life-and-death emergency.

'I've writing to do, love. I'm on a deadline.' In actual fact, Eve just cannot face driving to the Asian supermarket in stop-start traffic – they already went once this morning.

Izzy sees right through her. 'You're making excuses, Mama.' She pulls away from Eve's embrace and places her hands on her hips again, her face stern as she peruses her mother.

'What's this about excuses?' Joe is back from his run, sweaty and panting, smiling at his wife and daughter in turn.

'Dad, we need coriander and cashew nuts and saffron for the biryani. But Mama doesn't want to go to the Asian shop,' Izzy complains.

'Give me a minute to wash and change, sweetheart, and I'll take you,' Joe says and Izzy beams at her father, running to him with open arms and stopping just as he drops down onto his haunches for his hug.

'I'll wait until you've washed,' she says, making a face, and Joe's twinkling gaze meets Eve's and they both burst out laughing.

Knock. Knock. Knock.

Eve startles awake. 'Coming, Izzy.' The words die on her lips as the emptiness of the house slams into her, along with reality, breaking her heart afresh.

She's fallen asleep on the sofa.

Knock. Knock. Knock.

Someone at the door.

Not Sue. No cheery voice accompanying the staccato bursts of head-pounding noise.

Her head aches. Her heart aches. It's too cruel – to fall asleep, and to dream of her husband, her child. And not just any dream, but that one. The last time they were together, happy, alive, unbroken. A unit. A family. 'Don't go,' she should've screamed. 'We'll cook another recipe from Nana's book...'

Knock. Knock. Knock.

Eve sits up, feeling faint, light-headed. Her blurry eyes register flashes of colour. She blinks once, then again.

No, she's not seeing things, imagining things.

Her heart drums in terror. For, pulsing blue lights arc eerie blue and black shadows on her walls.

Her mind reels, stuck on that awful day when she'd waited in vain for her husband and child to come home. She'd seen the flashing blue lights, heard the sirens as they rushed past, and yet, she did not make the connection. Did not understand until much later that it was for them – her family as was.

And now, flashing blue lights outside her door once again.

Oh dear God. Something's happened.

Knock. Knock. Knock.

And then a child's voice, barely holding back tears. 'Please, Eve, open the door.'

CHAPTER 10

BINDU

1936

Bindu skips down the hill, between the fields, everything silent and baking in the blazing sunlight. She misses Dumdee beside her, but he's standing guard at home, like she asked him to, keeping Ajji company until it's time for Bindu to return home from school.

Attending school is sheer pleasure, for Bindu likes studying. She loves maths – knowing there's always an answer to every question if you follow the steps methodically, unlike life, which is messy and unfair. She likes history – past lives, involved human stories that show that however hard her life feels, others have had it so much worse. Her absolute favourite subject is English. She loves grammar, its backbone, rules and strictures scaffolding the language. Perversely, she delights in its idiosyncrasies, how some words that should rhyme do not, how there are always, always exceptions to the rule. She marvels at how twenty-six letters combine to produce such an intricate, beautiful language.

While lessons are fun, Bindu also looks forward to break times spent gossiping with Sunitha, her best friend. Sunitha hates lessons; her only goal is to get married. She is the eldest daughter and would rather be at home looking after her siblings – she adores children and wants several of her own – but she attends school because she thinks a command of English and sums will help secure a good match.

Sunitha was born with one leg shorter than the other. 'I'll not get offers for my hand because of my limp,' she cries, 'so I'm subjecting myself to this torture in the hope that *someone* will overlook my deformity and marry me for my English and maths skills. If they're illiterate, all the better, for they won't know that I'm not good at either.'

Bindu's reassurances fall on deaf ears: 'Don't put yourself down. You're beautiful, kind, caring. You'll find a man who loves you for who you are – if that's what you want. Personally, I don't think you need a man to make you happy.'

'All right for you to say. You're blessed with an abundance of beauty *and* brains,' Sunitha sighs.

There is no guile in Sunitha, no envy, only adoration and fierce loyalty, unlike the other girls, who are jealous of Bindu, making catty comments behind her back – and, every so often, to her face, which she parries sharply.

Yes, Bindu enjoys school, but there are days – like today – when she feels claustrophobic, when it all gets too much. She feels hemmed in, by the pressure to be a dutiful granddaughter and model student. And so, after lunch, when Sunitha goes back into class, Bindu slips away.

She will tell the nuns and Sunitha the next day that Ajji was ill and needed help. She easily catches up on the missed work, so the nuns can't complain; despite missing classes, she's ahead of her classmates and she aces any tests.

Bindu escapes school and walks from one end of the village to another. It is that time of day, after lunch when the sun is at its zenith, when all the villagers not at work are snoozing. At home, Ajji will have rolled out the fraying mat she and Bindu share at night and will be lying down beside the opening to their hut, the old sari that masquerades as a door swaying in the occasional breeze and caressing Ajji's face with dust and marigold-flavoured kisses. If Bindu was home, she'd be joining Ajji, after washing the pots used to cook lunch, and Ajji, while still asleep, would throw an arm round Bindu. Dumdee would sprawl across the threshold and, in minutes, his snores would compete with Ajji's.

This afternoon, Bindu is free to roam, all alone, this sun-battered, slumbering village that is her home, that she loves and loathes in equal measure.

Her steps take her to Sudhamma's compound. Sudhamma, the most vocal of the gossips, calling Bindu a demon with a goddess's face, her voice foul as a rotten egg, dripping with venom more poisonous than a cobra's.

The cow tethered to the post outside Sudhamma's hut is fast asleep, moist brown nose twitching as flies land on it. Sudhamma's saris wave cheerily from the clothes line strung beside the well, multi-hued flags, her husband's yellowed lungis, loincloths, looking wan and dirty in contrast. Two scrawny chickens peck half-heartedly at the dirt beside the well, scattering when Bindu approaches.

Ajji's long-ago warning, to deter toddler Bindu's curiosity, echoes in teenage Bindu's ears: 'Wells're dangerous. The silver-tongued goddess who lives there's partial to little girls, especially lucky ones with double crowns.'

The well is covered by a net. Bindu peers into its pixelated dark mouth, her hands slipping on the velvet moss of the well surround. It goes on and on, hypnotic wet darkness, cool and hushed, and there, deep within its mesmerising depths, a starburst silver twinkle.

Bindu steps away before the urge to give herself to the tanta-lising undulations, to explore those shimmering ellipticals, gets too much. She tiptoes past the hut, Sudhamma's snores reverber-ating from inside, to the cashew tree in her courtyard, flush with sunset-coloured fruit, sated bees drunk on juice asleep on the flowers, the scent of honeyed must. Bindu plucks a rosy cashew, juice exploding on her tongue, nectar sweet.

She's reaching for the fourth cashew when—

'Who's there?' An irate voice from within the hut.

She's been so absorbed in eating that she hadn't noticed the snores had stopped.

Bindu runs as fast and as silently as she can, trying to avoid her feet scrunching on the dry leaves littering the courtyard.

By the time Sudhamma is at the doorway of her hut, peering

blearily out, Bindu is squatting in the dirt at the base of the mango trees at the edge of the compound.

'I'll get you, thief, stealing my fruit,' Sudhamma cries, waving bony fists into the air, and the crows who were no doubt snoozing among the branches above where Bindu is hiding caw plaintively in complaint at their peace being disturbed so summarily.

Bindu is too absorbed to pay attention to Sudhamma's threats – she's busy gathering the raw mangoes that have fallen during the morning that Sudhamma hasn't got round to collecting yet. They're right beside where Bindu is hiding, like offerings from the gods. It's Sudhamma's fault she has left them here, for others – Bindu – to find. She'll save them for later – they're great pickled in brine and served with congee, they're wonderful grated in a chutney, but they're best in that spicy red chilli curry that is Ajji's trademark. They've been eating it plain as there's been a dearth of vegetables to add, but raw mango would give it a sour-sweet taste, plump it up nicely, add bite when consumed with rice.

Bindu collects all the mangoes and, with Sudhamma grumbling to herself while pottering about cluelessly inside her hut, she carefully makes her way to the courtyards of other villagers vocal in their disapproval of her in search of more bounty.

She's nearly at Kavyamma's courtyard – she has a glut of guavas that Bindu has set her sights on – when a whisper explodes loud as a gunshot in the somnolent, mid-afternoon torpor.

'I saw what you did.'

She swivels round, her heart drumming a staccato warning, the hand not holding her stolen goods reaching for her weapon of spice paste. This is the first time she's encountered anyone else out and about during these afternoon escapades. And of course, it has to be *him*.

Guru, the landlord's son, standing a good few paces away from her, a smirk in his voice. 'You're a thief in addition to being a violent criminal.'

'I'm no criminal,' she says even as she processes the implications of being caught by this boy. He knows she's stolen the fruit, but he doesn't know she's skipped school to do it. And in any case, what business is it of his?

'You assaulted me with spice paste, had me bed-bound for a week.'

Is he out for revenge? What can he do? Whatever it is, she'll not give in easily.

'That was your own fault,' she retorts.

'I just wanted to talk to you.' His voice rises in a whine.

She feels her heartbeat settle. He's just a man, like any other, taken in by her looks. She can deal with him. 'I wasn't taking any chances.'

'Well, I'm not taking any chances now.'

Yes, he's exactly like all the other men, scared of her wielding her deadly spice paste and yet ogling her from a distance, even when all that's visible of her is her eyes. Ha! 'I can see that. You're a good ten paces away.'

'And I'm keeping your hands in my eyeline at all times.'

She smiles.

'You're so pretty.' He sighs. 'Even with the veil covering your face. The prettiest woman I've ever seen.'

Her smile dries up. Why won't any of these men get the message? She's not interested. 'You said you're not taking any chances.'

'I'm not.'

'So, why're you here at all?'

'I was walking to clear my head when I saw you stealing.'

He needs to escape too?

'Why do *you* need to clear your head?'

'I'm fed up with my father's dictatorship.'

'Ha! You don't know the meaning of dictatorship. *We* suffer under your father's dictatorship. You're his son, his beneficiary.'

'I'm his prisoner.'

'*Please*! Don't expect me to be sympathetic.'

She sneaks a glance at him from under her veil. Has she gone too far? But no...

'I am,' he is saying, emphatically, his gaze imploring her to believe him. 'I have to do as he says, always. If I veer from what's expected of me, I'm punished, sent to boarding school, although thankfully that threat at least is in the past now. I cannot put a foot wrong.'

'And yet, from what I hear, you've put plenty.'

'All rumour. The few times I've tried, I've been sorely tasked for it. He is cruel, my father.'

'I agree. But at least you have water to drink, food to eat.'

'Is that why you were stealing, because you've no food to eat?' His voice gentle, understanding.

Perversely, it makes her mad. 'If that was the case, I wouldn't steal from people who're in the same boat as I am. I'd steal from *you*.'

She can't believe she's speaking like this, so openly, to the land-lord's son.

But he's not angry at what his father, she is sure, would consider insolence. Instead of retaliating, or stalking off to complain to him, he is curious.

'So why were you stealing from them then?'

'They deserve it.'

'Why?'

He seems genuinely interested in her answers. And the way he looks at her, adoration and attention – the landlord's son, heeding her opinions, responding as if they're equals – it's heady and flat-tering. He doesn't seem fazed by her stealing. In fact, he is admiring.

'They've been gossiping about me.'

'Do you always mete out justice to those who you think have wronged you?'

'Always.'

In the distance, the faint chiming of bells, indicating the end of the school day.

'I need to go,' she says.

'You've been skiving off school to steal?' He sounds even more admiring.

She nods. 'I stay until lunch and then I escape.'

'Why do you stay until then, why not skip school entirely?'

'For the meal, of course.'

'Oh.'

'Yes, not everyone has three meals on tap like you.'

He has the grace to look ashamed.

'Anyway, in spite of missing school, I top the class in all the exams – by a large margin at that.' She smiles. 'What, why are you looking at me like that?'

'You're even more beautiful when you smile, if that's possible.'

'You can't even see it.' She scoffs. 'I might be frowning for all you know.'

'Your eyes crinkle pleasingly when you smile.'

'But it's my brain I'm banking on. It'll take me far.'

'Not if you're caught stealing.'

'You won't tell, will you?' She bats her eyelashes through her veil. Any fear she had of him, any awe, is gone. He's just a man like the rest. But with one difference. He listens to her when she speaks – and it's wonderfully intoxicating. Until now, men have only responded to her beauty, but he is actually engaging her in conversation.

'I might. It's my fruit after all.'

'What do you mean, yours?'

'All the land in this village is leased by my father.'

'So that makes it your father's, not yours,' she snaps, astounded by his arrogance.

'I'll inherit it eventually.'

'Will you be as miserly as your father?'

'What do you mean, miserly?' His eyes flash and his jaw works furiously. She has touched a nerve.

'I thought you were angry with your father. You called him cruel.'

'He's still my father.'

'But that's no excuse! He measures how many ingredients he sends us when we prepare his orders. We cannot even taste the food we cook for him.'

'He pays you well.'

'He doesn't provide water for us to cook with even during the drought.'

'Why should he? He's paying you for your labour.'

She knows she should stop, his voice is getting increasingly heated, but... 'He's increased the farmers' rent.'

'He has to, it makes business sense.'

'Don't you see, he's taking from people who have nothing?'

'And you aren't?' Raised eyebrow as he looks pointedly at her bag of pilfered fruit.

The tinkle of voices wafts on the dusty, tamarind-flavoured breeze – her classmates walking home from school.

'I have to go,' she says.

'Enjoy the fruit. Don't worry, I won't tell on you.' He grins.

Bindu walks away, swaying her hips, just like the village women commented, feeling his eyes on her all the way, and liking it, enjoying the power she has over him, the landlord's son, when the landlord wields power over the entire village.

Perhaps her beauty has some uses after all.

CHAPTER 11

BINDU

1937

'Children, let's start the day with the hymn, "The Lord Is My Shepherd".' Sister Hilda claps her hands to begin class just as Bindu, who's been up since dawn preparing spice pastes, peeling and boiling vegetables, chopping and marinating meat – they've two orders to send out by lunchtime today, and she wanted to do her bit to help Ajji so she could attend school in good conscience – rushes in breathless and slides onto the floor next to Sunitha, who always saves a space for her. Sister Hilda raises an eyebrow at Bindu. 'What've we said about punctuality, Bindu?'

'I'm on time, Sister.'

'Just. Not to mention the number of classes you've missed.'

'Then why're you mentioning it?' Bindu mutters under her breath, while Sunitha nudges her with her elbow: *Don't court trouble.*

'Pardon me?' Sister Hilda's voice steely.

'I always catch up,' Bindu says.

'Yet still, you're in your matriculation year. The subjects are harder and the work more intense. You say you want to win a scholarship to study further.'

'Yes, I do.'

. . .

'Here at the convent, we teach only until matriculation, as you know, but if you continue performing at your current standard, you're almost assured of the top grades at the matriculation exams and that means you'll be awarded a scholarship to study further in the city,' Sister Maria Teresa, the headmistress, had said when she'd called Bindu in for a chat at the start of her matriculation year. 'But be warned,' Sister Maria Teresa was stern, 'you must attend and keep on top of *all* your lessons.'

'Yes, Sister,' Bindu had said, fidgeting with her veil, unable to meet the nun's censorial gaze. Then, a thought occurred to her, 'Will the scholarship cover my grandmother's...?'

'No. It'll only cover your expenses.'

'The nuns say I can get a scholarship to continue my studies in the city after matriculation,' she had told Ajji that evening.

'I'm so proud of you, my heart,' Ajji had cheered, gathering Bindu into her spice-scented embrace. Then, looking assessingly at her grandchild, 'Why aren't you pleased?'

'The scholarship won't cover your lodging and living costs.'

'Don't worry, I'll be fine here.'

'But, Ajji, you're not in the best of health...'

'I can manage. I've life in these old bones yet.'

'The orders... Your shakes... How will you...?' Bindu appeared to have lost the ability to form complete sentences.

'I can manage the orders for the villagers myself. They'll go easy on me. We look out for each other. For the landlord's orders, I'll ask someone to help me. I'll share the landlord's payment with them. Bindu, my heart, don't worry about me. Study further. Get a good job – that way, you'll make an even better marriage, maybe nab a prince.'

'I don't want to rely on a man, I'll provide for us myself. I'll build you a mansion in the city.'

Ajji beamed, her eyes glowing with joy and dreams, 'My star. You'll do anything you set your mind to.' Then, tearing up: 'I only wish your parents were here to revel in you. But *I* get the privilege. You're my good-luck charm.'

. . .

Now, Sister Hilda says, 'If you intend to win the scholarship, then you need to be focussed and diligent.'

'I *am* focussed and diligent.'

'But you miss too many classes – and not always with the intention of helping your grandmother, is it?'

'Yes, it *is* to help my grandmother,' Bindu says, but her heart is sinking, for she knows what's coming.

'Then why did someone see you by the lake when you were meant to be at school? And before you say you were fetching water for your grandmother, you were with a boy, I'm told.'

Her classmates gasp in shock. Sunitha looks at her, mouthing, 'Your reputation!'

'And not only that, there've been reports you've been stealing fruit from villagers' courtyards.'

More exclamations of exaggerated shock from her classmates.

'I don't believe it,' Sunitha, loyal to the core, whispers, her breath hot and sweet in Bindu's ear.

Who's been running to the nuns telling tales? Bindu wonders, feeling hot ire flood her mouth. Not Guru, she is sure. For he's the boy she was with – he's taken to joining her during her afternoon escapades. She sees that he, too, like her, feels trapped in his life, trying and failing to fit into the mould his father expects of him.

'He hates me,' he said the last time they met and Bindu heard the pain he was trying to hide behind a scowl, causing his voice to tremble. 'I'm not the son he expected.'

Although Guru clashes with his father, when Bindu tries to veer the conversation towards his father's misdeeds he clams up, gets angry, refuses to listen – or, worse, defends his father. And yet, the paradox is that Guru is the only one who understands the rebellious side of Bindu that tires of being the dutiful granddaughter, the good student, the good friend. He talks to her and, most of the time, listens when she talks, which is a novelty in this village, where everyone has an opinion of her and where they all expect her to behave in a certain way.

'Her beauty's gone straight to her head,' she's heard the villagers whisper. 'She's boasting of getting a scholarship from book learning. She claims she'll go to the city, become a doctor, cure her grandmother of her shakes and cough. Pah, big-headed pipe dreams. Bad luck dogs her like a cursed spirit. She can try but will never escape her dark destiny.'

It makes Bindu all the more determined to show them all, be independent, never rely on anyone for her livelihood, make her own money, provide Ajji with a comfortable retirement.

Bindu wants so *much*, but at times the pressure of trying to achieve it is overwhelming. She tries to be a caring granddaughter, but resents having to work into the night to spare her grandmother when they've orders the next day so she can attend school on a clear conscience, even though her grandmother neither expects it nor asks for it. She wants the scholarship so she can study further and rescue her grandmother from her life of drudgery, but she worries she may not be as good as she thinks. What if she doesn't get the scholarship? What if the villagers are right?

At times, while cooking, the scent of raw onions, sizzling garlic, caramelised sugar and proving dough surrounding her, she is tempted to empty the salt pot or pour a whole bowlful of crushed chillies into the dish she's preparing, overcome by an impulse to destroy, to ruin, to run from the village, the gossip, her life.

Someone saw her with Guru, but they want to protect Ajji – she is beloved in the village, having helped everyone at some point or another, while her feisty granddaughter, who teases the men from afar but assaults them with spices if they dare get too close, who challenges the women and steals from them when they gossip about her, is not. So, they came to the nuns bearing tales of Bindu's transgressions.

She hates this village and can't wait to get away. She'll study hard and move to the city, where she'll be anonymous. Just she and Ajji in a sea of people who don't have their noses deep in each other's business. But to do that, she must first get through school.

How to explain to anyone else when she can't quite understand it herself, that school, which she loves, gets too much sometimes – the rules, the strict rigidity of the nuns, even Sunitha's company, her unswerving admiration and loyalty – and she *has* to escape?

She needs a break, fresh air and space, some time to herself, a release from the pressure in her head, the desire to perform, to be something for everyone: dutiful granddaughter, star pupil, best friend.

She walks from one end of the village to another, stealing fruit from villagers' orchards as they snooze. She eats the stolen fruit and feels better at having got back at them for their gossiping, and whatever she cannot eat, she saves for Ajji for later, coming up with some excuse for how she obtained the bounty. Her grandmother trustingly believes her lies, thinking only the best of her grandchild, and this makes Bindu feel guilty – but not so much as to stop stealing. It is her outlet. Her secret rebellion, only Guru party to it.

Bindu enjoys the power she has over the landlord's son, how his eyes widen with admiration at her supposed fearlessness.

'I dare you to enter my father's compound. It's well guarded, you know,' he'd said the other day.

'Ha, a steal for me,' she'd declared.

She'd sashayed up to the guard, hips swinging, smiling at him, lifting her veil so he caught a glimpse of her face.

'I've a message for my aunt who works in the kitchens,' she'd said, batting her eyelashes seductively.

And that was it. She was in.

'He needs to be replaced,' Guru had said afterwards, 'if he is so easily manipulated.'

'Don't, it was my fault,' Bindu had remonstrated. 'He doesn't need to lose his job. It's his livelihood.'

'Well, his job is to guard my father's property,' Guru had retorted, eyes flashing, 'and he didn't do it. So why should he be spared?'

'Because he has a wife and children depending on him,' she'd countered.

'If he has a wife, he shouldn't be swayed by another woman, should he?'

'Why are *you* here, speaking to me, when you're all but betrothed to a princess, so I hear?' Muthakka had relayed this choice piece of gossip and, while Ajji had been excited, hoping for the landlord's custom and the renown catering for his only son and heir's wedding would bring, Bindu found herself wondering if Guru had had any say in the matter, whether he was pleased or felt even more trapped.

'You're different to any woman I've met. In any case, you haven't been updated on the latest news as regards the princess.'

'Oh?'

'I'm not in my father's good books right now.'

'Are you ever?'

He had smiled, but she saw pain flash in his eyes. He had told her often enough that he'd given up trying to please his father when he realised he never would. It had made Bindu realise afresh how lucky she was in Ajji. The villagers might condemn her as a harbinger of bad luck, a wild child, a seductress, but Ajji only ever saw the best in her: 'You're my lucky gift, beautiful inside and out, my heart.' Whatever happened, Bindu would always have her grandmother's force field of love. Even in the darkest of days, she glowed in the beacon of Ajji's devotion, always the centre of Ajji's world. Nothing and nobody could take that from her.

'What've you done to upset your father this time?' Bindu had asked Guru.

'Refused to marry that princess – the latest in a long line.'

'Why?'

'They're all the same. Beautiful and dutiful and filthy rich with it.'

'They sound perfect wife material for the landlord's son and heir,' she'd scoffed.

'I want someone different, someone with spirit.'

'Ah.' She'd arched an eyebrow at him.

'Someone fiery and feisty.'

She'd pulled out the chilli paste.

He'd laughed. 'Someone who makes me laugh,' he'd said, between chuckles.

'And cry.' She'd waved the chilli paste at him.

He had wiped tears of mirth from his eyes.

'Just to clarify,' she'd said firmly, 'you're my friend, that's all.'

'More than a friend, surely?' He'd twinkled at her.

'To me you're a friend, and even that's a bit of a stretch,' she'd said, yawning, although in truth she enjoyed his company, most of the time.

'Even if I refuse princesses for you?'

'I don't need a man – any man – to complete or define me. I'll make my own way in the world,' she'd insisted.

'You're confident,' Guru'd said, eyebrows raised, tone sceptical.

'I am. Mark my words, I'll ace my matriculation exams and win a scholarship to study in the city,' she'd declared, even as a small part of her whispered, *Then why did you get so nervous, so overwhelmed, that you had to escape school today?*

'You're quite something,' he had said.

'I know,' she'd replied, and he'd laughed.

'When you go to study in the city, will you forget me?'

'Of course. You're just someone to pass the time with.'

He winced. 'That's all I am to you?'

'That's all.'

'What if I arrange for my father to provide water along with the other ingredients required to prepare his orders? Will you remember me then?'

'I'd like all the villagers to have water, not just us.'

'You ask for too much.'

'Will you arrange it?'

'I can't. My father—'

She'd turned to leave. 'Goodbye. As I said, you're just someone to pass the time with.'

'Do you talk to other boys like you do with me?' Guru asked one time.

'What's it to you?' Bindu countered.

His eyes flashed fiery orange sparks. 'Are you a whore?'

'This conversation is over,' she said, walking away.

'I'm sorry. I just... I think we share something special and I... Where're you going?'

'I said, this conversation is over.'

His hand whipped out to stop her and, just as quickly, she took out her spice paste.

'Don't touch me.'

'So, it's fine to flirt with me...' he spat.

'I never flirted with you. I had conversations with you, on my terms.'

'You're a tease.'

'Goodbye.'

Bindu skipped school again a week later when she noticed that her Ajji was getting weaker – her grandmother was unable to disguise the limitations of her ageing body, however much she tried to keep her ailments from Bindu.

The previous evening, Ajji had tried to lift a pot she usually handled with ease and had nearly dropped it – if Bindu hadn't caught it in time, it would have smashed. Ajji had laughed it off: 'I was a hundred miles away – I really must pay more attention to what I'm doing.'

But Bindu could see her grandmother was shaken – she hadn't expected to lose control like that. It scared Bindu. She wanted *so* much for her grandmother to retire, to not have to worry about whether they had enough orders to see them through the week.

'Ajji, I'll stay home tomorrow, do the cooking. You must res—'

But Ajji hadn't let Bindu finish. 'You cannot afford to miss school, my heart. I'll manage fine.'

'Ajji—'

'I'm all right. You worry too much.' Ajji was firm, but in the tired lines crowding her eyes, the sighs that involuntarily escaped her when she thought her granddaughter was out of earshot, Bindu read the truth. Her grandmother was getting frail – she couldn't cope with the orders as easily as she'd done before. Cooking didn't afford Ajji the same joy it once had – it required effort and energy she no longer had.

But she wouldn't countenance her granddaughter staying home from school to help her, and so Bindu had waited until her grandmother was snoring softly beside her on the mat, and then she'd got up to prepare spice mixes and chop all the vegetables. She'd stumbled onto the mat beside Ajji when she could no longer stand up straight for exhaustion, and had woken again at 4 a.m. to finish off the last remaining jobs.

When Ajji woke to vegetables chopped and ready for sautéing, spice mixes prepared, rice picked free of stones and soaking in water, chapati dough risen, she was touched, even as she chastised Bindu gently, cupping her face, tears shining in her eyes: 'You're such a good girl, my heart. I'm so lucky in you.'

It made Bindu feel like a fraud, for while she was cooking, darkness pressing taut and fragrant with wistful dreams and ripe secrets, Dumdee's snores competing with Ajji's, her sleep-heavy eyes drooping, her body aching with fatigue, she'd resented every waking moment, silently screaming, *I don't want to do this. I want to be free. Free of cooking. Free of this village and its constraints. Free of the demands on me.*

She'd gone to school and her worries about Ajji's deteriorating health, the pressure to perform well in her exams, to win the scholarship, to rescue Ajji from drudgery, get her seen by an English doctor whose medicine, the nuns said, was backed up by science and thus effective, unlike the wise man whom she'd over-heard Sister Hilda call a 'quack' – a rarely heard note of disdain in her voice – had set up such a clamour in her head that she *had* to escape.

And when she did, Guru fell into step beside her.

She ignored him, their last conversation when he'd called her a flirt, a tease, a whore, rankling.

'Bindu, I'm sorry. I was out of order.' He was contrite. 'Please. Forgive me?'

She turned to him, eyes flashing. 'Rein your temper in when with me.'

'I will.'

'Why're you smiling and shaking your head that way?' She was curious.

'You're the first girl I've apologised to. Pleaded with. You're something special.'

'That I am.'

They were silent, content to walk companionably beneath the cloudless sky, shadows of birds slurs on its golden splendour.

After a bit, Guru said, 'Did you mean it when you said you do not need or want any man?'

'Yes. I'll make my own way in the world.'

'Can I convince you otherwise?'

'You can try. But you'll fail.'

He laughed.

As she was leaving, 'Friends?' he asked.

'Friends,' she agreed, to keep the peace, although he wasn't really, not the way Sunitha was. He was a spoilt rich boy who had a jealous temper and lashed out when things didn't go his way. He had no influence over his father, and when Bindu tried to tell Guru how his father's tyranny towards the villagers was squeezing the life out of them, he refused to listen, too in thrall to his father, no matter how much he complained about him: 'He doesn't listen to me. He doesn't care for me. I'm a nuisance to him.' Guru tried for nonchalance, but his voice was wounded all the same, bleeding hurt. 'Why do you think I'm here, running away from there? I'm a pawn to him, just like all of you.'

Guru refused to see how badly his father's selfishness affected the villagers. He didn't understand the way she and the other villagers lived – his life was too comfortable, too safe – and wasn't interested in finding out. He was, like she'd told him before, just someone to pass the time with, when others' expectations of her, and the pressure to meet the goals she had set for herself, got too much.

And now, someone has noticed and come to the nuns bearing complaints.

'You'll not miss class again without giving notice first,' Sister Hilda is saying.

'But I don't know when the orders—'

'We've let you get away with too much, Bindu. You might be bright, but if you want to study further, you need to attend classes more regularly. We'll not entertain you missing classes for no reason at all.'

'But—'

'If you do so again, you'll go straight to Sister Maria Teresa, who might decide to suspend you.' With this declaration, Sister Hilda turns to the class: 'Now, children, shall we begin singing "The Lord Is My Shepherd"?'

Sunitha squeezes Bindu's hand, offering silent comfort.

Bindu blinks away the hot moisture stabbing her eyes, tasting the hot briny bite of anger and upset, fiery chilli red.

Defiantly, she puts her hand up, the only one who does.

Sister Hilda's gaze sweeps over her raised hand. Bindu sees the nun deliberate whether to ignore her. Then, she sighs. 'Yes, Bindu?'

'Why do we have to learn about Jesus when we're Hindus?'

Beside her, Sunitha nudges: *Stop.*

But Bindu doesn't want to stop. She's been up since dawn cooking so she could attend school. She ran all the way here so she could make it in time, and even though she did, Sister Hilda took her to task about it. And she's angry with Sister Hilda for suggesting suspension. They might bluster about it, but they'll not suspend her, she's sure – why would they when she's their star pupil? She'll bring accolades and credit to their missionary school when she wins the scholarship.

Two bright pink spots adorn Sister Hilda's alabaster cheeks, a sure sign that Bindu is testing her patience to its very limits. 'I think you're being rude and insolent, but I'll answer your question,' she says rigidly. 'The only texts we've enough of for all the girls we serve in this school are Bibles and hymn books. Hence we use them to teach you to read, write and converse in the English language. If you do not want to learn the language, you can leave. Well?'

Sunitha nudges her again, but Bindu doesn't need her friend's caution; she knows she must rein herself in.

'I don't want to leave,' she says, mouth bitter with bile. 'And I do enjoy the Bible stories and hymns. I just wanted to know why we had to learn them.'

'And now you know. So, if you're quite done with your questions, shall we, at last, proceed with our hymn?'

'Yes, Sister.'

CHAPTER 12

BINDU

'Bindu, you've been summoned by the headmistress,' her classmates announce, as they swing from the low-hanging branches of the bimbli tree, their feet kicking up dust, faces scrunched up from the tart sweetness of the fruit they're snacking on, exotic birds displacing the habitual occupants who screech (the parrots) and caw (the crows) their outrage in green-winged, red-beaked and beady black flusters.

Bindu has arrived at school late and breathless as usual, having run all the way. She was up at four again this morning to prepare the masalas required for the day's orders, to spare her grandmother, whose cough is getting progressively worse, although she tries to hide it, who is shaking all over now – her hands, her head, her entire body.

Her classmates' voices are a mixture of avid curiosity and thrilling fear on her behalf, their inquisitive expressions asking, *What've you done* now?

Sunitha limps up to her, squeezing her hand, offering silent reassurance.

Perhaps Sister Maria Teresa is finally fed up with Bindu missing school and turning up late more often than not, Bindu thinks, tasting despair, bitter as methi seeds, in her mouth.

Oh, why did she have to skive off yesterday?

But, as the matriculation exams draw near, the pressure to perform is getting to Bindu and she has to escape, blow off steam, despite knowing that some busybody is watching and only too eager to report her misdeeds to the nuns, who have threatened her with suspension time and again. But, just as she surmised, the nuns haven't yet gone through with their threats, for Bindu is the star pupil on whom rest the hopes of the school.

But has she gone too far this time?

Once or twice, Bindu had tried to interest Sunitha in skiving with her.

'Why do you do it?' Sunitha asked. 'You know you shouldn't.'

Bindu did. But how to explain to Sunitha that it was a compulsion? That some days, her head felt like it was bursting, and although she knew she was risking her scholarship, courting suspension, she *had* to flee.

'In any case, even if I joined you,' Sunitha said, 'my limp means that I can't run if someone sees us. I'll be caught.'

'I'll carry you,' Bindu promised.

'You, slip of a girl?'

'I'm stronger than you think.'

'That I can believe. Mentally, you're strong. Anything you set your mind to, you do. You've the landlord's son besotted, I hear. You're the only one he respects, they say. You could marry him, if you wanted to. Imagine – you'd be the landlord's wife, lording it over us. I'd have to call you Memsahib.' Sunitha's voice thick with awe.

Bindu was unimpressed. 'First of all, I'm Bindu to my friends.'

Sunitha beamed with pleasure.

'Secondly, I don't want to marry Guru – or anyone else for that matter.'

'You're mad.' Sunitha's voice was even more awed. 'Why would you not want to marry the landlord's son, be set for life, not have to worry about where your next meal is coming from, have people wait on you?'

'I want to study, get a job, make my own money. Besides, I

don't love Guru.'

'Pah,' Sunitha snorted. 'Love is a luxury only the rich can afford to indulge in. When our stomachs are empty and throats are parched, where's the time to ruminate on love?'

Now, Sunitha whispers in Bindu's ear, her bimbli-scented breath hot and tart with fear on Bindu's behalf: 'I'm sure it's nothing. Sister Maria Teresa will issue another warning that you'll ignore.'

This makes Bindu smile, just as Sunitha intended, although fear bites her chest, palpitating yellow. *Please let me be allowed to write the exams, so I can win the scholarship.*

Why, oh why, has she been skiving when so much depends on her doing well in these exams?

But therein lies the bind – *because* it means so much, she gets scared, overwhelmed, doubts festering, nagging, choking the hope from her: *what if I can't do it?* And then she has to walk off the fear, the worry, parry with Guru, revel in his admiration, listen to him grumble about his life, so very different from hers, and feel her heartbeat settle as she finds herself again.

A parrot screeches somewhere among the fields and a cow lows mournfully. From the chapel in the nuns' convent, the bronze keen of bells mourning a death in the village. When someone local dies, the nuns dedicate a mass to the departed, accompanied by the soulful clanging of bells chiming goodbye and God bless.

Who is gone? Bindu racks her brain.

Ah, old Baiju, permanently doused and marinated in the palm toddy that he brews, whom the priests from the missionary house in town converted to Christianity when he was in one such daze, who has finally succumbed to his devotion to his one true faith – nearly 100 per cent proof palm toddy.

The bells continue their sombre song, the parrots joining in, beaks glowing red, bright green bodies vivid flashes among the orange-dusted foliage, the morning air, already infused with the heat of the day to come, vibrating, dust motes dancing in the golden haze.

Hearing the lugubrious sound makes Bindu's heart seize with

worry – will it be Ajji's turn soon?

Bindu wants to be able to afford English medicine, which the nuns and also the landlord and his noble and royal associates swear by – Muthakka again relaying gossip picked up while hawking fish under the peepal tree – for Ajji. But, perhaps because it's so successful, English medicine is exorbitantly expensive, which is why the villagers come to Ajji for herbal remedies – ironic, as her own remedies haven't done her any good – and, failing that, they turn to the wise man for potions and prayers, believing he has a direct line to the gods.

Bindu wanted to win the scholarship to provide Ajji with a comfortable retirement, but now it is *imperative* that she do so, for it is the only way she can get medical help for Ajji. But this means Bindu feels even more pressured and inevitably leads to her skiving off school even when in doing so, she is sabotaging the very thing she wants most in the world.

'You can't get away with this behaviour, Bindu. It'll catch up with you. You think you can do it all, miss lessons and still get top marks. It's not that easy. You cannot have everything,' Sister Hilda had cautioned, when, once again, Bindu was seen in the company of a boy when she should've been at school. And not just any boy, the landlord's notorious son.

'She doesn't care for her reputation,' Bindu heard the village women whisper, and this perversely made her want to do it all the more.

'Last warning,' Sister Maria Teresa had decreed at their previous meeting. So, she is to be suspended.

Bindu has inadvertently done what she feared – let her grandmother down instead of making her proud, when her grandmother has shaped her entire life around Bindu. She has lost the only opportunity to restore Ajji's health, better her quality of life, because the pressure got to her and she skived once too often.

With a heavy heart she makes her way to her audience with the headmistress, her classmates watching with fearful thrill, only Sunitha genuinely worried for her, the others thinking, like the villagers, that Bindu deserves it. *The gods have blessed her with beauty and brains to compensate for her bad luck, but the bad luck will always triumph.*

The sonorous gong of bells echoes Bindu's disheartening thoughts, sounding death knells on her future. She will not win the scholarship, will not be able to afford English medicine for her grandmother. This means, Bindu thinks, her heart wailing, soon those bells might toll for her Ajji.

No. *No.*

She will not go without a fight. She will beg Sister Maria Teresa, plead with her to keep her on. Bindu is so near to achieving her goal – she can almost touch it.

'Sister Maria Teresa looked more grim than we've ever seen her,' her classmates chant as Bindu takes reluctant steps towards the headmistress's office, which is, in reality, a corner of the school hut, situated in the convent compound, partitioned by cardboard for privacy, smelling of chalk and punishment.

Bindu is so weary, the calluses on her hands stinging, aware, suddenly, of her sari stained by mud and spices, fraying at the seams; aware of every pebble that has lodged in the welts and cuts of her bare feet as she skirted the stream that is now completely bone-dry, and through the fields, Dumdee howling the further away she got, having been instructed by her, with a kiss goodbye, to look after Ajji in her absence.

She hears the whispers of her classmates, the rustle and creak as they nimbly jump off the tree branches and follow her at a discreet distance. She has no doubt that they'll be listening, their ears peeled for whatever is going on inside the cardboard partition, even as Sister Hilda appears and claps her hands: 'Now, girls, it's time for our morning hymn and then we'll commence lessons. Chalks and slates at the ready, please.'

How Bindu wishes she was joining them, not facing whatever it is she'll hear from Sister Maria Teresa.

Behind her, her classmates stumble through the hymn as she knocks on the flimsy cardboard door. She knows that although they've to join their hands and close their eyes to observe piety, they'll be peeking at her from behind slightly open lids.

She recites the words to the hymn in her head. Although every so often, when Bindu is feeling contrary, she gives Sister Hilda a hard time about why they, as Hindus, must exalt a Christian god, she's willing to pray to any god as long as He or She will listen, deliver them from their day-to-day purgatory. But Bindu has realised long since that neither the Christian nor Hindu gods will do much for the likes of them, the poor and the needy. Like everything else, religion appears to be the prerogative of the rich. The gods, both Hindu and Christian, smile upon the rich. They heed their prayers first. If the poor want anything, they need to fight for it themselves.

'Come in,' Sister Maria Teresa calls.

Her room – or the corner of the school hut that she has appropriated for herself – is adorned with a statue of Jesus on the cross pinned to the wall behind the chair and the rickety little plank that passes for her desk.

Like her classmates warned, Sister Maria Teresa does look very grim indeed as she peruses Bindu from over the top of her glasses. It appears to Bindu that she sees right through her, to her doubts, her worries of whether she really is good enough to win the scholarship – and if she doesn't, what will they do?

Bindu feels sweat travel down her back, collect in between her breasts, bead the top of her lips. It tastes tart, of the raw mango she hastily munched on the way to school in lieu of breakfast, and pungent, from exertion and fear.

Sister Maria Teresa clears her throat.

Here it comes.

Bindu takes a deep breath, pushes her shoulders back, meets Sister's gaze as she prepares to fight. But...

'How're you, my dear?' Sister Maria Teresa asks and her voice is soft with concern.

Bindu is blindsided; the empathy in Sister's eyes makes her own sting. 'I...' Her voice is wet, thick with salt. She clears it. 'I'm fine, Sister.'

Outside, her classmates are reciting the poem they're all learning. Wordsworth's 'I Wandered Lonely as a Cloud'.

Bindu has never seen a daffodil, but Sister Hilda said they are yellow, like the promise of sunshine, bright like smiles. Bindu imagines they must look like the glow on Ajji's face when she is particularly proud of her granddaughter, when Bindu cooks something that tastes 'better even than I'd have made it. You've the gift, my heart.'

'Now, Bindu,' Sister Maria Teresa says. 'The matriculation exams timetable is announced. They're next month, from the second through to the fifteenth. You're our best student and, as you know, we've put you forward for a scholarship to the girls' college in the city, which is affiliated with our convent. It is, I might add, one of the best colleges in the country. While the scholarship will cover the cost of your education, along with a small stipend for books and other living expenses, we'll also apply for boarding for you. This will be free of charge as well. My girl, judging from your performance so far, I've no doubt that you'll win the scholarship. However...' Here, Sister Maria Teresa pauses and her voice is stern, 'It is *imperative* that you attend every single exam. And it goes without saying that you must work hard in the run-up to them. No skiving off at all from here on, understood?'

Sister Maria Teresa waits, looking at Bindu severely from over the top of her glasses.

Bindu does not mind, her heart abloom, like the sunny daffodils, she thinks, remembering Sister Hilda's words when explaining the poem to the class: 'They signify hope after a long and dreary winter.' Sister Maria Teresa did not call her in to expel her, to chastise her, but to encourage her, bolster her. The miracle she has been praying for is very much within reach.

'I will,' she says, her voice a bird soaring towards the sun on gilded wings.

'Remember, these are *matriculation* exams. They take place across the state at the same time on the same day for everyone who's taking them.' Sister Maria Teresa is firm. 'You *must* attend, at the given time and day, no matter what.'

'I will,' Bindu promises solemnly as, outside, her classmates chant the poem that echoes in her head, her heart, like a bright yellow daffodil.

CHAPTER 13

BINDU

Bindu's matriculation exams coincide with the landlord hosting a fortnight-long party extravaganza, with different guests every day – the Maharaja of Jabalpur one evening and the British Resident and his cohort the next. He wants Ajji to supply the food.

'We must cancel,' Ajji says worriedly, kneading her hands.

'We will not.' Bindu is firm. 'We've not had any orders recently and have run out of everything and are in credit to Dujanna. We need the landlord's custom.'

'But your preparation for the exams'll be disrupted by the cooking. Knowing you, you'll insist upon helping me and—'

'I'll study beforehand. Be prepared and ready. It'll be all right. I *will* get the scholarship.'

'I'll do all the work,' Ajji says determinedly. 'You'll not come near the hearth during your exams.'

But Bindu is just as determined *not* to let Ajji do all the work – in any case, she can't, what with her shakes and the constraints of her ageing body, no matter how much she tries to hide it, to convince Bindu otherwise.

As she has started to do when they've orders to deliver, Bindu wakes in the night after Ajji is asleep and completes the bulk of the work, preparing the masalas and spice pastes, peeling and chopping the vegetables and marinating the meats, roasting nuts and plumping raisins, caramelising sugar and boiling milk for the sweets.

The nuns shake their heads in upset, fingering their rosaries, and anxiously looking Bindu over when she stumbles in, tired but determined, to take each exam.

'How did it go?' Ajji asks, the nuns ask, Sunitha asks, after every exam.

'I think it went well.' She is cautiously optimistic.

When the exams finish, Bindu sleeps for a solid week.

Ajji visits the wise man who meditates by the lake, with offerings, hoping he'll negotiate with the gods on Bindu's behalf.

'You've done your best, I know, my heart; this is just insurance,' she reassures Bindu.

On the night before results day, Bindu cannot sleep. She tosses and turns as dark shadows dance upon the cracked mud walls of the hut, venomous monsters casting toxic aspersions on Bindu's rainbow-bright hopes.

Ajji caresses Bindu's head gently. She cannot sleep either. Is Ajji's skin warmer than usual, or is Bindu's fevered imagination conjuring up a fever that isn't there?

'You've nothing to worry about, my heart,' Ajji whispers, her breath hot – too hot? – and sweet, flavoured with neem and promise.

Bindu is startled – has Ajji read her mind? But then she realises that Ajji is talking about the exam results. And on the heels of that, another thought: why is Ajji chewing neem at this time of night? They usually use neem as a breath freshener – its strong, minty flavour masks other not so pleasant ones.

What is Ajji hiding from me?

'Ajji, are you all right?' Bindu asks, her voice loud in the hushed quiet, rife with anxiety.

'I'm fine, my heart. Excited for you,' she says, but Bindu, hearing the effortful catch in Ajji's voice, the way she has to pause after each word although she tries very hard for normalcy, is far from reassured.

Bindu must fall asleep eventually, for she wakes to the celebratory, burnt-sugar and honeyed-raisin scent of payasam. Ajji has obtained goat's milk from Chinnakka and nuts from Duja; God only knows what she has bartered for it.

'Eat up,' Ajji says, setting down a heaped bowlful of custardy payasam dotted with plump raisins drunk on nectar, cashew nuts roasted in ghee. 'To celebrate your scholarship.' She beams.

But she is very wan, her skin drawn, and Bindu's worries of the night before come rushing back, stabbing needles of trepidation all down her body, displacing her nerves regarding her results.

'Ajji, are you all right? You look—'

'I'm fine,' Ajji says firmly.

She must be, mustn't she, if she woke up to cook this feast of payasam for Bindu? Then what Ajji said – 'celebrate your scholarship' – sinks in...

'But, Ajji,' Bindu protests even as her cheeks lift in a smile for the first time since her exams, 'I haven't collected my results yet.'

Ajji takes Bindu's hand, places it upon her heart, which beats with love for her. But is it a tad too slow? 'You *have* won the scholarship. I know it here.'

Ajji's hand is very warm. When she turns away, Bindu notices that she sways on her feet.

The payasam tastes of salty anticipation, of nervous, thrilling hope and anxiety on Ajji's behalf.

Ajji, please be all right.

Bindu's feet drag as she nears the school.

Sunitha is waiting by the bimbli trees, looking anxious.

She squeezes Bindu's hand. 'I prayed for you.'

'What about for you?'

'Pah. I don't care about me. I bet I've failed. But you...' Sunitha leans forward, envelops Bindu in a fierce hug, 'I'm sure you've won it.'

Tears sting Bindu's eyes as she hugs her friend back, overwhelmed. Winning the scholarship means going far away from Sunitha and leaving Ajji behind here in the village while Bindu studies in the city, and yet both Ajji and Sunitha have only her best interests at heart. She is so lucky in them.

Sunitha and Bindu walk into the school hut together.

All the nuns are there, standing under the statue of Jesus on the cross, looking just as mournful as the dying messiah, his bleeding face framed by lank strands of sweaty hair, his head, pierced by his crown of thorns, falling forward in melancholy resignation.

Bindu's heart falls.

Then, as she crosses the threshold, they begin clapping and burst into song. 'Come, ye thankful people, come,' they rejoice in glorious harmony.

Sister Maria Teresa smiles for the first time that anyone can remember and this makes the girls gasp more than her announcement: 'You've done it, Bindu. You've scored the highest marks ever recorded in the matriculation exams. You've topped the state board and you've won the scholarship.'

Her headmistress's smile, Bindu thinks, as she tries to process Sister Maria Teresa's words, is as wonderful, joyous, hopeful and celebratory as she imagines a host of daffodils to be.

CHAPTER 14

When Eve throws open the door, heart pounding – did she hear a child calling for her, or was it just her imagination? – she is ambushed by small arms wrapping themselves round her legs.

Izzy.

Her beloved, precious girl.

Eve closes her eyes, rocks on her feet, overwhelmed by sensation. Relief.

It was all a very bad dream, of course it was.

She has been ill. She's had a breakdown of some sort. Joe and Izzy are fine.

In fact, her little girl is—

'Eve,' she hears and the tearful little voice jars into her fantasy, shattering it into a million mocking shards, each reflecting her foolish hope with bright, glaring scorn. 'Eve.'

She pushes her agony away, concentrating on the little girl from next door, her daughter's best friend, taller now than her own child was when she died – they were the same height then – her tearful voice pleading, 'My mum's ill. Can you come?'

'Of course, love.' Eve doesn't have to think twice, instinct taking over as she holds Maya's hand and turns to lock her front door behind her.

It is only when the fresh evening breeze deposits frosty

caresses – it might be spring, but the twilight air has a bite to it, winter prolonging its goodbyes for as long as it can – upon her cheeks that she realises she's stepped outside her house for the first time since the accident.

Eve suppresses the overwhelming urge to turn tail and run inside, shut the door on the world that stole her family from her, stay within her four walls that hold such bittersweet memories, but the child whose hand is trustingly tucked in hers is shaking with sobs, looking at her home, where an ambulance is parked, doors open, lights pulsing urgently.

Maya needs her.

'What's wrong with your mum, love?'

'She...' Maya says between hiccups. 'She's not been well for a few days and when I came home from school, she couldn't get up.'

'Oh,' Eve says, trying to keep the worry flaring at Maya's words from her voice.

'I called 999 and when the ambulance came, Mum said to fetch you.'

Eve's heart goes out to the girl, how she must have felt when she came home to find her mother so ill, calling the emergency services herself.

'It's going to be all right,' Eve says with firm conviction, although she perhaps knows better than anyone that there's no guarantee of any such thing.

Jenny and Eve are friends, and back when Eve's world wasn't splintered by tragedy, they'd share a drink and news in one of their gardens while the girls played together.

Jenny is bringing up Maya alone, her husband, Maya's dad, having succumbed to a heart attack when Maya was four.

'It came out of the blue. One minute he was fine, reading a story to Maya, the next complaining of chest pains, then dead,' Jenny had said, sniffing. 'He was the love of my life. I cannot countenance being with anyone else. I've been out with a few men, but none measure up.'

Eve had reached a hand out to Jenny, which her friend had

clasped as if it was a lifeline. 'I cannot begin to imagine,' Eve had said.

Now she can.

But even back then, as she held Jenny's hand, offered comfort, she had thought, shuddering inwardly, *Joe is the love of my life. I cannot think what I'd do if I lost him. I cannot imagine being with anyone else.*

'And there's no way I'll introduce anyone to Maya unless I'm completely sure,' Jenny had added, fiercely.

The setting sun – it was a lovely summer's evening – danced kaleidoscopic shadows upon the walls, bathing the houses beyond in a crimson gold glow. The air smelled of barbecues and languid laughter, sizzled meat, crisped onions, smoke and hops, caramelised apples and sweet nectar. The peacefulness was rent with the girls' shrieks as they tumbled on the trampoline, their hair, Izzy's straight and honey-auburn, Maya's dark corkscrew curls, shimmying around them, a tangle of limbs and gap-toothed smiles.

'We both came from broken homes, so we were determined to give Maya a secure, two-parent upbringing. Ha! Best-laid plans, eh?' Jenny had chuckled wetly, mirthlessly.

'Oh, Jenny,' Eve had said, patting her hand.

'I'll do it anyway, give her a happy, secure childhood. I *will* be enough,' Jenny had said fiercely.

'Ah, you're doing an amazing job,' Eve had reassured her. 'Maya's a well-adjusted, confident child.'

'She was very close to her father, a proper daddy's girl.' Jenny was wistful. 'She was devastated when he died, but she seems to've accepted it now.'

'Children are resilient,' Eve had said. 'I was adopted from India when I was around the age Maya lost her dad.'

'You were?' Jenny had looked at her, surprised.

'My dad grew up in India and worked there before the war. When war was declared, he signed up and when he was invalided out due to injury, he took Mum – she was the nurse who tended to him when he took a bullet to his thigh – to India. He wanted to show her the country he loved; it was the home of his heart. He'd have stayed there, if not for Indian independence on the heels of the war.'

'Ah.'

'I know you're wondering where I come into this. Bear with me. As an author, I like to set the scene.'

Jenny had smiled. 'I like it. I'd guess you were a writer if I didn't know it already – you're a born storyteller.'

Now it was Eve's turn to smile. 'You're too kind. And a great listener. I never tell this story to anyone. Only Joe knows it, really. I'd forget myself that I was adopted if it weren't for occasional letters and updates from my aunt...'

'Your aunt in India?'

'Yes. She's not really my aunt; she was my birth mother's friend. But I'm doing this all wrong.'

Jenny had laughed and, from the trampoline, the delighted giggles of their girls sugared the air.

'Now, where was I? Oh yes, my dad took Mum to India, to show her the places where he'd lived and worked. But the peaceful town he recalled was anything but, torn apart by communal riots, Muslims and Hindus who'd coexisted peacefully for centuries at loggerheads, and innocent people casualties of bloodshed and violence. Also, in parallel, there was the fight for independence from the British. Dad's quiet hamlet was now a very dangerous place.'

'Oh.' Jenny's eyes had widened with concern.

'Dad realised he couldn't stay and he and Mum made preparations to return to England. They booked a passage for two, but when they came home they were three. As my dad tells it, he couldn't live in India like he'd wished to, but he brought the best of India back with him.' Eve's father's eyes had shimmered and sparkled with love and pride when he'd said this, looking at her.

'Ah, that's so lovely,' Jenny was saying, eyes shining.

'Yes, sorry.' Eve had blinked, coming back into the moment. 'What I wanted to say, in my roundabout way, is that children adapt. I did. I lived in India until I was three but I neither miss nor yearn for it – I've only vague impressions of my time there. I coped with the upheaval of moving countries and adjusting to a new life, for I was loved. And so is Maya. An amazing girl just like her mother.' She had squeezed Jenny's hand.

'But, wait, I want to know how you came to be with your parents. What about your birth mother, your Indian aunt who's not really an aunt...?'

Before Eve could reply, the girls had skipped over to them, laughing and wheedling at the same time, 'We're thirsty. *And* hungry.'

Jenny and Eve had stood then, smiling at each other with one last squeeze of their joined hands, friends, connected by shared confidences and their children's bond.

They never did get round to finishing the conversation.

Eve's parents succumbed within six months of each other to different forms of cancer, the year before she lost Izzy and Joe. Loss upon loss. Her only consolation was that they'd gone before the accident – they didn't have to deal with the devastation of losing their son-in-law and beloved grandchild whom they'd absolutely doted on, in one heartbreaking swoop. Eve hadn't properly grieved for her parents, hadn't sorted through their things, had ignored their lawyer's repeated pleas and increasingly urgent summons for a meeting.

Jenny had been there for Eve when Eve lost her parents and after the accident that stole her family. She was as persistent as Sue, knocking every day, enquiring after Eve, leaving food and shopping on her doorstep. Calling through the letter box when Eve wouldn't open the door, 'I understand, to some extent, what you're going through. I lost the love of my life too,' Jenny's voice pulsing with pain and gentle with empathy. 'I've left some biscuits Maya and I made together – not as good as yours, Maya tells me.'

Oh, how I wish I could bake biscuits with Izzy, but I never will again.

And, as if she could read her mind, Jenny added, 'I know. I understand it's hard when Maya... I get it, Eve. Just wanted to say, we're here for you when you're ready. You're not alone.'

Now, Eve has to try very hard not to show her shock at the state of her friend. Vibrant, beautiful Jenny is wan, paramedics busy around her as they monitor the devices they've strapped to her body. She's struggling to breathe, even through the mask they've clamped on her face.

'Pneumonia caused by asthma and exacerbated by anaemia,' the paramedics say. 'You need to be in hospital for a few days.'

Maya sobs silently beside her mother, her small face drowning in tears.

Jenny holds her daughter's hand even as her eyes lock with Eve's. 'Please,' she manages between laboured breaths, her voice raspy through the mask. 'Can you look after Maya until I'm back from hospital?'

Both mother and daughter's hopeful, pleading gazes fix upon Eve.

She tries to find her voice in her suddenly dry throat. Look after a child, when her own... It would be torture.

'I wouldn't ask if I...' Jenny says, and in her friend's gaze Eve sees that, despite all she's going through, Jenny feels for *her*, knows what she's asking of her.

'Please, Eve,' Maya says in a small, broken voice. 'I don't want to stay with a stranger.'

How can Eve refuse?

CHAPTER 15

BINDU

1937

Bindu dances all the way home, unable to keep from smiling, imagining Ajji's expression when she relays the news.

Her first hint that something is wrong is when Dumdee doesn't come bounding up to meet her halfway along the fields like he usually does. Instead, he's standing at the entrance to the hut, whining mournfully.

'What's the matter, Dumdee?' she whispers, her voice in hiding, a small, cowering, frightened thing. 'Where's Ajji?'

Bindu hesitates on the threshold, her heart heavy, all the joy seeped from it like water from a holey pot as the worries from the previous night and this morning about her Ajji's health ambush her afresh.

She hears the villagers' voices, dripping poisonous conviction: 'She brings nothing but bad luck. She might flaunt her beauty and brains, but her bad luck'll always triumph.'

Not now, Ajji, don't go now when my dreams are within reach, when I can do for you all I've promised.

Ajji is on the mat, moaning in delirium, flushed with fever, burning to the touch. She must've held herself together this morning for Bindu's benefit. Did she prepare the payasam ahead of time wanting to celebrate with her granddaughter, knowing she wouldn't be well enough when Bindu came back, for she was sick-ening already?

Oh, Ajji.

With the water left in the pot – Bindu'll have to go to the lake to fetch more – Bindu fashions cool cloths to lay on Ajji's burning head to bring down the fever. She concocts potions with medicinal herbs and feeds them to Ajji. She has to shake Ajji awake to do so – her grandmother is scarily listless, barely conscious; Bindu has to hold the cup to her mouth and force her to swallow the mixture down. It ignites terror in Bindu, seeing Ajji like this – unrespon-sive, seemingly unaware of the world and even of Bindu. In all these years, Ajji, while ill more often than not, hasn't been this bad.

All day and through the night, Bindu changes the hot rags on Ajji's forehead for cool ones in a bid to bring her fever down. But Ajji's fever, far from dropping, keeps spiking, making Bindu terribly afraid.

Please, gods and goddesses, Jesus Christ, Mother Mary, she prays as she keeps vigil, *please spare my Ajji.*

In the morning, desperately worried, Bindu raids the mud pot they keep hidden in the rice sack and feed, every so often, with any spare change they're able to squirrel away. It's empty.

Ajji moans, rolling feverishly upon her mat.

Bindu feels like giving up, throwing her head to the unrelent-ingly dazzling heavens – the air heavy and humid and smelling scorched, not a cloud in sight, the monsoons delayed again, the earth cracked and powdery – and sobbing until she has no tears left. Instead, she shuts her eyes, takes a calming breath, then another.

She feels Dumdee's body against hers, his tongue soothing the blisters on her feet. It centres her and she knows then what she'll do. She makes her special spice mix – this one her own invention, not as spicy as Ajji's but with more of a bite – which is very much in demand, and goes to the wise man who meditates in the copse of trees by the lake that has shrunk to a quarter of its usual girth.

What'll they do when the lake completely dries up? Bindu shudders. She has enough worries already – she cannot get agitated about this too. Hopefully, the gods will heed the wise man's prayers and the much-awaited rains will come and fill up the lake and their wells. After all, every year of the drought so far, just as the lake's about to dry up, the rains have arrived. This year, too, it will be so, she tells herself firmly. And Ajji *will* get better. It's not time for her to go yet, not when Bindu has just won the scholarship – please, no.

Bindu waits for the wise man to finish meditating, catching her breath under the sweltering sun, feeling moisture pooling under her arms, between her breasts, arid earth, parched vegetation, sun-dazzled yellow, tasting prayer and desperation, the stark navy of nightmares.

He opens his eyes finally, says in a voice the solemn gold of sacraments, 'What is it, child?'

She holds out her spice paste offering, all the fear she's been keeping so tightly coiled within making her voice shake like a frightened child. 'My Ajji is grievously ill.'

He digs in the pouch beside him, hands her a stoppered vial of viscous liquid the colour of venom.

When she opens the bottle, the mixture slithers and hisses dangerously, emitting a dark blue odour that scratches at Bindu's throat.

'Feed her this potion twice a day with milk.'

'There is no milk.' Bindu sighs. Chinnakka's goat, along with the other village animals – and humans – is suffering in the drought, emaciated; with no fresh grass to enjoy, it is unable to produce milk.

'Water then,' the sadhu says.

Bindu thanks the sadhu and tucks the vial into her sari skirt pocket. She stops at the lake for water, glad she had the presence of mind to bring pots and rushes home praying, *Please, let this work. Let Ajji get better.*

As she nears the hut, her steps are weighted with trepidation and hope. When she arrives, she'll be greeted with the miracle of

Ajji up and about, her usual, albeit perpetually coughing and trembly, self. Won't she?

Then why is Bindu reluctant to enter, hope shrivelling acrid in her mouth, heart pounding, legs tremulous?

Dumdee is taking his guard duties seriously. He doesn't come up to her, instead lying at the threshold of the hut and whimpering mournfully. He too looks weary, lacking his usual vigour, his eyes lugubrious.

Taking a deep breath, shoulders pushed back, Bindu enters the hut, which carries the fug of illness, stale sweat and hot fever. Ajji is no better.

But... she is no worse.

Bindu mixes a few drops of the wise man's potion with water, the viscous drops swirling inky navy, adds a smidgen of powdered jaggery from their dwindling reserve to sweeten it and feeds it to a nearly comatose Ajji.

Please let the sadhu's vile-smelling potion work its magic on Ajji.

Afterwards, Bindu cooks. But even cooking doesn't offer the solace it usually affords. For their supplies are running low and they've no money to buy more – no orders from the landlord since the party extravaganza during Bindu's exams. Because of the drought, the chillies, herbs and vegetables they cultivate in their small patch of courtyard have dried up as well. Although Bindu meticulously waters them with some of the precious lake water, it is, evidently, not enough.

Bindu keeps vigil through the night, chanting, *Please let Ajji be all right*. Dumdee, loyal as ever, keeping her company, as the neighbourhood dogs howl at the moon while it flirts with the coyly dancing shadows, and the nocturnal animals slither and hiss and rustle, and the dry leaves whisper arid secrets even as they sigh for rain.

CHAPTER 16

BINDU

Three days since Ajji fell ill and she's showing no signs of improvement.

A new dawn streaks crimson gold over the horizon, washing the parched yellow fields in a creamy haze, making them glow serenely, belying their barrenness, the heartache of the farmers, who've no way of repaying their debt to the landlord.

Bindu has kept determined vigil by Ajji's side but, far from getting better, her grandmother's breathing has been more laboured, even as she's been getting more feverish. She called out a couple of times and Bindu was relieved, thinking her old Ajji was back. The one who would wake in the night and find her grand-daughter not sleeping peacefully beside her like she expected but cooking. Who would cry, 'Bindu, come lie down, you've school in the morning. There's nothing that cannot wait. Don't do this to spare me. You need your beauty sleep, you're a growing girl.'

But this Ajji was semi-comatose, calling out in the throes of delirium, in a fever-induced daze.

Bindu had ground potions, making cooling pastes with the dried-up and shrivelled, due to the drought, medicinal herbs and applying them, alongside wet cloths, to her grandmother's hot forehead. She'd prayed, a constant litany, *Please let this be just a setback and let Ajji be well.*

But to no avail. Ajji is very hot to the touch – the wet cloth Bindu had applied only an hour ago is boiling, the cooling paste on Ajji's forehead steaming from the heat of her fever-battered body.

This woman who has been her parent and guardian. Her protector. Her mentor. Her everything. She cannot *die*. Ajji has years to go yet. Whatever is happening to her, this listlessness, this unresponsiveness, is because of illness, not age. Once she's cured, she'll be *fine*.

Pushing all thoughts from her panicking mind, Bindu collects the last of the herbs from the wilting, rain-parched plants to make another medicinal potion. The sun is up. Skeletal cows have been led to pasture by despairing, jobless farmers and tethered there to munch half-heartedly at the bone-dry brush. The pebbles in the mud dig into Bindu's bare feet. The earth is heating up, the dew, if there was any, having evaporated already. The sky is cloudless, harshly bright. Another day of drought.

Bindu pounds the herbs in the pestle and mortar to release healing juices, praying all the while. She makes a wet compress with the last of the water – she'll need to collect more from the lake. She applies it to her grandmother, who moans and thrashes, her fever having spiked even more in the last few minutes, the cold compress turning instantly warm and sweaty. The wise man's foul-smelling potions – in exchange for more of Bindu's spice mixes – are not working.

'You must pray, that's all you can do.' His advice: the wise man, who deigned to come and see Ajji after Bindu bribed him with bisibelebath made from the last of their lentils and rice, only to have him shake his head, rub his beard and declare, 'Your Ajji must've angered the gods – or perhaps you did.' Looking at her speculatively, her uncovered head; in her panic and worry, Bindu had forgotten to drape her veil over her face.

In any case, he's a sadhu, she thought, *God's disciple.* What did a godly man care about her looks?

But she forgot that even the sadhu was a man, old and weathered and supposedly godly, but a man all the same.

She belatedly covered her face that made men, even this ancient sadhu, leer lasciviously.

'Ask for forgiveness. Perhaps the gods will then decide to make her better. Or...' Once again stroking his beard speculatively, 'If you give me money for puja, I'll pray on your behalf.'

Money. For this all-too-human sadhu's prayers.

Even if I had some, I wouldn't waste it on you, Bindu thought.

She understood then that the sadhu too was at a loss in the face of Ajji's illness. What her grandmother needed was an English doctor, a man of medicine.

Bindu knew the English doctors' medicines cured the seemingly incurable, from the nuns, who, when one of Bindu's classmates, Rupa, had died of snakebite, had been devastated.

Afterwards, when they'd prayed for Rupa with the girls and declared a holiday in her honour, Bindu, who'd run back into the empty classroom to collect her handkerchief, had overheard the nuns talking in Sister Maria Teresa's office.

'It's a travesty,' Sister Hilda had sniffed. 'A shocking waste of a life. A doctor, in place of the quack they consulted, would have saved her.'

'They cannot afford the services of a doctor,' Sister Maria Teresa had said with a sigh.

'Is there nothing we can do?' Sister Hilda had asked.

'I'll write to the abbess,' Sister Maria Teresa had murmured, sounding thoughtful. Then, the rustle of clothes as she stood up. 'Now, it's time to retire to chapel to pray for the poor girl's soul.'

The gossip at the lake, when Bindu went to collect water, was also about English doctors. Although the flavour was different, with talk of omens and miracles − a stark contrast to the straightforward concern of the nuns − the consensus was the same: English medicine *worked*.

'The landlord's wife was at death's door and only a miracle

could have saved her. The landlord had a puja to pray for her good health, inviting the most renowned sadhus in the country.'

Bindu knew this. She and Ajji had supplied the food, back when Ajji was well: chapatis, bitter-gourd curry, rasam, curd rice, drumstick sambar, beetroot salad. No sweets, as it was a sombre occasion.

'The sadhus had to admit defeat. Then the British Resident sent his personal doctor to see to the landlord's wife. The doctor prescribed these white pills, small as lime pips, to be taken thrice a day. And that was it. The landlord's wife was sitting up in two days and good as new in two weeks. These English doctors know black magic!'

Ajji needed an English doctor to perform a miracle. Bindu would get her one. Her grandmother had loved and protected Bindu all her life; it was Bindu's duty to do everything she could to save her, even sell her soul if that was what it took.

Sister Maria Teresa herself pays Bindu a visit, like that first time when she'd gifted Bindu her handkerchief and asked if she'd like to attend the school the nuns were starting at their convent. Sister Maria Teresa's pristine habit, her faultless cream complexion, her gentle demeanour all radiate serene calm, out of place in this hut, reeking of fever and desperation.

'Bindu, my dear, you were supposed to come to school to accept your scholarship.'

'My Ajji is ill.'

'We heard. We're praying for her. Now, I've the forms here for you to sign.'

Bindu looks at Sister Maria Teresa, who looks back at her, eyes shining with empathy.

'Is there any way I can defer the scholarship?'

Sister Maria Teresa wipes her eyes, her gesture weary. 'I wish I could say yes, Bindu,' she says with a sigh. 'But there's a long waiting list of deserving students who'll jump at this chance.'

'Even when Ajji gets better, this illness will have weakened her considerably.' Bindu puts into words the thoughts that have been going around her head as she has tended to her grandmother. 'I can't in all good conscience leave her here and study in the city. She's my only family. And the scholarship doesn't cover her lodging.'

'It doesn't, I'm afraid.'

Bindu looks at the forms in Sister Maria Teresa's hands, offering the tantalising possibility of a better life for her grandmother and for herself.

But the promise it offers is too far in the future. All their lives, Bindu and her grandmother have had no choice but to live in the moment, trying to survive the present, never knowing what the next day will bring.

Sister Maria Teresa leaves, and Bindu's star-studded constellation of dreams scatters like the grit whipped in the sudden dry sandy breeze that has started up in her wake.

When the nun is but a white speck swallowed by orange smog, Bindu squats down beside her grandmother, tenderly planting kisses upon Ajji's fevered cheeks, her throat tasting of the sea, her nose clogged with it. *You've been my mother, father, my biggest champion and protector, Ajji, and I'll do everything in my power to save you.*

CHAPTER 17

EVE

1980

As the ambulance bearing Jenny moves away, keening urgently, Maya launches herself at Eve.

And Eve's heart breaks all over again, even as it revels in this hug from a child, but not the one she yearns, as it mourns that she will never again be hugged by her own child.

I don't think I can do this.

She wants to help Jenny and her heart goes out to Maya. She understands where Jenny was coming from when she had said, urgently, to Eve while Maya was in the loo, even though she had trouble breathing and every word took effort, 'I know how hard this'll be for you. I wouldn't ask if I wasn't desperate but I really don't want Maya going into emergency foster care. They cannot guarantee she'll be placed with a foster family of her own skin colour. I'd much rather she was with you.'

This was the first time Jenny had referred to the racism she and Terry, both of Caribbean heritage, must have endured, that Eve has only guessed at, having suffered racism herself owing to her Indian roots. Eve suspected this was also why Jenny and Terry, like herself and Joe, didn't have many friends in the neighbourhood. They must've faced the same suspicion and mistrust when they moved in that Eve and Joe had.

The person Eve was before wouldn't have hesitated even for a second to have Maya stay with her. In fact, she'd have suggested it herself.

But now... To look after, care for, live with this child who grew up alongside her daughter, who is growing still while her daughter is not. This girl, who is looking at her with tear-adorned eyes...

Eve clears her throat, says to Maya, her firm voice belying the doubts swarming within her, 'Everything'll be just fine, my love.'

It's the least she can do for her friend and her child, her daughter's friend, although it feels huge, overwhelming, beyond her.

CHAPTER 18

BINDU

1937

'Who are you? Why are you here?' the gatekeeper at the ornate walled entrance to the landlord's vast compound barks.

The landlord is hosting a party – Bindu had singlehandedly prepared the order while also looking after Ajji, changing her cool compresses every few minutes and feeding her the wise man's ineffectual potions, hoping for a miracle – and the gatekeeper is busy waving cars in. He has little time for a woman on foot.

'I'm the cook who supplied the food for the party today,' Bindu says, pulling her veil down, only eyes visible, lashes lowered demurely as women are expected to behave in the presence of men. She considers flaunting her beauty, like before, when she'd gained entry to this compound because Guru had dared her to – it feels like that was another Bindu in another life – but she has her sights set higher this time. So now she'll be demure, behave like a shy rule-abider, if that's what it takes. Her legs and chest are cramped from running all the way here. The soles of her feet are burnt and bleeding, her hands chapped. But she's desperate. Ajji's not getting better. In fact, she's been comatose these last couple of days.

She tells the gatekeeper, 'I realised I didn't specify how to heat the biryani. I need to tell them up at the kitchen – it'd be a disaster if it burned.'

'Go on then,' the guard says, looking her up and down, the lascivious gaze she's used to.

She might be coy, thinking it best, but no matter how carefully she wraps her sari to not display even a sliver of flesh, she can't quite hide her figure and it always inspires this reaction in men – Bindu *hates* it, but she's also learned to use it for her own ends when necessary.

'Servants' entrance is behind the house,' he says, leering.

The landlord's compound is so huge, it could easily house the entire village and still have several fields' worth of space spare. The only other time Bindu passed through the imposing gates, she'd barely looked at the compound, triumphant at having won the dare, imagining Guru's reaction – she'd gone in and out again.

But now, she looks. And what she sees disgusts her.

Lawns stretch, immaculately mown, each blade of grass the exact height as its neighbour, as if none would dare be unruly enough to rebel against this pristine symmetry. The vegetation is lush green and fecund, fed by dancing sprinklers arcing sparks of silver spray. Fountains spill rainbows of water, gushing and gurgling in merry abandon. No sign of the drought plaguing the landlord's tenants here. Absolutely no dearth of the water they're all so desperate for at the village, that they'd give anything for.

Bindu thinks of the muddy dregs she's been lugging back from the lake, carefully sieving the red silt so that not even a drop is lost. Feeding the impure liquid to Ajji, whose lips, like Bindu's, are parched and cracked. She thinks of how she uses the moisture from the red silt dregs to make the cold compresses for her grandmother's forehead to ease her fever. And here, water is being *wasted*, used for decorative purposes, for lawns that are already so brightly emerald as to dazzle the eye.

Bindu is tempted for a long, lustful moment to stand under the fountain and drink to her heart's content. Her arid mouth salivates in expectation of unrationed slaking, finally, of what feels like permanent, never-ending thirst.

She swallows, her dry throat stinging, and forces herself to walk on. She needs to carry out her plan before she loses courage.

She marvels at the gardeners working the endless acreage, if only to distract her mind from dwelling on, getting agitated about, what she is to attempt. These men who work with this abundance of water, having to return each evening to their wives and children, gaunt and dry-skinned, their faces hollow with thirst.

Do they drink from the fountains, the cavorting sprinklers, when no one's looking? Do they smuggle some of this clean, pure, precious water home?

These considerations get her past the temptation of the water and up to the landlord's ostentatiously flamboyant mansion that glitters and gleams, vulgar gold, rivalling the sun.

Rumour had it that when the Maharaja of Jabalpur, known for his extravagant tastes — his gargantuan palace was said to be so crammed with antiques and knick-knacks that he was building an even bigger palace to exhibit the overflow — visited the landlord, he'd laughed, but it'd had an edge to it, declaring, bitingly, 'I'll take the fact that you've fashioned your home as almost an exact replica of my palace as a compliment, rather than an insult.'

The landlord had hastened to assure him that it was indeed a compliment, and had foisted several gifts upon the king, including his eldest daughter, who was then only twelve, as his bride.

After the king's visit, the landlord, it was said, had hired the ten best architects in the world and charged them with redesigning his abode in a completely original and unique style — also making it bigger, adding several new wings in the process — so that it wouldn't be accused of being a copy of any building anywhere in the world.

As Bindu reaches the entrance her steps falter, the gatekeeper's words echoing in her head: 'Servants' entrance is behind the house.'

Sleek motorcars, of the latest make and model, are pulling up, immaculately dressed chauffeurs helping out gentlemen in suits and glittering kurtas, women in kaleidoscopic dresses and matching hats, and others in gold-threaded, elaborately sequinned and intricately patterned saris, their arms and necks choked with jewellery. They might be the elite, but the Indian women, nevertheless, hang respectfully behind their men, their faces covered by their extravagant saris. Even though they are nobility, they still suffer the same fate as the likes of Bindu – nonentities secondary to their men, their faces hidden, personalities not in evidence.

And this more than anything makes up Bindu's mind, and her hesitant steps become assured strides as she follows the dignitaries and enters alongside them, confidently sidestepping the obsequious butler receiving guests at the door, her head, although covered by her old, frayed sari pallu, and out of place in these ostentatious surroundings, held up high.

CHAPTER 19

BINDU

As Bindu stands in the vulgarly over-the-top entrance hall, glittering with chandeliers, busy with knick-knacks from all over the world, staircases snaking up to various floors, carpeted in lush, exquisitely patterned runners, a phrase Sister Hilda was fond of, from the Bible, echoes in her head. 'My father's house has many rooms,' Sister Hilda would quote, smiling gently at each of her charges in turn, 'and everyone is welcome.'

Not so here, not everyone, only the obscenely rich and influential, Bindu thinks, even as she's assailed by a sudden pang of what she can only describe as homesickness for the school, its mud floors, the chalk Sister Hilda would distribute, with which they'd do their sums on the slates that she'd also give them. 'Easy to rub out if you make mistakes,' she'd say with a smile. Bindu only very occasionally had to. She loved the limestone scent of chalk, the crumbly feel of it, loved spitting into her pallu and wiping the slate clean after every lesson, a fresh start, loved how her fingers, stained turmeric yellow and chilli red when she arrived in the morning, would be powdery white when she skipped home through the fields after lessons.

That little school hut had felt like a second home.

Now, as she stands in the most luxurious surroundings she has ever seen – the landlord's home built on proceeds from ruthlessly

bleeding his poor tenants, and, mainly, from business deals arising
from the alliances he has carefully cultivated with royalty, the
kings of all the neighbouring kingdoms his friends, not to
mention the British Resident within whose jurisdiction his land
falls – Bindu is repelled. Being in these ostentatious environs,
seeing the supposed great and the good milling about, drinking to
excess, smoking and networking, she can see why Guru, heir to
this wealth and lifestyle, felt claustrophobic, stifled, and wanted
escape. There's space to spare here, but it's not welcoming; in fact,
it's the opposite. Now that Bindu has a glimpse into Guru's life –
used to everyone falling in with his wishes and to getting what he
wants – she understands why he was intrigued when a mere village
girl refused to acquiesce, bend to his will. She prays that now,
hopefully, this will work in her favour.

The main entrance hall opens onto a huge indoor courtyard
complete with a pool – a pool! – clean and sparkling, singing in the
sun that it reflects merrily from within its sapphire depths,
flanked by palm trees and more lush lawns and foliage, and even
more fountains, dancing rainbows in their bubbly carefree wake.
All this water and the villagers literally dying of thirst, scraping
the muddy bottoms of their wells in the hope of moisture, the
dregs of the lake that has nearly dried up, worrying what to do if it
does before the drought breaks.

The mansion is built around this courtyard – and others
dotted around the property, it appears – with ornate staircases
leading up several storeys that look down upon these open spaces.
There are sofas and divans set out on the lawns in the shade of
palm and fruit trees. A poolside bar does brisk business. A giant
chessboard with life-size pieces, each as tall as Bindu, occupies
one corner of the courtyard, within an arbour of banana trees,
their sweeping leaves swaying gently in the spiced afternoon
breeze like lovelorn ladies twirling in the arms of their men. A live
band performs on the bandstand beside the bar, rousing jigs
complementing the gushing abundance of water, parrots and
bulbuls cooing in the branches above, a tropical paradise.

Waiters circulate with trays of the tandoori chicken and fish
fry, cauliflower kebabs and spiced paneer cubes that Bindu herself

had prepared that morning, pounding herbs and marinating meat as Ajji's fever spiked and she moaned deliriously, Dumdee whining from the threshold, banana leaves tap-tapping secrets upon the soot-stained mud walls.

Others carry brightly coloured drinks in tall glasses, topped with slices of fruit and lime, condensation beading down the sides.

Bindu's thirsty throat gasps in anticipation and desire, but she ignores it. Now's not the time, and in any case, no drinks for the likes of her.

And as if someone has read her thoughts, picked up on the incongruence of a person of her lowly ilk mingling with this exclusive crowd in this hallowed setting...

'Who is she? What's she doing here?' A sharp cry cutting cleanly through the happy rumble of a successful gathering.

Accusing fingers pointing at her.

Even as she's speared by shocked and assessing gazes, the murmur in the courtyard and around the hall stopping abruptly, Bindu becomes aware that she's the only woman in here – no wonder she stands out. She's been so immersed in taking in the landlord's mansion, she has not paid heed to the crowd.

And now she sees that the women disappear almost as soon as they enter the grand hall, going, as if led by an unseen hand, or perhaps shepherded by one of the several uniformed servers, to a separate section for women, Bindu surmises, where, presumably, they can shrug off their veils and gossip about their men, much like Ajji and her friends used to of an evening after their chores were done back when Ajji was hale, although, of course, there's a world of difference in their settings.

There are only men in here, a mix of white and brown, suits and kurtas, crisp English accents, even from the Indians, interspersed with the odd Kannada exclamation. How did she not pick up on the deep growl of masculine talk and the low thunder of their laughter, unsweetened by the musical trill of feminine joy and conversation?

But now nobody is laughing.

Even the servants here are all men, and better dressed than Bindu.

'A maid? Why's she not in uniform and not in the women's section? Why is she *here* mingling with the guests?' The questions lobbed rapid-fire in English by a corpulent Indian man in a suit standing by the bar, buttons straining against a belly intent on freedom from constraints.

Bindu is hounded by the judgemental stares of everyone in the room and courtyard. Her heart beats so loudly, she's sure all can hear it.

She takes a deep breath. *You can do this, for Ajji's sake.*

The butler is advancing towards her purposefully, to lead her away no doubt.

A huge part of her is thinking, *If he throws me out, that's all right. At least I tried.*

You cannot give up now. Come on, for Ajji's sake, the other – braver or, perhaps, the more foolish – part of her chides.

She swallows, finds her voice. She does not shout and yet she knows she's heard by every single person in the giant entrance hall and courtyard, her voice reverberating in the shocked stillness, the kind that precedes a storm. 'I am the chef who prepared your food. I'd like a meeting with Mr Guru.' She speaks in the perfect enunciated English she's learned from the nuns. But while they'd have insisted on politeness, expecting her to add 'please' at the end, she deliberately doesn't.

Pandemonium.

'She speaks good English. But she's mere *help*, a chef.'

'She has delusions of grandeur. Chef! Fancy title for lowly cook.'

Then the same sharp voice that'd queried why she was here, the man standing by the bar, mocking, 'You'd like to speak to Guru, would you? I didn't know the host was in the business of arranging meetings with servants while he was presiding over a party. The cheek! What next? An audience with Lord Linlithgow, Viceroy of India?'

None of your business, she wants to spit at this bombastic man, even as others join in, spewing outrage while also leering at her, shocked by her sheer audacity, a member of the working class, a maid at that, someone whose job it is to unobtrusively make sure that everything is running smoothly while remaining invisible in the background, infringing upon an all-male gathering and demanding to speak to the host.

The butler is beside Bindu now, his mouth set in a thin, unforgiving line. 'Mr Guru is entertaining guests in the billiards room. He will not appreciate you making a scene in this way. I doubt you'll be receiving any more custom from him. In any case, since you're here now, you can address your query to someone in the kitchens. This way.' The butler's voice is harsh, clipped.

He turns abruptly, expecting her to follow, but is interrupted by a tall white man. He is young, Bindu observes, and not as nattily dressed as some of the others; in fact, his suit, while clearly expensive, is not pressed and his tie is askew. He's holding himself rather awkwardly, as if not used to his height, and when he speaks it's as though he's surprised by the sound of his voice, and he coughs violently a couple of times to clear it. 'Just a moment, sir, please, I'd like to talk to the lady.'

Is he calling *her* a lady? Is he being sarcastic?

The butler, clearly taken aback and wondering the same thing, harrumphs as he halts his stride.

The man approaches Bindu. Close up, he's even taller. His hair scruffy, unbrushed, a lock falling over his eyes, the colour of the sun-baked fields in the drought, wiry yellow. His face clean-shaven, except for a couple of spots on his chin where he's missed, patches of golden brush. And right where his chin clefts in a sharp dimple, a shaving cut resulting in a bright crimson clot of blood.

'Miss,' he says and his voice, despite the violent clearing, is rusty, as if he doesn't use it much. 'I think I heard you say that you're the chef who prepared the food today?' His accent is the impeccable one of Sister Hilda and Sister Maria Teresa, and brings to her mind, suddenly, daffodils, sunny yellow smiles, dancing on a crisp English spring morning, a bright blue sky punctured by rays of gold.

'Yes,' she says, chin up, her eyes, the only part of her face not hidden by her veil, bright upon his, ready to counter any abuse directed at her.

But the man's eyes, the colour of the lush, water-fed lawns here, a sparkling and vibrant green, are earnest, kind, not mocking.

Or is she reading too much into his gaze?

The annoyed uproar around them fades as, once again, Bindu is lanced by the attention of everyone in the room.

The man in front of Bindu clears his throat again before speaking. 'My name is Laurence Elliot. I'm a journalist and I've just launched a features and lifestyle magazine that'll be published monthly.'

He takes a breath. Jewels of sweat bead his face, under his chin and over his lips.

'I'm sorry, I'm making a mess of this, rather.' He takes a handkerchief from his pocket and wipes his face. She is somewhat sad to see the translucent pearls disappear. 'I can write, but I'm no good at conversation.'

She notes the fluster in his eyes and understands that he's nervous. Is this because he's going to complain about her food? She thinks not, somehow. In fact, she is convinced of it. And with that, another thought: *he is genuine*. He meant it when he called her a lady. It warms her heart.

The butler's face is set and his lips are a firm line of disapproval.

The guests are whispering among themselves while intently watching the scene playing out in front of them.

The man clears his throat *again*.

'Miss, your food, well, it is the best I have tasted.' His voice, his gaze, are earnest, those vivid green eyes emphatic.

She feels her heart swell, tastes joy on her lips for the first time since Ajji fell ill and she refused her scholarship and with it her hopes of a better future for herself and her grandmother.

'Several readers of my magazine's flagship issue have asked for a recipe section to be incorporated and I wondered if you'd perhaps share some of your recip—'

A hand claps his shoulder, interrupting him mid-flow.

'Mr Elliot. Glad you could make it.' Guru, dressed in a glittering kurta embroidered with gold thread and studded with pearls, sounding anything but glad. His English accent, interchangeable with any Englishman's, like ice cubes tinkling in a tumbler. 'And what've we here?' His gaze on Bindu, eyes like flint, the twinkling admiration she's used to not in evidence. 'Why are you here, causing a commotion?'

Complete silence as all eyes in the room focus upon them.

She holds Guru's gaze, failing to find in those forbidding irises any hint of the boy who'd regard her with such adoration. She takes a deep breath, gathering courage. 'I'd like a word with you.'

She hasn't seen him since Sister Maria Teresa's last warning a month before her exams, for then she'd stopped shirking and put her mind completely to her studies, the immediacy of the exams, while scaring her, also staying her feet from running away. When doubts threatened, she studied harder; in the nights when she cooked, she chanted sums and poems and that helped keep qualms at bay.

Now, when her only hope for Ajji was English medicine, she'd cast her mind about and thought of the only person who had the means to help – Guru. They were friends, of a sort, weren't they? she'd reasoned. He'd help, talk to his father on her behalf, wouldn't he? No matter what he said, when it came right down to it he must have *some* influence.

And so, she'd swallowed her pride and run all the way here, leaving a comatose Ajji unattended in the hut, albeit in Dumdee's care. Chinnakka had promised to look in when her husband made his daily jaunt to Anantanna's palm orchard to collect the toddy he illicitly brewed there.

But while in this Guru, face taut, jaw working furiously, she is hard-pressed to find the boy she'd roamed the village with on somnolent afternoons, she recognises the youth who'd lashed out when she said something he didn't like, when she challenged his father's actions.

'You'd like a word. So, you storm in here as if you're an invited guest.' His eyes flashing onyx sparks, his voice cold.

She's never heard it like this before, in all their time together, which, she sees now, was a few stolen afternoons of flirty conversation.

Why did I think this a good idea?

Because it's my only hope for Ajji.

So, although her heart is thundering furiously, she stands up straighter, determined to see this through. 'If you listen to what I've to say—'

'Why should I listen to you, mere servant of my father?'

How dare he? she thinks, ire replacing apprehension, fury biting chilli-hot in her chest. But even angry, she must accept that he *can* dare, for he's right: he is the landlord's son, while she's a lowly worker, in his father's debt. She is fuming because, when they'd meet in the village, he always reiterated that there was no difference between Bindu and himself – they were both oppressed by his father. Yet, now, here among his people, he's making their difference clear, putting her in place so very harshly.

'Now look here,' Mr Elliot says.

Guru ignores him, his flinty gaze fixed on Bindu.

Shamefully, Bindu wants to turn tail and run – all her bravado is deserting her. She does not know this man, even though she'd convinced herself she did. Like she'd maintained, even when Guru protested otherwise, he is not – and never was – her friend. But, for Ajji's sake she'd hoped Guru would recall his assertions of friendship. Her legs are shaking, her whole body trembling like Ajji's used to before she was rendered comatose by her fever. She hopes her shakes aren't evident to everyone. At least her voice is calm when she says, 'What I've to say is to your advantage.'

Guru's lips curl. 'Say it then.'

'I need five minutes with you in private.'

A gasp from the all-male audience, who've edged closer as the drama has been unfolding, drinks abandoned, discussions curtailed, business deals unbrokered.

Guru's eyes are steel but is that a glint of interest behind them? *Now,* she sees the boy who'd come to find her when she escaped school, the one who caught her stealing but kept it secret, and her flailing courage gets a fresh boost.

'You interrupt my party, upset my guests and have the gall to request an audience with me in private? I must say I'm intrigued.'

'I am too.' The portly man who'd first brought her to the attention of everyone in the room guffaws.

Guru ignores him, saying tightly to Bindu, 'This better be good. Five minutes. Come with me.'

She follows in his wake, as he strides purposefully through the room full of his acquaintances.

As she passes Mr Elliot, who smells of freshly mown grass and sunshine, her eyes connect with his. His green-gold gaze, lake water on a summer evening, is kind, offering quiet solidarity, and it momentarily soothes her apprehensive heart.

CHAPTER 20

BINDU

'Five minutes,' Guru says, shutting the door and turning to her, a muscle in his jaw working.

Bindu bites her lower lip hard enough to draw blood – it hurts, a welcome distraction from the clamour in her heart. What possessed her to do this?

This room too, like the rest of this over-the-top abode, is obscenely huge, packed with heirloom furniture, extravagant, jewel-studded collectibles, but it feels claustrophobic. Guru's impatience, Bindu's thudding heart, adrenaline and nerves – she can't breathe.

Bindu pulls the door open, just enough for people to see inside. Any of the servants rushing to and from the kitchen and the bar with drinks and platters of Bindu's food, curious as to where the landlord's son has led the upstart from the village, can have a look in, see that she isn't up to no good.

And she can breathe again. Sounds and scents of the party drift in – spiced meat and caramelised milk, the pungent tang of alcohol mingling with the sweet scent of perfume lingering in the hallway, relics of the women who entered in their men's wakes only to be spirited away again. Masculine laughter, perhaps at Bindu's expense. From somewhere to this room's left wafts the faint chatter of women, interspersed with giggles, the jangle of jewellery – the women's party sequestered nearby.

'As always, you've intrigued me,' Guru is saying, eyes raised in question. 'You never stop to think, do you? You decide on something and, bam, you do it without a second thought.'

'I did think long and hard,' she says, 'about approaching you.'

'*Approaching*?' A harsh bark of laughter. 'You infiltrate my party, make a scene and that's what you call it?' He shakes his head. 'You're lucky my father is away and I'm in charge. He would not have tolerated this insouciance, this *mad* behaviour, from a mere servant.'

Hearing this from him, away from prying ears, enrages her – when he'd meet her in the village, he'd call her his friend, but this is what he *really* thinks of her. 'So, it's OK for you to have accosted me in the village any time you liked, but *I* can't—'

'I didn't see you complaining. And *this* is an invitation-only party, to which I don't recall inviting you. *That* was wandering on land owned by my father.'

'One rule for you and one for the rest of us.'

His mouth a grim line, he bites out, 'I've no time for this. I have to return to my guests. What is it you had to say so urgently, Bindu, that you had to barge in here, caring nothing for rules, causing a right old fluster? How did you get past the guards? No, don't tell me, I can guess.'

'You didn't mind how I got the better of the guards when you were daring me to do so not long ago. But, in any case, this time I was demure.'

'Were you? I find that hard to believe, seeing as you boldly attend my party without invitation, and instead of retiring to the women's section you mingle with the men, and, when they question your presence, order you to leave, you've the audacity to request an audience with the host.'

Is that a twinkle in his eyes, the barest hint of mirth, lightness in the steel?

Emboldened, Bindu says, 'I did you a favour. Your guests were bored and I gave them something to gossip about. Your party'll be the talk of the town now.'

'I didn't quite see it that way.' He smiles and she recognises once more the boy who'd parry with her during languid, fruit-scented afternoons. 'You're right, you know. *And* it has the added bonus of annoying my father no end.'

And now she hears in his voice the wounded child angling for, but never winning, his father's approval, and so doing the opposite in the vain hope that his wild antics might at least snag his father's attention. Guru hasn't changed; inside, he's still the boy she recalls. It prompts her to say, one eyebrow raised, 'I'm always right.'

His smile grows wider. 'I've missed you, Bindu.'

'Funny way of showing it.'

His eyes flash with temper and she wonders if she's ruined her chances before she's attempted to do what she came for.

But then he smiles, shaking his head ruefully. 'I've an image to uphold, you know, especially when I'm the host.'

He preens as he says this – Guru might decry his father's high-handed ways when he's on the receiving end, but he revels in the power that comes with being the landlord's son and heir, she sees.

'So, you do it by insulting me in front of your guests,' she can't help saying, even though she wants him on side.

His eyes flash again. '*You* insulted *me* by deviously getting past my guards and into my home as if you were meant to be there. And if that wasn't bad enough, compounding it by bypassing the women's section – the lone woman souring the all-male gathering. I couldn't allow you the upper hand, undermining my authority – surely you understand that?'

'I take issue with *souring*. Surely *enhancing* is more like it.'

He smiles.

'I'm waiting for your apology,' she says, falling back to the repartee that has distinguished their meetings.

Again, he smiles. 'I'll apologise when I've had yours.'

'You'll be waiting a long time.'

Beaming widely, he cocks his head. 'You're looking good by the way, as always, owning that threadbare sari in a way that all those women' – he nods his head to the left, indicating the room where the women are gathered – 'can never do, never mind that each thread from their elaborate outfits must've cost more than your entire wardrobe, I bet.'

What wardrobe, she thinks. *I've two saris that I alternate between.*

Out loud, taking advantage of his improved mood, she takes a deep breath and launches into what she's come for. 'So, I did you a favour. Now I need to ask you for one.'

'Well?' he says, crossing his arms. 'Go on then.'

'My Ajji is ill. I need an English doctor to see to her.'

'Ha. And you've come to me. I remember you saying you wouldn't rely on anyone, that you'd make your own way in the world. All that skiving. You lost the scholarship?'

Pain stabs with sabre-toothed blades as she thinks of the scholarship. It *hurts*.

'You were so confident. Brought down a peg, were you?'

'I *won* the scholarship,' she throws at him. 'I got the highest marks ever recorded in the matriculation exams.'

And now she sees that admiring glint that she was used to when he'd accompany her during her escapades.

'Well, I expected nothing less of you.'

'Not what you were saying a minute ago.'

'I'm confused,' Guru says. 'If you won the scholarship, why're you asking me for help?'

'Because I declined it.'

She's succeeded in shocking him.

'Why?'

'My Ajji needs a doctor *now*. And I won't leave her and go off to study in the city.'

'Ah.' He looks assessingly at her. 'I didn't have you down as a self-sacrificing sort.'

You don't know anything about me.

'My Ajji sacrificed her life for me,' she says, tightly. 'So, will you help?'

'Let's say I do,' he replies. 'What do I get in return?'

'I'll cook for your father for free for a year.' As long as Ajji is cured, Bindu will manage somehow. She'll barter with the villagers, swallow her pride, live on credit for a time. She is prepared to use emotional blackmail on the villagers, bank on their affection and respect for Ajji to get them through.

But... 'No,' Guru says.

'No?'

'No.'

She's tried. And failed. She'll have to think of something else. Despair swamps her, nauseous yellow, as she thinks of Ajji, comatose with the fever that is showing no signs of breaking.

She turns to go.

'Wait. I didn't say I wouldn't help. I only said no to what you were offering in return.'

She takes a deep breath, annoyed that he's dragging it out, grateful that it isn't an outright no, and nervous as to what he might ask for. 'All right. What do you want?'

'You.'

She cannot deny that some part of her expected this. She recalls Sunitha saying, awe sunshine-bright in her voice, 'You've the landlord's son besotted, I hear.' And Guru himself had implied as much, more than once. But she'd hoped, and prayed, when she decided to come here and request his help to save Ajji, that he'd respect her boundaries, like he did when they'd meet up in the village.

She looks at him, crossed arms, twinkling gaze perusing her languidly – for him, it's a game. For her, this is bargaining for her grandmother's life.

'No,' she says, tasting salt and desperation. 'When we first met, I told you I'd never kiss a man who wasn't my husband. Do you remember?'

'I do.' He winces. 'And don't think I haven't forgotten what you did when I tried. That spice paste was lethal. The little I inadvertently tasted made my lips swell.'

'You offend me. I'll have you know I'm a very good cook.'

He smiles and, once more, he's the boy she remembers, the one she had sway over. *Please let it be so now too. Let me be able to convince him to help Ajji without having to do what he's suggesting.* But a part of her is resigned to doing anything – even what he's asking –

for the woman who has been mother, father, family, her all, although Bindu hopes it won't come to that.

The tinkle of glasses and a burst of masculine laughter drifts into the room on a gust of honey- and spice-flavoured air.

Guru's smile disappears, and he's all business. 'I've to see to my guests. I've spent too much time here already. I will be frank.'

Bindu takes a breath, meets his gaze. 'Please do.'

'I like you. I want you, have done so since the first time I saw you. And now you're as good as mine...'

'I am not...' She's nonplussed, too shaky to manage more than a weak retort.

'Let me finish.' Guru's voice sharp as a bee sting. 'Your reputation as a demoness with the face and figure of a goddess, casting devilish spells and hurting anyone who tries to get close, is well and truly shot. For you've ambushed my party, declaring to my guests, a roomful of gentlemen, in public, that you want to speak with me privately. That'll loosen a few tongues. Untouched witch no longer. Although there've been rumours floating around for a while now about our association, people seeing us getting close and flirty in the village—'

'Rumours started by you no doubt,' she says, her nerves making her impatient. 'Look, are you going to help me or not?'

He's quiet, looking intently at her, an assessing smile playing on his face. His scrutiny makes her uncomfortable, and she shifts her weight from one foot to the other, wanting, itching to escape this room.

Finally, 'Only if I can have you,' he says.

'I'll only allow the man who marries me to touch me,' she tries, tasting despair on her tongue. Why did she come here? Will she really do what he's asking of her for Ajji's sake, go from wanting to study to become a doctor and save people to being a fallen woman who cannot even save herself?

'Yet you've no qualms about flirting, flaunting your beauty.' His voice harsh, no hint of the boy Bindu had held sway over.

'Not if it opens doors, works to my advantage.'

'So why won't you go further? Perhaps you already have and this "untouched" vibe you give off is just a carefully cultivated lie.'

She shrugs with a nonchalance she doesn't feel. 'Believe what you have to. But I will say this. You spent many afternoons with me. The only man to do so. In all that time did I let you, even once, come close enough to touch me?'

His forehead furrowed in consideration, he is quiet for so long that she once again shifts from foot to foot, uncomfortable in the heat of his perusal. What is he thinking?

She's just about to tell him she's had enough when he speaks. 'So marry me.'

'*What?*' She didn't expect this.

'You're interesting. Bright. Beautiful. You intrigue me. I'm never bored with you. Unlike every other woman I've met – married and unmarried, princess and socialite. They're one and the same. Meek. Dutiful. Forgettable,' Guru is saying. 'I have to marry sooner or later, and if I marry one of the princesses or noblewomen my father keeps pushing at me, there'll be the tiresome business of keeping her family happy, placating her parents and brothers, being held to account for every supposed misdemeanour.'

He's thinking out loud and the more he speaks, the more she wants to run away, forget she ever came here, as it sinks in that this might actually happen – she might be joining the family of the man who represents everything she's against.

Bindu opens her mouth, finds her voice, which is playing truant in her dry, stunned throat: 'Will your father agree to you marrying a low-born villager when he has his heart set on a princess?'

'He already has a queen for a daughter. One of my sisters is married to the king of Jabalpur and the other to the wealthiest nobleman in India, one of the ten richest men in the world. As for money, there's plenty to be made from investments and property, given the volatile state of the markets here and abroad with threat of war in Europe and the independence struggle in India. I don't necessarily need it from in-laws who'd then expect to have a say in every business deal we broker. This is the argument that I suspect will sway my father – he doesn't appreciate anyone telling him his business. As for me, since I've no need for more money or status –

I already have more than enough – I might as well marry for beauty, and you're the prettiest girl in all of India by my reckoning.'

She is blindsided by this turn of events but, nevertheless, she counters, 'How would you—'

'I hadn't finished.' He grins. 'Even with your veil on, wearing that threadbare sari, you cannot hide the perfect contours of your body, that chiselled profile. And you forget that I've seen you without your veil twice, by my count.'

'Both times when you removed it without my consent,' she retorts sharply, unsettled and unnerved by his proposal.

'Well, now I'm asking for it. Will you marry me?'

Why is Guru's offer of marriage more shocking to Bindu than the proposition to be his mistress? Why is it harder to get her head around?

Because, her conscience supplies, she was expecting *that* proposition, used as she is to men objectifying her, checking her out like a piece of meat they'd like to sink their teeth into. They do not consider the fact that she has a brain, thoughts, emotions, that she is more than her beauty.

But Guru has. He always did, which was why she enjoyed his company on her jaunts – he'd talk to her, and, more importantly, listen when *she* talked. While he, too, like other men, was swayed by her beauty, he also valued her mind. She had enjoyed surprising him with her wit and intellect, seeing that admiring glint in his eye, not just for her looks but for her mind.

He has surprised *her* now, taking her seriously, on her terms. In a society where women, whether rich or poor, princesses or paupers, are disregarded, overlooked, considered mere props to their men, where their faces are hidden, alongside their personalities, their voices silenced, where they're just a means to an end – keeping house, providing and bringing up heirs – this is a novelty.

He grins at her, eyes bright. 'So, Miss Bindu, do we have a deal? Your Ajji can have medical help if you marry me.'

Her voice is in hiding and she cannot do more than nod. Is she really agreeing to this? Marriage into the family whose values are the opposite of hers? But what choice does she have with Ajji's life at stake?

But... Marriage is binding. Mistress is not. As mistress, she wouldn't be one of the figureheads for the family she hates. Instead she'd be just another of the many skeletons in their vast closet of sins. She could take that. But to actually *represent* the family... It appals her more.

'Lost for words? I never thought I'd see the day!' he teases. 'May I kiss the bride?'

'Not until we're married.' Is she really saying this? Is it really happening?

'I thought that'd get a response from you. So, all agreed then. I'll talk to my father. Not looking forward to that, I must say.'

'You need help?' She can't help asking.

He laughs. A genuine burst of mirth. 'You're the only woman – no, come to think of it, the only person – who can make me laugh, Bindu. Everyone else is a fawning sycophant – excepting my bully of a father, of course. I'll prepare for battle. I'm actually quite looking forward to it.'

'You're sure you'll win?' She wants him to, for Ajji's sake, even as her mind shies away from the prospect of marriage to the land-lord's son.

'Positive. He wants me to marry and provide him with a continuing line of heirs, and I'll reiterate that the only person I will do so with is you.'

Her mind cringes at the mention of heirs; it's a step too far. But... This man and what he's offering is Ajji's only hope. 'Well, good luck. But don't take too long. My Ajji—'

'I'll talk to him when he returns from meeting with the king of Chandrapur this evening, and if all goes well – and it *will* – the doctor'll be with your Ajji in the next few days.'

'Thank you.' Her gratitude is genuine, heartfelt.

'Now, I believe your five minutes are up. Goodbye, my betrothed. Are you sure I cannot bestow a token of my affection?' He is playful.

'Quite sure.' She turns to leave.

'There was just one thing...' Guru's voice stays her.

She swivels round to face him, her heart catching in her throat.

'You must promise something.'

Bindu's been through a gamut of emotions since entering this room: fear, worry, upset, despair, desperation, happiness at Ajji finally getting the medical help she needs. Then there are the emotions she'll unpack later, far from here, at what she's agreed to in return. And now, at Guru's words, worry again... She should've known there'd be a catch. 'What?'

'Promise me there'll be no spice mix anywhere near my body when we're married?' His eyes sparking with mischief.

Relief swamps her, honey gold, nectar sweet. 'I never make promises I may not keep.'

His hearty laughter follows her as she leaves the room, urgently scurrying servants breaking stride to hark at this unaccustomed sound of their master's unfettered chuckles, to stare at the slip of a girl in an old sari and bare, blistered feet who's provoked it, shaking their heads at this miracle of one of their lot – a woman at that – causing their famously tetchy employer to chortle like a naughty boy.

CHAPTER 21

EVE

1980

After her mother's departure in the ambulance, Maya appears to shrink into herself.

She looks at Eve with tear-bejewelled eyes, stark with apprehension. 'Is Mum going to die, Eve?'

Eve's heart goes out to this little girl. All her worries about how she'll cope, a broken woman in charge of a child who is a wounding reminder of her own lost daughter, disappear in the face of this young one's fear, her anxiety, her confusion. This vulnerable innocent, bereft without her only parent.

She sits beside Maya, puts her arm round her.

Maya snuggles into her side trustingly, sniffling intermittently. It feels so natural – Eve has done this a thousand times before with Izzy; it is both comfort and torture, inciting pain, while at the same time a balm to her yearning, devastated heart.

'Your mum's in good hands, sweetheart, in hospital, where they'll do their best for her. You did good by calling the ambulance.'

Against her, she can feel Maya nod, even as she sniffs.

Eve feels vindicated, a small relief that she's managed to say the right thing.

'It must've been horrendous for you,' she adds.

'Yes,' Maya squeaks. 'I... I thought she was going to die like Daddy.' And she breaks down, sobbing.

Eve holds the little girl, rubbing her small, juddering back, murmuring, 'There, there,' for the first time since the accident that stole her family setting her own grief aside to shoulder some of this child's despair.

CHAPTER 22

BINDU

1937

Bindu sleepwalks through her wedding festivities.

It's as if she's watching from afar the girl she was – apple of her Ajji's eyes, labelled bad luck by the other villagers out of Ajji's hearing – become wedded to the most eligible bachelor in the state, the landlord's only son, all the princesses and royalty and noblemen's daughters who'd been vying for his hand snubbed.

I don't want this, she's crying inside, mourning the life she could've had. *I never did. I wanted to make my own way in the world, to rely on nobody but myself. I certainly didn't want anything to do with the miserly bully of a landlord.*

Bindu and Ajji had been ordered to move here, to the landlord's residence, as soon as the landlord agreed to the wedding: 'My son and heir's betrothed cannot live in a hut in a village I own until the wedding! What'll people say?'

'I don't care what people say,' Bindu had railed at Guru. 'I never have.'

'Oh?' Guru had raised an eyebrow at her. 'Correct me if I'm wrong, but I recall you stealing the villagers' fruit because they were gossiping about you.'

She had flushed, looking away.

He'd smiled. 'You'll have to move in after the wedding, so why not now? In any case, it'll be easier for the doctor to attend to your Ajji – he visits my father every morning to check on his blood pressure, and at the same time he can look in on your grandmother.'

How could she argue with that?

The west wing of the mansion has been given over to Bindu and Ajji. A bevy of maids tend to them exclusively.

'We don't need maids,' Bindu had told Guru. She'd cringed upon seeing girls her age assigned to her and Ajji's care. 'I'll look after my Ajji. We managed just fine without maids in the village and we can do the same here.'

'Bindu,' Guru's voice tight, face grim, 'you're living under my father's roof and you'll abide by his rules.'

'But there's no need...'

'This conversation is over.' Guru turned away.

In rebellion, Bindu tried to do everything herself, but the maids hovered, looking piqued, and one morning, she overheard them grumbling: 'She lords it over us, when she was one of us just a few days ago, *and* she doesn't trust us to do our job properly.'

After which, hot tears pricking her eyes that she sniffed angrily away, she gave up, gave in, allowed the maids to do their job and sat vigil beside Ajji feeling like a spare part as they dusted and cleaned busily around her, missing her life in the village, which was harsh but full with the angst of surviving day to day, hour to hour, with little food and barely any water. Now she had all the food and water she wanted, but it tasted bitter, flavoured with the repercussions of her choice.

Dumdee and Sirsi were not welcome in the landlord's abode: 'No mongrels allowed, trailing diseases.'

Bindu had swallowed her pride and begged Guru, 'Please, won't you negotiate with your father?'

'He's allergic, Bindu.'

'To cats *and* dogs?'

'Yes. And to horses. That is why he owns several cars but not a single carriage.'

Bindu had wept as she'd handed Dumdee and Sirsi over to the

midwife – the very one who had, when Bindu was born blue and silent, tipped her upside down until she started wailing.

The midwife and her daughter, who is following in her mother's footsteps, having donned the mantle of village midwife after her mother retired, love animals and have a large collection of strays that they feed and house in their vast courtyard. Dumdee and Sirsi are happy there, with plenty of company, Bindu knows. Nevertheless, it doesn't ease the missing and she cries into the night, yearning for her loyal companions – Dumdee especially.

Ajji is being seen daily by the English doctor who performed miracles on the landlord's wife – he's prescribed medicine and advises patience, reassuring Bindu that the fever will break.

And the English pills seem to be working – once or twice, Ajji's eyes had fluttered open and she'd appeared to come out of the comatose trance induced by her raging fever, but before Bindu could rejoice, talk to her, spill her heart, Ajji's eyes had closed again.

But, nevertheless, this is a step forward and, along with the doctor's assurances, it gives Bindu hope that Ajji *will* get better, that her bargain with Guru has not been in vain.

Bindu wonders what Ajji will think of it – she has an inkling her grandmother will not approve. But that's all it is, for Ajji isn't aware that she's been moved into the most opulent surroundings possible, the softest bed. No more sharing a mat with her granddaughter. Bindu mourns the loss of this, even while knowing that everyone in the village would happily exchange places with them for the privilege.

The villagers think Bindu has landed on her feet, but Bindu hates being beholden to the landlord, tied to him. She mourns her scholarship and the future she once dreamed of.

One of the first things she asked of Guru as soon as she and Ajji moved here was if there was some way they could divert some of the water from the mansion to the village. It sickened her to wash in the luxurious bathroom – so unlike the little lean-to fashioned from coconut palm fronds that she and her grandmother had weaved into mats, where they'd washed using the bare minimum of rationed water Bindu had collected from the lake. Here, the water wasn't allowed to run out – servants refilled freshly heated water regularly in every bathroom in this vast mansion. As she tipped the pristine water, that wasn't scented with mud and sweat and lake dregs, but instead with sin and greed and other people's slog, over her body, guilt stabbed and lanced, and afterwards she felt dirty, even though she was the cleanest she'd ever been.

'The fields are lying empty and barren due to the drought. No crops, no livelihood. The wells are dry and now even the lake—' Bindu began.

'Stop right there, Bindu,' Guru had interrupted her. 'My father doesn't like anyone – and definitely not his son – interfering in his business decisions. I've already caused a furore by insisting I marry you. I've honoured my end of the bargain. Your Ajji is being seen to, regularly, by the doctor. Let this be.'

'How can I, when just days ago I was in the same plight and now I've the means to do something about it, make a difference?'

'You don't,' Guru said, a muscle in his jaw working. 'You can't.'

'But *you* can.'

His voice softened a tad. 'I applaud your belief in my supposed power over my father. Although he's come round to accepting that, at some point, he'll have to hand over the reins to me, and is grudgingly involving me in his affairs – as I said, he doesn't take advice from anyone.'

'He agreed for you to marry me.'

'That was a personal matter – *my* personal life, in which he wanted a say because it involves the future of his business empire. I had a hold over him; he needed me to marry, provide sons, in order to keep the business and wealth in the family.' The bitterness in Guru's voice barely disguised the pain at his father's continued lack of affection for his son.

'The villagers are desperate. Is it possible to provide them with one water tank?' Bindu begged.

His voice softened further even as he sighed. 'I'll try speaking to my father when he's better disposed towards me.'

'The villagers need water *now*.'

'They'll manage like they have before. I've no influence over my father right now, Bindu, not that I ever did. I've exhausted any goodwill I had by choosing to marry you.'

'I feel guilty about having water to spare when the villagers have none.'

Guru shrugged. 'It is what it is.'

'But your father can make a difference.'

'Enough!' Guru barked, his patience exhausted. 'There's nothing I can do right now, so there's no point going on about it.'

It is Bindu's wedding, but she, protégée of Ajji, famed cook whose dishes have been feted by princes and peasants alike, has not cooked a single dish for it. Bindu and Guru's wedding banquet is being supplied by a chef who used to cook for the king of Rampur but fell out of favour for adding cashew nuts to the king's favourite lamb biryani when the king had apparently expressly asked him not to (although, until that day, the king had liked cashew nuts in every single dish, sweet and savoury alike – the more, the better). The chef had managed to escape with his life, seeking allegiance with the British Resident – the king of Rampur was famous for having those who displeased him beheaded – and started his own catering business. 'Our only daughter-in-law will not darken the kitchen, do menial jobs when we employ a whole battalion of staff for that very purpose. Whoever heard of such a thing? Forget what she was, she's marrying into our family and must maintain a certain dignity,' Guru's father – Bindu still thought of him as 'the landlord' – had ruled.

The landlord's wife had no say – she was a mere woman, after all. Although, even if she had wanted to, she couldn't, as she was ill.

As for Guru...

'Why can't I cook at my wedding?' Bindu had stormed, bursting into his chambers, summarily ignoring the manservant who'd tried to stop her at the door.

This is how it was in this ridiculously huge mansion, everyone sealed into their own private spaces, rarely meeting – which, Bindu had to admit, suited her for the most part.

Guru, seated at his desk, poring over documents, had looked up in irritation, eyes hard and flashing orange sparks. 'You're disturbing me. In future, send word to my man asking for a meeting. You've enough maids at your disposal to do so. Where is he? Why didn't he stop you?'

'He tried. I ignored him.'

'I thought so.' Guru sighed, rubbing a hand over his face, the gesture weary. But the hardness had gone from his eyes, replaced by that twinkle she'd come to expect when he'd visit her in the village. 'You're irrepressible.'

'I'm to be your wife in a matter of days. I don't need to seek an appointment with you.'

'Good point, but remember it works both ways. I'll barge into your apartment whenever I feel like it.' A raised eyebrow. His lips rising in a playful smirk.

She ducked her head to hide her blush, even though her face was covered by the customary veil.

He noticed and snorted a bark of laughter, which made his manservant knock on the door and ask, 'Everything all right, Sahib?'

While Guru waved him off, Bindu wandered over to Guru's desk. 'What're you working on?' she queried, looking over the papers he'd been perusing. 'Plans for the expansion of your textile mills. But... these figures you've forecasted... you're *increasing* the hours of work for employees and paying them *less*?'

'Bindu' – his laughter evaporating, gaze flinty again – 'this does not concern you.'

'But these are people like me, like my Ajji. Human beings working back-breaking hours for a pittance and you... you're making them work for longer and...' Her voice broke in anger and upset.

He gripped her arm, none too gently, pushing her away from his desk. 'Do not – I repeat, do *not* – interfere in matters that are none of your business.'

'But—'

'And henceforth make an appointment when you want to see me.' And, his voice marginally less harsh, 'Now that you're here, what did you want?'

She stood up straighter, facing him. 'For you to drop my hand right now.'

He did, moving away behind his desk, a brief flash of mortification in his expression before it hardened again.

She resisted the urge to rub at her hand where he'd grabbed her.

'I'm busy,' he snapped. 'Was there anything else?'

She swallowed, her throat dry; she was unsure of him right now, and, she had to admit, a little afraid too. But she pushed her shoulders back and faced him squarely. 'Why can't I cook at my wedding? The landlord wanted Ajji and me to cater for all of his parties when we were his tenants.'

'I thought it was obvious.' Guru's voice was taut with irritation. 'But I'll spell it out. You're no longer his tenant but will soon be his daughter-in-law and it's not proper for the daughter-in-law of the landlord to engage in menial tasks. Now, if that was all, I'm busy and need to be getting on.' He turned his attention to the papers on his desk. She was dismissed.

But she refused to go quietly. 'Guru, those textile workers are human beings with families, children...'

He ignored her.

'Guru...'

He swatted in her general direction like she was a fly. 'You still here?' Not looking up from his papers. 'Don't you get the message?'

'Don't *you* get it?' she snapped, frustrated and furious. 'If it wasn't for the accident of your birth, you'd be one of—'

He laughed mirthlessly. 'I admire your persistence. But it won't make a blind bit of difference. Now, go away. It'd be a shame if I'd to ask my man to remove my future wife from my chambers.' He said it lazily, as if making conversation with a recalcitrant child not worthy of his time, his gaze never leaving his papers. This made Bindu all the more upset, ire and frustration bitter in her mouth. 'And don't come here again without an appointment.' Steel in his voice.

Bindu marched down the corridors of the mansion, past servants who looked askance at her, not paying attention to where she was going, getting lost more than once, her whole being shaking. He'd made her feel so small, so insignificant, this man she was to marry. But why should she be surprised, when he didn't care about the fate of his workers, about anyone, it seemed, except himself – his convenience, his time? Was this how it would be, for the duration of their marriage, Bindu ignored, sidelined, an irritant? What had she expected? Just because she made him smile, laugh at times, just because he let her parry with him, that he'd do as she asked? And would that change too now he was marrying her, would she lose what little influence she had with him, join the ranks of people he owned, to be used and discarded as per his whim?

Her feet led her to Ajji's luxurious room, knowing somehow that this was where her preoccupied, despairing self wanted to go; a room that could house two of their one-roomed huts easily. Bindu held her comatose grandmother's hand, drawing comfort from her papery skin, burning hot from the fever that still raged strong, all the while screaming in her head, *What have I done? What on earth have I signed up for?*

The next time Bindu and Guru met was at her husband-to-be's instigation, the day before the wedding, to detail what would happen during the ceremony.

It was as if his brusque dismissal of her the other day had never happened. It was perfectly possible he'd forgotten about it. *She* couldn't. For it had got her thinking about what she'd actually agreed to, when she said yes to marrying him. Up until now, she'd been pleased that Ajji was getting medical care; she'd been urging Ajji to get better quickly while also worrying about her grandmother's reaction, knowing she would be upset with Bindu for sacrificing her scholarship on her behalf; she'd been preoccupied with moving here, saying goodbye to, and sorely missing,

Dumdee, Sirsi and the village, even though while living there she'd felt claustrophobic and couldn't wait to get away.

But after Guru's cavalier disregard for her views, dismissing her so summarily and not even bothering to look at her while doing it, asking that she make an appointment to see him henceforth, she was beginning to realise that she hadn't given her marriage, and how it would play out, much thought, if any. All her focus had been on Ajji. Now she understood – why had it taken her so long? – that she'd be tied to this man for *life*.

Guru was unpredictable, selfish and, worst of all, callous. Like his father, those textile workers were not human beings to him, but mere pawns on the chessboard that was their business empire. And she was marrying him, this man who didn't see *people*, but instead manpower, like machinery, to squeeze the maximum use out of for minimum cost and then to discard without a second thought. If he thought of workers as mere cogs in the wheel of his business, how might he see her?

Lost in her musings, she almost missed what Guru was saying.

'Wait a minute, did you just say the women will be sequestered?' she asked.

'Yes, we'll be married by the priest and then you'll host the women's darbar.'

'Why?'

'What do you mean, why?'

'Why can't the women mingle with the men?'

'My father's old-fashioned. He likes women separate from the men.'

'Why?'

Guru's lips thinned in irritation, forehead creasing in a frown, 'So the men can have fun, drink and swear without having to be polite in the women's presence. Equally, the women can be free. No hiding behind veils. They can talk, laugh, gossip, let their hair down.'

'So, on my own wedding day, I'll be sequestered?'

'That's what I'm saying, yes.' His lips a grim line, a flash of temper in his eyes. 'It's how it's always been, during any and all gatherings conducted here.'

'And it can't change?'

Guru sighed. 'Why's everything a battle with you?'

'I thought you liked that I'm not meek and dutiful. I thought it was why you were marrying me.'

She worried that she'd gone too far – she wouldn't have considered that during their jaunts in the village, but, she was learning, everything was different now. Before, Guru would try to please her, woo her, win her approval, but now *she* was beholden to *him* and his father – and she absolutely *loathed* it. But that familiar twinkle appeared in his eyes and she exhaled in relief.

'I'm beginning to see the benefit of meek and dutiful.'

'You'd be bored.'

'But not constantly challenged.' He rubbed a hand over his chin, the gesture weary. 'Bindu, I've won one battle with my father by insisting on marrying you. I can't—'

'He's profited from the publicity – all the newspapers have reported about how the landlord's setting an example by his only son and heir marrying one of his tenants.'

One of the benefits of living at the mansion was that all the leading newspapers printed in both English and regional languages were delivered each morning. When she'd moved in, Bindu had asked if she could have them after Guru and the landlord had read them, and Guru had acquiesced, admiration in his gaze. She had taken to reading the papers aloud by Ajji's bedside and translating the English articles for Ajji's benefit, in the hope that even though she was comatose, she could still hear and be soothed by Bindu's voice.

'In fact, I read in yesterday's paper that major companies are lining up to broker business with your father because they're impressed by his integrity. What did they call him? *A principled man who leads by example, eschewing princesses in favour of a village girl for his only son.*' She'd flung the paper away in upset.

'The venom in your voice could poison an elephant!' Guru was smiling.

'You know what'll look even better, raise his profile even more?' The idea had come to her after she'd picked up the paper she'd thrown across the room and stared at the article again, her fury burning holes into it. But she hadn't been brave enough to barge into Guru's chambers after the last time. Now here was her chance. 'If the landlord, as a wedding gift to the village that gave him his daughter-in-law, pardons the rent of the villagers for this month.' It was the only way she could square her guilt at marrying the landlord's son, living in a mansion that represented everything she detested, not having to worry about food or water, Ajji being cared for, while her fellows suffered. At least the monsoons had finally arrived, so the villagers were all right for water for now.

'Bindu, I've told you this time and again: do not interfere in matters that are none of your business.' Guru's eyes shuttered.

She sashayed her hips, smiled up at him. 'I'm not asking for anything for myself...'

'You already have, if you recall. Your Ajji is receiving the best medical care. And your flirting won't work with me, for you'll be mine tomorrow.' He smiled.

A shaft of fearful apprehension lanced her at the thought of intimacy with this man who was, at heart, like his father, a ruthless businessman whose values were in opposition to hers.

She swallowed, tried: 'Please, Guru. The villagers—'

'It doesn't make business sense.' Guru brusque, dismissive.

'But pardoning their rent won't make even the slightest dent in your wealth—'

'My father's upset already at the wealth we've potentially lost by my not marrying into royalty.'

'But you're brokering new, better business deals with ethical companies who respect your father's values.'

They'll find out soon enough what his values really are when he hires workers for a pittance and makes them work heartless hours for it. She did not voice the thought – it made her heart bleed – and she was glad, for Guru's mood had changed in a heart-stopping instant.

'Enough with the mockery, Bindu, you're going too far.' Every word biting. 'He's been nothing but kind, setting you and your Ajji up here, making sure you want for nothing.'

He would, she thought. *For it adds weight to the new image he's cultivating. It's not kindness, it makes business sense.*

She took a breath, tried one last time, even though Guru's eyes were flashing with temper. 'Look, you have to admit, it'll be tremendously good publicity if it's reported that the landlord magnanimously pardoned the villagers' rent. It will not matter then that none of the villagers have been invited to the wedding, except in a menial capacity as servants to the guests...'

'They wouldn't report that.'

'Yes, because the articles are vetted by your father...'

'Bindu, I said *enough*,' Guru barked.

'Please float the idea to him and see what he says? In return, I agree to be sequestered in the women's darbar and to all the other antiquated traditions your father wants in place during our wedding.'

'You've no choice but to agree to them anyway. I've honoured my part of the deal, and now you'll honour yours. Goodbye. I'll see you tomorrow.' Guru turned away.

Bindu bunched her fists and clamped them into her mouth to hold her scream inside. She was frustrated, deeply upset that she'd failed to get through to him, that she couldn't influence him as she once could. It made her realise afresh that she was stuck in this situation, with no way out. She'd craved independence, financial and personal, which was why she'd tried so hard to win the scholarship, but when she'd agreed to marry Guru that was the very thing she'd sacrificed; she had signed away her freedom, any agency she might've had.

She felt claustrophobic, strangled by the weight of her choices, the direction her life had taken. The urge to escape, run, leave this mansion was so strong that she was almost at the main hall, her feet following her mind's unconscious urging, before she thought of Ajji. If she left, ran like she used to do at school, what'd be Ajji's fate? And where would she, Bindu, go? All the land around here, the village, her hut, was owned by the landlord. And, whether she liked it or not, she herself was too. She couldn't escape – she was well and truly trapped in this ostentatious prison, a veritable life sentence.

She turned round and, paying no heed to her hot, tingling eyes, leaking nose, the not-so-discreet gawping of the servants, she ran to the west wing – her home now – and into the courtyard.

Throwing herself down on the bench in the shade of the palm trees, she flung her head to the sky. Black silhouettes of birds dotted the sapphire gold canvas, flying free, and Bindu wished she was one of them. The fountain gurgled and hot air scented with mango and spices caressed her face, but all she could feel and hear was the clamour of her soul crying out for escape.

CHAPTER 23

BINDU

Now, on Bindu's wedding day, while her brand-new husband is busy entertaining his friends and business associates alongside his father, she's stuck in the women's room, being examined and assessed like a mango past its best at the market by noblewomen and princesses, who smile with their teeth but shoot acrid bullets with their eyes that could wound, if not kill. The landlord's son, the most eligible bachelor in the state, married to this... *nobody*. Ironically, despite the social and financial division between these women and the villagers, there's no difference in their scrutiny, their damning assessment of Bindu.

Whispers not quite quiet or discreet enough, meant for her ears: 'Unlucky, that's what she is.'

'Did you hear the landlord's wife's been confined to her bed? It seems she took ill as soon as the marriage was fixed and has got worse since, unable to attend her only son's wedding festivities.'

'Lethal, this girl. Causing havoc wherever she goes. Killed her father when in her mother's womb, and her mother as she came out of it.'

'What does he see in her, apart from looks?'

'She's weaved black magic on him.'

'It seems the landlord was apoplectic with rage. But when his only son went on hunger strike, what could he do but give in? And in return? His wife falls ill.'

'And Ajji, poor dear, on her deathbed when her only sin was to love the girl.'

'Whoever loves her is sentenced to death. It's only a matter of time before...'

Air, Bindu needs air. She's choking in the finery gifted by her husband, the jewels and fabric of which could purchase not one water tank but several, allow the villagers to live hunger-, thirst- and rent-free for a year at least.

She needs out of this room full of loathing barely disguised behind polite smiles, bared teeth, directed at her.

Normally she couldn't care less, but now... their poisonous barbs find their target. The knowledge that she's tied to Guru and the landlord for life slaps her with renewed force as she sits there under sufferance, having no recourse but to listen to their venom, for it's her *duty* to do so, part of the deal she wrought with Guru. It's also her duty to provide her husband − *her husband*, she who'd vowed to depend on no one, proudly making her own way in the world − with an heir.

Bindu has tried not to think of what that entails, but she cannot any longer, for it *will* happen in a few hours. She cannot even seek reassurance from her grandmother, for, while Ajji is definitely improving − her fever not burning furiously any more but milder, her eyes fluttering open for longer stretches each time − she remains confused, weak and unaware of her surroundings.

Bindu refused to take as a bad omen the fact that she participated in her wedding with no allies at her side. (If she'd married someone of her own ilk − a big if, as she'd not wanted to marry anyone at all − the entire village would have been in attendance.) She refused to think at all, trying to empty her mind of worry and doubt: *Ajji, am I doing the right thing?* even as − *especially* as − she walked around the holy fire, seven times, head bowed, behind Guru, binding herself to him like her elaborate sari, weighing almost more than she did herself, was bound to the shawl of his equally ostentatious wedding kurta, the priest chanting mantras as he threw ghee, rice and flowers into the hallowed flames, which hissed and spat in sacred celebration.

Afterwards, she'd looked out from under her veil and in the sea of attendees – all men, the women being sequestered as usual, as she would be when this ceremony was over – she found one familiar face. The tall journalist, Mr Elliot, who'd spoken to her that fateful day when she came to the mansion with a foolhardy plan to save Ajji, not knowing if it'd work but wanting to try all the same.

He stood right at the front, and while the other men were barely paying attention, chatting among themselves, some yawning, others eyes closed, mouths open, fast asleep as the rituals dragged on, his green-gold gaze was upon her, steady and kind.

When their eyes met he'd smiled and nodded, gently, and, flustered, she'd looked down, and had kept her gaze upon her feet for the rest of her wedding puja. But somehow this brief connection had comforted Bindu, her panic, her fear at what she'd let herself in for easing just a little.

CHAPTER 24

BINDU

Now, Bindu walks out of the women's party room, ignoring her guests, who ask, with mock concern, their eyes shining with the thrill of fresh gossip to be had at her expense, 'Are you all right?'

'Memsahib, do you need anything?' the servants ask obsequiously and Bindu has to stifle the urge to look behind her, see who they're referring to.

When she first moved here, she'd said, 'Call me Bindu, I'm one of you.'

And briefly, they'd dropped their servile manner, bared their teeth: *No, you're not any longer; if you ever were, that is.*

Showed your true colours, didn't you? is what they're thinking but refraining from saying. *You always thought you were better than us, flaunting those looks, swaying those hips, beguiling our men but declaring that you didn't need a man, that you'd drive your destiny yourself.*

Once out of the room, she careers blindly through this mansion's maze of corridors, feet clad in flamboyant but impractical gold sandals, courtesy of her new husband, that bite into her ankles, chafing skin, rousing blisters. She walks with such huge strides that she's almost running, all her jewellery chiming strident warning – the gold chains, diamond and pearl necklaces in addition to her mangalsutra, the auspicious thread Guru had tied around Bindu's neck binding her to him for life, silver and emerald rings, gold bangles and diamond earrings, gold-, emerald-, pearl- and diamond-encrusted headpieces, silver anklets – that her husband and in-laws had gifted her and insisted she wear (it was tradition apparently), weighing her down to this new life she's claimed for herself in return for Ajji's well-being.

When Guru gifted her the saris, sandals, headpieces and jewellery, the week before the wedding, Bindu had said, 'Instead of all this, I'm happy with a simple mangalsutra on a string. Please can you sell the jewellery and use the money to provide the villagers with—'

Guru cut her short before she could finish the sentence. 'Bindu, the jewels are family heirlooms and you, as the only daughter-in-law, are expected to wear them and pass them on to your – *our* – daughters.'

She blushed. He smiled.

Then, his voice gentler, 'Bindu, don't make this more difficult than it already is. We've had this discussion before.'

'Not this particular one. You didn't hear what I was going to say.'

'You wanted me to sell the jewellery and distribute the money among the villagers. I seem to recall that you hated them while living in the village.'

How to explain to this man, who had never experienced stomach-gnawing hunger pangs, or thirst so dreadful you couldn't think straight? How to make him see that now, with Bindu's hunger and thirst sated for the first time in her life, she was able to see what she couldn't then, hurting and angry and upset at those two-faced women who'd watched her grow, who were her grandmother's friends and compatriots, happily taking the spice mixes Bindu made, praising her in front of Ajji, agreeing that she was lucky because of her double crown, but, out of Ajji's hearing, damning her as a vamp who bewitched their men with her looks in order to circumvent her bad luck? Bindu had railed against their double standards, condemned their hypocrisy. But now, she understood that they'd needed something – anything – to take their mind off their misery, their children crying in hunger, insensible with thirst, their hapless husbands, plagued by drought, driven to drink, abusing them. Bindu was an easy scapegoat; in gossiping about her, they could escape their woes for a brief while.

'Look,' Guru was saying. 'Instead of heeding my suggestions, my father'll do the exact opposite just to punish me. Do you want the villagers to suffer?'

'You know I don't.'

'And please remember that I've kept my side of the bargain. You've to keep yours.'

'I *am* marrying you.'

'Yes, but there are certain rituals involved in marrying me. Wearing the jewellery and the saris we gift you is one of them.' He rubbed his face, sighing deeply. 'I don't understand you, Bindu. Any other woman would've been thrilled to be presented with expensive jewellery and saris.'

'I'm not any other woman.'

He smiled at her and, in addition to the admiring twinkle, there was another emotion she couldn't identify shining soft and bright in his eyes. 'Don't I know it!'

Bindu opens doors blindly and finally blunders into the courtyard in the west wing – one of the many courtyards around which the mansion is built – which, since running away isn't an option, is her haven when worries about her marriage to Guru overwhelm her. How many courtyards in this over-the-top manor? She can't get over the sheer size of this place, its grandeur, the dozens of rooms lying unoccupied, stuffed to the gills with antiques, not a speck of dust anywhere, thanks to the diligence of the army of servants, but soulless, lacking love, laughter, chatter, noise – the flavour that transforms bricks and mortar into a home, that had made their mud hut more comfortable and welcoming than this palace could ever be.

The courtyard hosts a glinting, gurgling fountain, surrounded by fruit trees: mango and guava, neem and banana, lazily waving in the sun-sizzled breeze. No one here, thank the gods. Right now, she's grateful for this haven of calm, an oasis affording brief respite from her wedding festivities, the animosity directed at her.

She throws the veil off her face. The monsoons are in full swing and it rained this morning, but now the sun's out. The fountain tinkles merrily and the water-fed grass is bright green, the trees shimmering with monsoon droplets. Birds fly overhead, dark slurs upon the blinding dazzle.

Finally, her face arced heavenward, eyes closed, Bindu can breathe – she opens her mouth and takes great gulps of fragrant air tasting of mud and rain, fresh and sweet.

And then, her solitude, the blessed peace encored by the music of the fountain, the sultry whisper of the moisture-laden breeze sharing secrets with the languidly swaying trees, the swish of wings above, is broken by a voice the bronzed gold of church bells.

'The food was good, but not a patch on yours, royal chef notwithstanding.'

Eyes flying open, she whips round, caught out, cheeks flooding with colour.

She should be irritated by this intruder interrupting her hard-won privacy, but, for some reason, she's not.

Perhaps it's his kind face that regards her with solicitude but not a hint of lechery, even though her face – she's suddenly aware – is exposed, unveiled. She doesn't feel the urge to rush to cover it, as she would in the presence of other men, even Guru, their lascivious gazes stripping her naked, making her feel dirty. This man's doesn't. He regards her steadily, but there's only kindness there, respect. It occurs to Bindu that, even though he's a stranger, she is strangely at ease in his presence.

And on the heels of this realisation, the words he's just said, spoken so earnestly, sink in and she sways on her feet.

His eyes, the colour of dew-jewelled moss, shine with concern, 'I say, are you all right?'

She nods, unable to find her voice. It's lost somewhere within the great big lump that's ballooned in her throat. She's not all right. She hasn't been since the day she found Ajji grievously ill and her dreams for a different life, a future of her own making, evaporated.

And yet she's kept on going, trying to be strong, to hold everything together, making mad choices, striking crazy bargains that she's been second-guessing ever since.

And now, this kindness, the compliment about her food, the simple but heartfelt question from a stranger – well, not a *complete* stranger, for she recognises him as the journalist, Mr Elliot, whom she'd met when she first came here to ask Guru for help, the man whose gaze had soothed her when she was floundering in panicked shock just after she was wedded to Guru – threatens to undo her.

'Come,' he says, gently approaching her. 'I'm sorry if I startled you. I don't know if you remember me but we've met before at a party here.' He nods towards the bench in the shade of the sweeping palm trees that Bindu favours when she escapes here for a respite from her qualms. 'You must sit down. I'll fetch you a drink.' He extends a hand to lead her to the bench, but she shrinks away, aware suddenly of her new status as married woman, of her reputation, alone with a man not her husband, her face uncovered.

He blushes, and she's fascinated by the colour flooding so visibly into his face, pink cheeks turning bright crimson, his neck and chin, dotted with blond stubble, blotching in purple hives.

His hand falls away as if his thoughts have taken the same direction as hers. 'I'm sorry, I didn't mean...' he says.

'I know,' she manages, even as she drapes her veil over her face. 'I must go.'

'Yes, of course.' He clears his throat, his face turning even redder if possible, his neck more blotchy. 'But before you do, I... I was hoping to talk to you, you see. That's why when I saw you leave the ladies' darbar, I followed. I-I wanted...'

Her heart sinks and she's tempted to walk away. She'd thought him different from other men. He hasn't once leered at her or behaved in any way so as to make her uncomfortable. So why has he followed her, a newly married woman?

'I...' He clears his throat again. He's nervous – she remembers, when he spoke to her before, how he'd cleared his throat multiple times then too.

It warms her, his anxious tic. She decides to wait and hear what he has to say.

'Your food, it's so good. The best I've tasted. I edit and publish a monthly magazine and we've a recipe section where I'd like to feature your recipes please, if you're willing?'

Oh. *Oh.* This, she wasn't expecting, although, come to think of it, now she recalls him saying something similar the last time they met, when Bindu had come to the mansion to ask Guru for help.

Her heart swells even as she regards him to check if he's serious.

He *is.* His emerald gaze so very sincere. He digs in his jacket pocket, plucks out a small rectangle. 'This is my business card with my address. If you're interested, please do write to me.'

She takes it, just as the merry chime of approaching anklets announces a maid: 'Memsahib, you're wanted by Sahib.'

And with a nod in her direction, 'Pleasure meeting you. And I meant to say, hearty congratulations.' His face flooding once again with colour, Mr Elliot disappears.

CHAPTER 25

BINDU

'On our wedding day,' Guru's voice is dangerously hard, his bloodshot eyes spitting amber sparks, his jaw working furiously, 'you abandon our guests to have a secret tryst with another man.'

'I needed air. I didn't know he...' Bindu is glad that she had the presence of mind to tuck Mr Elliot's business card in the paper bag containing her treasured keepsakes, including the few possessions she brought with her from the hut, before she met with her husband. For he's raging. He has many faces, she's quickly learning, and the one he's sporting now scares her.

He'd dismissed the maid without a second glance and locked the door, shutting out the sounds of the wedding celebrations still going strong, raucous masculine laughter and rowdy, inebriated chatter mingling with the pungent tang of alcohol, the fruity aroma of punch, the zesty bite of deep-fried sweetmeats, roasted ghee, caramelised sugar and spiced meat.

Guru stands with his back to the door, barring her exit. 'You've never voluntarily been without your veil in front of me, even since our betrothal, and I've respected that. But with him... A *white* man. A few hours after our marriage! Hedging your bets, eh?'

'No! How could you...?'

'What am I supposed to think? *My* newly wedded wife, instead of entertaining her guests, conducts a clandestine assignation with a man not the husband she's promised to be dutiful to.' His voice stumbles, the harshness cracking open to reveal the pain hiding beneath, and Bindu understands suddenly that Guru is raging out of hurt. Like when he speaks of his father, the surliness in his voice concealing a yawning wound.

And with this insight, her fear drops away. 'Guru, I did not—'

But he isn't listening. 'I've kept my side of the bargain. Your grandmother is getting the best medical care. She's improving, the doctor says, and her fever's not as potent as it was – he promises it'll soon bre—'

'You spoke with him?' She thought she alone was liaising with the doctor. She didn't know Guru was even aware when the doctor visited Ajji, let alone that he cared.

'I wanted to know how she was doing.' His voice was losing heat. 'She's your only family. It'd have been good to have her attend our wedding.'

He cares. This strange, complicated man she's wedded to, who's raging at her one minute and twinkling the next, has, like when he proposed, once again taken her by surprise.

'And along with keeping my side of the bargain, I've gone one further, negotiating with my father on your behalf, although, of course, I didn't tell him that.' Guru is yelling, but now Bindu is no longer scared of his spitting fury. 'It was a torturous enough discussion without informing him that you were behind my sudden interest in gilding his image, improving his profile. The villagers' rent for this month is pardoned. The textile workers' hours will not be extended. Instead, we're hiring more staff, so they'll be working shifts. Their salary remains the same, but in effect they're paid more for working fewer hours. The articles have already been actioned and will be appearing in newspapers tomorrow.'

Happiness floods her as what he's saying sinks in. This man, her *husband*, is different from his father – he has a heart. He *cares*.

She takes two steps forward, closing the gap between them, and brings a finger to his lips, stopping him mid-rant. 'Guru,' she whispers.

She's never been this close to any man before, but, strangely, she is no longer afraid.

He stares at her, finally quiet, her finger on his lips. His eyes are red and bloodshot. He smells of alcohol and sweat and woodspice.

'I was overwhelmed and needed air. I don't know the man and didn't plan to meet him. He was just there.'

Guru nods, his gaze softening as the anger leaves his eyes.

'Do you remember what I said when you wanted to kiss me?' His unexpected kindness gives her confidence, making her bold, even as fresh nerves flutter in her stomach.

His eyes darken as his lips tug upwards.

'I said I'd only allow the man whom I married to do so. And I'm married to you now.'

His eyes crinkle and his skin creases in a smile that lights up his face as his arms fold her into a hug. 'Promise me,' he whispers, 'no spice paste anywhere in sight?'

'I don't make promises I may not—'

She feels his laughter start in his belly and reverberate up his throat, her words evaporating as his lips claim hers.

Afterwards, he sleeps.

Bindu looks at him, this man who's a mass of contradictions. Slumber has evened the contours of his face; he looks like a little boy, gentle innocence.

He was tender with her just now. She hadn't known what to expect – Ajji wasn't well enough to assuage her fears and worries about what her wifely duty entailed, and there was nobody else she could ask. But when, after Guru had kissed her, he'd laid her down on the bed – strewn with rose petals, she belatedly noticed – and she'd started shaking, he'd held her until she stopped, whispering reassurances. He was gentle with her, warning her that it might hurt. And it had, but, because of his tender care, the intimacy she'd dreaded wasn't as bad as she'd feared.

He has treated her with respect, married her against his father's wishes, instead of keeping her as mistress. But he's short with her, and she fears he'll be even more so now they're married. He's unpredictable, quick to rage, jealous; he did not apologise for shouting at her when he presumed she was flirting with another man, and yet he forgave her easily when she explained. He longs for his father's respect and approval and yet he's willing to negotiate with him, incur his wrath, for her sake.

She thinks she understands why he's the way he is. Growing up in these luxurious surroundings, never being denied anything except the love and attention he craves from his father, everyone else obsequious, pandering to his whims, has made him selfish, thoughtless at times, expecting all to fall in with his wishes. No wonder he's angry when she challenges him, when she will not kowtow to him.

She thought he was like his father, and in some ways he is; but in the ways that matter, perhaps he isn't.

In his own way, he does care, she thinks, although he hides it very well. He can be kind.

Beside her, he emits a little whimper.

She surprises herself by reaching out, stroking his brow until the frown disappears and he's sleeping evenly again.

Eve holds Maya when she sobs and, afterwards, she wipes her face gently and asks, 'Would you like to stay here or at mine, love?'

Maya looks at Eve trustingly, 'I don't want to stay here without Mum.'

'All right, love, want me to help you pack what you need?'

'I can do it myself, thanks, Eve.'

Izzy was independent too, Eve muses, wanting to do everything herself, feeling frustrated when she couldn't manage it and had to ask for help. Like the time she had a day trip to the museum with her class and her bag, which she'd stuffed to the gills, just wouldn't zip up and she'd come to Eve in tears: 'It won't do as I ask.'

Eve had hidden her smile behind a purposeful frown as she'd helped Izzy rearrange the pencil case and the soft toy – Izzy's favourite rainbow-striped pony – and the storybook and the cardigan, refraining from saying, 'Do you really need all this?' until they were able to zip up the bag.

Izzy had beamed then, throwing her arms round Eve: 'You're the best mama in the world.'

It warms her heart, this memory of her child, lost until now in the recesses of her mind, suddenly vivid thanks to Maya.

. . .

When they get to hers, Maya sets her bag down and looks to Eve for direction.

'You must be tired, love, and hungry with it. Let me make you something to eat and then you can wash and go to bed. How's that?'

Maya nods, huge eyes ringed with circles of exhaustion and worry.

It prompts Eve to say, 'And, tomorrow, we'll call the hospital and find out what's happening with your mum and...' She takes a deep breath, but the child is looking at her so eagerly, so trustingly, the worry replaced by hope, that she has to add, 'We'll ask when we can visit, eh?'

Except for today, just to Maya and Jenny's next door, Eve hasn't stepped out of this house since the accident. For every time she tries, she sees her beloved family in her mind's eye, blood shadows on the road, a shrine of wilting flowers and soggy teddy bears bearing witness. It happened two minutes away from home, on the main road – which is usually clogged with traffic, but was traffic-free just when her husband and daughter were driving home, which was why that drunk driver was able to break the speed limit. If the road had been choked with cars, like always, it wouldn't have happened. If Eve had gone to the Asian shop with her daughter, or if they'd dissuaded Izzy from wanting to cook that particular recipe... If, if, if...

But now, she'll have to leave her house – she *must*. For this girl who nods, flashing Eve a wan smile. Then, softly, 'Can I have a sandwich with chocolate spread like I did the last time I stayed over?'

And Eve's heart breaks all over again.

It was the girls' first and, as it turned out, only sleepover, two months before the accident. They were so excited. For dinner, as a special treat, Eve had made them sandwiches with chocolate spread.

'Thank you, Mama,' Izzy had said, throwing her arms round

Eve. And turning to Maya, eyes sparkling, 'I'm *never* allowed chocolate at bedtime, this is *such* a treat.'

'It is a treat, so no asking for it until the next sleepover, you understand,' Eve had said, mock sternly, waving the knife with which she was slathering on chocolate spread at her daughter.

'I promise,' Izzy had giggled.

'You can have it when you come to mine for my birthday sleepover,' Maya had said.

But there wasn't another sleepover. Izzy never turned ten. When Maya did, Izzy was gone.

Now Eve summons up a facsimile of a smile. 'Let's see if I've any chocolate spread, sweetheart.'

She finds the jar at the back of the cupboard, gathering dust. It's about to go out of date, but when she opens the lid and sniffs, it smells all right. The gooey nuttiness takes her back to the sleepover, her daughter's happy grin.

'Aha,' she says, managing to inject some enthusiasm into her voice, even though her throat is salty with tears, her mind ambushed with images of Izzy so very thrilled at the decadence of chocolate spread sandwiches for dinner.

If I'd known, my love, I'd have made you these sandwiches every night. I agonised about your sugar intake, making sure you ate healthily, when there were far bigger things to worry about – like a speeding drunk driver travelling on the wrong side of the road and putting the brakes on your life...

'Can I help you make it?' Maya asks.

And once again Eve is waylaid by memories of Izzy, who'd stand beside her, or sit on the counter and help her cook.

'Let's use Nana's recipe,' she'd say, reverently turning the turmeric- and spice-stained pages of the treasured keepsake.

Eve's not been able to look at the cookbook since. It too is gathering dust at the back of the cupboard.

Together, she and Maya prepare sandwiches.

'One for you and one for me,' Maya says.

Eve smiles.

Making sandwiches with Maya is agony, heartbreak and comfort too. A strange, bittersweet mix.

Like the chocolate sandwich, which tastes of salt-stained loss and heartache, for she wishes Izzy was here to eat it. But it's an improvement on tasting nothing at all, the grey monotone that has monopolised her life.

Maya wolfs hers down, and when she's finished, a great big yawn escapes her.

'Right, young lady,' Eve says, once again assailed by how many times she's uttered this same phrase in another life to another child, 'bedtime.'

'But...' Like all children everywhere – like Izzy used to – Maya sets up a token protest, even though her eyelids are heavy and she looks about to fall asleep right there at the table.

'Have a wash first.'

'Ah.' Maya looks mortified.

'What's the matter?' Eve is worried.

'I forgot to pack my toothbrush.'

'Is that all?' Eve smiles, relieved. 'I'm sure we have a spare.'

The 'we' is automatic, even as she is reminded, with another flash of pain, that there's no *we* anymore.

'Thank you.' Maya beams, trustingly tucking her palm in Eve's and turning towards the stairs.

CHAPTER 27

BINDU

1937

'Bindu... Wake up.'

A male voice in her ear. A large, hairy hand on her arm, shaking her awake.

She sits up, startled. Where is she? Why's a man...?

And then, as Guru's features register, as does the sweetly musky scent of crushed rose petals, her sleep-addled brain recalls what happened and she can't help the blush setting her cheeks aflame.

Guru guffaws, winking at her.

Biting her lower lip, unable to meet her husband's gaze, which makes him laugh even louder, she concentrates on the faint sound of drunken masculine laughter wafting into the room, the clink of glasses, the aroma of spices and sugar, the footfall of servants rushing past... Her wedding night, the festivities still going strong.

Guru is saying, 'I must admit you look even better with your wedding finery all rumpled. I wish we could stay, but we've dallied enough.' He dusts down his kurta, holds out a hand to her. 'Ready?' he asks.

'For what?' She's puzzled.

'We've to mingle with our guests. We've been remiss in our duties, neglecting them while we...' He twinkles at her, indicating the messy bed.

She notices, mortified, that she's bled on the sheets, each of which must have cost more than what she and Ajji earned cooking in a year. Her cheeks are on fire again as she tries – uselessly – to hide the evidence from the servants, although she knows nothing is secret from them.

'Leave it. Not your job,' Guru says summarily. 'We've to go.'

'But...' In the aftermath of their intimacy, she's shy, unsure how to behave with her husband. The thought of once more enduring that roomful of women with their poisonous smiles, each nectary word laced with venom, turns her stomach. She wants nothing more than to wash and change into a less heavy, more comfortable sari and sit beside Ajji in peaceful silence. 'Do I have to...?'

'Yes,' Guru says shortly.

'I'd like to check on my Ajji.'

'She's being looked after, as per my part of our bargain. And now – I don't have to remind you, but I will – you've to honour yours.'

'But I thought...'

'As wife of the landlord's son and heir, you've to fulfil certain obligations, Bindu. If you don't honour your word, my father will have no qualms about kicking you and your Ajji out, daughter-in-law or not.'

She is blindsided by her husband's quicksilver moods, his gentleness when in bed with her no longer in evidence. 'That sounds like a threat.'

'You can't have everything your way. I've been very good to you. Made an honest woman of you. Seen to your Ajji. All I'm asking is that you do your part.' Now he smiles and holds out his hand again.

She doesn't want to take it.

'Hurry up.' He is brusque, smile gone. 'They're waiting.'

Returning to the women's darbar on her wedding night is as tortuous as she expected – knowing glances taking in the disarray of her clothes, toxic barbs and barely veiled insinuations of where she'd disappeared to, what she got up to, how she's trapped the most eligible bachelor in town.

Shaken by Guru's harsh reminder of what's expected of her, Bindu endures the endless night that veers long into the morning, the smile pasted upon her face threatening to droop, keeping her feet firmly on the lushly carpeted floor so they don't give in to the overwhelming urge to run from this life she finds herself living.

If she thought she'd have time to sit with Ajji, regroup, she's wrong. For there's no let-up. Each day following her wedding is packed with social engagements with the privileged elite – men and women segregated, of course. Bindu is shepherded to the women's section by maidservants as soon as she and Guru enter the mansions – each rivalling the other in flamboyant ostentation – where the parties are being held, as if she's contraband to be smuggled clandestinely away. If she's ever – briefly – in the presence of men, she's expected to be invisible, neither seen nor heard, blend into the background, although she cannot escape their leering gazes lingering a bit too long upon her body.

In the women's darbar, the ladies assess her with hard eyes and fake smiles. They're civil to her face but gossip behind her back, loud enough so she can hear every word. She's tempted to shut them up with a few choice words, these hypocrites, but the thought of Ajji stops her.

For there's a side to her husband, she's discovering, that's ruthless. And she's in no doubt that that side of him won't have second thoughts about carrying through his threat of sending her and Ajji away if she doesn't do what's expected of her.

She had power over Guru when he desired her but thought her unattainable. He was willing to do anything for her, then. Now, she is his and he wields all the power, and she hates how helpless this renders her. She yearned for freedom, independence, not being reliant on anyone. Instead, she's discovering that she is voiceless, at Guru and his father's mercy, and she absolutely loathes it.

. . .

Guru visits each night but Bindu cannot enjoy or take pleasure from their time together, for he makes no secrets about it being for the purpose of creating an heir – another example of her husband and his father's power over her. After Guru has been with her, he relays the timetable for the next day – more socialising, her days packed with activities she hates. She's not sleeping – her mind is whirling with frustration and upset at her bind. Moreover, she's not used to a man beside her in place of Ajji, whom she misses sorely. Guru's a noisy and restless sleeper, and when Bindu does manage to nod off, he changes position, jostles her, or stretches an arm, which catches her face and she startles awake, hands itching to push him away, legs itching to run away, head aching as it advises counsel, eyes stinging as she sees in the morning, which brings more engagements with women she doesn't like, who talk about servants as if they're vermin, and expect her to join in, even – *especially* – knowing that Bindu was one of them not so long ago.

They show off their wealth, thinking nothing of spending hundreds of thousands of rupees on house (mansion) extensions and renovations, and amassing jewellery and saris they don't need, and yet begrudge their servants their meals – leftovers that would otherwise go to waste. They revel in putting down those they think lesser than them, voices bilious bright with relish: 'She acts as though she's one of us, but word is her husband's lost all their money – they'll have to sell her jewellery and their house too without a doubt. I bet she'll convince him to move away rather than lose face.'

They look at Bindu when they say this, implying: *You too aren't one of us and don't dare assume you ever will be.*

It is all she can do not to snap, *I'd rather die than be one of you.*

The urge to run away threatens to get the better of her, her legs shaking with the desire to take off, the women looking askance at her, raised eyebrows, and so, to distract her mind, she busies herself with thinking of what recipes would suit each of these socialites best.

For the woman with the face like a dried mango seed, a

steaming curry with liberal amounts of chilli powder that will render her fiery red instead of wan and shrivelled.

For the woman who flashes ire at Bindu, cold congee spiced with plenty of cumin and fennel seeds; the laxative properties will relax her, ease that tight, wound-up look.

And so on...

When she tires of this game, she imagines the stories she'll tell her grandmother when Ajji is better, packed with detail – the flamboyant jewellery, the bedazzling saris, the constant one-upmanship, these women who've everything and yet none of whom appear happy. They find fault with the food – too hot, not hot enough, too spicy, not spicy enough, too sweet, not sweet enough; the servants – never good enough; the furniture – not comfortable enough; the ambience – not soothing enough, too soothing, not lively enough, too lively. They sigh and appear genuinely sad when they talk of their children. Their daughters fated for a life like theirs – for all their wealth, invisible, voiceless. Their sons packed away to boarding school when barely old enough to walk, and, when they return, only grudgingly visiting their mothers, treating them with the same contempt and disrespect their fathers adopt.

This is their life, and now it's also Bindu's. When she realises this, she feels consumed by a despair more potent than any she experienced while living in the village, no matter how difficult life was then. She longs to run, but she can't even leave the mansion without Guru's say-so. She tries talking to the servants, but they scuttle away, servile but monosyllabic, covering their faces to hide their disdain for this woman who's no longer one of them but tries to behave as if she is.

And were she to run, where would she go? What would she do? She's given up her scholarship, and her virginity. If she reneges on the deal she struck with Guru, she incurs the landlord's wrath. And he has a very long reach – he owns the village and surroundings, he knows the men who run the country. She'll not get a job, no matter how far she goes. How will she keep Ajji and herself?

She is trapped.

Oh, but she wants to run.
She wants to run.

CHAPTER 28

BINDU

'Bindu.' Guru's face is grim when he visits her a week after their wedding.

They've just returned from yet another gathering hosted in their honour by the landlord of Doddangadi. Spent from the sheer frustration of keeping her mouth firmly zipped as she was assessed and found wanting, smiling when she didn't feel like it, feet fixed to the luxurious carpet to stop herself fleeing, all Bindu wants to do is change and sit by Ajji's bedside. She hasn't been able to spend time with her grandmother since her wedding – even her chats to the doctor regarding Ajji's progress have been rushed and some days she hasn't been able to see him either.

And it appears that today, too, she'll have to give seeing her grandmother a miss, for here is her husband, earlier than usual for his nightly visit – another obligation she must fulfil as his wife.

'My father's not happy – it appears you've insulted the Maharani of Chandrapur.'

'Have I? How?' She casts about in her mind for what she might've done to cause umbrage, but she cannot recall which one among the melee of parties she's attended since her wedding was hosted by the Maharani of Chandrapur, or even which of the women she was; they all amass in her mind as a seething throng of sharp-tongued shrews. All she knows is that she's tried very hard to keep her mouth shut against the retorts sparking hot and fiery at the tip of her tongue, to smile and nod at appropriate times, to appear interested instead of bored out of her mind. She's not escaped into their gardens for a breather, hasn't even loitered in the – segregated – bathrooms long enough to be missed. And yet, it appears all her efforts have been in vain; she's *still* caused offence.

'She took the trouble to host a celebration in your honour – and she's famously choosy about whom she bestows favour upon; you were one of the lucky ones...'

Bindu stops herself from rolling her eyes, biting her lip to keep her sharp rejoinder to herself. *I was only invited because I'm your wife and your wealth rivals her husband's, even though he's a king.*

'And you insult her by attending in a sari you'd already worn to my sister's tea party.'

'*This* is why she's upset?' Bindu can't help laughing.

Guru, tight-lipped: 'It's no laughing matter.'

'Villagers are dying because they don't have enough water. And here, people get upset if I wear the same sari twice? I'd rather sell all my saris and give the money to—'

'You're not in the village any longer. You live here. You're my wife and you've my reputation to uphold. You cannot go about insulting maharanis, do you understand?' Guru bites out, teeth grinding.

No, I don't and I never will, she thinks defiantly, her laughter disappearing, fiery ire choking her throat.

'God knows my parents and I've gifted you enough saris and jewellery so you can wear a different set every day for a month and still have some left to spare. If you weren't aware of the protocol, you could have asked me, or one of the maids.'

'I—'

'And that's not all; the maharani also complained – and other hostesses, even my sisters, corroborated this – that you sit there with a face like thunder...'

'They're lying.' Her eyes sting with the unfairness of it.

'All of them?' Guru's jaw is working furiously.

'Yes. I smile all the time.'

'More like a grimace, they say. And, what's more, you yawn and fidget. When you're asked a question, you either ignore it or ask them to repeat it – it's clear you haven't been listening. You give the impression that you don't want to be there.'

'Too right, I don't.' She softens her voice, even though she's so angry she could scream, trying to appeal to the boy who used to roam the village with her. 'It's been a tiring few days and, Guru, to be honest, these gatherings are boring. Can I not—'

'No,' he snaps. There's no twinkle, no give in his hard gaze. 'It's what the wife of the landlord's son is expected to do. I married you against my father's wishes, the least you can do is make an effort.'

'I *am* doing so, but this isn't what I enjoy and I can't help it if it shows on my face,' she yells, completely losing her temper.

'Try harder. You can't always do what you enjoy. I don't enjoy pandering to my father, but I do it.'

'Guru, you married me because I'm different to—'

'Enough. You will be polite at the gatherings from now on. Now, enough talking.' He draws her into his arms.

She pulls away. How can this man dole out heavy-handed edicts one moment and expect her to submit to his kisses the next?

'I haven't visited my Ajji at all today,' she tries.

'The doctor's been to see her, like every day since she's been here. There are maids looking after her. Your duty is to your husband.' His tone brooks no argument.

'I'm—'

He kisses her, silencing the words she'd been about to say in a fit of unthinking fury – *I'm sick and tired of doing my duty*. As if he's heard them anyway. 'It's what you signed up for.'

He lays her down on the bed. Not roughly, but not gently either.

And as he settles on top of her, she shuts her eyes, but the tears come regardless. This life is so very different from the one she wanted – independent, doing her own thing, having financial freedom, not beholden to anyone. Instead, she's pandering to women she hates, wasting time listening to them compare wealth and complain about servants. And every night, disagreement or not, whether she feels up to it or not, she has to do her duty by her husband, to provide him with an heir.

Again, it's as if her husband reads her mind. 'Ah, Bindu, it's not so bad, is it? Your Ajji is recovering. You've all the luxury in the world. All you've to do is not appear bored at parties and dress up in a different sari each time – I'll gift you some more. Is that too much to ask?'

He gently kisses her tears away.

CHAPTER 29

BINDU

'Bindu, the women are complaining that you talk about politics and won't shut up.' Guru sighs, sounding fed up with this, the latest in the list of Bindu's supposed offences.

'*They* gossip about other women, sometimes right in front of them, or talk about clothes and jewellery, moan about servants and their failings, and won't shut up,' Bindu retorts.

She's decided that since she must endure these gatherings – and apparently smile more, fidget less and appear interested, for otherwise the socialites, her own sisters-in-law among them, will run bearing tales to her husband and father-in-law – she might as well talk about what *she* likes. And seeing their baffled faces as she witters on about what she read in the newspapers that morning, her smile comes naturally – she doesn't have to force it.

'But *politics?*' Is that a glint of amusement brightening Guru's impassive facade?

It's been a while since she's seen it and this prompts her to come clean. 'Guru, these women... they don't like me and don't hide it. I can't steal from them like I did from the women of the village...'

'Don't you dare!'

'So my revenge is to talk politics at them.'

He laughs, gathering her to him. 'You're one of a kind.'

'I know.' She beams, her heart lighter than it's been in a while at this brief connection with her husband, harking back to the boy she'd known.

But, a few days later...

'Guru, where are the newspapers? I didn't receive any today. I want to know the outcome of the anti-Hindi agitation...'

'Um...' Guru is uncharacteristically hesitant. 'My father's decreed that you're not to read newspapers. You're getting above yourself – his words. It seems that when you briefly crossed paths with the British Resident while saying goodbye after the party yesterday, you dared discuss the Indian independence movement with him.'

'He was impressed by it.'

'My father wasn't. It seems you undermined the point he was making.'

I got one up on him and he didn't like it. 'So, I'm not to read, then?'

'No.'

Despair, sickening yellow. 'So, what am I to do?'

'Well, there's a party tomorrow and one the day after and...' He's being facetious, while for her the newspapers are her lifeline – her only link to the wider world outside the claustrophobic confines of her life. She lives in a mansion with too many rooms to count and visits others the same, but the irony is that despite all this space she has no freedom – she feels hemmed in, closeted, imprisoned.

'And I'm to sit with the women while they gossip about me or ignore me altogether.'

Guru shrugs. He neither understands her desperation, nor cares, it appears.

'I... This is madness.' She's so angry she could cry. 'Guru, *please*, I need to read. It's my only outlet. Would you negotiate with your father on my behalf? Please?'

'Believe me, I tried. But it only made him more stubbornly determined.' His voice carries melancholy echoes of the boy who could never please his father.

'And yet you do as he wants. Why? There was a time when you wouldn't.'

'Rebelling against him didn't work. And since he's agreed to me marrying you, I feel duty-bound—'

'Ah, so it's my fault that you do everything he says.' She sniffs. 'And I suppose you're here now because he wants an heir.' She doesn't wait for his reply. 'I got the highest marks ever recorded in the matriculation exams and now I'm denied reading material. I dreamed of studying further, becoming a doctor, but instead my job is to socialise with women I've nothing in common with and to provide your father with an heir.'

'Not so bad, is it?' Guru says.

How can he not *get* it?

'I suppose the heir must be a boy.'

'That'll help.'

'And you'll do as your father wants.'

He sighs, and again there is that melancholy keen to his voice. 'It's easier than the alternative. I've tried going against him, it only makes life more difficult.' He gathers her in his arms, smiles at her. 'And, in any case, I enjoy this...' She cannot return his smile. How can he expect her to be intimate with him when he's denied her the one thing that made life here just about bearable?

'Come, Bindu, no need to be so gloomy. This life that you're complaining about was your choice.'

'It was my choice.' Her voice heavy, weary with the recognition that she only has herself to blame, but knowing she can't regret it, for what choice did she have, really, with Ajji's life at stake?

He bends down to kiss her.

'I don't feel like it today.'

'It's your duty as my wife. Your Ajji is getting—'

'I've had *enough*.' Her voice shrill. If she hears the word 'duty' again, she'll scream.

'That's enough, Bindu.' Voice sharp, smile replaced by a tight frown. 'No tantrums, please. You're not a child.'

How can he not understand? Where's the boy who listened to her? 'Guru, you'd escape to the village and join me because you said you felt trapped here. Can't you see I feel the same? Newspapers are my only reading material. I *need* them. Please...'

'Bindu, there's no need for hysteria. If you'd not wanted the newspapers banned, you should've been more careful and not talked to the Resident about politics – or anything at all – especially with my father present, bearing in mind he doesn't hold with the women of the family conversing with other men.'

'But the point your father was making was wrong. I couldn't help interjecting—'

'That's *your* mistake. I can't help, I'm afraid. You've turned him against you when you weren't in his favour to begin with. Now, if there's one thing that *will* placate him, it's a grandson and heir, so...' Guru smiles suggestively at her.

She turns away, for, at that moment, she hates him, more so because she knows he's right. She should've been docile and submissive and invisible in the Resident's presence, instead of antagonising the landlord.

'Ah, come now, Bindu, let me kiss your upset away.'

As if she's a child who can be placated with a kiss. *If you want me to stop acting like a child, then stop treating me like one.*

But now, too late, she keeps her mouth shut, even though she wants to scream, cry, run away. She submits to him, while in her head she escapes, picturing Wordsworth's daffodils. She imagines she is independent, that she's booked a passage to England with her own money – it's far enough away to be out of the landlord's reach – where her heart is at one with daffodils.

The next day, Bindu requests an audience with the landlord. It is denied.

It's only after days of persistent requests – he rejects, she tries again. And again. And again – that finally he allows her 'five minutes'. Like his son had that fateful day when Bindu came here uninvited and her life changed direction.

To a stranger, he'd appear harmless. Bald, small, withered-looking. Only his eyes, flashing hard and venomous, bitter black as he assesses Bindu, give an intimation of the evil lurking within his shrivelled body.

He's sitting on an upholstered chair as ostentatious as a throne. And although there are several chairs and divans dotted about the palatial suite, he doesn't ask Bindu to sit. Nor does he say a word, instead shaking his head and chuckling silently to himself – his eyes stone cold and flint sharp – as if to say: '*You* are the one my son gave up princesses and noblewomen for?'

Bindu pushes her shoulders back, her head veiled as he expects, but her eyes looking right at him. She will not be cowed by his animosity. 'I've been requesting an audience with you for days. You put out that you were busy.'

'I'm always too busy for the likes of you.'

'The likes of me? I'm your daughter-in-law.'

'By sufferance, not choice.'

'I'll be the mother of your grandchild and heir.'

'If you provide one.'

'And if I don't?'

'You're out.' He smirks.

'Does Guru know?'

'That's none of your business.'

'He's *my* husband so it *is* my business.'

'He's my son first and foremost. And he'll cease to be your husband if you don't provide me with a grandson within the next couple of years.'

She stands steady, holding his vile gaze, refusing to back down, look away, even as he grins at her. He's enjoying this. She will not allow the tremor rocking her entire being to show. Instead, summoning up all of her strength from within her, she laughs. It sounds weak to her ears, shaky. But it has the desired effect, for *he* stops smiling, glowering at her instead.

'What's funny?'

'You think you can control everything, even children and grandchildren, don't you?'

'I can and I will. Read my lips, wench. If you haven't provided me with a grandson two years to this day, you're out.'

She believes him. Too late, she realises that she shouldn't have come here. She's made things worse. And yet, still, she can't help saying, 'And if you have a granddaughter?'

He clicks his teeth. 'Are you thick? I'll say it again. If you don't provide me with a grandson...'

She tunes out his words, wanting away from this room, although she hasn't asked him what she came to ask. After this, it's pointless. But then, it was always pointless. He'd take great pleasure in refusing her – she'd known this really, but she was desperate and the more he declined to see her, the more she'd persisted.

She wants Ajji. When she talked to Ajji, all her problems seemed surmountable. Ajji would have advised against making mistake after mistake and compounding it by coming here. Ajji would have gently shown her the error of her ways, said, 'Your heart's in the right place. You're impulsive and that's mostly a good thing. But not in this case, my heart. Not in this case.'

Ajji, Bindu's only ally, while she is getting better, her fever falling more every day, is still too weak to make sense of her surroundings. And, in any case, Bindu hasn't had time since her marriage to spend more than a few minutes by her bedside. If she had, she'd feel better, less despairing. For talking out loud to her Ajji, sharing her problems with her, even if Ajji cannot respond, would have helped, would have been an unburdening, a relinquishing of her woes.

'Your time is nearly up,' the landlord – she cannot think of him as her father-in-law – snaps, jolting her out of her musings.

'Why did you eventually agree to see me?' she asks.

'Curiosity. You're nothing if not persistent. What do you want?'

She takes a deep breath and launches into the reason she sought an audience with him. It won't work, but she might as well ask now she's here. 'Reading material. I'd like access to newspapers again.'

'Ha, you'd like that would you?' He chuckles, mean and mirthless. 'No.'

'Why not?'

'Women are to do their duty and provide heirs. Not mouth politics.'

'Why not?' she repeats.

'You crossed me in front of the Resident. You will not do so again.'

'The Resident was impressed. I made a good point but you—'

'Get out of my sight! You talk too much. Can't see what my son sees in you. I'd much rather he'd kept you as his mistress. But no, he wanted you as his wife and I suspect that's your doing. You're supposedly a renowned beauty, but close up, you're not that great.'

'You're not either.'

His eyes flash noxious black. 'I can kick you out right this minute. I don't give two figs for you or your grandmother, ill or not. I could turn you onto the streets, put out word so no one in the entire country rents to you or offers you work or comes anywhere near you, soiled goods, disgraced ex-wife of the land-lord's son. The only reason you're still here is at my son's behest.'

'You do care for your son then.'

'That's none of your business,' he snaps. 'No newspapers. Do your duty. Give me an heir. If you don't manage it within two years, you're out.'

The words are out before she's thought them through – 'And what if *you're* out before then?'

'Are you threatening me?' He turns to one of the posse of servants hovering subserviently beside him. 'Get my son here at once.'

Guru does a double take when he sees her. 'What're you doing here, Bindu?'

'What use are you, son? You cannot even keep the woman you wanted for your wife in check. She threatened me. She's rumoured to bring bad luck and now she's cursed me.'

Bindu waits for Guru to say something, defend her, but he appears shocked into muteness, his apprehensive gaze flitting between his father and her.

And so Bindu says to the landlord, 'I didn't think you, renowned businessman, held with superstition.'

'I do now, seeing as my only son's been bowled over by the black magic wielded by you.' And, to Guru, who appears to shrink visibly in his father's presence, meek and hesitant, hanging onto his every word like the servants standing to attention by the landlord's side: 'You're just going to stand there gawping, are you, and let your wife speak to your father in this way?' Then, clutching his chest and turning to one of the servants, 'Get the doctor to me. Her insolence has caused my heart to palpitate.'

And now, Guru speaks: 'Bindu, how could you?'

'You believe him? Guru, you know he's more than capable of giving as good as he gets.'

'Bindu, his heart... What did you say to him?'

'Guru, I'm your wife. I'm telling you that he—'

'Leave,' the landlord barks, 'both of you. Take your marital tussles elsewhere. But don't let it interfere with your duty. I need an heir for the business. And you,' pointing at Bindu, 'remember what I said.'

She marches out of the room, not looking at him or gracing his taunt with a reply, not checking to see if her weakling of a husband follows.

In the event, Guru doesn't – 'I'll stay here until the doctor comes, see what he has to say.'

The landlord's triumphant laughter echoes in Bindu's ears all that day and into the night, when Guru visits and, tight-lipped, tells her off for upsetting his father – 'The doctor's prescribed a week's bed rest. You're not to visit him again, Bindu, am I quite clear?' – cutting her off each time she tries to speak – 'You've done enough!' – and refusing to take her reluctance into account when he expects her, despite everything, to 'do her duty' and provide his tyrant of a father with a grand*son*.

CHAPTER 30

BINDU

A week later, Guru storms into Bindu's chambers, slack-jawed with upset. 'My father's just had a stroke.'

'What?' She's taken aback. 'Is he all right?'

'Do you care?'

'Of cou—'

Guru's gaze lances her, accusation and pain mingling in his eyes. 'He's blaming you.'

'He can speak, then?'

'Barely. He's paralysed on his left side.'

'I'm sor—'

'You're not.'

Although Guru has visited her every night since her altercation with the landlord, he's barely spoken to her, cutting her off whenever she's tried to talk to him. She's never felt more keenly trapped and alone than this past week, especially when her husband's been with her, making it very clear that he is, foremost and above all else, his father's son. She knows the answer, but she can't help asking, 'You too think I'm to blame, don't you?' He doesn't reply, just runs a hand down his face.

'Guru?'

When he looks at her, he's the boy she remembers, trying to

hide his hurt behind bravado. 'What if I caused this by insisting I marry you?'

'Guru, you don't believe—'

'What am I to think, Bindu?' He explodes, his pain and worry igniting into anger. 'You curse him and, a week on, he suffers a stroke.'

'I didn't cur—'

'Perhaps there *is* something in what they say – that you bring bad luck.'

'Guru, how could you? You're my husband.' He's let her down time and again since they married and yet it still hurts each time he does.

'Perhaps that's where I went wrong.' Guru sinks onto the bed, dropping his head into the cradle of his hands. 'My mother falls ill as soon as my marriage to you is fixed—'

'She's all right now.'

'And now my father...'

'Guru, your father insulted me and you did nothing. And now, he has a stroke and you blame me. You're an educated man. How can you believe in superstition, especially when it comes to your wife?'

Afterwards, he sleeps and she lies there, staring at the ceiling until it blurs.

She'd wanted to be independent, but she's realising that she's the worst kind of dependent – voiceless, invisible, not allowed to express herself through her cooking, not even allowed any reading material any longer. She feels her brain stagnating with each passing day, trapped in this life, where her own husband believes she's the harbinger of bad luck, a witch who casts evil spells on those who cross her.

Before marriage, before he'd any hope of owning her, Guru had pandered to her. For she'd been unattainable and untouched, and that had its own allure. He'd tried, then, listened to her. She mightn't have had enough to eat or drink, but she'd had a voice.

Now, Guru doesn't have to listen to her any more, for she is his, a mere possession, part of the furniture, a beautiful collectible, on display like the antiques from all over the world gracing the many rooms of this mansion, her opinions shushed, ignored, unworthy. Her reading material taken away in case she might appear brighter than the men – her husband, his father. Like she had before when she felt pressured, she yearns to run, far away from her life. But... Ajji.

Ajji.

Bindu cannot sleep. She feels lost.

She goes to her wardrobe and digs about at the back, where, in a tucked-away nook, she's secreted the few meagre possessions she brought with her from the hut. Perhaps going through these mementoes from her life before will help her regain some sense of self?

Her fingers brush against the set of notebooks and pencils – the most precious of all the gifts from her husband when she first moved here, more valued than the jewellery and saris, these rooms and the maids at her disposal. She takes out the first notebook from the stack, runs her hand over it, marvelling afresh at its pristine newness, the scent of possibility emanating from the crisply blank pages, waiting to be filled. The irony's not lost on her – both she, who'd vowed to create her own destiny, not rely on any man, and the notebook, property of her husband.

When she opens it, a small rectangular card falls out.

MR LAURENCE ELLIOT. JOURNALIST AND EDITOR.

She'd tucked it in here for safe keeping when Guru had summoned her on their wedding evening right after her meeting with Mr Elliot.

Mr Laurence Elliot, the shy man with his anxious clearing of throat, who'd said, 'Several readers of my magazine's flagship issue have asked for a recipe section to be incorporated and I wondered if you'd perhaps share some of your recipes?'

Now, there's an idea.

CHAPTER 31

EVE

1980

In the bathroom, Eve finds the toothbrush she'd bought and hidden from Izzy – one of her presents for when her daughter turned ten. Izzy had coveted that toothbrush from the moment she'd set eyes on it in the supermarket, for it was more adult-looking – no princesses or teddy bears in sight – and, more importantly, it matched her parents' toothbrushes.

'We'll get it for when you reach double figures,' Eve had promised.

'But I've all my adult teeth already,' Izzy had protested.

'That's an exaggeration and you know it, cheeky. You've grown most of your adult teeth, not all. And you can wait until you're ten, just a few more months, can't you?'

Turns out she couldn't.

Now Eve hands it to Maya, still in its packaging, and helps her to open it, picturing Izzy's joy had she been able to make it to her tenth birthday. She'd have insisted on brushing her teeth right then – 'I've just had my birthday cake and my teeth're dirty.' Eve could imagine her daughter saying it, flashing an overexcited chocolate-stained smile.

'Wow, this is a really nice toothbrush, much better than the one I have at home. Thank you, Eve,' Maya says, eyes sparkling, a little of the girl she usually is emerging now she's eaten, her wanness having receded slightly.

Just like since she opened the door to this child a few hours ago, Eve is simultaneously touched and undone by loss and missing.

Maya brushes her teeth, and once she's done, she opens her mouth wide at Eve. 'All clean.'

'That's good.' Eve nods. Izzy also used to do just this – there's such comforting familiarity to this routine, guiding Izzy, night after night, through her bedtime, and it's as if she never stopped…

'And now to bed.'

And here, Eve is suddenly rooted, her feet refusing, unable to move. Why has she not thought about this?

For Maya makes straight for Izzy's room, turns to Eve, her hand on the doorknob, a question in her eyes. This is where she'd slept, on the bottom bunk, the last time she came round – Eve and Joe had bought Izzy a bunk bed with sleepovers in mind, and Izzy revelled in climbing the three steps up to the top, grinning at them, her waterfall of hair cascading down: 'Like Rapunzel, Mama.'

'Go on,' Eve manages, brine ambushing her mouth, a great big flood in her throat.

Eve had spent several nights on her daughter's bed, among her baby's teddies and ponies, pressing her daughter's sheets to her face, trying to find something of Izzy, her smell, her essence. But the room just smelled of her pain, her mourning, a pungent damp scent.

She still comes in here sometimes – this room is a shrine to her daughter, forever nine and three-quarters.

'I'll sleep on the bottom bunk, like I did before,' Maya offers, although she's looking longingly at the top bunk.

'Maya has just an ordinary bed, Mama, and she's so excited to sleep on the bunk bed with me. I've said she can sleep on the top bunk next time she comes round.' Izzy's voice in Eve's head, along with images of her daughter, her smiling face, her voice when she held her arms out every night: 'Goodnight, Mama.'

She imagines holding her daughter, breathing in her scent of strawberries and innocence.

She shakes her head to clear it, concentrating on this little girl, missing her mother, worrying for her. 'You can sleep on the top bunk, love. Izzy doesn't need it any more.'

And now, despite trying very hard not to, her voice breaks.

And suddenly Maya is there, throwing her arms round her. 'You must miss her so, Eve. I miss her too,' she cries. 'She was my bestest friend ever.'

Eve weeps along with this empathetic, kind child, big-hearted like her mother, offering comfort in the only way she knows how, even when she's going through such heartache herself. They stand in Izzy's room, Izzy's mother and her best friend, her belongings around them, and they sob together for a little girl who'll never play with her toys again, sleep in her bed again, open her arms out for a goodnight hug from her mother again. They weep for all that is lost.

'Thank you, Maya,' Eve says afterwards. 'Come, let me tuck you in.'

And these rituals that she'd performed every single night of her daughter's tragically short life give comfort at the same time as they stab and hurt.

'Now, what story would you like?'

She picks up the book on Izzy's bedside table that she was reading to her daughter the night before she died. '*The Borrowers*? That one was Izzy's favourite.'

And, somehow, talking about Izzy doesn't hurt as much as she thought it would, reading the story about tiny people living secretly in walls and under the floorboards that she'd read to her child so often that she knows parts of it by heart, to this different little girl sleeping in her daughter's bed in her daughter's place, but who sports similar expressions of intrigue and excitement, her eyes widening at the same parts of the tale that Izzy's would, her eyelids gradually getting heavier and drooping gently into sleep just as Izzy's would, doesn't hurt as much as she imagined. It is, once again, in a strange way, painful comfort.

When Maya is deeply asleep, Eve closes the book, tiptoes out of the room like she had a thousand times when her own child was sleeping here. At the door, she pauses and, looking at the sleeping child, she feels a tiny but imperceptible healing in the giant wound that is her heart.

CHAPTER 32

BINDU

1937

In her dream, Bindu is cooking in the one-roomed hut she shares with Ajji, frying cumin and mustard seeds and curry leaves in coconut oil, nutty sizzle and crispy crackle, sliced onions browning gold in the fragrant spiced oil, adding chopped ginger and crushed garlic, smoke from the hearth crumbling the mud walls of the hut and turning the hay-topped roof fiery red, Dumdee watching from the stoop, tongue hanging out in anticipation, Sirsi meowing plaintively from the banana trees just outside. Ajji smiling, exuding pride and love as she tastes the curry: 'The marriage of flavours – oh, my heart, you have the gift—'

Bindu startles awake to noise, chatter, the music of anklets. Golden spill of light edges in through the drawn curtains. Here, even the windows are clothed – the fabric rich and shimmering velvet – while the villagers make do with threadbare scraps to cover their malnourished, dehydrated bodies.

The space beside her is empty. Bindu has overslept. Guru must have retired to his rooms to catch up on work before leaving for the luncheon party they've been invited to. She should start getting ready.

But she's drawn to the maids' companionable chatter, bright as sunshine in the corridor, wanting to be part of it even though she knows they'll stop when they see her, their heads down, masks of dutiful diligence on.

Nevertheless, she pokes her head outside, and, sure enough, as soon as she opens the door they stop bantering and scurry past, the corridor emptying in a matter of moments. She sighs and is about to go inside when she locks eyes with a familiar face. The maid who's just turned into the corridor, hefting an enormous brass pot on her head, only her eyes visible. But Bindu would know that limping gait anywhere – Sunitha!

Most of Bindu's classmates are married now, those who dropped out before matriculation, already with children of their own, but seeing Sunitha here Bindu understands that her friend, whose greatest wish had been to get married and have several children, hasn't managed to find a man willing to overlook her limp as yet. Her heart goes out to her friend but Bindu thinks of the village women who'd come to her grandmother for healing potions after their men had vented their frustrations on their bodies, of herself trapped here, and she wonders if perhaps Sunitha's had a lucky escape...

Sunitha stops in her tracks, places the huge utensil from which steam emanates in swirling wisps – hot water for one of the bathrooms, presumably – on the lush carpet of the corridor, and beams at Bindu.

Sunitha's warm, hearty smile – how Bindu has missed it!

'I'm so glad to see you. I've been working here for days, and although I located your chamber easily – everyone knows the new mistress occupies the west wing – and have volunteered for all the jobs needing me to walk past your rooms, so I could "bump" into you, this is the first time I've managed it. Right time too. An excuse to set this monstrosity down for a minute.' Sunitha wipes her sweaty face with her pallu, still grinning. 'I hope you don't mind, Bin... I mean, Memsahib...'

'Sunitha! Don't stand on ceremony with me. I'm Bindu to you. And you don't have to ask permission from *me* to set your pot down!'

'Of course I do, you're the memsahib! Hearty congratulations on your marriage.' Sunitha beams, as always thrilled for Bindu, not a trace of guile or envy, no ill-feeling poisoning her wishes. It's a welcome change from the barely disguised loathing directed at her by servants and nobility alike. 'I told you, didn't I, that the land-lord's son had his sights set on you? I knew you'd come good, Bin — Memsahib.'

When Ajji fell ill, Bindu, occupied with Ajji's care, had lost touch with Sunitha. She'd heard from Chinnakka that Sunitha was similarly busy, looking after her siblings – she was the eldest of many, her youngest brother only two – and caring for her mother, who was ill. Then Bindu and Ajji moved here and she'd thought that Sunitha, like the other villagers, might resent Bindu for it. She's done her friend a disservice.

'Sunitha, please, I'm Bindu to you. I haven't changed.'

'You're my mistress, and I'll call you Memsahib,' Sunitha insists, beaming widely. 'Look at you, living here!' Then, her face falling: 'I'm sorry you had to turn down the scholarship, though. I know you wanted to study further, although why you'd willingly subject yourself to that torture I cannot imagine.'

Bindu tastes the familiar ache of loss for what might have been.

'But I'm so happy it worked out well in the end. Now, *this* is the life.' Sunitha gestures around her. 'All this, yours.' Her voice admiration and awe. And again, no guile, only pleasure on Bindu's behalf. 'And your Ajji on the mend now her fever's broken.' Her jubilation evident.

'Ajji's fever's broken?' Bindu is awestruck. Was it worth it, trading her freedom, tying herself to a man, something she'd adamantly vetoed, for the sake of Ajji? Of course it was. For, if Sunitha is to be believed, Bindu's Ajji is better. She is better. Bindu tastes happiness, festive payasam sweet on her tongue, and if there's a bitter niggle of querulous doubt at the back of her throat, she vehemently swallows it down.

'Oh, Bi— Memsahib, didn't you know? It broke last night.'

The English doctor is truly a magician. His pills, ground into milk sweetened with sugar – no poor man's knobbly yellow jaggery here, but rich folks' processed sugar, smooth and pristine white like the pills – fed to Ajji twice every day, have done the job, just as he promised.

'She was sleeping peacefully when I checked on her this morning,' Sunitha is saying.

'You checked on her?' Bindu is overwhelmed with joyful gratitude to her friend, while also ruminating on how much of a bind she's in, that the fact of her own grandmother finally being free of fever – the very reason she married Guru and why she's here living this life – is relayed by someone else. She should've been there, beside Ajji, but she hasn't had time and she'll most likely not be able to today either. She'll just have to take Sunitha's word for it.

'I've been visiting her first thing before I start work and last thing before I leave here. I fill her in on all the village gossip.' Sunitha beams.

Bindu quashes the envy almost as soon as it flares – Sunitha doing what she'd love to and cannot, sitting by Ajji and talking to her. Sunitha's free to leave the mansion, go back to the village, not trapped here like Bindu, with nothing to occupy her mind, no reading, no cooking. Only the forced company of ladies who despise her.

'Thank you, Sunitha,' she says.

'Don't thank me. Your Ajji means a lot to me – she's helped my ma with potions and food parcels enough times over the years.' And now, Sunitha's face falls, all the joy leaching from it, leaving behind pain and sorrow. 'My ma died a few weeks ago.'

Bindu reaches for Sunitha's hand, squeezes it. 'I'm so sorry.'

Sunitha gently frees her hand from Bindu's clasp, looking up and down the corridor even as she sniffs and wipes her eyes with her sari pallu. 'Better not, Memsahib. The other maids, they won't understand why I'm on such affectionate terms with you.'

'Ah.' Bindu gets it. All the other maids huff around her, shooting venom-drenched looks that declare, 'You're one of us, and now we've to clean and carry after you.' But they have to do her bidding and be civil, as she is their mistress. They'll have no such qualms with Sunitha if they think she's being singled out for attention by the despised mistress. They'll make Sunitha's life here hell and she'll have no choice but to leave.

It breaks Bindu's heart that even this simple gesture between friends is taboo because of Bindu's position – that she's lost this freedom too, alongside all others, and that this small token of friendship might cost Sunitha her job. The injustice of it makes her angry, want to scream. And, fuelled by the rebellious contrariness that ambushes her when she feels shepherded into a corner with no way out – unable to visit with Ajji, to even squeeze her friend's hand – she wants to reach across and hug Sunitha, to hell with the consequences.

Sunitha, however, knows her well. 'Memsahib, I need this job. It's down to me now to look after my siblings.' A note of warning in her voice for Bindu to not give in to impulse.

Sunitha's father was a hapless alcoholic who'd force himself on his wife when drunk, getting her pregnant with more children they couldn't afford. When he passed away a couple of years ago, Sunitha's mother had heaved a sigh of relief. And now she's gone too.

'Oh, Sunitha,' Bindu says, reading all that's unsaid in Sunitha's moist eyes.

You're not the only one whose dreams have had to be sacrificed. You've landed on your feet and Sunitha has the good grace to be pleased for you. You are lucky. So, instead of dwelling on what you lost, think of all you've gained. Medical help for Ajji, who's on the mend. No worrying about where your next meal is coming from. A husband who isn't a violent alcoholic.

Sunitha nods, then, once again wiping her eyes: 'I must go.'

Don't, Bindu wants to say. *Stay, please. I've just found you.*

Here in her father-in-law's mansion, there's every luxury. She isn't hungry or thirsty. But she's lonely. She understands this keenly since bumping into Sunitha – just five minutes of natter with someone genuine, someone who sees *her*, and she feels more herself.

Sunitha is setting the rolled-up cloth upon her head in preparation for picking up her pot of water.

Bindu's mind works busily as it comes up with a plan to keep her friend with her now that she's serendipitously found her.

'Sunitha, Ajji and I don't have a personal maid – I told Guru we didn't want one. But now, I'll tell him I've changed my mind, that I'd like someone to help me with Ajji as she regains her health.'

Sunitha cocks her head, and the cloth falls to the floor. She ignores it, hopeful eyes fixed on Bindu's face.

'I'll ask Guru to appoint you in such a way so as to not show favouritism, to put it about that he chose you because you'd had recent experience of caring for someone ill: your mother. That way, the other maids won't be put out.'

Sunitha's eyes glow. 'You could do that?' Her voice thick with emotion.

'Yes.' She'll plead with Guru, if need be. She'll wash and change and, although she wants to see Ajji more than anything, confirm with her own eyes that her fever really is gone, she'll instead request an audience with her husband before they leave for the party.

In the village, whole families crowded into a one-roomed hut, and in some instances, when there was rumour of a tiger prowling neighbouring villages, their animals too, everyone on top of each other, no notion of personal space. Here, in this vast house with space to spare, they have to make appointments to see each other.

Sunitha beams. 'It'll be just like old times.'

Bindu's glad to see the shadows that had briefly dimmed the light from Sunitha's eyes when she spoke of her mother's demise disappear, her sunny nature once again evident in her radiant face.

'Well,' says Sunitha, setting the rolled-up cloth once more upon her head and bending down to pick up her pot, 'I better get this to the downstairs bathroom in the north wing before the water goes cold. Can you imagine the amount of water they have here – they don't need to worry at all.' A pause, a blush colouring her cheeks. 'I mean, you don't need to worry. I mean...'

'I know what you mean. I can't get over it either.'

With an effortful grimace, Sunitha hefts the pot onto her head. 'See you soon, I hope, Memsahib.'

'Call me Bin...'

But with a cheeky smile, Sunitha limps away.

CHAPTER 33

BINDU

Exactly a week after their first meeting, Sunitha starts work as Bindu's personal maid.

Soon after Sunitha left, hefting the pot of water on her head, Bindu had requested an audience with Guru.

He was busy with paperwork. 'What is it that's so urgent it couldn't wait until we leave for the party?' he snapped, barely looking up at her. And then, a self-important tone entering his voice, a sheen of smugness − 'Now my father's bedridden, I'm handling all business affairs.'

So, his stroke worked to your benefit, Bindu thought but, since she needed his help, did not say out loud.

'Although, of course' − and here the familiar bitterness seeped through the nonchalance he tried to affect − 'he insists on reviewing every single thing I do.'

She knew she shouldn't, but she couldn't help it − 'And does he approve?'

'What do you think?' Guru barked and, in his eyes, she glimpsed the wounded child forever trying to please his father and failing, and she experienced remorse for needling him.

She went to him, placed a hand on his arm. 'He's lucky in you and foolish not to see it.'

He twinkled at her then, the heaviness easing from his gaze. 'What do you want, Bindu?'

She told him.

'Is that all?' He laughed, gathering her into his embrace.

'The other maids, far from being jealous, are admiring of me! They're being very nice in the hope that I'll put in a good word and they too might get a promotion.' Sunitha beams. 'Thank you, Memsahib, and many thanks to Sahib too.'

'Sunitha...'

'You'll always be Memsahib to me.' Sunitha smiles.

Bindu sighs, letting it go, and asks the question foremost in her mind – the one she'd chastised herself sorely for not thinking to ask Sunitha when they met before. 'How is Dumdee, do you know?'

'That mongrel that followed you everywhere?'

'Yes.' She tries and fails to sniff away the moisture crowding her eyes. 'Have you happened to see him?'

'He's happy, don't you fret, Memsahib.' Sunitha's voice is affectionate. 'He's causing havoc alongside the other neighbourhood dogs, strutting around as if he owns the village.'

Bindu smiles through her tears.

'Although he did pine for you dreadfully, still keeps vigil every night at the hut, drives Chinnakka's drunk of a husband crazy.'

Bindu snorts, salty brine. 'Serves Chinnakka's husband right.' *Oh, Dumdee.*

'And your snooty madam of a cat has taken up position under the peepal tree, eyeing Muthakka's sorry excuse for fish.'

Bindu laughs and cries again. When she's managed to compose herself somewhat, she goes on, 'How're the nuns, do you know?'

'You caused them enough headaches when you were at school and now you miss them?'

True, Bindu thinks. She'd rebelled against the nuns' strictures, bristled at what she thought of as their rigid disciplinarianism. But now, she misses them – not just the nuns, but the villagers with their gaunt bodies and prematurely aged faces ravaged by permanent hunger, the menagerie of scrawny animals stalking the fields in the hope of sustenance, the village itself, beautiful and terrible, the harsh but full life.

'The nuns weren't bad,' she says to Sunitha.

'No, they really weren't, considering they never once went bearing tales of your escapades to your Ajji, even though they weren't bound by loyalty towards her like the villagers.'

'Yes,' Bindu agrees, recalling how she'd acted out with Sister Hilda and yet the nun had been patient with her, kind.

'School... just the thought gives me nightmares.' Sunitha shudders. 'But my younger brother is really good, like you.' Pride gilds her voice. 'The priests've put his name forward for the scholarship.'

And Bindu's wound of ache for what might have been throbs and bleeds, even as she says as enthusiastically as she can manage, 'That's wonderful, Sunitha. Good for him.'

'I don't know how people like you and my brother can like book learning.' Sunitha grimaces as she dusts the room. 'Not for me. I'm happy here.' She runs her duster dramatically over Bindu's dressing table, striking a pose, and Bindu laughs. 'Bhanuakka says the nuns were very upset that you gave up the scholarship, crying, "Oh, that girl, what a missed opportunity!" Now, Memsahib, why are *you* crying?' Sunitha tuts. 'Your tears're very close to the surface, aren't they? If only we could use them as a water source for the village, we'd never have to worry about the drought.'

Once again, Bindu smiles through her tears.

'Look around you.' Sunitha is on a roll. 'Now this is what I call opportunity.'

But whereas others would have said it with envy tinting their voices bilious green, Sunitha's is matter-of-fact, merely reminding Bindu to count her blessings. And this is why Bindu loves this girl and is so grateful and happy that she's here.

On the subject of blessings, Sunitha definitely tops the list.

. . .

Each day, Sunitha updates Bindu on Ajji's health, having liaised with the doctor on her behalf. Bindu, while grateful to Sunitha, is saddened and frustrated that she must rely on her friend for this, while she's forced to spend her time pasting a smile on her face and nodding along to the inane conversation and catty gossip of bored socialites. She visits Ajji when she can, but the brief snatches of precious time with her grandmother are never enough. Ajji is getting better, but she isn't out of the woods yet. She's still very weak and confused. Once or twice she has smiled at Bindu, the gleam of love in her cloudy gaze, but before Bindu could make conversation, Ajji's eyes had closed and she'd fallen back asleep.

The doctor, a thin, unprepossessing white man not much taller than Bindu, who nevertheless performs miracles, promises: 'Your grandmother will get better, but, mind you, she has several complications – not just as a result of this illness, but also due to long-term starvation – which need to be dealt with.'

Long-term starvation. *Oh, Ajji.* Her grandmother going without so Bindu could eat, grow. Her grandmother sacrificing her own health for her grandchild's well-being.

'She'll need ongoing medical care,' the doctor warned.

And Bindu marvelled that she didn't have to think twice about agreeing. Selling her soul and losing her freedom by marrying the landlord's son had paid off if it meant Ajji was guaranteed medical care for as long as she needed it.

Each morning, Sunitha pushes open the curtains and sets Bindu's chambers in order, nattering as she works. She'll not countenance any help; when Bindu tries, she's gently rebuffed. 'This is my job. I enjoy it. It makes me feel worthwhile. Isn't it time you were getting ready for your party?'

I miss cooking, concocting pastes and spice mixes, seeing the joy on people's faces as they sampled my curries. It made me feel worthwhile.

Sunitha notices her melancholy but misunderstands the reason for it. 'Memsahib, why the long face? Your Ajji'll be right as rain, don't you worry. She's just biding her time, and why shouldn't she?

She's lying on a soft bed, not a care in the world, finally resting after a lifetime of cooking and anxiety, all her needs met. I know Chinnakka'd give anything to take her place. Do you know what her husband did...?'

And as her friend talks, Bindu decides that Sunitha's right about one thing: enough with the moping.

CHAPTER 34

EVE

1980

As Eve crosses the corridor outside her daughter's room, where Maya sleeps in her daughter's place, she hears Izzy's voice: 'See, Mama, this is why I didn't want you to die. You had to be here for Maya.'

And she smiles as she enters the bedroom she shared with Joe – the love of her life.

In the early days just after the accident, she'd alternate between her daughter's room and this one, sleeping on Joe's side of the bed, holding his pillow, trying and failing to conjure his presence.

Now, once more, Eve lies down on Joe's side of the bed, her head on his pillow, and she fancies she can smell her husband, ginger and lime, hear his voice, 'Sleep now, my love, you've a long day tomorrow.'

'Eve?' A small voice.

Eve opens her eyes to sunlight edging in through drawn curtains, a little girl standing beside her.

Izzy?

She squints, for her daughter appears different.

Eve is sleeping on Joe's side. Where's Joe? He hasn't already left for work, surely? Or perhaps he's gone for his run? And why's Izzy awake before her? Why didn't her alarm go off? What is the time?

'Eve.' A child's voice. But not her own little one's.

And then it slaps her, the knowledge, all at once.

But she cannot give in to grief, for Maya is looking to her for direction.

She'd set her alarm for the first time since the accident, for she has a little girl she's responsible for, again, albeit temporarily this time. But also, for the first time in forever, she slept through it! She, who hasn't slept well, certainly not for hours at a stretch, since the accident.

'Eve, do you think I can stay home today?'

A little girl who, like children everywhere, is looking for an excuse to skip school.

'I think you should attend school as normal, Maya,' Eve says, sitting up and stretching.

'Do I *have* to?' Maya's face falls. 'I'm late.'

That emphasis on 'have'. That cajoling tone, that pleading expression with those downturned lips, all stabbing at Eve's heart, for Izzy would regularly employ them too.

'I'll call the school, let them know you'll be in late.'

Maya still appears miserable, so Eve says, 'Tell you what, I'll make you a chocolate sandwich for lunch just this once and you can have Coco Pops for breakfast too.'

She's pretty sure there's half a box of Coco Pops languishing in the pantry. It was Izzy's treat for the weekends. Irrationally, a stubborn part of Eve had fancied that if she kept hold of Izzy's favourite cereal, her daughter might come back.

Well, now she's glad she saved it, for Maya beams in delight, saying, 'All right, I'll go get ready.'

Ah, the innocence of childhood, Eve muses, where worry and pain can be deferred by the promise of chocolate.

At the door, Maya turns. 'Eve, I can walk to school on my own. My mum lets me,' her voice, charged with pride at her independence, wavering slightly as she mentions her mum.

Again, Eve's heart goes out to this girl even as she experiences a fresh pang of loss that Izzy will never walk to school on her own, get to experience the many heady freedoms on the journey to adulthood, of growing up and away from her parents.

Izzy had been pestering Eve for weeks before the accident, to be allowed to walk to school independently. 'All my friends do.' Her lower lip jutting out in defiance.

'Not Maya,' Eve said.

'She'll be allowed to when she's ten.'

'You can when you're in Year 6.'

'But that's *ages* away.'

'Not really. Only a few months to go.'

But Izzy never got to Year 6.

Eve is jolted from her ruminations by Maya's voice.

'After breakfast, can we please call the hospital, find out what's happening with Mum, when we can go see her?'

Eve's stomach clenches at the thought of venturing outside. But Maya is looking at her, expectantly, and so she nods. 'That's a plan.'

CHAPTER 35

BINDU

1937

'Can I help you with work?' Bindu asks Guru.

Now that the landlord is indisposed and her husband is in charge – although the landlord is loath to accept it – 'He "corrects" everything I've done,' Guru sighs when he visits Bindu – Bindu has decided that, instead of bemoaning her lack of independence and agency, she'll take action. She'll try appealing to the boy her husband once was, who'd admired her intelligence.

Guru looks up from the papers he's perusing, irritation flashing in his eyes. '*No*, Bindu. It's a daily uphill struggle to try to get my father to accept *my* help, let alone yours.'

'He needn't find out.'

'He *will* find out. If anything, he's more adamant about having things done his way. He's afraid of losing control and wants to hold on to it for as long as he can.'

'Given the escalating tensions in Europe, the anti-Jewish campaign in Germany, all signs pointing to war' – Bindu hasn't had access to newspapers – or any reading material for that matter – since she crossed the landlord in front of the Resident, but she's determined not to let her brain stagnate, so during the interminable socialising she has to endure she ruminates on all she'd read when she did have the luxury of daily newspapers – 'with the

Indian National Congress in power and the communal strife here, I thought you could expand...'

'Bindu, when I'm landlord, perhaps.' A weary sigh. 'But my father is even more dictatorial than usual and I can't...'

'Why can't you? He's ill.'

'Exactly so. His body's not in his control – he's paralysed on his left side and has little use of his right arm. The only thing he can do is supervise the running of the business. I cannot take that away from him.' Guru rubs a hand across his eyes.

Although he disguises it behind his brusque manner, his quick-silver moods, Bindu is reminded every so often that her husband has a heart. And, right now, she sees that it bleeds for his father. All his life Guru has yearned for his approval and he's still trying, still hoping.

But this is bad news for her, for it means he'll not let her help with work, for fear word will get back to his father, which is frustrating beyond belief.

While she tastes the bitter bile of defeat, Guru smiles, once again affecting that disconcerting switch from ill temper to good humour. 'He keeps asking when we'll provide him with a grandson.'

A grandson to carry on the family line, to keep the business empire in the family. 'Tell him I'll provide him with a grand-daughter.'

Guru chuckles, although she wasn't joking. It makes her *mad*. Why won't he even try to see how bored she is, how useless she feels?

'I miss cooking. Can I at least supervise the servants—'

His laughter turned off abruptly, a scowl warps his features. 'You know how—'

'Yes,' she snaps. 'Your father's house, your father's rules.' Then, 'How about if I make spice mixes and food parcels for the villagers?' she tries. 'It'd raise the landlord's profile even further if it was reported that he was helping out his tenants this way.'

'Bindu, he grumbled that pardoning their rent for a month set us back gravely, that instead of bringing dowry, you've proved to be a money drain,' Guru says tightly, expression grim.

And again, she says, 'He needn't know.'

And again, he replies, 'He *will* know. All the servants report to him.'

'So, it's a no, then?'

'For now, yes.'

'Guru, I'm so *bored* with nothing constructive to do. I can help with—'

'I said no.' Guru's eyes flash furious orange sparks. 'If you've time to spare, arrange a meeting with the Maharani of—'

'But that's all I do, all day. Socialise with women I've nothing in common with.'

'You said you want to help. Well, this will help cement our alliances and partnerships, bring about more business,' Guru barks.

She sees he's dangerously close to losing his temper. But *she's* angry too, and desperate with it. Why can't she get through to him, this man who, just a few months ago, would listen to her, commiserate with her, understand her, the only one who did? And so, despite knowing she should stop pushing when he's in this mood, she says, 'Why did you marry me if you wanted someone meek and unquestioningly obedient? My mind is stagnating. I've nothing to read. I don't even have time to visit my Ajji—'

'And I don't have time to listen to you whining like a child.'

She's *incensed*. 'I'm trying to tell you—'

'Go away, Bindu,' he snaps, his face a snarl. 'I'm busy.'

'And I'm not. If I just—'

'Enough.' Guru is out of his chair and looming over her as he yells, 'Get out before I ask my man to forcibly remove you.'

She's too angry to be scared at her husband's transformation into a growling monster. She marches away, fuming, throat clogged and eyes burning with upset and resentment.

Soon she'll have to change for yet another party, and, upon her return, her husband will visit her in her chambers and kiss her and be with her as if nothing's happened, as if they haven't rowed, as if he didn't shout her out of his room like she was an annoying pest, and she'll take it, for she has to do her duty, provide the landlord and his son with an heir, fulfil her part of the bargain she struck with Guru.

She is trapped and cannot see a way out of this bind.

Or can she?

She hasn't lost *everything*.

She picks up the notebook into which she's tucked Laurence Elliot's card. Until now, although she's toyed with the idea of taking up the journalist on his invitation, she hasn't acted upon it for fear it would anger her husband.

But now, she doesn't care – she's losing more of herself each day and she's desperate to salvage something of who she once was: the stellar cook whose recipes made Ajji proud, the bright spark who'd achieved the highest ever marks in her matriculation exams – before she loses herself altogether.

She stares at the card, seeing in her mind's eye a tall man with hair the colour of sunburnt hay, eyes the shimmering green-gold of monsoon-burnished fields dancing in the rain, neck and face blotchy red as he cleared his throat and handed it over, and she knows just what she will do.

CHAPTER 36

BINDU

Bindu should be getting ready for the party, but instead she pens her recipe for *sambar pudi* – vegetable soup spice mix – in her notebook, imagining she's cooking it on the hearth of the one-roomed hut she shared with Ajji, Dumdee watching from the threshold, the cat sunning herself on the moss-encrusted well surround and the dry wind making the coconut fronds dance, the parrots screech and the mynah birds sing, the air smelling of raw mango and ripe guava, zesty sweet.

Decisively, she tears off the recipe, and another blank page from her notebook, in which she writes:

This is the recipe to make a spice mix for sambar – vegetable soup – that is beloved by everyone in my village. It works well with any combination of vegetables. You can even use meat, fish or lentils. It works well on its own too, if you don't have any vegetables, as was often the case with us. You can store the spice mix for up to a month. Use as per taste – I recommend two teaspoonfuls if you like your sambar mild and three if you prefer it with a kick.

Here's my recipe for sambar:

Heat one tablespoon of coconut oil in a pan. (Feel free to substitute coconut oil with any other oil/butter/ghee.)

When the oil is hot, add a pinch of mustard seeds and another of urad dal. (You can skip the urad dal, but I like the crunch and flavour it adds to the oil. However, I've made the sambar without urad dal and it tasted fine. Also, once, when I ran out of mustard seeds, I cooked it without and that was all right too. As you can see, this is quite a forgiving dish.)

When the urad dal and mustard seeds are spitting in the hot oil, add chopped onions, green chillies, ginger and garlic. Fry until golden and the raw smell is replaced by the delicious aroma of sizzling onions, garlic and ginger in spiced oil.

Now add your sambar mix to taste (two teaspoons for mild, three for a kick).

Fry until the onions, ginger and garlic are coated in the roasting spices. Now add drumsticks, aubergines or any vegetables, lentils or meat you prefer, with a tumbler of water. If you have coconut milk, you can replace the water with it.

Cover and bring to a simmer.

Add salt to taste.

Serve with rice, chapatis or any other pulses/grains of your choice. Also perfectly tasty and filling on its own.

She bites her pencil once she's done, thinking, considering. Then, at the bottom of the page, she writes:

I hope this is what you asked for. If you wish me to continue, and/or if there are any specific recipes you require, please do let me know. Please address any letters to:

The Missionary Girls' School
Ursuline Sisters Convent Compound
Suryanagar

She trusts the nuns will forward any post in her name to Sunitha, who'll bring it to her.

But as Bindu folds the sheets of paper, she is pulled up short.

For how to post the letter? She has Mr Elliot's address but no envelopes, nor stamps, nor means of buying them. She might be living in a huge mansion, she might have grand clothes and never have to worry about her next meal, but for all that she's at her husband's mercy, his possession, just as much as her clothes, her jewellery, even this notebook and pencil. She owns nothing except for the small paper bag of odds and ends she brought with her when she came here. She doesn't have any money and if she asks Guru, he'll say, 'Why do you want money when you have everything? Whatever it is you need, tell me and I'll have my man get it for you.'

She hates to be beholden to him, to have no independence, no agency of her own. It makes her even more determined to send this letter, carve out something private, just for herself. As she casts about in her mind, and comes up with a plan, she feels, for the first time since she arrived here, like herself, the old Bindu – feisty, determined, refusing to allow anyone to get the better of her.

CHAPTER 37

BINDU

Before leaving for the party, Bindu tells Sunitha, 'I've a favour to ask of you.'

'Yes, Memsahib?' Sunitha is curious.

Bindu presses two gold-lined, jewel-encrusted saris from her wedding trousseau – gifted by her in-laws and neither of which she's worn – into Sunitha's hands.

Sunitha looks at her, shocked, and for once tongue-tied. After a couple of tries, she finds her voice. 'Mem... Memsahib, what's this?'

Bindu has thought long and hard. She knows that, while jewellery will be missed, saris won't – one expensive, gold-embroidered sari looks much the same as another and she now has quite a few. 'One of these is for you and the other... Is there a way you could arrange for it to be sold so you won't get in trouble?'

Sunitha is still staring at Bindu open-mouthed and so Bindu takes a deep breath and continues.

'I remember you telling me your father knew of moneylenders who'd take anything and not ask questions as to their provenance. Is there some way you could pass the sari on to them? Sunitha, if there's even the slightest danger of you getting in trouble, then of course don't do it – but if you *could*, I'd be so grateful.'

'Memsahib,' Sunitha finds her voice, 'what's got into you?'

'I... Sunitha, this life... I've no freedom, I'm just...' How to explain to Sunitha that sometimes this mansion with its endless rooms gets so claustrophobic that she struggles to breathe? 'All this' – she sweeps a hand around her to indicate their luxurious surroundings – 'it's not as great as—'

'We don't have enough to eat or drink, Memsahib.' Sunitha's voice is uncharacteristically (but understandably) sharp.

'I know,' Bindu says softly.

'I know you do.' Sunitha's voice is just as soft, a contrast to her previous tone. 'And I do understand that your life is not all the villagers think it to be. But nowhere's perfect, Memsahib, especially for a woman, and this is better than most.'

'I know,' Bindu repeats, twirling the pallu of her grand sari, one she hasn't worn before so as not to insult the hostess.

'Memsahib, you're like my sister, so I'll say this. Tell me to shut up if I'm crossing lines here, but don't sack me please, I need this job.'

'But you'll still say what you have to?' Bindu smiles.

'I must. For you're my friend.'

Friend – it warms Bindu's heart. 'But you still call me Memsahib.'

'Look' – Sunitha takes a breath, unsmiling – 'you've a tendency to rebel against constraints, see how far you can push boundaries. But you've landed on your feet here, Memsahib. You'd be crazy to jeopardise all this.'

Suddenly it is imperative that Sunitha understands. 'It's just that I... I need *something* for myself. I loved... love cooking. I miss it. I'm going to write and post some recipes, that's all.'

Far from understanding, Sunitha looks perplexed.

'Please, Sunitha. It'll be my lifeline. I'm going crazy here.'

'Memsahib, you're crazy to risk your life here.' Sunitha wrings her sari pallu in upset.

'Please.'

'Even if I say no, when you get that determined look in your eye you'll find a way to do what you've set your mind to. And I'd rather I was on board than someone else who doesn't have your best interests at heart. What would you like me to do?' Sunitha sighs.

Bindu smiles, her heart swelling with relief. 'I'd like you to sell one of the saris if you can and use some of the money to buy envelopes and stamps, please. The other sari and the remainder of the money from the sale of this one's for you. But, as I said, I don't want you getting in trouble.'

Sunitha sighs again. 'I won't, but that doesn't mean I'm happy doing this.'

'I know but—'

'...You'd like me to anyway,' Sunitha finishes for her. 'My uncle enabled my father's alcoholism and ignored my mother's pleas. Now he's repentant. He'll sell the saris for me. I'll sell both, for, much as I'd like to keep this' – she runs her hand gently over the smooth silk of the sari, her stern expression briefly wistful – 'it's too grand to wear and it would raise too many questions. No, I'd rather sell this one too and use the money for food and any left over for a rainy day.' She takes a breath. 'But I'll say this again, Memsahib, think carefully about this. If your husband finds out, you'll be in trouble. And I will too.'

'I'll make sure you don't get in trouble, Sunitha.'

Her friend only rolls her eyes.

'How'll you smuggle the saris out without being caught?'

'Don't you worry, I've my ways.' Sunitha winks. 'I've the gate-keeper in the palm of my hand.'

'Thank you, Sunitha,' Bindu says, tears in her eyes. 'For being my friend and ally.'

Sunitha tuts, clicking her teeth. 'I'm the one taking all the risks, what're you crying for?'

When Sunitha returns a few days later with the envelopes and stamps, Bindu secretes all but one set away in the small bag, nestling at the very back of her wardrobe, where she's carved out a hidey-hole – one of the first things she did when she was assigned this room. Even if a maid was to stumble upon it, they wouldn't, she's sure, set much store by the torn paper bag. It's incongruous, and they'd know at once that it contains sundry items of sentimental but no real value from Bindu's former life.

In any case, just to be safe, she deposits the envelopes and stamps at the very bottom of the bag. Then, carefully placing her sambar recipe and notes inside the envelope she's kept back, she copies Mr Elliot's address onto the front, attaches the stamp and seals it.

When she hands it to Sunitha, asking her to please post it, alongside gifting her another sari as thanks, she feels her heart lift. For, until now, Bindu has felt frustrated, restricted, having to fall in line meekly with the landlord's rules. Now, she's taking back control in some small way.

Sunitha raises an eyebrow, shaking her head as she tucks the envelope into her sari skirt pocket. And just in case her feelings weren't clear: 'It might just be recipes, but your husband, if he finds out, will take it as a betrayal,' she says, and, 'What's this for?', looking at the sari.

'For your trouble,' Bindu says. 'I know what you're doing is not as easy as you make out. And I appreciate it very much, Sunitha.'

It is all Bindu has to give that won't be missed – and it isn't hers either. But, alongside writing the recipe and posting it, sharing the landlord's token gifts to his daughter-in-law with someone deserving makes Bindu begin to regain her sense of self, for she's *doing* something instead of bemoaning her fate.

'A reply should arrive at the convent in a few days. Please will you drop by there to check next week?'

Sunitha sighs, shaking her head. 'When I left school, I never thought I'd set foot back there again.'

How Bindu wishes she could visit the convent! If she had her time at school again, she'd never skive off.

'It gives me nightmares,' Sunitha is grumbling. 'The things I must do for you! Next week you said?'

And Bindu smiles.

. . .

A week after she posted the letter, Bindu's heart lifts in tentative hope as she waits for Sunitha to arrive, even as she tells herself that it doesn't matter if he replies or not, the journalist with eyes the colour of moss who liked her cooking and wanted to publish her recipes.

'No post, sorry,' Sunitha says.

He might not have recalled asking you for recipes, giving you his business card, sampling your cooking and loving it. You're just one of the many people he meets during his busy life, Bindu castigates herself.

But, just as when she'd skive from school, the very act of writing to Mr Elliot, sending the recipe, conducting a clandestine, albeit one-sided, correspondence unbeknownst to her husband has given her a thrill, a reminder of her former self.

And, a small voice in her head pipes, *there might be something tomorrow.*

This prompts her to say, 'Will you drop by again tomorrow, Sunitha, please? I know you've to leave home earlier to make the detour to the convent, and that it's a longer walk for you.' Especially given Sunitha's limp. 'I'm really grateful.' She is, alongside a flare of envy, quickly squashed, for Sunitha's freedom. Bindu doesn't allow it access, for it's wrong to think this way – Sunitha's life is fraught with worries, as hers was when she lived in the village. Then, she couldn't wait to get away.

But now...

Now what wouldn't she give to live in the village, hungry, thirsty but free again.

The next morning: 'I don't have the letter you were expecting, but here is something from the nuns.' With the panache of a conjuror, Sunitha retrieves a small package from her sari skirt.

Handwritten notes from the nuns, asking after Bindu, which make her cry.

'I knew it. I came prepared.' Sunitha hands her a scrap of old sari masquerading as a handkerchief, but it only inspires fresh tears, recalling as it does the handkerchief Sister Maria Teresa had given Bindu when she and Sister Hilda came to her hut and asked

if Bindu would like to join their school. The much-washed handkerchief, no longer pristine white but dirty yellow, is in the torn
paper bag tucked into the back of the wardrobe, containing her
most precious possessions, all she owns from her previous life,
which feels so far away.

CHAPTER 38

BINDU

'Here, Memsahib' – Sunitha whips the envelope from her skirt with a flourish – 'what you've been waiting for!'

Mr Elliot has replied!

Bindu runs her hands over his neat, precise handwriting in delighted wonder.

Sunitha tuts, shaking her head, as Bindu tucks the letter into her sari skirt, where it nestles alongside his card. 'Memsahib, this man must be something else.'

Bindu is aware of hot colour flooding into her cheeks. 'No, I... It's my recipe, he...'

'Memsahib, I hate to harp on a sour note when you're so happy, but as your friend and with your Ajji still not quite well enough to advise or caution, I must warn you...'

'Yes, Sunitha, I know that if my husband finds out...'

'You are lucky, Memsahib.' Sunitha takes Bindu's palm in both of hers, looking into Bindu's eyes, her gaze earnest, 'I know you're not happy here, that you feel trapped. All this, which would make most women very content indeed, doesn't satisfy you. You want more. At school, you'd run away, steal fruit. Now, you're doing this – only recipes, perhaps, but still. Writing to another man, unbeknownst to your husband, is a recipe for trouble, as I see it. Be careful. Please. Act with your head, not your heart. You are *lucky*.

You've a roof over your head, enough to eat and drink. Your Ajji looked after. Your husband isn't the worst—'

'I know, Sunitha.' Bindu retrieves her hand, impatient, and wanting, desperately, and for the first time since Sunitha came once more into her life, some time alone from her friend. 'I'll be in the garden while you dust here.'

'My dusting never bothered you before,' Sunitha calls after Bindu as she all but runs into the little courtyard adjoining her rooms – well, little in comparison to some of the other courtyards in here, big enough to easily contain five of the villagers' abodes – where she met Mr Elliot on her wedding day and he handed her his card. 'Please think about what I said.' Her friend's warning echoes in Bindu's ears as she shuts the door behind her, the hot tart air, baked earth and green mango depositing humid kisses on her flushed cheeks.

Bindu sits on the bench snug within the embrace of the gently weaving palm fronds, their green susurrating rustle complementing the gurgle of the fountain, the swish of bird wings across the dazzling-bright awning above. She likes this seat, for it affords privacy, of a sort. All the courtyards in this mansion are rectangular in shape, the house rising around them, and the servants walking past in the corridors upstairs can see all the happenings below. But here, Bindu is hidden within the palm bower. Thus ensconced, she takes out the letter.

Mrs Ramraj
The Missionary Girls' School
Ursuline Sisters Convent Compound
Suryanagar

Mrs Ramraj. It jars, seeing herself addressed by her husband's name, in Mr Elliot's precise handwriting. It underlines what she is – Guru's possession, even her name gifted by him. But she won't let it mar the excitement, the sheer joy, of receiving a reply from Mr Elliot, journalist and magazine publisher, when she'd all but convinced herself he wouldn't bother to respond. He must be so busy, and yet, he's taken the time to write to her and she's heartened by it.

She pries open the envelope carefully, heart pounding with nerves. Has her recipe passed muster?

Dear Mrs Ramraj,

Thank you kindly for your recipe.

It is exactly what I envisioned for the cooking section. Readers of the magazine will be very happy indeed. I will send you a copy once it is published and also your remittance with it.

Oh. Bindu clutches the letter to her chest, overwhelmed. Her recipe is to be published – *and* she's to be paid for it! Somehow, she hadn't thought of that aspect of it. She'll have something that's just hers, unconnected with the landlord and Guru – *her* recipe in print, money that *she* has earned. It's gratifying, liberating, exhilarating. For even the envelope and stamp she's used to communicate with Mr Elliot are from money obtained by selling a sari gifted by her in-laws and that grates on Bindu. In future, instead of presenting Sunitha with saris, Bindu will be able to reward her for her trouble with *her* money and then perhaps Sunitha will understand why Bindu must do this.

Bindu shushes the voice in her head that questions if perhaps there's something to Sunitha's warning. She'll never be found out – and, after all, what harm is she doing by sharing a recipe or two? She turns her attention back to the letter.

If you find the time and have the inclination to send more recipes, I would be most grateful. The magazine is a monthly publication and the cooking section will be, I dare say, a popular feature once your recipe is featured.

He would like more! Bindu is thrilled. A means of independence. What she'd hoped to achieve with her scholarship, doing things her way, and not having to rely on anyone. This is not the same, of course – she's still reliant on Guru – but it's *something*.

May I also compliment you on your command of English and your handwriting – both exquisite.

Thank you so very much for taking the time to write to me.

Yours respectfully,

Laurence Elliot

Enthused and very pleased – *I'm no longer voiceless, Guru. No matter how much you and your father try to reduce me, render me invisible and mute, I will find a way*. Bindu composes a reply at once:

Dear Mr Elliot,

Thank you so much – for your reply and for featuring my recipe in your magazine! It is very exciting and I am thrilled.

Thank you, too, for your kind words about my command of English and my handwriting. I went to the missionary school run by the nuns at the convent where you address your replies. I owe a lot to them.

Now, here's my recipe for rasam, spicy tomato soup...

CHAPTER 39

EVE

1980

Eve rings the school to say Maya will be late, while Maya is spooning Coco Pops into her mouth. The number comes to her as soon as she begins dialling; she'd done this several times over the years with Izzy and learned the number by heart.

Her own daughter had loved Coco Pops, savouring every one, slurping down the chocolatey milk after, sporting a creamy moustache and grinning. The image is vivid in Eve's mind's eye even as the school secretary picks up, her voice familiar, her name coming to her in Izzy's voice: 'Mum, Miss Aldridge says we can wear fancy dress for mufti...'

After the call, Eve feels tired, like she's lived through a whole day already. This rollercoaster of emotions is taking its toll on her. But before she can dwell, Maya is pushing her bowl, clean to the last milky drop, aside and asking, 'Can we call the hospital now, Eve, please?' Hope and worry war in the little girl's eyes.

Eve takes a deep breath, chastising herself for her self-indulgence, focussing on this child who needs her. 'Of course, sweetheart.'

And then, sending a prayer heavenward – she doesn't believe in God, but it's for Jenny's sake – Eve picks up the phone again.

She's redirected to the nurse responsible for Jenny's care. 'Jenny's sleeping, but she's left a message for you. She'd very much like to see Maya to reassure her she's all right – visiting hours are between five and six p.m. She said to tell you she knows how hard it'll be for you to make the journey and that it's OK if you can't. She understands.'

Eve sets the phone down, marvelling at Jenny's empathy – so ill and yet worrying for Eve venturing outside her house. She *will* go – she owes it to her friend and her child. And like Sue has reiterated, time and again, she must go out sometime.

She smiles at Maya, who's watching her, wide-eyed with anxiety, and says, brightly, 'Your mum is asleep now, love. But she's asked for you to come see her after school. We'll go together, all right?'

Maya's beaming smile is a gift, warming Eve's broken heart.

CHAPTER 40

BINDU

1937

When Bindu pops in to check on Ajji – her few snatched moments of peace before the day's socialising duties – her grandmother is awake, eyes bright as they take in her surroundings properly for the first time since she moved here.

She glows when she sees Bindu. There's no other word for the transformation on her grandmother's face, crinkling in a smile that lights up her whole body.

Bindu blinks, rubs at her eyes, even as her heart sings. 'Ajji!'

'My heart.' Her voice a weak whisper. 'Am I dreaming?'

'No, Ajji,' Bindu reassures her, although she too feels as if she's in a fantastic dream. She takes her grandmother's hand, deposits soft kisses on Ajji's face, feeling the happiest since she moved here.

'Where are we?' Ajji asks.

And taking a deep breath, Bindu tells her.

The doctor comes to check on Ajji and pronounces her 'as well as can be expected, under the circumstances. She still needs treatment, mind you. I shall look in on her every other day.'

Sunitha is exultant, she and Ajji chatting away, wiping each other's tears when Sunitha tells her of her mother's passing.

. . .

That evening, after Bindu's socialising duties are done, and before
Guru is due to visit, when Bindu rushes in to see her grandmother,
a part of her wanting reassurance that she wasn't dreaming, that
her grandmother truly is returned to her, Ajji pats the space
beside her. 'Come, I need to talk to you, my heart.'

She cups Bindu's face and Bindu is overwhelmed by love and
gratitude. Oh, how she's missed Ajji's touch.

'You gave up your scholarship.' Ajji's voice is sad.

'Yes.'

Ajji's eyes shine with tears.

'But I have all this,' Bindu tries, but Ajji sees right through
her.

'You're not happy, are you, my heart?'

'I...'

'Does he hit you?'

'No.'

'Hurt you?'

Does he? *Yes.* 'With words. He has a temper.'

'But not physically?'

'No.'

'He respected your wishes and married you rather than
keeping you as mistress...'

'Yes.'

'I sense a but,' Ajji, always perceptive, says.

Bindu takes a deep breath. Should she tell Ajji?

'My heart, what's bothering you?' Ajji prompts, once again
intuiting her thoughts.

And Bindu, in a breathless gush, unburdens her soul. 'I've no
agency, no voice. I dreamed of being independent, self-sufficient,
of not relying on anyone. I wanted to make a difference, to matter.
Instead, I'm doing nothing, feeling my brain erode more every
day. I'm banned from reading, from making intelligent conversation, from doing anything at all.' She sounds like a sulky child, she
knows, but she cannot help it. She's finally giving vent to the
miasma of resentment and anger festering inside of her. 'I want to

do something useful, Ajji, instead of pandering to the same group of spoilt rich women, none of whom like each other, delivering barbed compliments behind fake smiles.'

'Ah, my heart.' Ajji sighs. 'Do you remember the village women coming to me for potions for their bruises and to stop them having children as their husbands would come home drunk, beat them black and blue and force themselves on them?'

'Yes.'

'They'd no choice in the matter. They were given away by their parents as soon as they came of age to the first man who offered for them, never mind if he was three times their age, twice widowed, an abusive drunk. That's what your fate would have been if you weren't beautiful, or smart, if you hadn't won the scholarship.'

'But I rescinded the scholarship.'

'I know, my heart, and I'm sorry. But what I'm trying to say is that you had the option of another life. Most women of our ilk don't. And poverty... It's terrible. Soul-destroying.'

'I know.'

'I know you do, which is why you worked so hard to win that scholarship. Most women in our society, even the rich ones, don't have that opportunity, the possibility of a different life. They must marry the man their parents choose for them. Growing up, they've no choice but to do as their parents ask and, after marriage, as their husbands say. Rich or poor, husbands can be brutal. If they're not, you're lucky.' Ajji is looking at Bindu with all the love in the world, her gaze tender. 'What I'm saying, my heart, not very well – this illness has muddled my brain – is that women don't often have options. You're lucky that you did. The boy you used to meet when you were bunking off school and defying the villagers...' Ajji's eyes twinkle.

'You knew about that?' Bindu asks. The villagers and nuns had conspired to protect Ajji from Bindu's transgressions, but...

'Nothing much escapes me, my heart.'

Bindu is surprised into laughter.

Ajji chuckles along too, which morphs into the cough that would make Dumdee...

Bindu sees her pain and loss reflected in Ajji's eyes. She squeezes her grandmother's hand.

'Sunitha said that he's happy where he is.' Ajji's eyes are shining.

'I miss him, though.'

'I do too.' Ajji takes a breath. Then, 'Anyway, what I was saying is that you escaping school paid off, for, being the spirited girl that I love, you impressed the landlord's son.'

'Yes.' The word is weighted with Bindu's disappointment, her frustration. Impressing the landlord's son hasn't been the boon her grandmother implies. Ajji of course picks up on what Bindu's not saying. 'You're here now, *this* is your life.'

'I don't agree with the landlord's—'

'My heart, the landlord is old, and ill with it. Guru will take over soon and you've influence over him. I hear from Sunitha that you've already made a difference in the village through him. The landlord pardoned a month's rent upon your marriage to Guru and the workers in the textile mills are being paid the same for working fewer hours *and* he's employed more people, thus providing jobs for those farmers affected by the drought.'

'How did they—'

'Oh, they know it's all your doing. Word was that the landlord was bent upon increasing the hours of work with no increase in pay. Then you marry Guru and, suddenly, the landlord executes an about-turn alongside pardoning the villagers' rent.' Ajji's face is radiant with love. 'You say you want to make a difference. My heart, you already have. You sacrificed your dreams to save me. That's impressed the villagers; so too has the landlord bringing about changes he would never have before. I know you, my heart, you'll make the best of this situation. You already are and you'll continue to make even more of a difference to the villagers, our fellows.'

And now, Bindu, instead of fixating on what's holding her back, all the things she *can't* do, looks at her situation through Ajji's eyes. 'I will,' she vows.

'So, you see' – Ajji smiles – 'you missed out on the scholarship, but you're still changing lives for the better, including – especially

– mine. I don't want for anything. I've all the food and water I need, the best medical care. I am ensconced in luxury, resting my tired bones, a woman of leisure.'

Bindu smiles. She might've given up the scholarship but she *has* done for Ajji what she hoped – liberated her grandmother from a life of struggle, so she can live out her last years in comfort.

'My heart' – Ajji's voice is tender – 'you may not become a doctor, but in your own way you are, and will continue to save lives of those who matter to you and me. The villagers hailed me as someone who could be relied on to always help those in need and expect nothing in return. And now, instead of railing against you, crying that you're the devil's spawn, bad luck personified...' And seeing Bindu's expression, 'Oh yes, I knew about that too. In any case, Sunitha tells me they've changed their tune.'

'Have they?'

'Now they declare that you're your Ajji's granddaughter – kind and wonderful and giving.' Ajji chortles and coughs and Bindu gently rubs her grandmother's back until her fit passes, her mind fired up, working furiously as she thinks of ways she can help make more of a difference to the villagers.

Reading her mind as she's always been able to do, Ajji cups Bindu's cheek and beams at her, her gaze aglow with love and pride.

CHAPTER 41

BINDU

A few weeks after her talk with Ajji, Guru pays Bindu a visit mid-afternoon. 'We've been invited to the Resident's summer ball. Wear the gold sari I gifted you last week.'

'You're taking me?' Bindu's surprised. The landlord doesn't approve of parties where women are allowed to mingle with men and so, since her marriage to Guru, while she's had to socialise endlessly as part of her duties as the landlord's heir's wife, they've all been gatherings where the women are segregated from the men. 'Defying your father?'

'Do you want to come or not?' Guru snaps.

'You're finally growing a backbone then, now he's bedridden and cannot police you. Better late than never, I suppose.' The words are out before she can take them back, although, after talking with Ajji, she's decided she'll be more canny and less impulsive to get what she wants.

Predictably, in response to her outspokenness – the very quality that Guru used to like before their marriage – her husband's eyes flash dangerously.

'What?' she says, again not able to help herself. 'Touched a nerve, did I?'

'Bindu' – his jaw works furiously – 'don't provoke me.'

'I specialise in provoking you,' she retorts. 'And I recall you used to like it.'

'We leave in an hour. Don't be late,' Guru says tightly before walking away.

Afterwards, on their way back, 'You were wonderful.' He beams.

And Bindu sends a little prayer of thanks to Ajji in her head. For, after the rocky start, when Guru had ignored her all the way to the Resident's ball for her needling him about defying his father, she'd decided to implement Ajji's advice.

'Ajji, I hate having to sit with those spoilt rich women while they make thinly veiled references to my humble roots. It gets to me that I've to listen to them put me down, and grumble about their servants, and can say nothing, for otherwise they'll complain to the landlord,' Bindu had moaned.

'My heart,' Ajji had said, smiling, cupping Bindu's cheek with her gnarled palm. 'You're direct, which is well and good. But to get your way with these women, and with your husband, you must learn to be subtle. Be nice, be kind always. Praise them. Appear to agree with them while quietly pushing your own agenda.'

'But—'

'When they complain about their servants, smile sweetly and say, lightly, "Oh, I never have that problem. Even though they resent me for daring to aspire above my class and succeeding..."' Ajji had chuckled at Bindu's expression, her mirth morphing into a cough. When she'd stopped coughing: 'Yes, my heart, these women skirt around the topic, try to shame you, so *you* bring it up, own it, show that far from being ashamed, you're proud...'

'But I'm not,' Bindu had cried. 'I hate that I'm one of them.'

'You should be proud of what you did, my heart, of where you are. For you did it out of love. For me. *I'm* proud of you.' And, her eyes shining, 'Anyway, where was I? Oh yes, say to them, "My servants resent me, but they do as I say." Stop there and smile placidly at them and wait for their questions.' Ajji had chuckled and coughed again, and when the fit had passed: 'For they won't be able to help themselves. And then, you beckon them closer and whisper, as if you're sharing a great secret, "I reward them with more food, more breaks, other small gifts and sanctions that I won't miss but will make a world of difference to them. And this way, they're loyal, they do anything I ask of them.'" Ajji had smiled fondly at Bindu. 'This'll work, I promise you. And this way, you're tricking them into being kinder to their servants.'

And it *has* worked, Bindu having applied it at the parties she's attended since her talk with Ajji. The women are easier with her now, and Bindu, while not quite enjoying the parties, is able to endure them, for it engages her brain to direct the conversation subtly, to take charge in such a way as to give the other women the impression *they* are in charge.

And now, Ajji's advice with regards to Guru appears to have worked too.

'With your husband too, appear to do what he wants, all the while getting him to do what you want,' Ajji had said. 'I assure you this will work better than your forthrightness...'

'He liked it when he was wooing me. It's one of the reasons he asked me to marry him,' Bindu had protested.

'Suitors like a girl with spirit. Husbands, on the other hand, want a meek and dutiful wife.'

'Don't I know it,' Bindu had grumbled.

'My heart, I'm not saying your direct manner is wrong but, with husbands, tact is essential. Their ego needs to be nursed. You must rein in your temper no matter the provocation, use charm instead of fury. The trick is to put forth your opinion in such a way as to make them think it's what they meant all along.'

'But you talked too much at the table,' Guru is saying. 'You must watch that.'

Bindu bites her lip to stop her retort from escaping, like she's done several times over the course of the evening. *See, Ajji, I'm learning.*

'Some of your points were quite good,' Guru acknowledges magnanimously.

I bet they were the ones where I backed you up.

Sure enough – 'We make a good team.' Guru's voice is puffed

with self-importance. 'Everyone said so. "Your wife is not only easy on the eye but intelligent too. She complements you perfectly in looks and mind. Don't hide her away, old chap, bring her along to more of our dos. As a pair, you're formidable." These were the Resident's exact words,' Guru crows.

And again, Bindu thinks, *Ajji, how right you were. How wise.* Out loud, she says, eyebrows raised, 'So, can I expect to accompany you to more parties where women are allowed to mingle with the men?' If it wasn't for Ajji's words of caution at the forefront of her mind, she'd have asked, instead, 'Does this mean you'll defy your father more?'

In response to her diplomatically worded question, Guru smiles at her instead of snapping or cutting her down. 'Yes. But, as I said, perhaps don't talk quite so much.'

Make no points of my own, instead just back up yours, you mean. Be dutiful but not original. Don't think for myself but agree with all your thoughts and opinions.

'Your father won't be happy when this gets back to him, if it hasn't already. And he definitely won't be pleased if you take me along to more of these gatherings,' she says, testing the waters.

'It's time he realised I'm going to take over and that I do things differently.'

Ah, Ajji, you were right again. He's willing to stand up to his father if he thinks I'm supporting him. Now that Guru is not quite so in thrall to his father, Bindu risks being arch. 'That wasn't the tune you were singing, as I recall.'

Guru sighs and smiles, both at once. 'All right, I admit I was giving in to him rather a lot...'

'All the time,' Bindu mumbles and he laughs.

'Have it your way. But it was just after the stroke, when he was hell-bent on micromanaging all things pertaining to the business. Now he's conceded that he needs to take a step back.'

'Is he going to retire?' Bindu asks, hearing Ajji's words in her head: 'My heart, the landlord is old, and ill with it. Guru will take over soon and you've influence over him.' When Ajji had said this, Bindu had doubted her grandmother on both counts. The land-lord was still reigning supreme from his sickbed and his son wasn't the boy who'd been smitten with Bindu but a husband quick to anger and cut.

'That's what he's promised,' Guru is saying. 'Whether he'll really do so is another matter. That stroke scared him.'

'He's still blaming me?'

'Vehemently so. But I feel like the luckiest man alive to be taking home the loveliest woman in a room full of society beauties this evening.'

'Only in the room?'

He laughs, eyes twinkling, and, after what feels like forever, she's in harmony with her husband. It's like when they used to spar verbally in the village during indolent, spice- and dust-laden afternoons.

'You're looking especially beautiful right now, your face silhouetted by moonlight.'

'What moonlight? There's barely even any starlight. You're no poet, Guru,' she teases.

'I never claimed to be one, although your beauty inspires poetry.'

'Ah, stop.'

Darkness streaks past the windows, greeting the navy awning of sky, which gushes with radiant tributes of stars. Yellow light pools on the road from the lamps of the car and it feels to Bindu that the ginger-and-musk solidity of her husband is the only real thing in the world.

'Can I kiss you?'

'That depends...' she says, thinking of Ajji's words: 'I know you, my heart, you'll make the best of this situation. You already are and you'll continue to make even more of a difference to the villagers, our fellows.'

'Oh, Bindu, now what?' Guru sighs, not so much with irritation as with desire.

'The villagers'll soon be facing drought again. An irrigation system would—'

'Bindu, I can't in all honesty justify—'

'Three wells then and a water tank. They won't cost much and they'll make a huge difference.'

'I'll talk to my father.'

'You don't need to talk to your father. Like you just said, you've basically taken over.'

'I haven't *yet*. And you know how everything is an uphill battle with him.'

'This battle is worth fighting. It's water for your tenants who'll otherwise die of thirst. You can come up with something that'll sway him. Didn't you, after all, win the battle of marrying me against his wishes?' She bats her eyelashes at him.

'That was different. This—'

'Well then, it's a no to the kiss and anything else that might lead from it.'

'You're my wife.' A schoolboy whine.

'So, are you going to force me then?'

'Bindu, don't...'

'You'll be making a difference to several lives. *I* will be in your debt.'

'For how long?' Eyes bright with interest.

'A week.'

'Only a week? For three wells and a water tank.'

'Two weeks then.'

'Three.' A hint of a smile, reflected in the twinkle in his eyes.

'Three.' And Bindu, while experiencing a sense of accomplishment, is also disappointed at how easy it is to manipulate her husband with wiles that don't come easy to her, following Ajji's advice to broker deals for the greater good.

CHAPTER 42

BINDU

The work on the wells and water tank begins. The newspapers applaud the landlord's generosity.

'You're a miracle worker!' Sunitha throws her arms round Bindu, but not before making sure the door is shut first and the other maids do not bear witness to this blatant crossing of boundaries, one of them on such intimate terms with the mistress of the house. 'We'll have water even during the drought! Thank you, Memsahib.'

Ajji cups Bindu's face in her palm. 'That's my girl,' she says, glowing.

And through it all, unbeknownst to Ajji, Bindu continues to write to Mr Elliot, with only Sunitha party to her subterfuge. With every letter, she feels she's reclaiming the part of her that she lost when she gave up the scholarship.

After a month of back and forth with Mr Elliot, his letter arrives with her payment – crisp notes, money all her own! – and a copy of his magazine: *The Sentinel*.

After weeks of no reading material, to hold an actual magazine packed with articles in her hands is a blessing, a gift, sheer joy and celebration. The cover depicts a fan fashioned from peacock feathers, arranged on a coffee table. Classy yet compelling. Even though the photograph is in black and white, the beauty of the image is such that Bindu's imagination supplies a host of iridescent sapphire and emerald gold eyes winking against the burnished wood.

She opens the magazine: contents listed on the first page, with a small insert featuring those involved in the publication of the magazine.

Editor: L. Elliot.

She glances at the contents with honey-sweet anticipation.

Editorial notes. News in brief. Features on art, politics, sport, home decor. A fiction section featuring a short story. Advertisements. Indian cookery – page 22.

She'll read all the features at her leisure, but first...

Hands shaking, it takes her a few tries to open the magazine to the relevant page.

And there is her very first recipe.

How to make sambar (spicy mixed vegetable soup)
Recipe for spice mix and sambar provided by Mrs Ramraj

She runs her hands over the printed words, her Ajji's recipe with some flourishes of her own, now being tried out by this magazine's readers. Bindu's notes, her suggestions on what works best and what could be used instead, have also been printed alongside, word for word.

The recipe blurs before her eyes, choked as she is by emotion.

'Not crying again!' Sunitha sighs.

Bindu cannot speak, so she points at the magazine and Sunitha peers over her shoulder.

'You're not making me read English, are you? I thought I'd left that punishment behind when I left school,' Sunitha grumbles, squinting as she carefully mouths the English words. Then she gasps, clapping a hand over her mouth: 'Memsahib, it's... *your* recipe?'

'Yes.' Bindu's voice is wet.

'Did you also supply the photograph? From where?'

And, at this, Bindu's attention, until now upon her words, is captured by the photograph accompanying the recipe. A dish of sambar dotted with vegetables, a bowl of rice beside it adorned by a hibiscus flower. As with the cover, although the image is in black and white, the skill of the photographer invokes the turmeric gold of the curry, the contrast of the crimson hibiscus petals with the fluffy white grains of rice and the glossy vermilion sambar. Bindu can almost smell its zesty aroma, taste its mellow spiciness, visualise the steam rising off it. It brings to mind pounding spices with Ajji in the courtyard, shelling tamarind, grating coconut under the mango trees, parrots screeching above, Sirsi snoozing on the well surround, Dumdee asleep at their feet, nose twitching and tail swishing when flies dared alight upon either, hot air flavoured with grit and drunk on ripe cashew caressing their cheeks. 'I didn't send the photo, just the recipe.' Bindu's voice is soft with awe.

'He must've taken it himself,' Sunitha exults.

By publishing her recipe, this journalist has – in addition to, in some small way, helping her to realise her dream of independence – provided her with a tangible legacy of sun-drenched golden childhood days with Ajji.

'Don't you want to show it to your Ajji?' Sunitha asks, eyebrows raised.

'I... I'd rather not.'

'Because she'd tell you not to jeopardise what you have,' Sunitha says, not looking at Bindu, pretending to polish the dresser. 'This is well and good, Memsahib, but if you're caught, can't you see how it'll look?'

'It's a recipe in a magazine, Sunitha. It's harmless.' Isn't it?

Bindu negotiates with Guru on behalf of the villagers but this... her correspondence with Mr Elliot, being published in his magazine and getting paid for it, is something just for her. With one snag – the name accompanying the recipe is hers, but not. Mrs Ramraj. Guru's name. The landlord's name. She hates being defined by her husband, linked to his father, especially when this is *nothing* to do with them. In fact, if it wasn't for Mr Elliot, her dishes would be forgotten, relegated to Bindu's memory. Her past identity as cook is, for all intents and purposes, effectively over-written by who she has become. Except for this journalist who's trying to keep it alive.

But, more than that – and she hates to admit this, even to herself – for all her bluster to Sunitha, her rebellion against the strictures of this life, it scares her, her husband's name in print for all to see. She hadn't considered this. Surely no one will make the connection, join the dots back to her? In any case, she resolves to ask Mr Elliot, in her next letter, to use a pseudonym. Perhaps Mrs R? Or, A Devoted Cook? Yes, that'll do.

'Memsahib, do you really want to pursue this?' Sunitha is saying. 'You're putting all the good work you're doing in jeopardy. It's like when you'd run away from school.'

'That worked fine.'

'Did it?' Sunitha raises an eyebrow, her gaze censorious. 'Something in you wants to make trouble when everything is going smoothly. And there's so much more at stake here. Not only all this' – Sunitha waves her hand around the opulent room – 'but the difference you're making to so many lives.'

Bindu's had enough. All her joy leached from her by Sunitha's lecture. More so because she knows there's truth in it but she doesn't want to acknowledge it. And so, 'Don't you have work to do, Sunitha?' she says, tightly.

'I'll shut up, Memsahib, but let me just say this: you're playing with fire. Beware. You might get burned.'

'I'll take my chances,' she bites out, even as a voice inside her warns: *She's right. She's a good friend. You're risking everything, like you'd risk being suspended and losing the chance to win the scholarship at school, and for what? What happened to turning over a new leaf, playing the long game, taking Ajji's advice?*

She impetuously ignores the caution of her conscience as she has Sunitha and storms into the garden, taking refuge on the bench under the palm trees.

When Bindu reads the magazine from cover to cover, she discovers that Mr Elliot is, in addition to being the publisher and editor, a great writer besides. His editorial is thought-provoking and perfectly judged. The short story that appears in the fiction section is his too – and it's thoroughly absorbing.

It touches her that this man, with his beautiful gift of words, has printed hers.

Afterwards, she hides the magazine and the money – *her* money, half of which she's decided she'll give Sunitha for her part in all this when they've resolved their tiff – at the back of her wardrobe, with her meagre possessions.

Thank you so very much, she writes in her reply to Mr Elliot.

It was a real privilege to see my grandmother's recipe, with minor embellishes from me, in print. She taught me to cook, imparted to me the joy of mixing the right ingredients together to create magic, feed people, show our love for them in this way. I may not cook any more, and I miss it greatly, but knowing that my Ajji's recipes are inspiring others to cook is gratifying.

I loved the photograph accompanying the recipe. The sambar looked just like the one Ajji and I used to cook together on our hearth. It's a visual reminder of our time in the village where I grew up – I have many happy memories there.

Thank you very kindly for the generous payment, Sir. It is greatly appreciated.

I have one request. Please, henceforth, instead of printing my name, could the recipes be published as contributed by 'A Devoted Cook'?

The magazine itself is so beautiful – I love the title and the cover is so inviting. I enjoyed reading every single article and I'm humbled to have my recipe featured alongside such informative articles.

And, may I say, Sir, that, in my humble opinion, your writing is exquisite and thought-provoking with it. I especially liked what you said in your editorial column about freedom and the meaning of it, personal freedom and the freedom of a country, a people. With

Indians fighting for freedom from British rule and with Hindus and Muslims increasingly divided, with communal riots and nationalism, and in the wider world, the threat of war in Europe, it's a very timely piece. I liked how you put forward an impartial yet considered argument.

I also very much enjoyed your short story. You're a man of many facets, Mr Elliot – writing compelling articles about the political situation internationally and here in India and wonderfully light-hearted fiction too, plus also editing and publishing a magazine. I have to say the ending of your short story was a little ambiguous for my liking. I like my stories to have a definite, preferably happy, ending. But yours was very clever, true to life. For, in real life, there's no well-defined happy ending, is there? Life goes on, we meander through, don't we? And then we die – a sad ending if ever there was one. Your story made me think – which was the point, I gather. You wanted the reader to arrive at their own conclusion.

And then, before she can stop herself.

I feel so proud to know you. You with all your words and you've published mine! Thank you.

I'm sorry I have gone on, rather. I'll stop now.

Here's my recipe for green masala chicken spice mix and curry...

His reply, a week later:

Thank you for your letter and for the recipe for green masala chicken. It sounds absolutely divine. And yes, of course, Mrs Ramraj, henceforth the recipes will be printed as shared by 'A Devoted Cook'.

I'm thrilled that you were happy with your sambar recipe in printed form. I'm especially gratified that the photograph accompanying it met with your approval. It took me several tries before the

sambar I made looked as good as it tasted. And it took an entire
roll of film to make it look inviting on camera. Not your recipe's
fault by any measure but that of an inexperienced cook and novice
photographer.

Bindu pauses in her reading. *He* cooked it? Never in all her
years has she come across a man willing to cook, and to be seemingly accomplished at it, despite his humble exhortations. Mr
Elliot is a man of many talents.

I warmly appreciate your kind words about the magazine and,
especially, about my writing. I've very much enjoyed your astute
observations. I'm crafting a new story now and will take your
opinion on board.

Colour floods to her cheeks as she clutches the letter to her
heart, which swells as it dwells on his words: *will take your opinion*
on board. After she sealed the letter, she'd worried that perhaps
she'd been too open, said too much. But: *I've very much enjoyed your*
astute observations...

She throws her head to the dark green canopy above, criss-
crossed with gold, and smiles. She has escaped, once again, to the
courtyard with his letter, reading it while reclining on the bench
camouflaged by palm trees, fronds depositing green caresses
alongside bursts of baked earth and ripe jackfruit-flavoured
breeze, fountain gurgling, silver blue, gilded rays filtering through
the palms, glittering her hot cheeks with sprays of golden dazzle.

She tries to picture Mr Elliot, but he's just an impression of
height and kindness, and all she can envision are his eyes, twinkling bright green as ears of paddy singing in the rain.

Mrs Ramraj, if you'll permit my saying so, you write very well. I
look forward to the vignettes that you provide with each recipe
almost more than the recipe itself. When you described pounding
the spices for your green masala chicken under the mango and
tamarind and guava trees in the courtyard of your childhood
home, I could picture it all – your dog warning the cat off, the

gritty breeze spiced with earth, parrots screeching above you, the smoke of the hearth adding to the flavour of the curry.

The feedback from readers to your sambar recipe has been over-whelmingly positive – every one of them wrote to say that the recipe worked beautifully, that it was delicious and easy to prepare and that they especially liked the notes accompanying it. I look forward to their reaction when your chicken recipe is published.

In my humble opinion, Mrs Ramraj, along with cooking, you also have the gift of words.

She closes her eyes, touched beyond measure. Hears Sister Hilda's words after reading a story Bindu had composed upon her slate: 'Shame this'll have to be rubbed out. It's very good, Bindu. I rather think you've the makings of a writer.'

If you do try your hand at writing, that is – if you haven't already, of course – we're always looking for contributors to the magazine.

As what he's saying sinks in, she is overwhelmed, his words blurring, her whole being aglow. He's suggesting that, in addition to her recipes, he's happy to consider her writing for one of the other slots!

Corresponding with this man affords Bindu the same heady buzz as when she attended school, opening possibilities, giving her hope.

The next day, watching Sunitha go about her work, humming as she dusts, her anklets chiming a unique tune, keeping time with her limp as she carries water into the bathroom, the germ of the idea Bindu woke up with takes a life of its own as a poem in her notebook.

There had been tension between them after Sunitha warned Bindu about writing to Mr Elliot, but Sunitha's nature was such that she couldn't sulk or nurture a grudge, and on the third day, she'd come up to Bindu and said, 'I hate this, Memsahib, can we be friends again?'

'We always were, Sunitha, and always will be. You can speak your mind with me.'

Sunitha squeezed Bindu's hand, eyes shining. 'I'm so lucky in you.'

'It's the other way round.'

Sunitha laughed, happy relief.

Bindu composes a reply to Mr Elliot:

Thank you for your kind words. They've given me the confidence to start writing in earnest – stories, poems, little snippets. I'm not ready to share them with you yet, but I've discovered that I enjoy the process of writing very much indeed. I thank you greatly – without your encouragement, I would never have chanced upon this wonderful habit that brings me joy and fulfilment.

Mr Elliot, I cannot believe you try out my recipes yourself! I've never come across a man who's willing and happy to cook – is there no end to your talents?

Mr Elliot's response, a week later, does not disappoint.

It gives me a great deal of pleasure that I've inspired you to start writing. I understand your reluctance to share your efforts with me – I speak from personal experience when I say that there is no greater critic of their work than the writer themselves. But believe me, Mrs Ramraj, I don't think you need to worry on that score. I edit work from experienced writers and amateurs alike, and from what I've sampled of your writing in the vignettes that accompany your recipes, I believe that it's very good. I'll wait to read your work when you're ready to share it with me. And even if you never do, that's all right. What matters is that you enjoy doing it.

As always with Mr Elliot's words, Bindu is touched. He knows just what to say to boost her confidence, bolster her belief in herself just as it's in danger of flagging. She had reread one of her very first stories before his letter came and thought it was rubbish. Why was she even bothering? But after reading his latest missive, once she picks up her pencil and opens her notebook, the words arrive as if they were waiting just for this. It's like when she'd pick up the onion that was on its last legs or walk around the vegetable patch plucking the drooping sprigs of coriander, the flagging mint thirsty for rain, and she'd be floored by the compulsion to cook, a recipe arriving in her head. And this man – he *understands*.

She returns her attention to his letter.

And yes, I cook. I live alone and have become accustomed to fending for myself. I suppose I could employ a maid, but I've always valued my independence a bit too much.

Bindu experiences a shaft of envy. She'd wanted to be independent too. She'd fancied a life like this man's, where she'd fend for herself, make her own way in the world, relying on nobody but herself.

In fact, I've rather shocked society here by eschewing help. I must say, I've begun to quite enjoy cooking. Although, when I try out your recipes, I do sometimes wish you were there in person to show me how to do certain steps – for example, are the onions golden enough, has the spice mix fried enough, is it supposed to smell smoky or is it burnt?

Bindu smiles at that even as she has a sudden vision of herself cooking alongside this man whose features she cannot quite recall, but whom she considers, in her heart, her friend.

CHAPTER 43

EVE

1980

After waving goodbye to Maya, Eve comes back into the silent house, but now the silence has a different quality. It's no longer pungent, pickled in grief. There is sorrow, but there's also *life* in the debris scattered round the kitchen, the chocolate-covered knife, the cereal bowl on the table, Maya's belongings scattered around. The house echoes with a child's recent occupation. It is busy, purposeful. It has lost its mournful air.

You're being fanciful, Eve tells herself, shaking her head.

She calls the school, just to check that Maya's arrived safely. She knows more than anyone what can happen during an ordinary journey, what can go wrong.

'Shall I walk with you?' she'd asked Maya.

But, 'I've been walking on my own to and from school since I turned ten. Mum lets me.' Maya sounded so proud of her independence that Eve didn't insist. And she was a coward, a part of her grateful that she could postpone braving the road where her daughter and husband had lost their lives until later.

'Yes, she's here. She's all right. A bit wobbly but all right,' Miss Aldridge informs her.

Eve sets the phone down and, filled with a sense of purpose, does a recce of the kitchen cupboards. She usually makes do with the groceries Sue brings – she's been eating to live, taking no pleasure from it, whatever's easiest, sandwiches mostly.

But now she has a child to feed.

Izzy had always been 'absolutely *starving*, Mama,' when she got home from school and she knows Maya will be too.

There's nothing else for it: she needs to do a grocery shop.

The local shop, run by Mrs Lewes, is, thankfully, in the opposite direction to where the accident happened. Eve will have no choice but to pass the spot this evening on the way to the hospital – the bus stop is right there. But, for now, she's spared.

Walking down the street for the first time since the accident is not as daunting as she expected. She keeps her head down, tries to think of nothing at all, and her feet take her by rote to the shop she'd frequent almost daily in another life.

The spring sun on her face is a blessing and she thinks, *Why didn't I do this earlier?*

Mrs Lewes beams when the bell above the door announces Eve by clanging a merry tune. 'Nice to see you back, Mrs Snow.'

Oh, the irony of that moniker! Joe is gone. But she's still his wife and Izzy's mother.

She manages a smile for Mrs Lewes. 'Thank you.' The woman is being kind, although she hadn't given Eve the warmest reception when she and Joe had moved in.

Once again, her feet lead the way, taking her to the requisite aisles of their own accord, her hands picking up the things she'd usually get for Izzy.

'I heard you took on the little girl next door. Good of you,' Mrs Lewes says as she bags up Eve's groceries.

They live in the biggest city in England and yet here, in their slice of it, news travels fast.

'Just until her mother gets better,' she says, thinking, *And you will, Jenny*.

'Good of you all the same,' Mrs Lewes declares, handing Eve her bag.

CHAPTER 44

BINDU

1938

'Bindu, what is this I hear?' Guru is annoyed.

'What is it you've heard?'

'The servants we employ are paid generously to work, not sit around wasting time.'

'They're not wasting their time. They're learning. I'm teaching them to read and write in English.'

Writing to Mr Elliot has allowed Bindu to find herself again and she's decided that she'll share with the servants the freedom and pleasure that reading and writing affords her. When she writes, she can process what she's feeling, whether it is through the medium of journal entries, poems or short stories (although she's still not brave enough to share them with Mr Elliot), and when she reads, she has access to different, wonderful places and events. She wants the servants to experience this too.

Ajji reminded her often, especially when Bindu was feeling fed up with the direction her life had taken, that the poor had few options, that they didn't have the luxury of choice, or the time to ruminate on how their lives had turned out. Bindu has decided that she'll try to provide them with the means to escape, briefly, into different worlds when their own gets overwhelming. This way, she'll be making good use of the time when she's not socialising.

She has co-opted Sunitha as her (reluctant) assistant. 'If I'd known this was what I'd have to do, I'd never have come to work for you,' Sunitha tutted when Bindu floated her idea, but she was smiling.

'Why're you doing this? Is it your mission to anger my father?' Guru asks now.

The landlord keeps making noises about retiring, but he's still reigning strong from his bedside.

'My world doesn't revolve around your father, like yours does,' Bindu snaps. She tries hard to follow Ajji's advice and be tactful with her husband, but at times her impetuous nature wrestles back control.

'But you're keeping the servants from their work.'

'Surely you and your father can spare them for an hour each day?'

'If you teach them English, they'll get ideas above their station.'

'That's the point.'

'They'll leave for other jobs.'

'Good for them.'

'How will we manage if they all leave?'

'I personally think you and your father keep far too many staff and we'll be perfectly fine with a quarter of—'

'Bindu!'

'But, if necessary, we can always employ others. There're so many who'd be grateful for the opportunity.'

'Who'll also leave once they've mastered English if you persist in doing this.'

She can see her husband getting frustrated, about to lose his temper, and *now* she employs the tact and caution Ajji preaches. She goes up to him, takes his hands in hers. 'Is it so bad, Guru, if their prospects widen? If their life, instead of being narrow and one-dimensional, opens a bit? Learning to read and write gives them access to so many worlds. Yes, they might use their new-found knowledge to secure better jobs and leave here, but equally they might not. Instead, they might just glean pleasure from a story. A poem.'

His gaze softens. 'This one, by Elizabeth Barrett Browning, is my favourite: "How do I love thee?",' he says, reciting the opening and kissing her.

Afterwards, she says, 'I was thinking—'

'Do you have to?' He sighs.

'We cook far too much every day, Guru, and I've heard from questioning the servants that a lot of food is wasted…'

'Are you teaching them, or quizzing them on what goes on behind the scenes here?'

'We're conversing in English!'

He smiles. 'Go on, what were you thinking?'

'So, the food that's left over each day, why don't we distribute it among the villagers?'

'That *is* a good idea. I don't know why I didn't think of it.'

She refrains from pointing out that she'd floated a similar idea before (perhaps not quite so diplomatically) and he'd vetoed it. 'Say that again.'

He appears confused. 'I said, I don't know why I didn't—'

'No, the other bit, where you acknowledged that your wife always comes up with the best ideas.'

He's laughing even as he kisses her again, Bindu joining in his mirth, kissing him back, happy that she's finally managed to put the wastage that has irked her here at the mansion since she moved in to good use, for the villagers' benefit.

CHAPTER 45

BINDU

'That was fun, wasn't it?' Bindu asks.

They're returning from a party hosted by Captain Lennox, first cousin of the Resident, and while these events are more enjoyable now Bindu uses them to her advantage, Guru is uncharacteristically subdued.

'You're quiet,' she says.

A muscle works in his jaw. 'Perhaps my father has a point when he insists upon segregating men and women.' Moonlight highlights the rigid planes of his face, the scowl marring his features. 'Who was that man you were dancing with?'

'Ah, so *that's* what's—'

He grips her arm in a vice.

'That *hurts*, Guru.' She pulls away and he lets go.

But he brings his face very close to hers, his breath pungent with alcohol and jealousy. 'Who was he?'

'You know perfectly well. The colonel.'

'He was flirting with you.'

'That's all it was, a mild flirtation.'

'So, you agree.'

'I'm married to you. I'm coming home with you.'

'His gaze followed you all night.'

'That's not my problem.'

'You're not accompanying me again.' His voice tight.

'Ah, so you'll keep me prisoner.'

'If I have to.'

And now she loses her temper, and, with it, all intent of following Ajji's advice. 'You're behaving like your father.'

'Don't bring my father into this.'

'You like it when they compliment you on your wife, say I'm intelligent and charming.'

'I don't like it when they flirt with you. Look at you as if they want to devour you. Dance with you, their hands on your body.'

'Tough,' she says coolly, turning away.

He grabs her arm again, tighter, turns her round roughly to face him. 'Remember *I'm* the one paying for your Ajji's ongoing treatment. The one helping your villagers. The one who negotiates with my father and placates him on your behalf, allowing you to get away with teaching the servants and your other mad schemes.'

'They're not mad...'

'Without me, you're *nothing*.'

Tears prick her eyes. She'll not let them fall. She thinks of Mr Elliot, her published recipes, the money she has tucked away. Now, there are twelve magazines featuring Bindu and Ajji's recipes, each with Bindu's little notes about how they came about, reprinted word for word, and accompanied by Mr Elliot's glorious photographs. They're hidden in the secret nook at the back of Bindu's closet, in the bag with half the money she's earned – the other half she gives to Sunitha for her help in supplying Bindu with envelopes and stamps, posting the letters and collecting replies – and the few things she'd salvaged from the hut she once shared with Ajji, so meagre and falling apart and precious; relics of her life before this one.

I've something that is mine alone.

'Why're you smiling?' Guru yells.

He kisses her hard.

She struggles away from his grasp. But he grabs her harder, pulls her closer, kisses her again.

'You are mine. You will not flirt with anyone again. If you do,

I'll stop your Ajji's treatment, put an end to all your schemes for helping the villagers and the servants. Remember, I've given generously, but I can just as quickly take it all away.'

She sobs in Ajji's arms. 'I was just beginning to relax with him, think he's all right, and then he does this.'

'He cares. And he doesn't know how to show it. He's never learned to show affection,' Ajji says, gently stroking Bindu's hair.

'That *wasn't* affection,' Bindu cries.

'No, it was jealousy,' Ajji confirms.

'I hate him,' Bindu rages. 'I hate him, hate him, hate him.'

When she finally falls asleep, she dreams of the village women.

'He kissed you without your consent? Told you he owns you? So what?' they say. 'He's your husband, that's what they do. What did you expect? You're lucky he didn't take it further,' they cry. 'Our husbands beat us ruthlessly, mapping their frustrations, their anger at their lot in life, upon us with their fists, their feet, their bodies. Some of us have delivered at least a couple of children before we reached your age, and do you think that was with our consent? You've seen us come to your grandmother for medicinal pastes to alleviate our pain, soothe our bruises. We've begged her for something – anything – to stop us getting pregnant yet again as there's nothing worse than your children who you've grown in your womb looking at you with hungry eyes, dehydrated bodies, begging for a drink, for sustenance you cannot provide. You won't have to watch your starving children lap up the dirty, bug- and silt-ridden lake water during the drought and catch diseases, wither and die a horribly painful death. No wonder we're bitter. No wonder we lash out, in our turn, like our husbands do to us, at any available target – in our case, you. You with your looks that've opened doors we're denied. What've you got to complain about? You've as much food as you want. You don't have to worry about water running out. You've clothes, jewellery, a room of your own – correction, an *entire suite* of rooms, the west wing in that huge mansion. You've maids pandering to your every need. Your grand-mother is being seen to by an English doctor. Do you think we had that luxury when we watched our loved ones die of thirst, of hunger, of diseases contracted from consuming mud and dirt in hungry desperation? Does your husband beat you? He is rough, perhaps. Aren't they all? You've everything *we* want. A roof over your head. Shelter. Food. Water. You're being waited on hand and foot. What more do you want? You have made out your life in the village to be so romantic. Was it really so? Don't you get it, Bindu? It's only when all your physical and material needs are met that you've the luxury of complaining about boredom, loneliness, being unfulfilled. Do you think we have the time to think about that when we're just trying to make it through each harrowing day?'

The next day, Guru comes to find her.

'I'm sorry. I was out of order, accusing you of flirting with the colonel. What can I do to make it all right?'

This is a new side to Guru that's emerged since Bindu took Ajji's advice and began to support him instead of fighting him. During the early days of their marriage, when he was in his father's sway, and she, hating it, would lash out, he'd never have apologised, tried to placate her.

The dream is loud in her head, the village women's voices clamouring to be heard. *Do you think our husbands apologise after they've been rough? They just get drunk and do it all over again.* 'The villagers...'

'Not for the villagers. For you.'

'You'll make me happy if you pardon their rent for this year.'

'Too much.' He is firm.

'Pardon their rent this month and freeze it for the rest of the year. No hike.'

'All right. And a new sari for you?'

'I've enough saris. But you will not touch me again without my consent.' The words are out of her mouth before she can take them back, her hot-headed side winning again like it does every so often, no matter how much she tries to rein it in.

Predictably, Guru's eyes flash and his jaw works furiously as his temper rises. 'I'm your husband. It's my right. And yet, I've said sorry.'

'I'm supposed to be grateful?' Bindu snaps, although a voice in her head that sounds very like Ajji cautions, *Is this wise?*

'Yes, for I'm doing what I can for your blasted villagers.'

'They're *your* tenants.'

'Yet they're more important to you than your own husband.'

And with this, Guru turns on his heel and storms off, leaving Bindu grinding her teeth in agitated frustration.

A few weeks later, Guru says, 'The colonel is hosting a tennis party and we're invited.'

'I can play?' She's surprised.

'Of course not,' Guru scoffs. 'Your accompanying me to these parties where women aren't segregated has caused enough furore as it is. If you play that would be one step too far.'

His high-handedness gets on her nerves and she forgets, once again, to be tactful. 'What's the point of attending a tennis party if I can't play the game?'

And now cold amusement glints in his eyes. 'Do you know how to?'

She juts out her jaw. 'It's a game. I'll pick it up.'

'No, you won't. You'll sit with the women and make pleasant conversation and cheer me on while I play.'

His dictatorial laying down of the law grates on her, but she grits her teeth, bites her tongue, takes a breath, and another, and says, sweetly, 'And if I do, what'll I get in return?'

'Does everything have to be a bargain with you, Bindu?' Guru sighs. 'If the colonel hadn't insisted you accompany me – he's quite taken with you' – raised eyebrows – 'I'd leave you behind.'

Again, she's tempted to snap, 'Then do. I don't want to attend just to sit there twiddling my thumbs and cheering you on when I don't care one way or another if you win or lose, as I'd rather be playing myself.' But she manages to swallow the words and smile placidly – she hopes. 'An irrigation system for the fields in the village, in return for my attendance?'

'They've a water tank, they no longer need worry about running out of water,' Guru says, frowning in bemusement.

'But the sheer effort involved in lugging the water from the tank to the fields... Guru, an irrigation system will make *all* the difference.'

'Bindu, the cost...'

'Do we have a deal?'

'I'll think about it.' His voice tight to signal an end to the discussion.

Afterwards, she says, 'I kept my part of the deal, now you've to honour yours.'

They're in the car, pressing night susurrating around them, scented with roses. The navy awning of sky is studded with stars. The air that strokes Bindu's face is fragrant, tasting of wistfulness, ache for something she cannot name.

Guru does not reply, or offer any indication that he's heard her, his gaze fixed upon the darkness rushing past.

Nevertheless, she presses, 'So, irrigation system?'

'It doesn't make business sense,' he says, shortly, still not looking at her.

'We had a deal!'

'We didn't. I said I'd think about it. In any case, even if we had, you rescinded it when you put me on the spot, declaring at tea, in front of the Resident, the colonel, the king of Jabalpur and the rest, that I'd fund scholarships for deserving children among our tenants,' he says coldly.

Ah, that's why he's so prickly. She'd thought it was his jealousy flaring again.

'They were very complimentary and thought it a great idea,' she placates, for Bindu has been cunning, deliberately touting the scholarships – an idea that's been brewing in her head for a while – as agreed upon in front of Guru's friends and betters, knowing Guru would not entertain it otherwise.

'They think it's a done deal when we haven't even discussed—'

'We're discussing it now.'

'I meant with my father,' Guru snaps, rubbing at his jaw in frustration.

'You heard them agree that it's a noble thing you're doing.' She is meek, her voice gently soothing, employing all the tact in her arsenal. 'It'll raise your father's profile even further, engender more business deals.'

'Bindu, if I've told you once, I've told you a thousand times,' he explodes, 'don't meddle where you're not—'

'I'm your wife,' she says, simply.

'That's exactly it, you're my wife, not my business partner. You don't know the financial ins and outs of the business.'

'Then explain them to me,' she says, playing to his pride.

'It's not your—'

'Guru, what's the harm in helping deserving children, sponsoring their education?' Her voice rises, patience exhausted.

They've reached the mansion and Guru storms out of the car without helping her out. She waves the chauffeur aside and jumps out herself, running to keep up with Guru's agitated strides, the servants pausing in their tasks as they surreptitiously watch the goings-on while trying to appear as if they're not.

'Look around you, Bindu, all this is only because we've invested wisely.'

'At the expense of the poor,' she snaps, having had enough of playing tactful, massaging his ego.

He swivels round so quickly that she's winded, his face upon hers, contorted with anger, voice a snarl. 'Do not,' he says, jaw grinding, 'poke your nose in affairs that don't concern you.'

'So, you want me to make intelligent comments when it suits you to augur approval and compliments, but do nothing that matters.'

'Yes, that's exactly what I want,' he spits.

'You're no different from your father.'

'Enough,' he yells. 'Do not get above yourself. Go away, I've had enough of you.'

'And I of you.'

But he's already entered his chambers and shut the door in her face.

'I hate him, hate him, hate him,' she cries to Ajji.

However frustrating and constricting she might find life here, Bindu's grateful to be able to vent after those months of feeling so alone when her grandmother was lost to her. And although Ajji is far from her old self, still being seen by her doctor each week, she's happy to rest in comfort and luxury, keeping abreast of village gossip via Sunitha.

She smiles gently. 'Hate and love are two sides of the same coin.'

'Ajji, what're you saying?' Bindu's shocked. 'He's a tyrant.'

'Aren't you being a little unfair to him? He lets you do what you like—'

'Does he? I can't read, cook, visit the village or help with the business. Instead, I've to do what he wants, always.'

'To get what *you* want,' Ajji says, smiling tenderly at Bindu. 'It's what you do best. Giving him the illusion that you're acceding to his wishes, all the while arranging matters to your benefit.'

'Not this time. He refused to even entertain the idea of awarding scholarships to deserving children.'

'You did put him on the spot, declaring he was doing so to his friends and betters without discussing it with him first.'

'Why're you always on his side?' Bindu marches out of Ajji's room to the bench in the courtyard, where she begins a letter to Laurence Elliot. The one friend who is on her side, it feels sometimes, with both Ajji and Sunitha seemingly in Guru's thrall – although, if he's done anything at all for the villagers, it's been because of *her* input.

Laurence – he's asked Bindu to address him so, but she hasn't felt able to in their correspondence as yet, although, in the privacy of her head this is how she thinks of him – makes her feel good about herself. At times, it feels like he's the only one who does.

They discuss the features in his magazines; they have lively debates about the current political situation in India and abroad. Via his magazines and letters, Laurence has provided thought-provoking reading material just when Bindu was going mad without anything to stimulate her mind.

I agree with Churchill, he writes. *The Munich Agreement's an unmitigated disaster. There's no appeasing Hitler. War is, sadly, inevitable. I plan to return to England to do my bit.*

Don't leave, she wants to cry. *What'll I do if I don't have you to share recipes and thoughts with? Your friendship, writing to you and – thanks to your encouragement – writing for myself, plus the stipend from getting my recipes published in your magazine, have fostered my confidence, given me back the self I lost when I rescinded my scholarship.*

His letter: *I disappointed my father when I didn't follow in his footsteps to Sandhurst, for since I learned to read, enchanted by the power and beauty of words, I've wanted to write, not fight. My father didn't consider my profession manly enough – although he never said so, it was always implied. His only child and I wasn't the son he wanted. I like to think that were he alive, he'd be proud of me signing up to fight for my country.*

Although selfishly upset that he's thinking of doing so, Bindu is also touched. She understands that she's being taken into Laurence's confidence.

There's something about the medium of letter-writing, she's found, putting pen to paper and sealing the envelope shut, that invites the spilling of secrets, the sharing of thoughts that haven't been openly voiced before.

She tries to picture Laurence, but he's a hazy silhouette – she can't quite recall his features. She remembers that he was tall. A bit awkward, perhaps. His eyes the colour of coriander leaves spangled with dew. She thinks of his feeling he has failed his father, wanting to please him even though he's long dead. And although she's furious with her husband, she thinks of Guru, also perpetually trying to please *his* father, win his affection, and failing. And she feels a little softening of the hard ball of anger in her heart.

She's annoyed with Ajji for always taking Guru's side, but she must concede that she's very lucky in her grandmother. Ajji is her only family, but Bindu's never once felt the lack of her parents. Her grandmother has always made Bindu feel like she's her world, like nothing Bindu does would ever disappoint her, that by her very being she makes Ajji proud. It is a precious, beautiful gift.

Forgive me if I'm speaking out of turn, she writes in her reply to Laurence, *but I think your parents would be very proud indeed of their only son, who's singlehandedly launched a magazine that is a runaway success, breaking records by becoming one of the top publications in India in just over a year. A man of words, who, through his articles and the insightful features he edits and publishes, touches so many, making laypeople and state leaders alike consider their choices, question their actions, think before they act – crucial and necessary during these uncertain times.*

In their letters, they discuss the communal riots in India, Muslims and Hindus turning on one another amid their fight for independence from the British. Bindu wishes she was having these discussions with Guru. He'd enjoyed conversing with her once, his eyes twinkling with admiration and awe. Now, he only likes her to back up his points when in company or else shut up.

'You talk too much,' he says, when she can't help putting forth an argument or making a point of her own. 'If you'd like to accompany me to more of these parties where women are allowed at the table with the men, you must behave more like the other women.'

'Smile and look pretty but be mute, a tablepiece to be admired and ignored like the antique vases or the silver candelabras,' Bindu opened her mouth to retort, but then shut it again, biting her tongue to hold her anger and upset inside, behaving just as he wanted her to, a beautiful but dumb accessory to her husband, and hating every minute of it.

The ball of anger fists in her chest, choking her heart of any softening of feeling towards her husband.

It's shocking and extremely upsetting to hear about the riots in our city, she writes. *Neighbours and friends killing each other in the name of religion. But I do understand – desperation, hunger, anger, oppression are a potent combination, causing one to lash out blindly, taking casualties.*

Their correspondence makes Bindu feel understood, her opinion given weight by a man of words, a respected journalist.

With Laurence, she feels heard, feels like, finally, she's using her mind and is applauded for it, as opposed to Guru, with whom everything's a battle.

She picks up her pencil and adds, *You're the only one I can share my thoughts and opinions with. I'm deeply grateful for my correspondence with you. When I write to you, when we discuss politics and poetry, I feel like I matter. Thank you for your friendship. It allows me to face each day with a smile on my face and a spring in my step.*

As soon as she sets her pencil down, she wonders if she's shared too much, if she should strike the last few sentences off.

Then she thinks of Guru: 'You're my wife, not my business partner.'

Ire once again flaring fiery crimson in her mouth, she deliberately leaves the last paragraph in and seals the letter.

A fortnight after their argument regarding the scholarships Bindu promised on his behalf, Guru says, 'I'm sorry if I was harsh the other day.'

An apology. At last. She doesn't know what he's apologising for, but it doesn't matter. 'You were,' she says, not looking at him.

'Look' – he sighs – 'I've arranged it with my father to fund scholarships for deserving children – two a year.'

And now, she turns to him. He appears tired, weary lines crowding his eyes, and she's beset by an unexpected urge to smooth them away. She entwines her hands on her lap, bites her lips hard enough to draw blood until the impulse passes. 'How did you do that?'

'I've my ways.' A smile gilding his voice, twinkling in his eyes.

'You paid journalists to trumpet his generosity, didn't you?'

'I went one better. They're coming to interview him tomorrow. One of them will take him to task about providing his tenants with an irrigation system given how much they struggle to water their fields...'

She smiles.

'Happy now?' Guru beams at her.

'Not quite,' she says. 'Only two scholarships a year?'

'Bindu.' Her name is a lament, a plea. 'You madden me. You're feisty and passionate, you care so deeply, but unlike other wives who want jewellery and gold, saris and material things, you want to help those less fortunate. Everything you fight for with your all is for everyone else.'

'This *is* for me,' she says softly. 'Every child who wins the scholarship is me.'

'Ah, Bindu,' he says, opening his arms.

She goes into them, resting her head against his shoulder, his scent of musk and ginger, even as, for the first time since she started her correspondence with Laurence, her heart dips with guilt, for her last letter, while still innocent, had strayed a little too far into the personal: *You're the only one I can share my thoughts and opinions with.*

Outside, dusky twilight purrs in heady anticipation as it angles to meet the horizon, where beacons of stars twinkle in seductive flirtation.

Eve has milk warmed up, and raisins, and apples cut into slivers ready for Maya by the time the clock chimes half past three.

She watches out the window, curtains wide open to the chatter of children returning home from school, although her own child will never again walk home, nattering with her friends, on her own like she'd wanted to without Eve trailing a few paces behind.

Maya turns the corner, head down, strides brisk. Her steps falter as she nears her own house. She stops in front of it and then, taking a deep breath, she squares her shoulders and walks past and up the steps of Eve's house – Eve moves away from the window just in time so as not to be caught snooping – and knocks on the door, calling, 'It's me, Eve, back from school.'

Eve opens the door and bends down to drop a kiss on the girl's head, her hair mussed up now, most of it having escaped her scrunchies. She smells of apple shampoo and the outdoors, of sweat and innocence.

'How was your day?'

'All right.' Maya shrugs.

Izzy would chatter away the moment she saw Eve at the school gates and drop her school bag onto the carpet as soon as they reached home.

Maya is quiet, setting her bag down carefully beside her

belongings. But, once she has drunk the milk and eaten her fruit, she says, 'Everyone knew about Mum.' And, softly, 'Will she be all right, Eve?' Looking at her with such concern in those liquid brown eyes.

'Of course, love, she'll be right as rain and back home in a few days. As she'll tell you herself. Once you wash and change out of your uniform, we'll take the bus to hospital, eh?'

Maya doesn't need to be told twice. Flashing Eve a smile, she's off to get ready.

It is Eve who dallies, dreading the ordeal of walking past the spot where she lost her family to get to the bus stop.

CHAPTER 47

BINDU

1939

'Guru!'

It's barely dawn.

Guru has just left Bindu's chambers and she's made her way to Ajji's room, a habit formed in the last few months.

For Ajji's been sickening again, getting frailer every day. Her cough is worse than ever and the doctor's magic pills aren't helping.

'It's my time, Bindu,' she said gently when Bindu ranted about the medicine not taking effect.

'Perhaps he needs to prescribe stronger pills,' Bindu had said.

'I'm not getting any younger. This body has reached its limit.'

When Ajji speaks this way, it terrifies Bindu. She'll not countenance a time and a world without her beloved grandmother in it. 'Don't say that, Ajji. You can't go yet. What'll I do without you?'

'You'll manage. You'll thrive. You're my star, my heart.'

'Don't go, Ajji,' Bindu has pleaded, cried, coaxed, cajoled. 'Not yet. I need you.'

But as much as she tries to ignore it, Bindu cannot miss the exhaustion in Ajji's eyes, etched into the grooves of her face, the sheer effort it takes her grandmother to get through each day.

Ajji is sleeping more and for longer every day and is less alert even when awake – not quite all there, her eyes cloudy and memory foggy. She never fails to recognise Bindu, her face glowing at the sight of her granddaughter – Bindu spends every spare moment with her – but she's forgetting other things, mixing up facts, losing her thread of conversation. She was never this fatigued even when run ragged by orders when they lived in the hut in the village, even when she was coming down with the fever that floored her, and this worries Bindu. She hates being away from Ajji, having to smile and make inane conversation at the parties she's duty-bound to attend when the weight of her worry is a stone sitting on her chest, stealing the breath from her.

A bed is set up in Ajji's room for Bindu now – the room is easily large enough to host five. Bindu sleeps next to Ajji – side by side but not sharing a mat like they used to – after Guru leaves her at dawn to get on with work. Her husband is extremely busy now that he's finally taken over from his father – the landlord had another minor stroke a couple of months ago, which prompted him to actually retire instead of just saying he would. But no matter how well he and Bindu are getting along, no matter how sweetly persistent she is, Guru will not countenance Bindu's help – 'You're my wife. I don't want you interfering in business affairs.'

'I won't be interfering, I'll be *helping*. It'll take the pressure off you.' She wants to shout, to snap, to bite, but manages to regulate her voice just in time, practising the caution Ajji has always preached.

But in this matter it fails to work.

'Bindu, I've said this often and I'll do so again: no.'

Guru might be busy, but he visits Bindu every night without fail – now that he's taken over as landlord, he wants an heir as much as his father does. When he leaves with the dawn, Bindu goes to Ajji's room, slipping into the bed set up for her, so when Ajji wakes she sees her granddaughter first thing and her warm smile makes Bindu glow.

But this morning when she enters Ajji's room, she is aware of stillness.

'Guru,' she cries.

Her husband is panting, having run all the way back down the corridor, heeding her distressed call. 'What's the matter, Bindu?'

She cannot put it into words. Her mouth chokes with salt and despairing incomprehension as she takes in Ajji's small form on the huge bed. Her chest unmoving. Her breath non-existent. A small smile on her weathered face, which is unlined in repose. Peaceful.

She steps aside, so Guru can look, a meagre sliver of hope in her stricken chest. Perhaps she got it wrong?

But... 'Oh, Bindu,' Guru says.

At the look on Guru's face, the silver bloom of hope droops and dies.

Her husband opens his arms.

And in his spice-and-sweat embrace, Bindu howls her loss in endless, enervating keens.

Each day without her grandmother is long and dreary and colourless. Bindu sits in Ajji's chambers, staring at her grandmother's empty bed, wondering, *Where are you, Ajji? How can you be gone?*

Each despondent, directionless, empty hour bleeds into another and Bindu is unable to rouse herself from her melancholy. Everything feels like effort. She stares at her notebook and thinks, *What's the point?* Ajji – who taught Bindu to cook as an infant, so her earliest memories were peopled with spices, rich and hearty with goat's milk pedas, honey-sweet with jaggery-stuffed coconut dumplings, flavoured with curry leaves and sizzling onions and the right consistency of spice paste and the crackle and spit of mustard seeds in hot oil – is gone.

Guru is gentle, tender, patient, visiting as soon as he's finished work, holding her when she cries. But she is numb when she is with him. And sometimes she is angry, so angry that it takes every ounce of her willpower not to push him away. She married him for Ajji's sake and now her grandmother is no more – she is no more – and Bindu is stuck in this life she doesn't want, with this man who thinks he owns her.

Sunitha chats, jokes, grumbles, regales Bindu with gossip in a bid to rouse her from her malaise. Bindu knows Sunitha's worried – her cheerful friend no longer hums as she works. She's looking extremely glum. Bindu guesses that while part of it is grief – Sunitha was close to Ajji – mostly it is because of her, but she cannot bring herself to do anything about it. It's an effort just to exist from day to day.

'Your Ajji wouldn't be happy seeing you like this,' Sunitha sighs each morning when she arrives to find Bindu in Ajji's chamber, staring at her grandmother's empty bed as if she can bring her to life by the sheer force of her longing.

Only writing to Laurence Elliot offers Bindu solace. He is kind and generous in his replies. And while their correspondence doesn't cross the bounds of propriety, it's intimate, tender, just what she needs. Corresponding with him is her comfort; her rambling feelings of how empty she feels, her lack of purpose now her only family is no more and her boundless sorrow shared with him.

I'm sorry if this letter doesn't make sense. The world doesn't make sense to me now my Ajji's gone. Without her, it lacks flavour, vigour, seasoning. It's bare, not vivid but vapid. I cannot conceive of cooking. I'll send recipes across when I'm able.

And he, in his reply:

I understand. I felt just so when I lost my parents. Please don't apologise – I feel privileged that you can share your grief with me. Please don't worry about sending recipes. You've sent plenty during the course of our correspondence that I haven't published yet – I'll use those. Please take as long as you need.

She does not feel much, but she does experience guilt when she pours her heart out to Laurence and seals the envelope. They're not improper, just sharing in the manner of friends. He is her outlet and she needs one now her only kin is gone. But she feels guilty anyway and she wants to talk to Ajji, yearns for Ajji's voice of reason. Grief stabs afresh and she picks up her pencil and begins a new note to Laurence.

There's a gift enclosed with his reply: a poetry book, with his annotations in the margins. *This is one of my favourite collections. Please forgive its appearance – it's worse for wear, for it has travelled everywhere with me, has seen me through some challenging times. The power of poetry to soothe, to pacify, I think is unparalleled. I hope this will help, and that it offers you the solace it has given me.*

Bindu is touched beyond words – this man whose features she cannot recall, who has, during the course of their communication, become her cherished friend. This man who restored her sense of self when she was feeling trapped by the strictures of marriage to the landlord's son by publishing her recipes and paying for them. This man who's been there for her during this, one of the most trying times in her life. This man who's inspired her to write and supplied her with reading material in the form of his letters and magazines and, now, his treasured poetry collection, with his thoughts annotated in the margins, offering comfort when she most needs it. This man who's not her husband but knows her better than anyone else.

CHAPTER 48

BINDU

Bindu knows Sunitha and Guru have been conspiring to bring her out of the fug she's descended into since Ajji's passing.

And now, here is Guru, and Sunitha is smiling – relief and hope.

Guru takes Bindu's hand. 'Come with me, I'll not take no for an answer.'

She doesn't have the strength or energy to protest and allows him to lead her through the mansion, past the ostentatious show-rooms bursting with antiques, scented with rose and jasmine and luxury, the vast corridors narrowing as they enter the parts of the mansion not for show, the carpets threadbare and worn here, where only servants tread.

The servants move out of the way in shocked surprise, as their master and mistress occupy these unhallowed portals where the stultifying aroma of opulence is replaced by the hearty sizzle of onions, roasting garlic, burnt sugar, crisping dough.

Bindu breathes in deeply of these scents of her childhood and, for the first time since Ajji died, she feels close to her again.

'Have you been here before?' she's moved to ask of her husband.

Guru turns in the narrow corridor profuse with the aromas of cooking, the walls not adorned with paintings or tapestries or elaborate mirror work, but painted in earthy colours garnished with smoke-doodle frescoes, and smiles at her, eyes tender. 'Never. The things I do for you, woman!'

She smiles.

He bends down to kiss her, beaming even as his eyes shine. 'I've missed your smile.'

When they enter the vast kitchens of the mansion, Bindu feels finally able to shed that untethered feeling of floating in an incomprehensible plane and take a tentative step into a world where her grandmother no longer exists.

'Look,' Guru says, 'I know my father said no daughter-in-law of his would demean herself by cooking. But he's retired. Would it help if you prepared your Ajji's recipes?'

She can only nod, her fingers already itching to pick up a knife and begin chopping onions, peeling garlic, crushing ginger, tempering mustard seeds in coconut oil, just like her grandmother had taught her.

She opens her mouth and, instead of tasting keening despair, she samples possibility, a different, blander future without Ajji in it, perhaps, but a means of moving on.

And with it, guilt flaring bright purple and damning, for her indiscreet, intimate communication with Laurence Elliot, for cherishing his gift of the poetry book, for sharing her grief with and seeking solace from a man not her husband, when her husband has surprised her by being so thoughtful and kind. She might not have crossed the bounds of propriety, but she has to admit – only to herself and in secret – that she's been unfaithful all the same, confiding her deepest feelings and thoughts to someone whom she has allowed to mean so much to her while keeping her husband at arm's length, rebuffing his attempts to console her, to help her navigate her sorrow. Yet, he's the one who has known how to reach her, to give her something of Ajji back.

I must stop writing to Laurence.

The thought makes Bindu's heart dip, but she tells herself again, with firm resolve, *It's the right thing to do. I* must *stop and I will.*

. . .

Bindu takes the very first meal that she cooks in the landlord's kitchens – she has cooked hundreds of meals for the landlord, but it was always in the hut with Ajji by her side – to her husband.

Guru is in his chambers, scowling at the document he's perusing. He smiles when she enters. 'Whatever it is smells divine.'

'Potato and spinach curry with red rice – the first meal I cooked with Ajji.' Her voice stumbles.

'Ah, Bindu.' He opens his arms.

She shakes her head. 'You can comfort me later. Now, eat before it gets cold.'

'It's delicious,' he exults through stuffed mouthfuls. 'A far cry from my first experience of your culinary skills. That spice paste completely put me off your cooking – I didn't realise what I was missing. This is heavenly.'

Just as she's resolved to stop writing to Laurence, Bindu has decided she'll focus on her marriage, on her husband. And when he's like this, open and effusive, thoughtful and kind, it's not effortful. In fact, it feels natural, right, to loop her arms round his neck and kiss him, convey her feelings, her full heart, in this way.

'As I was cooking, I heard Ajji's voice; it was like she was there, cooking alongside me.' She'd picked up the knife – an expensive, shop-bought one, as opposed to the ones made by Sivanna, who was very good with his hands, that Bindu and Ajji had used (bartered for Ajji's curd rice) – and it was like she'd never stopped, the copious onion-induced tears healing. She cooked in the landlord's well equipped kitchen, servants dancing attendance, but in her head she was in the hut she'd shared with Ajji, her grandmother coating vegetables in gram flour paste dotted with mustard and methi seeds, Bindu rescuing from the hot oil in which her Ajji had fried bondas the globules of gram flour that'd escaped the coating, and dousing them in jaggery caramel to make boondi, honeyed bites, Dumdee's nose twitching at the scents of a feast in progress that painted the air outside the hut shimmering rainbow.

'Thank you,' Bindu says.

Guru beams.

CHAPTER 49

EVE

1980

The spot where they died is a shrine to Eve's family. Images of her husband and child smiling from the lamp post, surrounded by flowers and soft toys. Sculptures of angels. Poems and letters from Izzy's classmates, carefully written in best handwriting in coloured marker, drawings of stick-figure children cuddling, hearts and flowers, encased in polythene so they're weatherproof. Teddy bears. So many, many flowers. All fresh – someone is taking great care to replace wilted blossoms with fresh blooms. Candles, potpourri and plant pots. Eve is touched.

She reads every message, every heartfelt eulogy, including a beautiful letter from Sue to Joe and Izzy and an emotional poem by Jenny. She marvels at the tributes by Izzy's friends, a lovely poem from Maya among them. Maya has drawn the two girls, arm in arm in a field of daffodils as they were Izzy's favourite flower; Eve's too.

'It's all right, Eve,' Maya says, putting her small arms round Eve's neck like Izzy used to. Eve and Maya were on their way to the bus stop to head to the hospital, but the tributes waylaid them and they've now missed the bus; but Maya's been so patient, allowing Eve to take her time.

'I'm humbled, Maya, by the effort you and Izzy's other friends and classmates have put into your messages.' Their crossed-out words, their colourful writing, their spelling mistakes making it all the more poignant.

'She was our friend,' Maya whispers. 'I miss her so.'

Eve sobs and the tears are cathartic. Why didn't she do this before? This is beautiful. So many people loved her husband and child. They miss them too. They're keeping their memory alive.

Yes, perhaps this road will always be where they met their deaths. This is where Eve will see, in her mind's eye, her vibrant husband and child lifeless, her daughter's cream dress with yellow daffodils, splashed with blood; but those images are now over-ridden by these tributes to her family. Beautiful words of missing, of love, showing how many people they touched in their short time on Earth. She's been hiding away, hugging her grief selfishly to herself, when perhaps if she'd shared it, it wouldn't have felt so overwhelming, so disabling.

While Maya is staying with her, Eve decides she'll cook some-thing from Izzy's nana's cookbook – it's been gathering dust, she hasn't been able to even look at it since the accident. But cooking from that book was what Izzy loved to do, her favourite pastime. And like these poems, drawings and gifts, it'll be Eve's tribute to her daughter.

She's been postponing walking past this road that claimed her family, but it has helped her to do so, a balm to the wound that is her heart. Perhaps cooking from Izzy's nana's book will also, instead of hurting, heal.

CHAPTER 50

BINDU

1939

Where are you? Bindu has wondered every day since Ajji's been gone. *Are you with your son, my father? Can you see me?*

She has her coping mechanisms now when grief threatens to engulf her. She writes, stream-of-consciousness musings on grief and loss.

She cooks and it is then that she feels closest to Ajji. She sees her smile, hears her voice, 'My heart, you have the gift.' But when she samples the food she's prepared, she finds it bland, although all who try it declare it's exquisite, the best they've tasted.

She prepares all the recipes she would with Ajji in their one-roomed hut in the vast kitchens of the landlord's mansion – she still can't think of it as hers. She makes food parcels, which are distributed among the villagers. Bindu would've preferred to do this herself but of course that is one step too far, even for Guru, allowing his wife to mingle with the villagers, even though she was once one of them.

In the afternoons, after the servants have had the lunch she's prepared, she takes lessons, instructing them in English, reciting poetry to them. But she can't find the joy she used to in imparting her love of reading and writing, of prose and poetry. Even Wordsworth's daffodils cannot stir her; she can't picture their yellow dancing heads any more.

Bindu tries her hardest to be a dutiful wife and kind benefac-
tress, to do what's expected of her, but, like before, when she felt
hemmed in from the pressure of being a caring granddaughter and
good student, now too she feels restless. For she liked the secret
thrill of writing to Laurence Elliot – something for herself alone –
and she misses it. She misses him.

The day after Guru granted Bindu free rein of the kitchens,
she'd written to Laurence that she was taking a break, that there
wouldn't be any more letters for the foreseeable. It required all
her willpower and she changed her mind several times, but in the
end she sealed the letter and handed it to Sunitha: 'There, that's
it. The last letter you'll post for me.'

Sunitha threw her arms round Bindu. 'Good for you,
Memsahib. You were taking great risks writing to him – I've been
so worried.'

Although sorely tempted several times, Bindu hasn't asked
Sunitha to stop by the convent and collect Laurence's reply – if
there was one. She's made her choice; she must stick to it, keep
her vow to herself and to Guru.

Bindu has never been on better terms with her husband and
yet, she feels lack. An ache for more. She itches when Guru
touches her, is with her. For she can't help thinking, *Is this it? My
life? Yes, I'm doing good work, helping the servants, teaching them. I'm
cooking and distributing food among the villagers. I'm a dutiful wife. But
what about my aspirations, what I wanted before Ajji fell ill and I gave
up my scholarship? Now that Ajji's gone, I don't have to stick to my side of
the bargain – I could leave Guru. Go abroad, to England, see daffodils,
read poetry, study, work. I've money saved up.*

But then Sunitha hums as she goes about her work, one of the
servants thanks her for the food parcel Bindu distributed to her
family, another for the scholarships she instigated that have
helped her son study further, yet another for the irrigation system,
which has proved to be a godsend. Guru beams as he samples the
food she's made, helping himself to more: 'I'm full but I can't
resist.' And she knows she cannot leave. She's trapped by her good
deeds as surely as she was by the bargain she'd struck with Guru.
And this makes her even more desperate to escape. She wants to

be free, not bound by her loyalties, by the change she's effected, by the lives she's touched. She wants out: she wants her self back.

The servants, who now look up to her, their beloved mistress, instead of resenting serving her, report that the landlord grumbles about Bindu no end from his bed.

'Two strokes since she married my son, each worse than the last. If only I'd foreseen this, I'd never have let him anywhere near her. She's cast an evil spell, rendering me bed-bound because I dared threaten her with eviction if she didn't provide me with an heir within two years of marrying my son. Well, now the two years are almost up with no sign nor rumour of an heir. And now I hear she's not only demeaning herself and our good name by cooking with the servants, she's also giving the food away. It was bad enough when she was parcelling up the leftovers, but the mistress of the house cooking and serving fresh, wholesome food prepared with the choicest of ingredients, dishes that wouldn't look out of place at the Resident's table, gourmet delicacies fit for kings, to servants, distributing it among my tenants! Whoever heard of it? She's throwing away my hard-won money, and does my son see it? Witch, that's what she is, a demoness who's enchanted my son, made him blind to her faults. Oh, I'd rather die than be a party to this.'

'He says he'd rather die, Memsahib,' the servants sniff. 'But the moment he experiences so much as a twinge, he sends for not one but three doctors!'

And Bindu hears from Guru: 'He *says* he's retired, but he expects me to update him on business affairs twice-daily, if not hourly. How am I supposed to do any work?'

'I can do it for you,' she says.

He laughs: 'Ha, nice try. That *will* do for the old man.'

Best outcome all round, Bindu thinks but has the good sense not to say out loud.

Bindu now has the servants' unquestioning loyalty and respect, Guru on her side, as opposed to his father's – but without Ajji, it feels hollow, insubstantial. Why is it not enough? Why does she feel unfulfilled? Why does she crave more, different? Why does she experience an uncomfortable niggle when the servants narrate what the landlord's saying about her, as if there might be some truth to his caution after all, as if the old man is the only one who can see through her to her self-destructing core?

She reads the poetry book, Laurence's annotations in the margins, when ensconced in the bench in the palm tree bower, and she yearns for more. Something other than this life she feels stuck in. Something for herself.

She picks up her pencil and her notebook and begins a letter to Laurence. She will not post it, so there's no harm, is there?

But when she's written it, jotted down her thoughts, telling him how much his poetry has helped, how much writing has helped, when she tells him she's cooking again and pens the recipe for spiced cauliflower with peanut rice that arrives in her head, she thinks, *what's the harm in sending it?*

Sunitha's lips disappear, her features distorted by a scowl, when Bindu hands her the letter to post. 'Memsahib, why? Why do you always want to jeopardise things when they're going smoothly? What is it in you that wants to flirt with danger, push your boundaries to see how far and how much you can get away with?'

'Sunitha, I don't want a lecture, I just want you to post this. Here's money for you to—'

'I don't care about the money, Memsahib. I care about you and what you're doing...'

'Sunitha, please. Stop. I *know* I'm gambling with danger, taking unnecessary risks. But I've got away with it until now, haven't I?'

'That doesn't mean you'll do so forever.'

'Please, Sunitha, enough.' *Sunitha*, she thinks, *what I'd rather do is run away, far from the responsibilities and loyalties binding me here. Instead I'm easing my restlessness by writing to Laurence. It's the lesser of two evils.*

But is it really?

For in the letter, by way of explaining to Laurence why she took a break from writing to him, she's poured out her heart in a bid to make him understand. Been too personal and indiscreet. She's shared her conflicted thoughts, her desire now Ajji is no more, to be free, someone other than wife and daughter-in-law and Memsahib, someone in her own right. And in this way, she knows she's being unfaithful, not only to Guru but to the servants too. Perhaps it is not the lesser of the two evils after all.

CHAPTER 51

EVE

1980

Jenny is sitting up in bed.

A day in hospital and she already looks better. She's breathing easier and is not as wan.

'Mum,' Maya says, throwing her arms round her.

Jenny beams. She glows.

Over her daughter's tousled head, her gaze meets Eve's. 'Thank you,' she mouths. And her friend's heartfelt gratitude humbles Eve all the more.

She's been indulging in the luxury of grief, spending months shutting herself away from the world. There are worse tragedies, innocent victims caught up in wars, earthquakes, tsunamis, who lose everything – their families, their home, their country, their way of life. At least Eve has a roof over her head. She has good friends who care for her, love her despite her selfish foibles.

'*I* thank *you*,' she says. 'And Maya, who gave me a hug when I was overwhelmed by the tributes at the place Joe and Izzy died. I thought that I couldn't bear it, that it'd destroy me. But I was wrong. It was, contrary to what I'd expected, a healing and illuminating experience. They touched so many lives.'

Jenny nods, eyes shining.

'Your poem is beautiful and Maya's tribute made me cry.' She takes her friend's hand in hers. 'How are you, Jenny?'

'Much better. They say I'll be discharged within the week. Is it all right to have Maya until then?'

'Do you even have to ask? Your daughter is quite something. An empathetic, kind, brave, wonderful girl. It's an absolute pleasure having her,' Eve says and both mother and daughter burst into happy laughter, their giggles festooning the air in rainbow celebration, echoing in Eve's heart, brightening it.

CHAPTER 52

BINDU

1939

Bindu throws her head to the heavens, drizzles of gold filtering through palm fronds, coy dance of dappled light and shadow, birdsong mingling with the fountain's silvery siren call as the water dances and glitters, sending iridescent spray her way. The sky, white gold, shimmers, and Bindu breathes in the zesty scent of spices and earth. Warm air deposits humid kisses upon her cheeks and she imagines it's Ajji's caress as she smiles fondly at her. Settled on her favourite bench tucked within the embrace of the bower, composing a letter to Laurence, Bindu is momentarily at peace, her restlessness, the urge to run away temporarily assuaged as she pens a recipe for Laurence's magazine.

Here's a recipe that sings hope to me: sago payasam.

Ajji would make it when she was able to barter one of her dishes for goat's milk from Chinnakka, and when the warming scent of sweetened milk spiced with cardamom rose from the hearth into the fruity, fermented air, I knew we were in for a festive treat.

'What're we celebrating?' I'd ask, bounding in from the fields where I'd been playing with Dumdee, and Ajji would laugh, cup my face

and say, 'You, my heart. We're celebrating you, us, family, love, togetherness.'

If I knew then that my time with her was limited, I would have celebrated every single moment. But as children we never think ahead to a time without our loved ones, do we?

In any case, here's the recipe for sago payasam; when cooked, it looks like jewels of stars dotting a creamy sky, heralding hope and good omens.

Yours,

Bindu

Sago Payasam recipe: So simple, so delicious, fit for any celebration, easy on the eye and a healthy treat for the body.

Three cups milk

One cup sago – soak in three cups water for two hours or overnight

Half-cup sugar or jaggery

Cardamom seeds from six pods, crushed

Cashew nuts and raisins to garnish if you have them. If not, delicious on its own without.

One tablespoon ghee

Heat the milk with the sago until the sago resembles translucent pearls and the milk is bubbling in happy anticipation. Add the sugar/jaggery and crushed cardamom seeds. Stir until sugar/jaggery is absorbed.

*If using nuts and raisins, roast them in a tablespoon of ghee until
cashew nuts are golden brown and raisins are plumply drunk on
ghee. Add to the payasam and serve.*

Can be eaten hot or cold. A festive treat to brighten one's day.

She seals the letter and is about to call for Sunitha when the
glue of the envelope, slickly pungent, assaults her nose, turns her
stomach, and she runs to the bathroom and is promptly sick.

'What's the matter, Memsahib?' Sunitha frets as she gently
leads Bindu to a chair, handing her a tumbler of water. 'How
long've you been feeling like this?'

'Oh, for a while now. Ever since Ajji died. A symptom of grief,
I suspect. One of the more unpleasant ones.'

Sunitha continues to look assessingly at her.

'I know I'll be grieving for Ajji for the rest of my life, but I do
hope this stops soon. It's been months!'

Sunitha, that pondering look still on her face: 'All day or more
so in the mornings?'

'Well, any time... anything can trigger it. Smells, mostly.'

Sunitha's gaze taking in and resting on Bindu's stomach.

Bindu's eyes follow Sunitha's, with bemusement, at first, until,
suddenly, she understands...

Her sari skirt's been increasingly snug recently and she's been
puzzled as to how she's gained weight when she's sick more often
than not. 'Oh.'

'My cousin was exactly like this with her first, sick all through
her pregnancy.' Sunitha beams.

Since Ajji passed, Bindu's been wondering, *Why, Ajji? Why
leave me now?* But now she understands. Hence the sago payasam
recipe – her subconscious is dropping hints that a celebration is in
order. Ajji bestowed her a gift and then passed on. Bindu strokes
her stomach, experiencing awe, wonder, and something else,
something sour that she pushes away and yet it blooms, a dark
flower casting shadows upon her joy: *I can never escape now.*

Much as she tries to ignore the bitter aftertaste to the sweet
happiness making her body sing, it slurs her pearly joy, casting

aspersions on the dark navy of nightmares: a child of her own to love and cherish – but also an heir to the landlord's empire. And if it's a girl, then, like Bindu, will she too be doomed to this life of constraints, prison bars of rules defined by men, a trapped bird in a gilded cage, never free?

CHAPTER 53

EVE

1980

It is Saturday, Maya's first weekend without her mother; Eve's first weekend with a child in months.

'Shall we bake biscuits?' Eve suggests when Maya wakes and comes downstairs, mussed hair, sleep-sticky eyes.

'What about something from Izzy's nana's cookbook?' Maya says. 'I used to love cooking from it with her when I came over.'

And Eve recalls her resolve to cook from the book when she and Maya had visited the site of the accident.

Each night of her stay here, Maya has slept on Izzy's bunk, Eve reading her stories from Izzy's bookcase, then going to her own bedroom and falling asleep on Joe's side of the bed. She dreams of Izzy and Joe, and on waking, she's consumed afresh by grief; but not for long, for there's Maya's morning routine to follow. For breakfast, Maya has cereal – not Coco Pops now, but cornflakes – and afterwards they make a sandwich, ham and cheese or tuna, for her lunch. And once Maya leaves for school, there's shopping to do, cleaning. And writing.

Much to Sue's delight, Eve is writing again. Tentatively, just stream-of-consciousness journaling. Memories of Joe and Izzy that she's taken to jotting down. Letters to her family that they'll never read but are therapeutic all the same – it's like having conversations, albeit one-sided, with them, her mind supplying their replies, vivid and clear. It's her way of keeping them abreast of, and involved in, her life now.

Eve and Maya find the cookbook at the back of the cupboard. Maya carefully blows the dust off it, opens it reverently.

It smells of happy times; it is a repository of memories, a sensory feast, recalling Izzy's peals of delighted laughter when Eve misread coriander as cucumber: 'Now, why would she ask me to garnish with a few sprigs of cucumber?' The sugar- and spice-scented pages, gluey with gram flour, tattooed with turmeric thumbprints and a small chilli-stained handprint, perfectly preserved. Her daughter has left an impression on these pages that represent Eve's only connection to her birth mother. This recipe book carries the imprint of three generations in different corners of the world and afterworld, who will never meet again.

'Izzy loved cooking from her nana's book,' Maya says.

And looking at the girl, golden sunrays angling in and high-lighting her rich coffee curls, wearing her daughter's apron, dotted with daffodils, Eve feels, not sad, but thankful.

Morning sunshine accentuates the cobwebs in the ceiling, dust motes shining bright as jewels. But Eve doesn't see that. She looks at the cookbook, relics of joyful times together, creating food and memories with her family. *We were happy. It was short, the time we had together, painfully so, but we were happy.*

And for the first time, she dwells on good times, on what she had rather than what she's lost, and she's deeply grateful for it.

They decide on spicy omelettes – 'suitably breakfasty,' Maya says earnestly, and Eve nods, hiding her smile behind her hand.

Maya rushes about the kitchen collecting all the ingredients. She's cracking eggs and Eve is chopping onions and sniffing vigorously when the shrill ring of the phone cuts across their busy industry.

'I'll get it, love. You continue with what you're doing,' Eve says.

But Maya has stopped, 'It might be news about Mum. Perhaps they're calling to say she can come home?'

'I should be discharged in the next couple of days,' Jenny had said when they visited the previous evening, speaking nearly effortlessly now. She didn't need the breathing mask any more.

'It might well be so,' Eve agrees, as Maya follows her into the living room, hope and anxiety tangoing across her face.

Maya waits, her gaze never leaving Eve's as Eve wipes her hand on her apron, says, 'Hello?' into the receiver.

As soon as she sets the phone down, 'Is it Mum? Is she all right?' Maya asks.

'She's been given the all-clear and is coming home this evening,' Eve says.

Maya lets out a shriek of delight and launches herself into Eve's arms. Then, taking Eve's hands in hers, she leads her in a dance merrily across the room.

Eve laughs, sharing in Maya's infectious joy even as her heart dips. Jenny coming home means Maya going home too. Eve will miss her sorely, this little girl who's changed her life, made her discover purpose, even joy at times, inspired her to write again.

She will miss her.

CHAPTER 54

BINDU

1939

'You're smiling,' Guru says when he visits that night.

'Don't flatter yourself,' Bindu teases. 'It's nothing to do with you.'

He mock-frowns. 'I'm disappointed.'

'I tell a lie, it *is* to do with you, but...'

He takes her in his arms, kisses her deeply. 'I've missed your smiles.'

'I miss Ajji,' she whispers against his chest. 'But I know why she went when she did.'

He looks quizzically at her. 'It was her time?'

'She's left me a gift.'

'She has?' His face bemused.

She does not say a word, just raises her eyebrows while patting her stomach.

'Bindu! You mean...' His voice awed.

'Yes!'

'Oh, Bindu.' His eyes are soft and shining with joy as he gathers her in his arms.

He's thrilled. She's torn. With Ajji gone, she's resented being trapped in this life that she chose for her grandmother's sake. And now, she's bound by even stronger ties to this world that's never felt like hers. Ajji's gone, but there's a new life tethering her here.

Despite her apprehensions, she loves this child, Ajji's gift, already, but she can't help wondering whether growing up here, with over-the-top privileges and unshakeable prejudices, the excesses and the differences, the incontrovertible dogmas the landlord preaches, is in their best interests. But then is the alternative, the childhood she experienced – filled with joy and warmth yes, but also hardship and struggle – any better? Or can she find a middle ground?

'I'm going to be a father!' Guru beams, kissing her stomach.

And seeing Guru's elation, her doubts are momentarily assuaged. Guru is *not* his father. He's no longer in the landlord's thrall. Bindu will work with him to make sure their child is not subjected to the landlord's high-handed rules and narrow-minded dictums. She'll curb her restlessness, stop fantasising about running away to a different life and put down roots for the sake of her child. She'll effect more change for the better here in the landlord's mansion, which will no longer be the landlord's but hers, Guru's and their child's. *This* is the middle ground between her childhood and Guru's, what she wants for her child – filled with love and opportunity, devoid of the constant struggle for survival.

She tastes hope, bright white and pure, as Guru kisses her.

Guru leaves at dawn but pays Bindu a visit mid-morning, bearing fruits and nuts. 'For the beautiful mother of my child.'

'Guru, I'm not an invalid. If I want something, I can get it myself.'

Her husband has sourced the juiciest mangoes. They're nectary, her mouth exploding with syrup. And yet, they leave an acrid aftertaste. Is this how it's going to be from now on? Will even her freedom to choose what to eat, how to treat her own body, what to feed it be taken from her, her body now a receptacle, a machine that will grow and deliver her husband's heir?

Bile rises, nauseous blue, strangling the breath from her, the hopefulness she'd felt when she shared the news with Guru replaced by an almost uncontrollable compulsion to turn tail and run. To put as much distance as possible between herself and what's expected of her. The fact that she can't makes her more distressed, the impulse even stronger.

With difficulty, she pastes a smile on her face and swallows down the bitter gorge.

Guru gently caresses Bindu's stomach and she resists the urge to bat his hand away, bunching her hands into fists and sitting on them.

'Hello, my son,' Guru says.

'What if it's a girl?' she counters fiercely. *Your father and, by extension, you make the rules on how I must behave and live here, and now you also dictate the sex of our child?*

'Bindu, a girl next time. This one's a boy. I'd like my father to have his heir. It'd make him so happy.'

All the uncertainty, the angst, all her confused feelings, even more mixed after discovering she's pregnant, her agonising doubts and agitated worries, the claustrophobic choke of feeling trapped exploding from her in a shrill screech. 'What're you *saying?* Our child's not a tool to placate your father, feed his ego...'

'He's been through a tough time, with his strokes, and being bedridden. He's had to retire, and even though he doesn't show it, he's quite down. It'd lift his spirits if this was a boy, that's all I'm saying.'

'And if it's a girl, he won't be happy? Surely he shouldn't care what sex his grandchild is?'

'Bindu, you're being unreasonable,' Guru huffs.

'*I'm* being unreasonable?' She's *furious,* but, if she's honest, it's at herself more than anything. Why is she so frustrated? What is it about her that she can't simply be happy, enjoy her pregnancy, her husband's obvious joy, his solicitous care? Why does she have to analyse and worry about every little thing that may or may not happen? Why, like Sunitha frets, does she yearn to escape, crave something different, other, when things are going smoothly? Why the impulse to jeopardise, to rebel, to change, to run? Why can't she just accept what is and get on with it? Why can't she be like the other women, any of the village women, who'd have given anything to be in her shoes, with every luxury, more than enough to eat and drink, husband dancing to her tunes, spoiling her, waiting on her because she's carrying his heir? Why does she always want more? Why does she create problems when there aren't any?

The rage bubbles inside of her, needing an outlet, and Guru's right in front of her. 'Tell me, Guru, do you want a son too?'

Guru's eyes are flinty, his chin jutting out, lips disappearing into his frown. 'For my father's sake, yes. He asks me for a son every time I see him. It's his greatest wish, he says, to hold his grandson in his arms before he dies.'

'And if he has a granddaughter? He doesn't want to hold her?'

'You're deliberately misreading...'

A part of her knows that Guru's right. The landlord's always made it clear that he wants a grandson – he's never pretended otherwise. He even gave Bindu an ultimatum when she confronted him about banning newspapers in the early days of her marriage – but his stroke soon after, for which he blamed her, had put paid to that; he never threatened her again.

Now, she's deliberately causing an argument because she's angry at herself and at circumstance. She's been so since Ajji died. She chose this life for Ajji's sake, but Ajji is gone and here Bindu still is, stagnating in a life she didn't want. She's tried to keep a rein on her fury, but right at this moment, all the resentment and upset is spewing from her. She wants the life she gave up for Ajji and she can't have it, even more so now she's going to be mother to the landlord's grandchild. She loves this child, but she also wants to be free to do what she wants, to go after the life she dreamed of. She is tied when she wants rid of all ties, and she hates it even as she loves her child. She wants Ajji, who was her voice of reason, who knew just what to say to her granddaughter, tempering Bindu's hard edges with calm reason seasoned with fond affection.

Yes, Guru, although Bindu hates to admit it, is right. She's being unreasonable, but she can't seem to help it. She knows she should be happy – she has a loving, if at times intractable, husband, and a baby on the way – but she's not. She's angry, spoiling for a fight because she wants Ajji and instead she must make do with Guru.

'What am I misreading, do tell? He doesn't care about a grand-daughter, he only wants a grandson. If it's a granddaughter, will he shun her?'

'Of course not. Why're you being like this? He wants an heir for the business, that's all. There's no great conspira—' Guru is saying tightly, but Bindu's heard enough.

'Why can't a girl be the heir?'

'You know why. Because it's always been this way for genera-tions, the business passing from son to son.'

'It's also always been the tradition to marry nobility. But you changed that by marrying me. Can't it be the same with this child?'

'Bindu, my father's already made several compromises...'

'So, I'm a compromise? This child, if it's a girl, is a *compromise?*'

'Again, you're purposely misunderstanding...'

'Guru, forget your father. I'm asking *you*: do you want a son?'

Guru's face rigid, lips thin, he turns away. 'I can't talk to you when you're like this.'

'You didn't answer my question. Do you also think that the business should be passed on to a son?'

'That's the way it's always been.'

'I didn't think you were this narrow-minded...'

'It's not a question of narrow-mindedness. It's tradition. The business has always been handed down from son to son.'

'So, if this is a girl, she doesn't get anything?'

'She'll be married to a landowner who'll have his own wealth. Plus, we'll be bestowing substantial wealth upon her in the form of dowry. With all this in place, why should my daughter's husband also get *our* family business? We've worked hard for it, it should remain in the family, go to my son.'

'I cannot believe I'm even having this conversation with you. Guru, you're an educated, intelligent man and—'

'And I'm saying that it's been this way for generations and it's worked.'

'Only because nobody's questioned it before. Nobody's made the change. Do you want your daughter to feel she's not good enough?' *Like me. I could have made something of myself. Instead, I've*

been made to feel I'm not good enough, banned from reading newspapers or
helping with the business, nothing to stimulate and occupy my mind.

'That's rubbish. My sisters never—'

'How do you know? How on earth do you know? Did your
twelve-year-old sister have a say when she was married off to the
king who was thirty-six at the time and already had three wives?'

'She's happy. She's—'

'*How do you know?*'

'Why're you shouting? Calm down.'

'I cannot believe you...'

'Bindu, this screaming and temper tantrum is not good for you
in your state.'

'Don't you dare presume to know what's good for me.' She
shouldn't have started this. For having her husband's innate sexism
thrown at her is like he's punched her in the stomach, right where
their child nestles. She'd dared hope she might affect his decisions, bring about change now he's taken over from the landlord.
Granted, she hasn't followed Ajji's advice just now, but she understands that, for all her effort, whether she follows Ajji's advice or
not, she cannot change Guru's mind once it's made up. However
much Guru might humour her in small things, in things that
matter, the important things that *should* change, he is rigid, his
father's son. The realisation is exhausting. She hasn't made even a
dent in anyone's opinions, certainly not the landlord's, and
although she'd dared hope, not Guru's either. She feels light-
headed, woozy. Her husband is no different from his father, a chip
off the traditional, uncompromising, pig-headed old block.

'What's got into you? You're hysterical,' Guru is saying. Then,
alarm in his voice, which is fading, suddenly. 'Bindu?'

Has he left? Why is her vision fuzzing?

'Bindu. Bindu...?'

She is accosted by a blur of concerned faces. Guru, tight-lipped,
Sunitha wringing her sari pallu, and the doctor who'd tended to
Ajji, all hovering over her.

'Wha...' Her mouth feels inky.

'You had a bad turn,' the doctor says.

She's lying in bed, she realises, even as fear kidnaps her heart in frenzied ambush. 'The baby?'

'Is fine,' the doctor reassures her. 'But you must rest for the foreseeable. I'll check on you every day. No exertion, please.'

Sunitha's face worried. Guru's impassive.

Bindu looks away from her husband, at the doctor, as what he's saying registers. 'My cooking. My classes...'

'Bed rest for now. In a few weeks, we'll see.'

'A few *weeks?*' All these ties to the mansion had chafed but, now they're in danger of being taken away, she wants them – these small things that helped her pass the time, justified her being trapped in the unwanted and much-resented role of landlord's daughter-in-law, made her feel useful, as if she mattered in some modest way, as if she was making a difference. She hadn't become a doctor, saved lives, but she was still effecting change, she'd thought. But now even that is to be stopped. *All* her freedom taken away.

'You heard the doctor,' Guru says, voice clipped.

I hate him, Ajji. I hate, hate, hate him.

CHAPTER 55

EVE

1980

'Eve,' Maya says once she's polished off the spicy omelette she helped prepare with happy gusto, 'let's cook something from Izzy's nana's cookbook to welcome Mum home.'

Maya decides that her mother will love the sambar – the spiced vegetable soup.

And as Eve and Maya follow Eve's mother's recipe, step by step, like Eve used to when cooking with her daughter, as they chop and peel and temper and sauté, Eve, just as when she read the tributes to Joe and Izzy at the site of the accident, far from feeling sad or upset or sorrowful or distressed, is happy. Revelling in Maya's joy. Hearing her own daughter's laughter, seeing her face vividly, as if she was standing beside her, her tongue poking out of her mouth in focussed concentration as she measured out the ingredients, her sweet voice ordering her mother about bossily.

She realises when she tastes the sambar, the explosion of flavours in her mouth, that she's thoroughly enjoyed cooking this recipe. That this sambar has never tasted better.

Until now she's eaten for the sake of it, not deriving joy from it. But now, every mouthful is pure joy.

'Why did it take you this long, Mama?' Izzy giggles in her head, her daughter's laughter like sun-splashed jewels.

CHAPTER 56

BINDU

1939

Guru visits every day, along with the doctor. He is solicitous, but Bindu can barely stand to look at him, answering his queries, after the doctor has left, about how she's feeling in monosyllables.

Finally, 'What's the matter? Why're you sulking? Is it the pregnancy making you moody?' he asks.

'How dare you blame the pregnancy, call me moody! And what do you mean, what's the matter? Have you forgotten already?' Bindu, on the other hand, has been going over every word of their argument, her resentment, anger and sense of claustrophobia festering as she lies here with no means of escape, utterly trapped.

'Now, Bindu' – he looks alarmed – 'don't get yourself into a state.'

'Don't you dare patronise me, you...' She pauses as she feels her vision blurring again.

The next thing, Guru is calling for Sunitha to send for the doctor and Sunitha and the doctor are fussing around her, Guru standing beside her bed, arms crossed, face a mask.

His apology, or even an acknowledgement about what was said, never comes. Bindu knows she'd behaved unreasonably too – she must've been sickening, her emotions all over the place, but that's no excuse – but she'll not apologise either. For why should she make herself even smaller than they make her feel, her husband and his father, holding all the power, and she rendered powerless, thinking they can determine even the sex of her child by wishing it so? No, she'll not apologise, even though she screamed like a banshee, caused an argument when Guru was being kind, bringing fruit to his pregnant wife. But, she tells herself, it was on condition that this child is a boy.

Just the thought makes her angry, her heart palpitates dangerously. She takes deep breaths until she calms down. She will not apologise.

While Bindu's on bed rest, Guru has asked Sunitha to stay overnight with her.

'Your siblings...' Bindu says.

'My sister's finished school now. She's like me, never took to book learning, but she's very good with the younger ones. My brother, on the other hand – thanks to you, Memsahib, the scholarships you tricked your husband into providing – is doing so well. He's the first of my family to study further and will be the first to get a job in an office.' Pride and love glow in Sunitha's eyes as she squeezes Bindu's hands. 'Thank you, Memsahib. You gave up your dreams, but you've helped others follow theirs.'

Bindu's eyes shine. 'Ah, Sunitha, it was nothing.'

'It was everything. You've adjusted to this life that you didn't want, and in doing so you've changed all our lives. I'd stay any number of nights with you, Memsahib.'

Bindu sniffs, feeling unworthy. *I haven't adjusted to this life, Sunitha, not really. I still fantasise about running away.*

'In any case,' Sunitha continues, 'staying with you overnight is no hardship at all. In fact, it's luxury. Your husband's paying me very well, Memsahib, for a full night's sleep, undisturbed by children's wailing and petty fights.'

'You love looking after your siblings.'

'I do.' Sunitha's face softens. 'But I love you too.'

'Ah, Sunitha.' Bindu's eyes water. 'I'm blessed in you.'

'It works both ways, Memsahib.' Sunitha smiles, enveloping

Bindu in her spice-scented embrace, whispering in her ear, 'I'm the lucky one.'

You're not. I am and yet I'm constantly beset by the urge to throw it all away, chase the dream that was to be my life, once.

Each week, Bindu asks if she can get up now. She's had enough.

But the doctor decrees that she must continue with her bed rest.

Bindu's bored out of her mind.

'If I can't cook, can I at least teach the servants from my chambers?'

'Only the women,' Guru says.

'Why not the men?'

'In your private chambers? Don't be deliberately obtuse, Bindu.'

'You're being stubbornly narrow-minded, like your father.'

'Enough.' He storms off, leaving her winded. Sunitha rushes for her medication.

Bindu teaches the maidservants in the mornings, rests in the afternoons, writes to Laurence Elliot in the evenings. This means of communication with her friend is more important than ever now she's laid up.

War is inevitable, Laurence writes. *I'm leaving for England in a few weeks to sign up. I'm looking for someone to take over the magazine, but have had no luck so far.*

I could do it, Bindu thinks. *I wish I could.* Feeling guilty for the thought, she caresses her bump. *I love you, my babe, even if you tie me to this place. I will love you like Ajji loved me, with my all, and hope it's enough to counteract your father and grandfather's disappointment at your sex.*

For, increasingly, she's convinced that this child's a girl.

She's angry with her husband, the affection that had kindled following his kindness after Ajji passed, sloughed off by his stance on the sex of his child. His visits with Bindu are short and awkward; he's brusque, distant, afraid to say anything that might rouse her temper and harm his child. They are formal, like strangers.

'I can help with the business,' she'd said, setting aside all the subtle ways preached by Ajji. For what was the point? She'd tried being sweet and smilingly obedient, hoping Guru might take her ideas into account, that together they could change the way things were done – and it hadn't worked.

'You're bedridden,' he'd countered.

'So's your father. But he's been running the business from his bed, until recently. If you brought me some papers to look at...'

'Leave it, Bindu.'

'Why, because I'm a woman and the business can only be handled by a man?'

'Enough.'

'Why do you do it, Memsahib – deliberately provoke him when he comes to see you?' Sunitha sighed after Guru had marched off.

'He's maddening.'

Sunitha shook her head. 'He might say the same about you. You complain that he has a temper. Don't you see that you do too? If he's dangerous when he's angry, you're even more so.'

'Enough, Sunitha.'

'See, you're exactly like him, both of you just as bad as the other, neither giving an inch,' Sunitha tutted in exasperation.

In the evenings, after dusk, Sunitha helps Bindu into the courtyard – the doctor has mercifully recommended a small walk each day. The fountain ripples seductively, every so often glimmering with the reflections of the lit lanterns the guards use as they pace the west wing walls, as they do all the walls of the mansion through the night, a dancing constellation of jewels flirting with the reflections of palm trees.

If Dumdee was here, he'd have bounded to the fountain, lapped at it noisily like he used to drink from the stream during those brief joyous weeks when it was pregnant and overflowing with monsoon water. Bindu still misses Dumdee, aches for him, even after all this time. When, a few weeks back, Sunitha informed Bindu that Dumdee had died of old age, it had exacerbated her sorrow at Ajji's loss and she'd grieved terribly, writing so many tributes to her beloved pet that she'd filled an entire notebook.

The sky is dark and cloudless, unlike the clouds that mar her own thoughts. Guru's words reverberating in her head: 'She'll be married to a landowner who'll have his own wealth. Plus, we'll be bestowing substantial wealth upon her in the form of dowry. With all this in place, why should my daughter's husband also get *our* family business? We've worked hard for it, it should remain in the family, go to my son.'

Bindu is furious and upset at Guru's refusal to see anything wrong with his views. This means that if their child's a girl – and Bindu is convinced so – she's doomed to be second best, not good enough, and she'll know it. Just like Bindu, always having to kowtow to men, to shut her mouth and keep her opinions in check. Her daughter won't have the freedom to be herself, just as Bindu couldn't be who she wanted to be. Her daughter will be trapped in this life, just as Bindu is. Not the coveted heir, just a girl, to be paraded among women at parties and married at sixteen – or earlier – to a wealthy suitor who'll treat her like a possession. A childhood not wanting in material comforts but offering barely any freedom. Forever the intimation that she is 'only' a girl, groomed to marry well, valued only by the match she'll make.

Not if Bindu has anything to do with it. Bindu wants for this child what she herself had: schooling, and with it the potential for freedom and independence, unbeholden to any man, alongside the certainty that she's loved.

This child will be the centre of Bindu's world, but she'll always feel the lack from her father and grandparents, and how will it affect her?

And what if this child is a boy? He'll be cosseted and spoilt, denied nothing, like Guru was. Bindu will try to ground him, but she'll only have him until he's five, or at best seven years old, after which he'll be sent to boarding school; and then, when he returns, he'll move into his father's quarters, visiting his mother every so often and then only cursorily.

No, *never*. Whether girl or boy, this child will not suffer the fate she's envisioning, Bindu vows. This is *her* child and she'll fight with her all to give her babe a well-rounded childhood, instil in him or her the right values. But she can't see it happening in this house.

What should she do?

She looks at the dancing water of the fountain. It twinkles with merry nonchalance.

She wishes Ajji was here to advise. She cannot ask Sunitha – her friend would think her mad to even countenance denying her child a life of ease here at the mansion. And so, Bindu picks up her pencil and begins a letter to her only other friend, who's always treated her as an equal, who's never made her feel second best, who has, in publishing her recipes and paying for them, through his magazines, his gift of the poetry book and his letters, given her agency, returned to her some sense of self. Her friend, who'll be leaving for England very soon to do his bit for the war effort. The thought of being stuck here without Laurence to write to makes her want to scream: *Take me with you. I'd love to travel to England, see daffodils. Be free.*

Dear Laurence, she begins. They've been addressing each other by their first names for a while now. *I've a hypothetical question. What if I wanted to go away, leave here with my child? How would I go about it?*

Once she's finished, she chews the end of her pencil. She doesn't need Sunitha to tell her that if she posts this letter, it's the ultimate betrayal and impropriety. For she's asking another man for advice on how to leave her husband, taking their child with her. Hypothetically – but Laurence will see through that, of course.

But she's just setting her thoughts on paper. She won't post the letter.

Or will she?

CHAPTER 57

EVE

1980

Maya and Eve decide, after the success of the spicy omelette and sambar, to make vegetable pakoras, using peppers and aubergines.

Unlike Izzy, who insisted that they stick religiously to her nana's recipes, Eve and Maya use what they have, experimenting when they can't find an ingredient, using poppy seeds instead of cumin, ginger powder instead of fresh ginger.

'Mama, the taste won't be the same!' Eve hears her daughter's voice in her head, spiky with outrage.

'Izzy wouldn't be happy. She liked everything just so,' Maya says, as she adds spring onions in lieu of red onions to the pakora mix – they used up the red onions for the sambar.

And Eve smiles.

It is lovely reminiscing about her daughter with her best friend. It is wonderful cooking from her mother's book, touching the pages that bear the imprint of her daughter's sticky fingers, hearing her voice in her head.

As they wait for the oil to reach the right temperature, Maya asks, 'Was your mother a chef?'

'I don't know, love.'

'You don't?' Maya's surprised.

'All I have of her is this cookbook. My adoptive dad, who was a

publisher, collated her recipes and notes and published them in
book form as a keepsake for me.'

Maya considers this, even as she keeps a beady eye on the vat
of oil. 'Your mother was Indian,' she says after a bit.

'Yes.'

'Have you been to India?'

'No.'

'Why not?'

'Never had the time. Or the money for it.' The lines she always
uses, blithely finding excuses for not making the trip. But, she
thinks now, perhaps she's done so because she'd been happy, loved,
secure, content with her parents, and with Joe and Izzy, the family
she made, and hadn't wanted to rake up the past.

Maya puts her hands on her hips. Her cheeks are dotted with
gram flour. A curl has escaped the imperfect plaits that Eve
braided this morning and rests upon her forehead. 'Izzy told me it
was her dream to visit India.'

'It was?'

'She said you were all going before she started secondary
school.'

'That was the plan, yes, if we'd managed to save enough by
then.' Eve hadn't known Izzy was so interested in visiting India. It
was always Joe, who'd no connection to the country whatsoever,
who'd been most enthusiastic about it. 'Aren't you even a little bit
curious about your family?' he would ask. And Eve would reply,
simply, 'You are my family.' Now, she sees with sudden insight that
she was subconsciously aware she'd had more than her fair share
of happiness and was apprehensive of doing anything to rock it,
tip the balance.

'Izzy said you'd read the stories about her nana's childhood
accompanying each recipe in this cookbook together and that
made her want to experience it for herself,' Maya is saying.

Eve's throat is clogged up. She cannot speak.

But Maya doesn't require her to. 'Eve,' the little girl says gently,
'you should go to India.'

She'll be lonely after Maya goes home. She's brought joy into

Eve's life, given it purpose. Since Maya came to stay, Eve is writing again.

I can write from anywhere. And where better than India? she thinks. *I will go. I've no excuses not to any more. I've all the time in the world. I've the money from Joe's insurance.* A painful pang at this. *I'll finally meet the aunt who's been writing to me, inviting me to visit for as long as I can remember. My mother's best friend. I'll find out about my mother.*

She realises that now she wants to know more about this woman whose recipes her daughter loved. She's not been curious before. She had her mother's book. Her aunt's letters. She had two loving, supportive parents, a doting partner and a wonderful child. Her life was full and happy. But now, she's ready to find out more. To discover where she came from, how she ended up here, living this life.

'You know what, Maya?' she says, 'there's an idea.'

Maya smiles. Then, 'Eve, I think the oil's ready for the pakoras.'

CHAPTER 58

BINDU

1939

Increasingly, especially since her estrangement from Guru, Laurence Elliot is Bindu's lifeline, her connection to the world outside these four walls. With Laurence, as they discuss the inevitability of war in Europe, India's fight for independence from British rule, the communal riots, Hindus and Muslims turning on each other, the solace of fiction and poetry when the world is falling apart around them, Bindu feels seen, heard, understood, valued. In his eyes, she is an intelligent and articulate person who contributes to his magazine and has opinions that are valid, rather than a mere woman. She shares her conflicted thoughts with him, how she feels trapped, how she cannot be true to herself here in the mansion, and he understands.

Society needs to change, afford women a voice, he writes, *both here and in England. I know this doesn't help you in your situation, and I wish I could do more than offer a listening ear.*

His words give her hope that perhaps when – if – she needs his help to leave the mansion, he will offer it.

'Memsahib,' Sunitha says when Bindu hands her the latest letter to post, 'you're with child. Should you be continuing this...?'

'Yes. It's something for me.'

She hasn't posted the letter she wrote asking Laurence for suggestions about how she and her child could – hypothetically – get away from Guru and this mansion. But she's saved it and is still deliberating about whether to send it. In the meantime, she has some ideas about what she'll do. She has the money from the publication of her recipes, minus what she's given Sunitha for her help. She could use that to book a passage to England – Laurence would help with that, she hopes. Once in England – *England!* – she will work. She could use the money from the sale of the jewellery and saris Guru's gifted her during their marriage to tide her over until she finds a job. She could be a nanny, a cook, a writer, a maid. She's willing to do anything at all. Just the thought of it – freedom to work, to live her life *her* way – gives her the same exciting thrill as when she was a schoolgirl studying for a scholarship and dreaming of independence, agency of her own.

She knows there are obstacles, of course – how would she leave without Guru knowing? How would Laurence help if he was already in England? Even if she got to England, how would she find work in a country at war? Would it be safe for her and her child? And even if it was, how would she manage to work as well as care for an infant?

But still... imagining freedom, escape, gives her hope, bright as a shiny new coin.

Sunitha's voice cuts into her daydream. 'You have so much. This could jeopardise—'

'I know, Sunitha. All that I have is thanks to my husband, subject to his whims. This is why I *need* something that is only, exclusively, mine. If he crosses the line once my child is here, I'll take her to England, the land of Wordsworth. See daffodils for real, instead of picturing them in my mind's eye.'

All the maidservants now know Wordsworth's 'I Wandered Lonely as a Cloud' by heart, thanks to Bindu.

Sunitha smiles, her face softening. 'You'll go to England, will you? With your child?'

'With my child,' Bindu agrees, stroking her stomach.

'Memsahib, you're bright, intelligent, amazing. You've done so much for us, changed our lives for the better, and yet you're also like a child. You don't see when your actions might cause...'

'What'll they cause? I'm corresponding with a man who pays me for my recipes. I'm earning my own money so when my husband is high-handed, reminding me that I owe everything to him, I can take comfort from the fact that at least I've *something* of my own. I'm teaching my daughter how to be independent even when all avenues appear closed.'

'But, Memsahib, don't you see how much it would hurt Sahib if he found out? He has a temper and is prone to lashing out, as several servants have found to their detriment...'

'Don't I know it! But Guru won't find out.'

'Memsahib—'

'In any case, Laurence is signing up for the war effort in England. He's not found someone to take over the magazine, so it'll most likely fold. So, my days of clandestine correspondence are numbered. Now, are you going to post this or what?'

'Memsahib...'

'Yes, I know that I'm playing with fire and might get burned.'

Sunitha does not utter another word, but her expression says it all.

CHAPTER 59

EVE

1980

INDIA

Four weeks after Maya goes home to Jenny, who returned fit and hale from hospital, Eve exits the airport in India, into a maelstrom of khaki-clad men, yelling, 'Taxi, ma'am, me speak English, good price!' A bemused Eve, dazed from jet lag, dazzled by sunlight, teetering from this eager onslaught, picks one at random.

The taxi driver immediately takes control of her luggage, lifting her suitcase onto his head as if it weighs nothing, and leads her to the car, a compact, rusted vehicle that looks like it might fall apart any minute. He then proceeds to heft her case onto the roof, securing it in place with a fraying rope. Noting Eve's concern, the driver grins, displaying a cave of a mouth, rotting stumps of teeth, 'No worry. No fall.'

The car takes three tries to start and, when it finally leaves the airport behind and Eve is afforded her first proper glimpse of India, she stops minding if they break down or her case falls off the roof, her belongings strewn on the road – it's all part of her adventure in this tropical country, so wonderfully, noisily different from England.

London, despite its big-city vibe, seems tame in comparison to the sheer life and bustle here. People and animals crowding the streets, a welter of colour and sounds. Hawkers in the dirt by the roadside, their wares spread out on newspapers flapping in the humid breeze: baskets of exotic fruit and vegetables; fish with glinting scales, unseeing eyes, bloody innards; glass bangles catching the light and twinkling seductively; teetering piles of coconuts; kaleidoscopic mounds of spices. The scents: manure and fermented fruit and drains and spices. Everything coated in an orange haze of dust, the white-gold brilliance of sun.

People cooking, drinking, eating, laughing, defecating, tending to children and animals, right there on the streets, living in tents fashioned from colourful saris propped up by tree branches, which wobble precariously as bullock carts and buses and rickshaws and lorries and cars career past, each trying to overtake the other. Cows, dogs, hens, monkeys, even camels, *elephants*, a peacock or two, sharing the road with vehicles and pedestrians. Eve's taxi in danger of overturning into ditches overflowing with rubbish, she thinks, until the pile of scraps moves and she sees it's a *person*, coated in dirt and dust, his body riddled with festering sores, wounds of eyes. Emaciated children, gaunt faces, haunted gazes.

Eve is distressed, overwhelmed, thankful for the life she's had. *I've suffered tragedy, but this puts it in humbling perspective.*

Barely ten minutes into their journey, to Eve's amazement, the taxi driver careens to a juddering halt beside a family risking their lives by standing very close to the dangerously packed road and waving their hands frantically at passing vehicles, nearly bumping into the autorickshaw that has suddenly braked in front. A heated exchange of words follows between the taxi driver and the rickshaw driver before the rickshaw driver spits on the road in fury, jumps into his vehicle and speeds away.

The taxi driver grins at Eve, holding up his finger, 'One minute,' and climbing out.

He gestures to the family group – a mother, father and two small children – and the next minute, he's loading their bags onto the roof.

Shocked, Eve climbs out, tapping the driver on the shoulder.

He turns, nearly dropping the bag he's affixing atop of Eve's case upon her head, managing to catch it just in time.

Eve, startled, steps away, onto the foot of one of the young children, who promptly starts crying, regarding her with wide-eyed reproach.

'I'm so sorry,' she says to the child, who bawls even louder.

'What's happening?' she asks the driver. She has to shout to be heard above the cries of the child and the whispers of the crowd that has gathered, all in the space of a minute, it seems, around them.

'They coming.' The taxi driver grins cheerily, wiping sweat off his face with the sleeve of his khaki shirt, nodding his head in the direction of the family.

'But...'

'They going same place.'

It would require energy Eve doesn't have to ask the driver to retrieve her case from the roof rack and find another taxi to take her. In contrast to the sheer choice at the airport, here she spots rickshaws and lorries and buses clogged with too many passengers, a raggedy cat, two scrawny dogs and a hen pecking half-heartedly at the mud by the roadside, but no other car in sight.

Defeated, Eve climbs in and the family bundle in next to her, body odour and dust, the children both crying now, the car windows open and whipping grit and spices and noise into their faces, the taxi rattling and rutting over potholes. Eve is jolted along, falling against the family and vice versa as the car swerves, the driver stopping once more for two men who climb in next to him, nearly sitting atop him, their luggage on their laps. How he changes the gears and navigates through traffic, she shudders to imagine.

Eve is just deciding there's nothing for it but to go with the flow, ignore the aches and pains she's experiencing on this roller-coaster of a journey, when, with a screeching of horns, just as they're navigating a bridge with no railings, their ramshackle taxi decides to overtake a lorry overrun with people – several are hanging off the roof. Of course this foolhardy manoeuvre causes the taxi to veer into the fast-flowing river below, two wheels going

off the road, teetering over the water, the men in front shouting
and gesticulating frantically, the children beside Eve, who'd just
stopped crying, starting again. The driver with great skill manages
to right the taxi just in time, thank goodness, all four wheels back
on solid ground. But barely has Eve's heart settled than he is over-
taking bullock carts and autorickshaws, buses and pedestrians and
animals who walk without a care in the middle of the road, even
children barely older than Maya and Izzy hefting little ones on
their hips. The taxi races through narrow roads meant for two
vehicles but hosting five at least, not counting people and animals,
flanked by huts and hawkers, spices flavoured with grit painting
the dusty orange air all colours of the rainbow as vehicles thunder
past.

CHAPTER 60

BINDU

1939

In Bindu's eighth month of confinement, Guru extends an olive branch.

'I know that despite teaching the maids, you've been bored.'

'Ha, you noticed! Should I applaud you on your observation skills?'

'Why're you like this, Bindu?' he sighs.

'I've always been like this.' *Except for a brief interlude when I took Ajji's advice. But now Ajji's gone, I no longer bother with it.* 'You used to like it once upon a time.'

In fact, one of the reasons he'd married her was because he liked her spirit, but he's spent their marriage crushing it. And she's had enough. She'll not let her child suffer the same fate and she'll not tolerate her child witnessing Bindu being put down by her husband. For what sort of example will that set for her child?

'Bindu, the reason I came' – he runs his hand down his face, the gesture tired – 'is to say we'll host a party here. To celebrate our child's imminent entry into the world.'

'Even if it's a girl?' She's deliberately needling him, for she's bored out of her mind. He won't let her help with the business. She has so many ideas, especially now with England at war, the Indian independence struggle ramping up, the communal riots between Hindus and Muslims getting heated, but, like his father,

Guru won't listen, will not accept that she might have points of value, for she's a mere woman, her only job, in his eyes, to grow his child. She's tired of being overlooked and undervalued, fed up of being caged, Guru her captor, her opinions ignored, her voice silenced. Her only sport is baiting him, seeing him try to rein in his temper for fear of causing damage to his unborn child in her belly.

'Stop, please,' he says, sounding weary.

We're having a child together, she thinks, *yet we can't conduct a single meaningful conversation any more.*

'I've not hosted a party since taking over as landlord. And with war in Europe and many of our friends leaving to sign up...'

Bindu feels a pang as she thinks of Laurence Elliot.

'We might as well have a big celebration before all the doom and gloom,' Guru's saying.

'Will women be allowed to mix with men?'

'Bindu,' he sighs like she's a child who's pushing his buttons. He doesn't even try to understand her, figure out why she's being so ornery. He cannot know how frustrated she is, how torn, how powerless she feels, because he's never had his hands tied, his freedom curbed. The few times when he was younger and his father expected him to do things his way, Guru had rebelled and come complaining to Bindu, but he's conveniently forgotten that.

'A valid question, which you're deflecting,' she says. 'Which leads me to deduce—'

Predictably, he cuts her off. 'You're still on bed rest, so you'll be unable to mingle as you'll be reclining for the duration of the party. Given this, it's best for the women's darbar to be separate.'

'So, at your first party as landlord, you're continuing your father's tradition of segregating women, using me, pregnant with your child, as an excuse. Nice.'

'I did think it'd be a nice gesture, something that'd make you happy, alleviate the monotony of your days. I was, clearly, wrong,' he says tightly, face grim, as he walks away.

Guru, do you expect me to applaud? Praise your thoughtfulness? Why won't you try to understand your wife? You married me because I was different from the other women, but you've spent our marriage trying to mould me into one of them. Well, I refuse. You think a party would help? I've always hated parties, especially those where we're segregated from the men, and you know this. I'll only be happy when I'm free and my child is too.

'The party's going ahead?' she asks his rigid back.

'I've already sent out invitations.'

'So, telling me was just a formality. It wasn't something you organised for my benefit. You'd already decided on a party, whether I agreed to it or not.'

He doesn't reply.

She is raging, incensed, absolutely *furious* with her husband. She wants some semblance of agency, wants to stop feeling useless, a mere prop in his life. And so, she writes to Laurence, inviting him to the party. *Please come. I'd like to thank you in person for all you've done for me before you leave for England.* She also wants to ask his advice on how to escape – she never did send the letter with her 'hypothetical' query – for she's decided that she *will. I'll contrive to meet you in the courtyard in the west wing where we met before. Time and details to follow in my next letter.*

And as she seals the letter and hands it to Sunitha, who takes it, not knowing what it contains, she hears her friend's refrain strident in her head, 'You're playing with fire.'

CHAPTER 61

EVE

1980

The taxi weaves between bullock carts topped to twice their height with hay, buses and lorries, with people dangling off the yawning openings that pass for doors, seemingly balanced on just one leg and one hand, jostled by the dust-laden breeze and other vehicles, more people spilling from the roof, all to the accompaniment of ear-splitting horns, as the sun sizzles gold from the endless white canopy of sky. A coconut hangs from a telephone line like an afterthought.

Eve keeps her fingers crossed that she arrives at her destination in one piece.

How Izzy would have marvelled at the mad chaos around her, the helter-skelter taxi ride! And Joe... He'd always wanted to come here.

And now here she is, funding this trip via the pay-off from her husband's life insurance policy.

Oh, Joe.

'Izzy and I are here in spirit,' he whispers, she imagines. 'We're seeing it, experiencing it with you, through you.'

And finally, the driver comes to a stop by the side of a road with small cottages scattered beside it. The men in front jump off. The parents beside Eve gently rouse their children, who'd only just fallen asleep in the adults' arms, tears drying in salty tracks on their faces; upon waking, they start sobbing again.

Eve stretches as she blinks at her surroundings through the grainy haze of red dust, the blistering dazzle of sun, hot air enveloping her in a humid embrace. The aroma of spicy fried food mingles with the reek of drains. Izzy would have absolutely *loved* this, Eve thinks, hearing her daughter's delighted giggles in her head, seeing her face lit up in absorbed wonder.

The taxi driver unties the rope holding the luggage in place with a flourish, handing Eve her case, which, like her, has arrived bruised and battered but in one piece. Pocketing his fare, grinning widely at Eve's generous tip, he beams: 'You take autorickshaw from here to Suryanagar.'

CHAPTER 62

BINDU

1939

The party's in full swing, but Bindu can't settle, obsessively watching the clock, trying to do it as discreetly as possible, even as she attempts to engage in the requisite small talk.

She's feeling on show, decked out in her husband's over-the-top gifts of jewellery, the women's eyes drawn to her bump – the new landlord's heir.

Bindu can hear their thoughts: *This mere servant elevated to wife of landlord has waited long enough to do her duty. Will she give him a son, or will it be the disappointment of a girl child?*

She wishes she was with the men, discussing politics and world events, seeing their expressions change as they realise that she is more than a pretty face, someone whose opinions, which they were resigned to suffering for politeness' sake, far from being vapid and inconsequential, actually carry weight; that she is as good as them, if not better.

Or, better still, she wishes she wasn't here at all but somewhere on her own with her child, a success in her own right, living an independent, fulfilled life of her own choosing.

'We heard you've had to rest for almost your entire pregnancy. Are you all right?' The women can't quite hide the relish of gossip from their voices, sizzling on their avid tongues, even as they try for concerned.

Wants the world to revolve around her, they're thinking. *Women give birth all the time, but this one must make a production of it.*

She hears their murmurs, even as they call for maids to bring chiwda, bondas, coconut chutney, chicken pakoras, lime sherbet, cinnamon and ginger tea, paan, another chair – actually, a divan would be better – some cushions, a fan.

Everyone has children. These village girls are supposed to be hardy. What a fuss she makes, carrying a child, and that too one she took so long to conceive.

Bindu becomes progressively quieter and wilts in her seat as around her the women laugh and gossip, nudging each other as they point to her, whispering, *Look at her, what a weakling. The landlord's had a rough deal with this one. Now, if it was my daughter he'd married, she'd have produced a couple of robust boys by now, at the very least...*

Bindu surreptitiously watches the clock and at the time agreed with Laurence Elliot, she beckons to Sunitha: 'I'm not feeling up to it, I'll go for a lie-down.'

I know it's against protocol for us to meet in private, Laurence had written in reply to her invitation:

> *but I cannot let this opportunity pass me by when I'm leaving the country to fight a war on the other side of the world and there's a distinct possibility we might never cross paths again. Over the course of our correspondence, you've become a special friend and it would be my privilege and honour to meet you in person, albeit to bid adieu.*

Sunitha is saying, 'I'll accompany you, Memsahib.'

'No, you're needed here. Stay. It's just a few paces to my chambers, I can manage.'

'I'll come to check on you soon.'

'I want to sleep. Give it an hour at least?'

There will be gossip, even more so than usual, at Bindu bailing on her duties as hostess and leaving the party early. She knows it won't go unnoticed, that it might get back to Guru. She hears Sunitha's voice in her head: 'You're playing with fire.'

Yes, Sunitha. Perhaps I want to.

For now that she's set things in motion, a big part of her *wants* to be caught, wants an altercation with her husband. With her child imminent, she's reached the point of no return, absolutely fed up with her lack of agency – her difficult pregnancy and enforced bed rest not helping matters. She's too frustrated with her life to continue as it is. She wants change – some change, any change – especially once her child is here, for she doesn't want her child to live in this house if the rules continue as they are now, rigid and uncompromising, women treated as second best, dumbed down, hidden away, ignored, and servants even worse – although she's tried her hardest to change that, it's not nearly enough. She'll tell Guru so if it comes to that, tell him she wants to leave. She's ready for it – she hopes Laurence will help, perhaps even agree to book a passage to England for herself and her child.

Bindu leaves the ladies' party suite, walking unobtrusively but as briskly as her bump will allow down the corridors – she hasn't worn her anklets, presents from her husband and in-laws, the better to be quiet. She avoids the passageways frequented by the servants weaving to and from the kitchens with platters of food and trays of drink, staying in the shadows so that the guards patrolling the corridors upstairs don't see her.

And finally, she's at the courtyard in the west wing, her own private garden, her respite. She sits down, catching her breath, glad Laurence is not here yet. She needs a moment to herself – unused as she is to exertion, having been on bed rest all this while. Her baby responds to her touch, but is she not as sprightly as usual, or is that just Bindu's imagination? And those sudden sharp twitches in her belly, which she's been experiencing all morning with increasing frequency, as though someone is prodding it – are they normal? Are they the cramps the doctor said she might experience as she gets closer to labour – her body rehearsing for it? She'll be sure to ask him when he visits tomorrow.

She throws her head to the heavens, twinkling bright gold through dappled palm fronds. She is spent – what she told Sunitha wasn't a lie. She really is not up to it and is relieved to be free of the gaggle of women, in this green-gold haven, fountain burbling, honeyed, earth-spiced air stroking her face. Until Laurence gets here, she's alone; all the maids are busy serving the party guests. She sits discreetly in the shade of the palm trees, her green sari blending with the fronds, the gold border looking like splashes of sunshine, waiting to finally, properly, meet the man who has over the course of their correspondence become a very dear friend.

CHAPTER 63

EVE

1980

The crew of rickshaw drivers lounging lazily on their vehicles, smoking roll-ups and gossiping, stand to attention as Eve approaches, all talking at once: 'I speak English, ma'am.' 'I take you anywhere.'

The taxi driver, who's now finished collecting payment from the other passengers, bounds to her side like a modern-day saviour, self-importantly looking over the noisy huddle of rickshaw drivers and singling one out, with whom he converses rapidly in the local language, musical but incomprehensible to Eve.

The back-and-forth continues, with the other rickshaw drivers joining in. One of them pushes the taxi driver and he pushes him back and a squabble ensues, a crowd forming to watch. While some intervene to pull the fighting parties apart, others egg them on. Even though Eve doesn't understand the language, she can deduce from the cheers, the yells and – ouch, it's now escalated to blows delivered to and fro – what's going on.

What on earth have I got myself into? she muses.

But then she hears Izzy's voice in her head, agog with wonder: 'What an adventure you're having, Mama!'

And this allows her to relax, let go, enjoy what's going on, instead of fretting about whether she's done the right thing in coming here.

Finally, with intervention from the crowd, well-meaning onlookers physically holding back the taxi driver and the sparring rickshaw drivers, the physical fight devolves once more into rapid-fire exchanges of heated words. Again, even though Eve cannot understand, she misses nothing, thanks to the violent body language and raging expressions of the warring parties straining against the arms preventing them from launching themselves upon each other.

Meanwhile, through the pungent spice and body odour press of the crowd, Eve is aware of a gentle tap on her shoulder. A small man with kindly eyes beckoning to her: 'I take you.' She hesitates, unsure, but he smiles at her and something in the way his eyes crinkle reminds her of Joe, even as she hears Izzy's voice in her head again, vivid as anything: 'I'd trust him, Mama.' She nods and, beaming, the man picks up her case and manoeuvres her unobtrusively through the mob intent on the fight. Quietly, they slip away from the mayhem to the man's autorickshaw resting in the shade of a huge tree.

Once she's seated, her case stowed beneath her feet, the driver takes off. The still-arguing taxi and auto drivers and the huddle surrounding them become aware of them only once they're some distance away and stop arguing at once, united in their surprised outrage as they run behind the rickshaw yelling, 'Hey!'

They can't catch up and recede into the distance, their faces contorted in anger at this sneaky trick played by one of their own, shaking their fists and shouting what are no doubt insults, until they're obliterated by the cloud of orange dust left in the wake of the autorickshaw wheels churning up dirt on the mud road.

Eve is hot and bothered and sweaty, yet she can't help laughing and the rickshaw driver joins in. And, looking up through the autorickshaw canopy's see-through plastic to the cloudless gold sky above, Eve realises that, in this moment, she's utterly *happy* in a way she hasn't been since she lost her family and thought she'd never be again.

She asks the driver, 'Won't you be in trouble with them?'

He turns to look at her and the rickshaw judders over a pothole and tilts ominously.

'Please concentrate on the road,' Eve says.

He looks back at the road, but asks, 'What you say, madam?'

She smiles. 'My name is Eve.'

'Eve.' The rickshaw driver nods vigorously while grinning at her in his mirror. 'Nice name. What it mean?'

'It means life.' Her dad would reiterate, often, 'You brought life into our lives, Eve, love.'

'Good.' The driver nods.

'What's your name?' Eve asks.

'Sundar,' he says. 'Mean beautiful.'

'Pleased to meet you, Sundar.'

'I like how name sound when you say.' He grins. He repeats his name, mimicking Eve's accent. 'Sundar. Nice. I say this way now on.'

Eve laughs.

The rickshaw driver grins. 'What you ask before?'

'Won't you be in trouble with the other rickshaw drivers?' Eve repeats her earlier question this time speaking slowly, enunciating each word.

'No, no.' He gesticulates with one hand while shaking his head vehemently, almost running over a chicken pecking at something right in the middle of the road, which squawks indignantly as it hops away. 'I buy them tea. With tip. You give good tip, no, madam?' He grins cheekily at Eve in the mirror.

She laughs. 'It depends on whether you get me there in one piece.'

'One piece?' He looks puzzled.

'Safely.'

'Ah.' He nods so enthusiastically that the rickshaw veers off course, nearly falling into the ditch. 'I very careful driver.'

He continues nodding happily even as he rights the rickshaw, which judders over a stone the size of a brick lying on the mud road and once again almost overturns, into the ditch on the other side of the road this time.

Eve hears Izzy's laughter echoing gold as sunshine in her head. Throughout this journey she's felt neither alone nor lonely, for she's heard Izzy's voice, pictured her child's amazement and wonder, her husband's joy and excitement. It's as if her family are sharing this with her, accompanying her every step of the way. And it is solace and comfort – her husband and daughter watching over her, during this, the greatest adventure of her life.

CHAPTER 64

BINDU

1939

Footsteps approaching. Trying for stealth, but their heavy tread gives them away.

A man.

For a brief moment, sitting there, her face to the sun, just Bindu and her child in quiet solitude, palm trees swishing languidly in the humid, fruit-scented air, the fountain gurgling a lovelorn melody, birds flying above, black blemishes upon a blue gold canvas, feeling a strange languor even as her stomach twinges with cramps every so often, Bindu is loath for anyone, even the man she's here to meet, to disturb her peace. For then she'll make decisions, set things in motion and, like the struggle for India's independence, prepare for battle for herself and her child's freedom.

She smiles even as she winces at her belly cramping again – she is being dramatic, over the top in her comparison. But who knows how Guru will respond to her decision to leave him – for she will, unless he changes, and things change here, that is the ultimatum she'll set him; she's decided.

'Bindu.' Her name in his voice flowing gold.

She turns, takes him in.

Tall. Hair the colour of sunflowers.

Stubble like shorn hay dotting buttermilk cheeks.

Guava-pink lips lifted in a shy smile.

Eyes the green-gold of dewy moss reflecting sunshine.

Her heart lifts, fills, overflows, her momentary reluctance quite gone.

He's here. Her friend. She'd struggled throughout their correspondence to remember his features but now, here, he's as familiar as her own self in the mirror. The one man who respects her for her mind, who values her opinions, who's inspired her to write, who's been her sounding board and solace after Ajji died. He is her hope for a different life, although he doesn't know it yet. She'll ask him if he can book a passage to England for herself and her child. She will retrieve the money she's kept aside, the money he paid for her recipes, from her chamber to pay her way if he agrees to do so.

'Laurence,' she whispers, standing to greet him.

A spell of dizziness floors her, even as her stomach cramps sharply, but she manages to keep her balance. *I'm not used to exertion, that's all. I walked all the way here from the party suite, a longer walk than usual.*

He enters the dell, so they're encased by palm fronds, which swish gently in the sun-sizzled breeze. His ginger-and-lemon scent spices the glen, flooding her senses.

What does he see when he looks at her? She's wan, tired circles crowding her eyes. And she's pregnant, obviously so – but he knew that.

Is he disappointed upon seeing her in person after their intimate correspondence? Will she live up to the person she comes across in her letters? But how could she even try, in these stolen moments together? Why is she even thinking like this?

Because she's shy, nervous about what she wants to ask him – so much depends upon it. Most of all, she is blown away by his presence, this man whom she cares for, who's become such a dear friend, who's gifted her a means of independence in a challenging, stifling marriage. Whom she'll miss dearly when he leaves for England... But not if she soon follows, when her baby is born.

But can he really help? And is it safe to go to England with the country at war? She's not really thought it through – she wants escape so badly that she can taste it on her tongue, as tantalisingly delicious as Ajji's payasam.

She feels her eyes prick, overflow.

'Ah, Bindu,' he says, taking a step closer. Raising his hand as if to touch her, then dropping it again. Clearing his throat even as he smiles, eyes shining, the creases around them crinkling pleasingly, 'Am I that much of a let-down in person?'

She laughs, her doubts and worries temporarily eased, and he glows. 'Your laughter is poetry,' he says, smiling tenderly at her.

She beams at him, still not quite able to believe the wonder of this man standing here, in front of her, close enough to touch. This man who knows *her*. Her friend and confidant. His kind eyes the colour of wet moss warmed by sunlight.

'I'm glad we could meet properly at last,' she says. 'Especially since you're leaving soon.'

Take me with you.

He clears his throat and she recalls his nervous tic.

'We can still continue our correspondence,' he says. 'I'll write to you care of the nuns as always and share my address.'

On the third of September, England had declared war on Germany, and the very next day, Laurence had booked his passage home.

I haven't found anyone to take over the magazine, so sadly it will fold. I'll miss trying out your recipes greatly.

In polite society, I'm awkward and something of an outsider but with you, I'm myself in the truest sense of the word. It is a privilege and a gift. Over the course of our correspondence, you've become my cherished friend. And you'll always have a friend in me, distance and war notwithstanding. If there's anything you need at any time, please say and I'll do everything within my power to make it happen.

She'd read that last and thought: *There is. I do need your help, desperately so.* She opens her mouth to tell him about her bind, ask him for help – even if he can't give it, she will have tried – but her stomach cramps so fiercely, her words are usurped by a whimper.

'Bindu, are you all right?' Concern in his eyes.

'I—'

Another cramp, more painful than the last.

She clutches her stomach, sways on her feet. 'Nothing... It's... noth... Oh—'

Another cramp, more violent, if possible.

Laurence puts his arm round her, sitting her down, gently, on the bench where she reads his letters and writes to him.

'I'll get help,' he says.

But just as he turns to leave, another cramp, so ferocious it steals the breath from her. She holds on to him for dear life, waiting for it to pass.

Worry threads through her friend's voice, giving a lie to his reassurances even as he says, 'It's all right. I'm fetching some...'

She doesn't hear the rest. His voice fades into black.

CHAPTER 65

EVE

1980

'Here we are. This Suryanagar,' Sundar says, coming to a halt under a huge tree with a giant trunk that seems to have split into tributaries like a river, all the many tributaries having grown their own roots so the whole tree takes up most of the roadside, the split trunks meeting to create a vast and shady canopy.

A fisherwoman, head covered by her faded yellow sari, a very lined face, leathery skin, desultorily hawks sad-looking fish, glassy eyes glinting silver-grey in the sun, laid out on what looks like some sort of tree bark placed atop a woven basket. From the boughs above swing monkeys, jumping nimbly from branch to branch, hanging upside down, babies clutched to their stomachs, chittering nonsense all the while and regarding them brazenly. A man stands beside the fisherwoman, operating a machine that looks like a sideways bicycle, between the wheels of which he feeds long, knobbly tubes, white frothy liquid smelling nectary sweet dripping from the other end into a bowl, a great big cloud of flies buzzing around it. Into this, he squeezes lime and adds sugar, as the monkeys dangling from the trees eye the concoction with unabashed curiosity.

'Sugarcane juice,' Sundar explains.

The sugarcane vendor holds up two fingers, grinning at them, open-mouthed, displaying a completely toothless cave, blackened gums.

'Two rupees only,' Sundar translates.

'I'll try it later,' Eve says, wary of upsetting her stomach.

She turns to take stock of this village where her mother once lived, where her aunt still does.

CHAPTER 66

BINDU

1939

A booming cacophony of voices. Loud. Angry.

Fading in and out with the pain that clamps and seizes, twisting Bindu inside out and, when she cannot take another searing second of it, offering brief, glorious respite before starting up viciously all over again.

She hurts. She *hurts*. She's being torn apart by agony.

'Please, Sahib, she needs the doctor.'

Sunitha?

Her usually happy friend, sunny like her name, sounds different, her voice wet and desperate with tears.

Oh, the pain. The pain. Endure it. You can do this. For the baby.

The baby.

'What's this? Letters. She's been writing to him. I cared for her. *Loved* her. She wanted for nothing...'

Guru?

He sounds angrier than she's ever heard him and that's saying something.

Another wrenching, breath-stealing wave of pain.

When it's over and she has a brief breather before the next, the shouting slams into her. Her husband's incandescent fury. '...Was in his arms. He was the one who called for help. The cheek.

Carrying on, in her husband's, *my*, house, right under my nose, with one of my guests...'

'Sahib, the baby, your child, is coming. Memsahib's had a difficult pregnancy. She needs help...'

'Not mine. His, by all accounts. Look at all these letters. Pages and pages of correspondence with him. It's been going on for as long as we've been married! She met with him on our wedding day. I caught her. And yet I allowed her to feed me a mouthful of lies, willingly swallowed them. More fool me.'

'Please, Sahib, the doctor...'

'I cared for her. And I was stupid enough to think she reciprocated my feelings. But she... With her, I was my truest self and I dared to hope she was the same with me. And all the time she was playing me.'

'She's not been unfaithful to you, Sahib, I swear on my siblings' lives. The baby is yours.'

'How did she get the letters to him? You knew, didn't you? You were in on it.'

'Sahib, please, I beg you, please send for her doctor. The baby's coming.'

'I don't care. It's not mine.'

'Sahib, it's your child. She's not been unfaithful to you.'

'What do you call this then? All these letters, addressing each other by first names. A poetry book in her possession with love poems underlined and annotated by him...'

'It's not...'

'I recognise his handwriting from the letters. It even has my favourite poem, by Elizabeth Barrett Browning, which I'd recite to her. *Romantic love's ideal*, he's written next to it. How they must've laughed together at her naive cuckold of a husband.'

'Sahib, it's not what you—'

'And what's this tucked inside this envelope? I don't believe it! He's been sending her money? She's stooped that low?'

'No, Sahib, you've—'

'My father was right. I was swayed by her, completely taken in. I should've known when she asked me not to segregate men and women, when she picked fights with me, when she flirted merrily with men at parties. She never cared for me. I should've known when I found her, on our wedding day, with him.'

'Sahib, please...'

'I'm done. Lock her up.'

'But, Sahib, she's about to give birth. She needs medical help. You can't—'

'Enough. You're sacked. Get out.'

Wave upon wave of pain.

She can't take any more. She can't...

Blessed blackness carrying Bindu far away from this hell.

CHAPTER 67

BINDU

Pain. Tearing her apart. Accosting her in bands of tightening, excruciating agony.

She drags her eyes open. It is dark. Shadows slither down the walls, haunting the room, sinister, snake-venom black.

The pain is a savage attack, intense, enervating, focussed. It ambushes and batters Bindu like waves at sea, relentless as the tide. She has time to breathe when the band releases its hold before it clamps her stomach again in a vice even more intent on suffocation.

Her baby is coming. She's coming – now!

But where is the doctor? Guru? Sunitha? Anyone?

There's nobody here. She's on her own.

And then, all at once she remembers.

The party.

Meeting Laurence.

The pain starting then. Not as bad as this, but bad enough that she'd fainted.

And...

Hearing Sunitha crying... Her happy friend.

Pleading with Guru. His monstrous rage.

Bindu has learned during the course of her marriage that Guru is angriest when hurting the most, a furious front to hide his desperate pain. And that is also when he lashes out, blindly, raging hurt making him lose any objectivity he might otherwise have employed.

Her husband yelling at Sunitha, 'You're sacked.' And, 'Lock her up.'

He meant me.

And now, as the pain briefly loosens its hold, her eyes having adjusted to the darkness, she looks about her room. It appears ransacked. Her clothes spilling out of wardrobes, strewn on the floor. And the letters. Her correspondence with Laurence... Ripped to shreds.

'You're playing with fire. Beware. You might get burned,' Sunitha had cautioned repeatedly.

Oh, Sunitha, it's all my fault. You warned me and I didn't listen and you got burned too. I'm so very sorry.

What's the point of being sorry now? her conscience chides.

Another cramp takes hold. They're nearly on top of each other, barely any breathing space in between – her babe's arrival is imminent; she needs help. She gets up from her bed, the movement making her dizzy. She holds on to the bed until the spell passes and walks – drags – herself to the door, tries to open it.

It won't budge. It is, as she expected, locked from the outside.

She grits her teeth against a contraction, leaning against the door until it passes, and then, she raps on the wood, 'Hello, anyone there?'

'Memsahib.' A voice she recognises as Madhu's. She's taught Madhu English, read poetry to her, right here in this room. 'I'm on guard duty.' Madhu is apologetic, her voice tearful.

'I'm not your memsahib, Madhu. I'm your prisoner. Call me Bindu.'

'I'm so sorry, Memsahib.' Madhu too, like Sunitha, persists in using her formal title even though it no longer applies.

'Madhu, please send word to my husband. My baby – *his* baby – is coming. Please tell him I need help as soon as possible. *Now.*'

Madhu, sounding distressed. 'He... he knows, Memsahib. Sunitha tried before...'

Bindu fills in the pause, closing her eyes. *She was sacked* is what

Madhu is hesitating to say. Bindu is in intense physical pain, the likes of which she hasn't endured before, but this hurts too.

'He... he... insists the child's not his. He said we're not to help you. If we do, we'll not only lose our jobs but neither ourselves nor our families will find work again. Sorry, Memsahib.'

Pain. She gives in to wrenching, mind-twisting agony, holding on to the door, biting her lips until the wave passes.

'It's not your fault, Madhu,' she manages, before making her shuffling way back to bed.

My child is ready, but I'm not. I'm scared. Terrified. How can I do this on my own?

And then, even as she bites her teeth and fists her hands to endure another contraction, a miracle. Her beloved grandmother's voice: *Don't give up before you've begun. Take this in your stride like you've done everything else life has thrown at you, my heart.*

Has Bindu gone mad? Hearing her dead grandmother's voice in her dark prison of a room populated by ghosts, smelling of pain, fear, trauma.

Beeramma's daughter had given birth all on her own, she recalls suddenly, and it's as if her grandmother has planted the memory in Bindu's pain-ravaged mind. The baby arrived in the middle of the drought. Beeramma had come to Bindu and Ajji, asking for strengthening foods for the mother so she could produce good milk for the child. 'My daughter was all alone while giving birth. Her husband was scouting for work in town. I couldn't get to her, as I was ill. She did it through sheer strength of will – both mother and child are fine,' Beeramma had said proudly.

My baby will be fine too, Bindu tells herself now, fiercely.

And she hears Ajji, a smile in her voice, *That's the spirit, my heart.*

Another contraction takes hold, this one more painful than anything Bindu's ever experienced. Once again, she bites down on her lips until she tastes blood, even though every instinct in her wants to scream her pain out. But with great effort she holds it in, knowing Madhu on the other side is feeling bad enough that she cannot give Bindu the help she needs. She does not want to make her feel even more guilty and upset, which she will do if she hears Bindu cry out.

And as contraction upon contraction – they're fast and furious, one on the heels of another – tears her, ruins her, so she is gasping, her hands bunched into fists, nails digging into and breaking skin, her mouth bleeding from holding down her scream, this pain that feels like it is destroying her – a terrible, terrible thought: *What if, like my mother, I die giving birth? What of my child then, when her father refuses to acknowledge her, doesn't want her? What if she's born blue and I'm gone and there's nobody to dangle her upside down, jolt her into life?*

Another contraction.

And another.

She is spent.

She can't hear Ajji any more. Everyone has abandoned her.

She might as well give up.

But…

Her baby…

I will not be defeated. I will fight till the last. This child's father has disowned her. She has only me. I'll be there for her. I will not give up. Thousands, millions, of women give birth alone. I can do this. I will live to see my child. If she's blue, I'll hold her upside down until she cries. We'll be fine, both of us. We will.

But she is so tired. She yearns to give in to the inviting, glorious oblivion hovering just at the edges of her eyelids.

But no. *No.*

My baby needs me.

And so, she pushes, she fights against her agony, the desire to give up, give in, close her eyes and sleep away the pain, even as her body is squeezed in a pincer vice, ripped from the inside out.

Another contraction. And another.

She is so very tired.

Her eyes closing of their own accord. She cannot hold them open. The blackness winning…

And now, Ajji's voice once more, coaxing, gently, *You can do it, my Bindu. You are lucky, my heart. My best girl. You* must *do this for your very own best girl.*

Ajji holding her hand, there when she needs her. *Push, my heart, just a little more, a little longer. The last stretch. Almost there. Come on, you can do it.*

And in her mind, instead of the welcoming oblivion, she focusses on Ajji's voice that has blessedly returned to her.

And in this sweat- and blood- and angst- and terror-infused battleground of a room, her prison, she pushes with all her might and finally, a slippery gush.

A cry.

Not hers. A reedy mewl. Just as Ajji described when narrating the story of Bindu's dramatic birth. Her baby.

Her baby.

With great difficulty, her whole body protesting, she sits up, gathering the tiny sproglet emitting plaintive cries that simultaneously rend and thrill Bindu's awestruck heart, lying in a pool of blood and gore, to her heart. Carefully, she wipes her child's face, her body, with her sari pallu. A girl. Of course. Minuscule mouth open and screaming, her tiny perfect face scrunched up in outrage at having to exit her mother's womb so violently, so disgracefully.

Ten curlicues of baby-snail fingers and toes. Glorious tendrils of wispy black hair. So exquisitely delicate. So amazingly perfect. *Her* miracle of a child. Her skin a healthy, furious gold.

There. Ajji's voice festive with joyous delight. *What did I tell you? You are strong. You are amazing. You did it, my heart. She's beautiful. A feisty fighter. Just like you.*

Gently, Bindu pats her baby's tender head, silky clouds of ebony erupting from a nest of two whorls.

And if Bindu didn't know before that this little one was Ajji's last, most precious gift to her, she does now.

Double crown. She's lucky, Ajji says, smiling tenderly, *just like you.*

CHAPTER 68

EVE

1980

Suryanagar is quiet. Quaint. Tiny. Beautiful.

Eve's heart does a strange little flip – is it recognition? Is this where she was born?

Fields stretching as far as the eye can see, on either side of the mud road, bordered by coconut trees, with storybook-pretty hamlets dotted here and there. Green ears of paddy, dusted with the ubiquitous coating of mud dancing in the sun-baked breeze.

It has a timeless feel to it – Eve imagines it's pretty much unchanged from her father's time. How did he meet her birth mother? How did they come to exchange recipes? Did he come here? Why? He was a journalist; what occasioned him to venture to this small village in the middle of nowhere? So many questions and she wonders why it hasn't occurred to her to ask them before. She makes up stories for a living, but as to the story of her provenance, her own life, she's been decidedly uncurious. No longer. Now, she's determined to find out. She doesn't want to get her hopes up, but she *is* hopeful, now she is here.

CHAPTER 69

BINDU

1939

Her baby cries constantly and Bindu places her at her breast, but she can't do more than that. She doesn't have the energy. It seems to have dissipated after the terrible trauma and exquisite joy of giving birth. Darkness crowds the edges of her eyes, blurring her vision, pulling her eyelids closed. She feels drained. Burning hot one minute, shivering cold the next.

Her baby cries and Bindu wants to placate her, but she can barely hold her.

She loves this child with her all, but doesn't seem to have the strength to do anything other than clasp her to her breast. When she tries to rock her, she feels faint, pitching forward, even though she's sitting down and nearly keeling over.

She holds her crying child and tries feebly to bat away the darkness that shadows her vision, rendering her dizzy.

What is wrong with you? Where's your oomph? Soothe your child. Be the mother she needs.

She tries to – she tries – but she can't.

She no longer hears Ajji's voice, but at the dark edges of her faint spells, Ajji waits, smiling at her warmly with that love- and pride-filled gaze that assured Bindu she was the centre of her world.

My child is the centre of mine, Ajji, but I can't help her. I can't stop her crying, for my energy, my life force is bleeding from me.

For Bindu's been bleeding continuously, excessively, since she gave birth. She knows post-partum bleeding is normal, but not like this, not this much.

Ajji smiles tenderly at her. It's as if she's conveying something, but Bindu can't read what her grandmother's trying to say.

Bindu had tried standing up after her baby's birth, clutching her infant to her chest, but the dizziness that she can't seem to shake had propelled her to her knees. She had dragged herself with all her rapidly waning strength to her dresser, her babe in her arms. But this too, like the rest of the room, has been subject to Guru's rage, ransacked, its contents strewn haphazardly across the floor.

Scrabbling around, she'd found her little brass pot of kajal under the carpet. She'd picked up the kajal, which she used as eyeliner, and recalled how she and Ajji used to make their own with sandalwood paste and castor oil.

'Natural beauty product,' Ajji would say, beaming. And, once she'd prepared it, she'd apply it under Bindu's eyes, on her lashes and, for good measure, behind her ears, plus a tikka on her forehead: 'To ward off the evil eye, seeing as you've grown into such a beauty, as I always knew you would. My Bindu, beautiful inside and out.'

And now I've a daughter of my own and, although this kajal is not made by me, it's all I have, and hopefully it will protect my child, Ajji.

She had dipped her pinkie finger in the kajal and applied it gently to her baby's forehead, and behind her ears, plus one tikka on each cheek, perfect black circles on her child's downy, sweet-smelling skin, to ward off evil. Bindu had dropped kisses on her baby's kajal-dotted cheeks and the little one had opened her eyes and squinted up at her, her cherub lips curving upwards briefly. A gift.

You're perfect, my love, Bindu had thought then, *but I'm not. I'll try to protect you to the best of my ability, but I fear it may not be enough.*

Madhu had called from the other side of the door. 'I heard the cries, Memsahib. Everything OK?'

'I've a baby girl,' Bindu had marvelled. She was resting against the door – after she'd grabbed the kajal pot, she'd not been able to move further than the door, the small exertion of finding the kajal and applying it to her child having exhausted her. 'She's perfect. Beautiful.'

And she heard Madhu's awe, even as she sobbed. 'You're amazing, Memsahib. You did it all on your own. I wish I'd been able to help. We're not even allowed to give you food, Memsahib. You're only sanctioned one chapati and a tumbler of water each night, I'm so sorry. You must be so weak and needing sustenance to feed the baby. I wish I could help.'

Now, hours later, the baby's not stopped crying and Bindu is devastated that she cannot console her child, for she is weary to her very bones and even this simplest act of love, soothing her upset babe, seems beyond her.

The kajal has now been rubbed off by her baby's tears and Bindu's kisses. She applies it again, having kept hold of the pot.

Her baby wails.

A knock at the door.

Madhu. Madhu's voice, distressed earlier with the pain of not being able to help, now sounds resolute. Determined. 'We went to your husband.'

'*We*?' Bindu whispers. She's slumped against the door, still unable to garner the energy required to move to the bed, and can hear Madhu on the other side.

'All of us servants employed here. We petitioned, pleaded on your behalf. Assured the Sahib that you'd been faithful to him, that it was his child, a baby girl you'd birthed on your own. That you and the baby needed to be seen by the doctor. But he won't see sense. He says he doesn't care what happens to you or the child.'

Bindu is too exhausted to feel animosity or anger towards Guru, too spent for anything but remorse that she cannot comfort the child she loves more than life itself, love her like she aches to.

'But, Memsahib,' Madhu is saying, 'that doesn't mean we can stand back and watch you and your cherub suffer, you who've done so much for us. If anything happens to you or the child, we couldn't bear it. We don't want it on our conscience.'

And now Bindu is moved to say – a throaty whisper all she can manage – 'But he said...' She summons the energy to speak louder, to be heard above her child's wails, but it hardly makes a difference.

Madhu hears her all the same. She must be crouched on the other side of the door with her ear pressed to it. 'Yes, Memsahib?'

'He said that you'll never work again and neither will your families.'

'He cannot sack *all* of us. And even if he does, thanks to you, Memsahib, teaching us to read and write in English, we have avenues. We'll go someplace out of the landlord's sphere of influence and find jobs – we can do that now, because of you.'

Madhu's words a balm, a brief distraction from her fatigue, her distress at being unable to soothe her child's cries. Then, a thought: 'But the village is your home.'

'Yes, but it was also our prison until you, Memsahib. You've given us freedom, opportunity, agency.'

The freedom Bindu had wanted, yearned for, because of which she's here now, under literal lock and key. She has felt trapped in this mansion, by the rigid constraints of her marriage, but even so, she has managed to provide the servants with a means of escape. Madhu has given her a gift. She's in enervating agony, physical and mental, but even so she tastes happiness, bright gold, briefly on her tongue.

Madhu is saying, 'We can move out of the village if we want to, while before we couldn't – we were stuck here, beholden to the landlord, forever in his debt because of his atrocious rent, no means of paying it back because our husbands' hands were tied in the drought. Now, due to the water tank and the irrigation system, our crops are always good and not subject to the whims of the monsoon, so we can pay the landlord's rent. Our children are winning scholarships and going on to study in the city. All thanks to you, Memsahib. We can't stand back and watch this atrocity when you've done so much for us. We're determined to help.' Madhu takes a breath and now, her voice gentle: 'The reason I knocked is to ask you to move away from the door. The butler has given us the key and he's going to distract your husband while we look after you. We are coming in.'

And then the door is opening and Bindu can hear the servants moving around her, sense the shock they're trying, and failing, to hide.

Gentle arms holding her, but she holds tight to her baby.

'Oh, Memsahib,' they cry. 'Oh, Memsahib.'

'I'm nobody's memsahib,' she whispers. 'I cannot even care for my child whom I love more than anything.'

'You saved her by giving birth to her all on your own. You've saved an entire village. You've saved all of us. You are our memsahib.'

They carry her gently to the bed.

She holds on to her child.

'You need medical help.' Madhu's voice is quivering with upset. 'One of us will go to your doctor, beg him to talk sense into the Sahib and allow him to visit with you.'

Bindu grabs Madhu's arm – it takes utmost effort. 'My child...' Her voice shaking. 'Is she OK?'

'She's perfect. She's just upset that her mother is ill.'

But Bindu can hear worry in Madhu's voice, the fear she is trying desperately to hide.

She tries to focus on Madhu's face, but it blurs before her pain-assaulted eyes. 'Tell me the truth. You've been present at many births. Your siblings, your own children. Is my child all right?'

'She's absolutely fine. You've done brilliantly, Memsahib.'

She believes Madhu and feels relief, payasam-sweet despite her body giving up on her.

'What about me?'

Madhu's eyes fall away. 'The doctor's coming. You'll be all right once he's—'

'Ah,' Bindu says, holding her sobbing child closer to her, dropping a kiss gently upon her downy head. It requires all of her strength to do so, but she does it again and again, savouring the feel of her baby's hot little body against her own weak one, her cries so full of energy, of life.

Now, Ajji hovering smiling at the edge of her hazy vision makes sense.

And it also makes sense why her child hasn't stopped crying since she arrived in the world. Her baby senses their imminent parting.

'They're wise souls trapped in infants' guises. This is why in their first few days, and especially when they exit their mother's bodies, they look so old and wrinkled – they still carry the imprint of their previous lives upon their faces,' the midwife would opine.

Oh, my love, how I wish I'd more time with you.

'Please take her to Sunitha. She'll look after her,' she says to Madhu, and those few words – every one of which she means – take everything out of her, for this is goodbye.

'Don't give up, Memsahib,' Madhu cries, but there is no fire behind her words.

And if Bindu didn't know she was dying before, she definitely knows now. Her pregnancy was difficult, risky, which was why the doctor had advised bed rest. Giving birth on her own did for her. But she's managed to save her child, like her own mother did for Bindu – dying just as Bindu had exited her womb.

'I love you,' she whispers, dropping another kiss onto her child's head. The kajal has washed away again, a casualty of her tears and her child's. 'Listen,' she whispers to her daughter. 'I was brought up by my Ajji. I never knew my mother but I never felt the lack. You won't too. It's what I wish for you and it *will* happen.' She looks at Madhu. 'Won't it?'

'We'll make sure of it,' Madhu promises fiercely.

'I'd like her to be independent, free to study, to work, to live her life *her* way. I'd like her to discover the powerful wonder of poetry. To visit England one day. See daffodils.'

'She will, Memsahib.' Madhu is crying openly now.

Gently kissing her child, Bindu picks up the kajal pot and draws a round tikka on the babe's forehead, behind each ear and on each cherubic cheek.

'This will protect you, even when I'm not there,' she whispers, trying and failing to hold back the tears that smudge the sooty kajal on her child's cheeks.

And then, Bindu hugs her little one to her heart, whispering endearments and her wishes for her child.

She commits her baby's face, which is already stamped in her heart, to memory, the feel of her child in her arms.

The kajal will keep you safe, it will keep you from harm. I love you, my heart, now and always.

She turns to the waiting servants, who'd resented her when she arrived here, but are now her very own army.

'We'll keep her safe. She will be loved, don't you worry, Memsahib. But don't give up yet, the doctor'll be here soon to see to you – we'll make sure of it.'

It's too late for me, Bindu thinks, and sees that truth reflected in Madhu's eyes.

Madhu holds her arms out for Bindu's babe.

No. I don't want to.

Her daughter emits a keening, heart-rending wail of protest, different from her sobs of before, as Madhu takes her from her mother.

It breaks Bindu's already broken heart. Her body feels bereft. Her arms wanting to hold her child. Her whole being arching towards her baby, aching with yearning.

Give her back. She's mine.

She's mine.

And then her baby is gone and Bindu is in that room, smelling of death and birth and violence and love and pain and loss and heartbreak. It's as if her heart has been wrenched out of her and taken away and she is but a shell, pining to hold her child just one more time.

She hears Madhu's receding footsteps and she thinks, *I'll never know what happened, but I can hope. She's Ajji's gift. She has the lucky*

double crown. She will know love. She will be loved. She will enjoy a
profession that fulfils her, a partner who makes her happy, children who
complete her and bring her joy. She will live a full, free and happy life.

She can no longer hear Madhu's footsteps. And now, with her
daughter, her life, her heart, her love gone, she finally lets the
tantalising darkness that has been nudging at the edges of her
consciousness take over and it is comforting as Ajji's embrace.

CHAPTER 70

EVE

1980

'Fifty rupees, madam, plus tip,' Sundar, the auto driver, grins at Eve.

'Wait. Aren't you taking me to the Bindu Charitable Institution?'

'You say Suryanagar.'

'Please could you take me to the Bindu Charitable Institution? It's in this village.' It's run by Aunt Sunitha and it's also where she lives and works.

He scrunches up his nose, shakes his head. 'I no live here. I not know where it is. I ask.' He turns to the man hawking sugar-cane juice and the fisherwoman, who's been regarding Eve unashamedly since they got off the rickshaw with the same unblinking curiosity as the monkeys and talks to them rapidly in their sing-song language.

The fisherwoman nods busily and, turning to Eve, grins widely. The monkeys jabber among the tree branches. Spiced, fruit-scented air strokes Eve's face with humid caresses.

The fisherwoman stands up with an audible cracking of her knees. She rolls the sheet on which the fish basket was resting into a ball, plants it upon her head and then hefts the fish basket atop it.

Sundar beams at Eve. 'It nearby. Shortcut through field.' And, nodding at the fisherwoman, 'She take you.'

The fisherwoman turns to Eve, eyebrows raised as if to say, *Coming?*

'But what about her fish?' Eve asks.

'Give her tip, like you give me.' Sundar grins and, with a cheery wave, starts up his auto to a screeching din from the monkeys.

The sugarcane juice man sighs and Eve, feeling sorry for him, presses a ten-rupee note into his hands.

He folds his palms in thanks.

The fisherwoman rocks on her feet, shaking her head, her expression clearly implying, *Are you coming or not?*

And, picking up her case, Eve follows her down the rough path between fields, ears of paddy gently swishing her legs in velvet reassurance, feeling energised, for she is finally here, in the land of her birth, something she wouldn't have imagined a few weeks ago, excitement unfurling, bright and hopeful.

CHAPTER 71

EVE

The path between the fields is precarious, only wide enough to walk single file and place one foot in front of the other. While Eve concentrates with all her might, the older fisherwoman dances ahead, hips swaying elegantly despite the basket of fish balanced on her head, hands swinging freely by her sides. She waits every so often for Eve to catch up.

Crows natter and parrots screech from among the branches of the trees lining the fields. Cows moo and a dog barks. A branch strokes Eve's cheek, nectar-sweet, the tree laden with ripening yellow fruit. Mangoes!

They come to a gurgling stream, a narrow tree branch laid across it serving as a bridge.

A hill rises from the stream and atop it are perched several cottages nestling among a cornucopia of fruit trees.

The fisherwoman pirouettes across, her bare feet barely making contact with the branch, and waits for Eve on the other side.

As she carefully navigates the makeshift bridge, Eve catches glimpses of fish, silver-bright in the stream. And is that...? Oh! A water snake, navy velvet skin glinting and glimmering as sunlight shimmers, twinkling gold on the water.

Eve pictures Izzy's delighted amazement, Joe's happiness, and she feels buoyed. Something about this place inspires her, making her feel hopeful for the future. For during this journey, she's felt her husband and child's presence more keenly than while at home, she's heard them in her head saying, 'Move on, live your life, for we're right beside you every step of the way, experiencing life with you.'

Perhaps she needed to get away, travel here, to learn this truth – that she has lost her family only in *this* world, that they are not with her physically, but they are also always with her, watching over her, by her side.

A rough track, hewn by hordes of feet, leads up the hill.

Eve lingers briefly at a tree halfway up, fascinated by its knobbly brown fruit that smells sour *and* sweet. She racks her brain. Ah, tamarind.

The fisherwoman watches her from atop the hill. She's had to wait for Eve several times, but the smile's never left her face, which is creased like a very lined sheet of paper.

Eve encounters a pepper tree further up the hill, rife with red and green peppercorns, their potent spice tickling her nose.

At the crest of the hill, a courtyard, replete with more exotic fruit trees and shrubs. Rosy yellow pineapples, like starry gifts.

A dog comes bounding up, barking at first and then, when the fisherwoman chats to him, licking the dust off her feet and doing the same to Eve, staring up at her with huge, befuddled eyes when he encounters the hard, leathery obstruction of shoes.

'Hello there.' Eve bends down and pats the dog, who licks her hand and jumps up to lick her face vigorously.

Eve cuddles the dog and takes in her surroundings avidly, spotting banana trees and others bearing saffron and peach fruit shapely as a woman's torso, with a grey shell dangling down. They smell of liquor, alcoholic, fermented. Eve feels a thrill as, all of a sudden, she recognises the fruit. Cashew! And the hard grey shell encases the nut she loves. It's immensely rewarding and satisfying to actually encounter these fruits she's only read about and seen on television until now.

And then, her attention is snagged by a round cement surround, a cat sunning itself languidly upon the rim, net on top from the front of which dangles a spinney with a pail and rope attached.

An actual well! Eve cannot resist walking towards it for a closer look.

As she approaches, the cat stretches sinuously, cool orange gaze regarding her with disdain before it morphs into a snarl for the dog, who's followed Eve and who barks and prepares to give chase. But the cat is fast and has disappeared even before the dog's taken a single step towards it. He comes back to Eve's side, having apparently decided that she's his new friend.

Eve peers through the net into the dark, seemingly endless tunnel that appears to be the entry to hell itself, repelling the cheerful dazzle of sun, permanent night within its hellish depths. But there, a twinkling glimmer of silver undulating through the interminable shadowy navy.

Satisfied by this tantalising glimpse of water at the base of the well – and, she has to admit, a tiny bit spooked – Eve turns back to the courtyard.

Hibiscus flowers sing in crimson exuberance. Sunny marigold smiles greet her cheerily. Colourful saris, faded cream vests and chequered cloths sway on a washing line strung from the well to one of the coconut trees rising above the hill at the edge of the courtyard. Multi-hued butterflies and moths flit among the foliage, shiny beacons.

The fisherwoman leads her up the path in this lush orchard, which widens as they approach the cottages. Bright yellow walls contrast sunnily with red-tiled roofs.

From the chimney of the cottage nearest to Eve, zesty steam rises, heady and scented with caramelised sugar, sizzling onions, roasting garlic, heralding a feast. The smells remind Eve of cooking with her daughter from her mother's recipe book a world away – she knows them, but out here, they're all the richer, more potent, soaked in radiant sun-crisped sweetness.

A patch of earth in front of the cottage is swept clean and on this, on mats woven from coconut fronds, neat lines of red chillies dry in the sun. And beside it, a woman squats atop a stool, pounding herbs and spices into a velvety green paste.

The woman looks up as they approach. Her face, upon seeing the fisherwoman, lights up in recognition and she smiles, saying something in their language. Then her gaze lands on Eve and her mouth opens in an O of shocked surprise, her eyes shining and pooling with tears.

'Memsahib,' she whispers.

Eve clears her throat, bemused by this display of emotion.

'My name is Eve,' she says. 'You must be Aunt Sunitha.'

The woman stands, comes to Eve, walking with a limping gait. She raises a trembling hand up to Eve's cheek, cupping it. Her tender touch feels to Eve like benediction.

'You're the image of your mother,' she exults in halting English, her voice bright with awe and wonder.

CHAPTER 72

BINDU

1939

Arms round her.

A voice: 'Bindu.'

Familiar. One she recognises.

From where?

She should respond.

She tries.

But...

Her whole body heavy. Eyelids weighted down. She cannot open them.

'I'm so sorry, Bindu.' Wet drops dotting her body. Cool on her hot skin, but why then does she feel so agitated?

She's missing something. And the loss *hurts*.

She wants to speak, ask for explanation. But her mouth is a wound. Her tongue won't cooperate. It feels like her heart's been wrenched away, her body flayed open.

'Please don't leave me. I couldn't bear it. You're the only woman, the only person, I've loved completely, with my all. That is why I did what I did. I couldn't bear the thought of you with someone else. I'll regret it all my life. I... I just hope it's not too late, Bindu. Please let it not be too late. When Sunitha came to me...'

Sunitha. There's something Bindu needs to remember. Something of hers, entrusted to Sunitha...

'The guard had let her in while the butler was distracting me. All the servants, Bindu, they've ganged up against me, on your behalf. They're your soldiers. They don't take orders from me any more.'

The man is sobbing and laughing at the same time.

Sobbing...

Sobbing like her heart was breaking and it broke Bindu's heart for she couldn't console her.

Oh. Oh. Oh.

The missing. The ache. Her body bereft. Empty. Yearning. Wanting.

In vain.

Her baby. Her child.

Gone.

'You're quite something, Bindu. Inspiring loyalty, love, a following. "You've sacked me, so you've no power over me. I'm here to give you a piece of my mind and you *will* listen," Sunitha said, "for the memsahib, my friend, is dying and you're the cause."'

I am dying. My child is gone. Entrusted to Sunitha.

What Bindu has done. Best for her child. Even though it's hell for Bindu.

Hell.

Sunitha, my friend, I know you'll love her like Ajji loved me, with your all. She'll have the freedom I wanted for her.

'I was so shocked,' Guru – for Bindu now knows it is her husband – is saying, through his tears, 'that I did listen. And I am sorry. I wish I could go back, Bindu, undo my last few actions...' Guru takes a shuddering breath. 'The anger. It blinded me. You see, you're the only person who has ever seen the real me. My father has never cared for me. My mother was too meek, too passive. She loved me but gave in to my father always, let him bully me, stood back and allowed it. She was bullied by him too, so I don't blame her.'

'I know, Guru,' she'd say if she had the energy to speak.

'I yearned for my father's love, hankered after it. I told myself I hated him, but I loved him. I love him.'

I know.

'Then you came along – the exact opposite of my mother – refusing to be bullied or cowed, fiery and feisty, and all that unreciprocated love I had in me, I transferred to you and I hoped that you'd love me back, unlike my father. This is why I'd get so angry when I thought you were flirting with other men, when I suspected you cared for the villagers more than me... I knew I couldn't force you to love me and that made me hurt and upset and I lashed out. But I hoped that I wasn't entirely unlovable – that you, the only one to see the real me, would grow to love me.' A shuddering breath. 'When you started cooking again, there were a few months when I allowed myself to believe that you had...'

I did love you, I realise now. Especially when you showed me kindness after Ajji died. This is why it hurt so much when you were heavy-handed like your father, refusing to let me help with the business, expecting me to conform. This is why I was so angry and resentful, why I picked arguments with you, why I lashed out time and again.

Laurence was never my love. He was my friend. He offered me the independence I craved. I wouldn't have left my marriage, for I was making a difference, bringing about change for the villagers. But I liked flirting with the idea. Having it as an option. Seeing the money I earned by publishing my recipes grow and thinking I could leave, travel to England and the independent life that had always been my ideal if I wanted to. I wouldn't have walked out of my marriage until I found out I was carrying our child and then... then I wanted to give her the freedom I'd been denied.

As if following her train of thought, her husband is saying, 'But then you found out you were pregnant and, instead of bringing us together, it pushed us apart. You picked arguments with me every time I visited. I put it down to pregnancy hormones – I was so excited about our child that I consulted the doctor and read up all I could. I hosted a party, thinking that would cheer you up. It was meant to be a surprise, which was why I'd already sent the invites.

I told you about it at the doctor's say-so; he warned me that a big surprise was not advisable at this stage of pregnancy.'

You were being thoughtful. But, Guru, it was too little too late. I took it as just another instance of your high-handedness and in retaliation I wrote to Laurence, inviting him to the party.

'And then I discovered that at the party I gave for you, celebrating our baby, you had a liaison with Laurence Elliot. You fainted in his arms. And it didn't stop there. I discovered your letters – you were corresponding with him throughout our marriage...' Raw hurt in his voice. 'And the poetry book, with the poem I'd recite to you, that for me encapsulated our love, annotated by him. I saw red. I wasn't thinking straight – I decided that the reason for your distance during pregnancy was because it was Laurence's child, that you were planning to run away with him the night of the party – I found the money too and that gave credence to the idea – and that your plans were foiled because your labour started.'

Oh, Guru, we got it so wrong.

'I was *so* angry. I loved you. You were all I had. And you... I thought you'd betrayed me. That you did not love me. That I was unlovable...'

If she was able to, she'd say, *You're not unlovable. You have too much heart, but I refused to see it, for, as Sunitha pointed out, we're each as stubborn as the other.*

'I couldn't handle it, Bindu, I couldn't.' He sobs. 'I wanted to punish you just as much as I loved you. I was hurting and I wanted you hurt too. But not this. I don't want this. How do I live without you, especially knowing I caused this?' He takes a shuddering breath. 'Sunitha told me that you've entrusted our child – and I know now she is *our* child – to her and her fellow villagers. I will honour your wish, Bindu. I'll pay for our daughter's upkeep, love her from afar.'

Ah Guru, it's for the best. Darkness threatens, as she feels the last of life drain from her.

Her husband is sobbing even as he recites the lines of the beloved Elizabeth Barrett Browning poem.

She thinks of her legacy. Her child. Rescued by servants who once resented her but came through for her when she needed them most, her very own army. Her child she has bequeathed to the village Bindu wanted to escape, where she'd felt claustrophobic, the village where she was free and happy – she realised only after she left – the village that she won round.

She had craved a different life, but as she nears the end of this one and prepares to meet Ajji in the afterlife, keep a watch over her child from there, she thinks, *I didn't do so badly in this one.*

She might not have had the independent life she'd craved, but she managed to bend the fierce, temperamental man she married to save her grandmother to her will, many a time. She had manipulated the landlord, whom she'd hated, who had made their lives a misery, to help the very people he'd terrorised and bullied. She might not have made a success of her life in the manner she wanted to, but she paved the way for others to do so. She instigated scholarships so other village children would follow their dreams. She installed a water pump and an irrigation system to help with the drought. She *has* made a difference, made the most of the cards she was dealt. She has left a legacy. Ajji's recipes with her tweaks published in magazines. A child. A village changed. A husband who loves her. But whose love ultimately became their downfall.

With the last remaining ounce of her strength, she squeezes her husband's hand, which is holding hers tight, his tears anointing it.

And like that, her hand joined with her husband's, their child in Sunitha and the villagers' care, Bindu travels towards Ajji, who is waiting with a couple she doesn't recognise but feels drawn to and a dog who makes her heart swell and sing, joy and love.

'Come, my heart.' Ajji beckons to her. 'Dumdee and I feel it's time you were reunited with your parents. We'll keep watch on your cherub together. Isn't she lucky to have so many people to look out for her in her world as well as in the afterworld?'

And now, at last, Bindu is free.

'This is the boys' orphanage,' Sunitha says, leading Eve through rooms that are brightly painted and partitioned into cubicles, with a table, a chair, a wardrobe and bed in each one. 'And that cottage next door is the girls'.' Sunitha points. 'That's the kitchen,' she adds, indicating the cottage from where zesty aromas spice the air, honey-sweet and chilli-hot mingling to create a mouth-watering, stomach-rumbling celebration of flavours. 'It was where your mother's hut was.'

'Oh.' Eve breathes, overwhelmed.

'I was tempted to leave her hut as is, for purely sentimental reasons,' Sunitha says. 'But it wasn't practical – the hut was only one room, for a start...'

'She lived in one room?'

'We all did.' Sunitha shrugs. 'Everyone in the family – parents, grandparents, children, even animals, in some cases, when there was a tiger prowling...'

'A tiger!' Eve is awed.

Sunitha smiles at Eve's expression. 'In any case, the hut your mother had shared with her grandmother was falling apart. It felt fitting to build the kitchen cottage, sturdy brick and mortar in place of mud walls that leaked during the monsoons and cracked during the drought, here, as cooking made your mother's soul sing. She was happiest when she cooked for people.' Sunitha's eyes shine.

Eve squeezes her hand. In the tree branches above them, birds twitter. The jackfruit-scented air that strokes Eve's face is soothing, a perfumed caress. *Are you looking on, Ma? Is this your way of telling me you can see me?*

Eve shakes off the whimsy, but she can't help but feel comforted, convinced that on some level her birth mother, whom she never knew, is here with her, feeling connected to her in a way that she's never experienced before. Yes, she had the recipe book and always felt a link to her, but here, her birth mother's presence feels tangible, vital, real.

The dog, who'd run off to growl at a parrot that dared alight on a scarlet hibiscus flower, bounds up to her.

'This is Dishoom, Dumdee's descendant. He's become your shadow. It's fitting, no? Dumdee never left Bindu's side and now Dishoom has declared allegiance to you, although I'm the one who feeds him.' Sunitha laughs, her entire being aglow, and Eve is floored by affection for this woman who was her mother's dearest friend, whom Bindu loved.

'Now, that cottage near the well' – Sunitha points – 'hosts the bathrooms, laundry rooms et cetera. Those cottages over there on land acquired from Chinnakka and her good-for-nothing husband – for a very good price, mind you, and yet still he complained – are the women's refuge. Chinnakka ran it after her husband finally met his maker. Not soon enough, in my opinion. Now she's retired, yet still bosses everyone around.' Sunitha chuckles. 'Good for her. She took enough flak from her husband, time she did some bossing of her own.' She barely pauses to take a breath. 'The women are having their siesta now, but you'll meet them soon.'

'Ah,' Eve says, taking in the buildings nestling among an abundance of fruit trees, green foliage swaying in the spice- and grit-laden breeze under the bright white canvas of sky, gilded light filtering in through branches, dancing on red-tiled roofs, spilling buttery-bright down yellow walls. A tropical paradise. 'This is wonderful.'

'All thanks to your mother,' Sunitha says softly, eyes shining.

'She was an amazing woman. In her too-short time on this Earth, she changed all of our lives for the better.'

I wish I'd known her, Eve thinks, identifying the warm swell of her heart as pride for the remarkable woman who'd birthed her.

Sunitha sniffs, wipes her eyes with her sari pallu. 'The children are at school, but they'll be here soon. They've their routine: eat, play in the orchard, homework, wash, bed.'

Eve smiles – it almost exactly mirrors her routine with Izzy, with Maya.

'The nuns still run the village school, although they take fees now, out of necessity, as it's expanded so. But we, the Bindu Foundation, provide scholarships and bursaries for children who cannot afford the fees. And we cover the fees for all the children in our care.' Sunitha beams at Eve.

Tour over, they sit in the courtyard, side by side, Eve and her mother's best friend. Around them, the coconut, mango, guava, jackfruit, cashew and banana trees sway in the grit-soaked breeze. Crows cast black scowls upon the jewel-bright sky. The air that strokes their cheeks tastes of spices. Gilded rays of light dapple the water of the stream, so it gleams like a twinkle in a lover's eye.

'Tell me about Bindu,' Eve says.

Sunitha tells of a girl who was feisty and fiery and extremely bright, who wanted to forge her own way but changed tack to save her grandmother's life. Who refused to be cowed by circumstances, instead making the best of what she'd been dealt, in the process changing countless lives, even as, ultimately, she lost her own. She tells of a couple each as stubborn as the other, a man blinded by love, turned mad by jealousy, with devastating results.

'I loved her,' Sunitha says. 'She was my best friend, the sister of my heart. I still miss her and will do so every day I'm alive.' She takes a breath. 'She changed our village for the better. She gave us confidence, showed us we could do anything we set our mind to, in any circumstances. She showed that we always, always have hope. That we can make a difference, whatever happens.' And then: 'Wait here. I'll be back in a second.'

Dishoom settles at Eve's feet, keeping her company as above them, among the branches of the mango tree, parrots call, and in the fields, peacocks dance, showing off their kaleidoscopic plumage. Sitting where Bindu must once have done, Eve feels a kinship with her mother. A conviction she can't explain – the certainty that she's watching, and that she's happy Eve is here.

'Here...' Sunitha is back, holding out a stack of notebooks.

'Are these my mother's?' Hope flaring in Eve's heart. *Please say yes.*

'Yes,' Sunitha says. 'She was always writing, jotting down ideas and recipes. She'd several of these notebooks. When Guru found the letters, I grabbed as many as I could and hid them in my sari skirt. He destroyed the others.' She sniffs.

Eve takes them reverently. 'But you kept these.' She runs her hand gently over the notebooks her mother once touched, containing her writings, in English. Beautiful cursive handwriting, the script faded but legible. 'Thank you,' she breathes, tasting gratitude and anticipation.

Her mother, she sees as she tenderly flicks through the pages, was a writer. Poems. Stories. Beautiful vignettes describing this very village and featuring Ajji alongside a vast array of characters, the villagers Bindu grew up among, Eve surmises. Almost an entire notebook devoted to Dumdee.

'Here...' Sunitha points to a notebook that looks marginally less worn than the others. 'This one contains her writings from when she was pregnant with you.'

Eve's fingers tremble as she lets the notebook open randomly onto a page.

I know you're a girl, my heart. I will call you Eve. I loved the name from the first time I heard it. The nuns told me it means 'life' or 'living'. For that is what I want for you: the freedom to live a full, happy, fulfilled life of your choosing. I wish for you, my heart, to know love and to be loved completely and uncon-ditionally, like I was, like you are the centre of someone's world.

She was. Her parents loved her like that and so too did her husband and child.

I also wish for you:

Daffodils, which, I believe, are bright yellow heralds of sunny promise, in every season.

To discover the healing power of poetry, the transporting magic of words.

The freedom to be who you are, to be, always, true to yourself, to live life to the full.

Ah... Eve is overwhelmed. *I have been loved. I have loved. I've had a fulfilling life and it's not over yet.*

'You were loved by a village, guarded fiercely by all of us when communal riots and the fight for independence tore our village apart,' Sunitha says. 'It was mayhem. So many people dying needlessly, neighbour turning on neighbour, such unwarranted bloodshed. We wanted to protect you – you were orphaned by then, both your parents gone. And so, when Laurence Elliot returned from England asking after Bindu, wanting to introduce his wife to her, we entrusted you to him. Your mother had trusted him, loved him like a friend. But not only that, we could see that both Laurence and his wife fell in love with you at first glance. His wife, like Laurence, was gentle, capable, kind. A nurse who'd tended to him when he was wounded in the war – he attributed his recovery to her. They loved you. It was good enough for us.' Sunitha takes a breath.

I lived here until I was three and yet I've no recollection of it at all, Eve marvels. There are fuzzy impressions, certain scents triggering déjà vu, but nothing concrete, except, now she's here, a sense of connection – to her mother, and strangely to her husband and daughter too.

Sunitha's faraway gaze settles upon Eve, a smile creasing the lines on her face. 'Nevertheless, I said to them, "If you don't look after her, love her, like Memsahib wished, you've not only myself but the entire village to answer to."' Sunitha's laughter festoons the air, iridescent gold. Then, 'We missed you dreadfully.' Her eyes shine. 'We pined for you. But, like your mother had, we gave you away to protect you, keep you safe. We did the right thing, didn't we?'

'You did,' Eve says, squeezing her hand, thinking, *I've been blessed many times over, loved so very much.*

'She'd wanted you to go to England, see daffodils,' Sunitha says softly, her gaze once again parting the mists of the past.

'They're my favourite flower.' *Izzy's too.*

'There, I'm glad.' Tears glitter pearly silver on Sunitha's cheeks. She makes no move to wipe them. 'She'd have been *so* proud of you. An author. She was so good with words. She was good at anything she set her mind to. She married to save her grandmother, even though she wanted to be independent. And then she made it her crusade to save us. She hated being fortunate while we were suffering. She never forgot her roots.'

'She sounds a remarkable woman,' Eve says. Every one of Sunitha's letters reiterated this, but now, having seen and experienced, first hand, her mother's legacy, she truly understands the sentiment.

'She was. She had her faults too, of course.' Sunitha laughs. 'She was stubborn, headstrong. Once she set her mind to something, she wouldn't listen to sense. She was hot-headed, overconfident, but kind, loving, fiercely loyal with it.'

Eve thinks of Izzy. She was just like her grandmother. *Izzy, are you with her? With Bindu?*

The air once again deposits mango-flavoured kisses on her cheeks. A blessing. An affirmation.

'My father?' she asks. It occurs to Eve that while the recipe book and her aunt's letters have forged a connection to Bindu, there's never been such with her birth father and perhaps this is why she's not thought of or considered him until now.

'He... After Bindu died, he lost himself in drink. He died

almost exactly a year to the day Bindu did, a few months after his
father passed away, leaving the entire estate to Guru. Bindu was
the love of Guru's life and he could not get over her death.'
Sunitha sighs deeply. 'He paid for your upkeep, and he visited you
during those brief spells when he was relatively sober. We tried, all
of us, to get him to give up drinking, and bless him, he did
attempt to do so, for your sake, but he could never sustain it for
long enough – he was consumed by guilt and remorse. He died of
a broken heart.'

'Oh.' Eve is saddened.

'Such heartbreak,' Sunitha says, shaking her head. 'And all
because two equally stubborn people wouldn't, couldn't, communicate with each other.' A pause, then, 'But good came out of it.
After his father's death, Guru wrote off the debts of all the
farmers indentured to the landlord, allowing them ownership of
the land they lived on outright. He left the mansion to the
villagers, care of myself, to do with as we wished. It's a hospital
now, providing free medical care to the poor. He also left half his
business empire to the villagers for improvements, such as Bindu
would have wished. That's exactly what he stated in the will, and
he made me the executor.' Sunitha sniffs. 'So, the irony is that
the wealth that Guru's father had so scrupulously guarded and
amassed at the expense of the poor is now distributed among
those very people, and it's saved and transformed countless
lives.' She waves her hand around the compound, lush with fruit
trees, a haven for people in need. 'Thus all this is your mother's
legacy.'

Eve is awed afresh, and again, she feels her heart balloon with
pride. *My mother, in her short life, did this.* And on the heels of that,
another thought: *I've lived longer than my mother did on this Earth. I'm
alive but, recently, I haven't really been living. I've been wallowing, directionless. But here is my direction. I must continue what Bindu started.
And there's still much to do. My daughter might not need me any longer,
but other children do. I couldn't save her, but there are several others who
need saving.*

She thinks of the children she saw begging on the streets on
the way here, their emaciated bodies, their gaunt, bedraggled

faces, sunken gazes pleading for deliverance, that man sleeping in the ditch who'd regarded her with wounded eyes.

'And the other half he's left to you, in trust,' Sunitha is saying. Her words jolt Eve from her rumination.

'What?'

'I thought you knew.'

'I didn't.'

'I was the original trustee, but when you were adopted, I made Laurence the trustee. He didn't tell you?'

Her father had been notoriously impractical, not caring about material things, content to live in a world of words. He'd ignore his finances until he had no choice but to tackle them and then both Eve and her mother knew not to disturb him, for he'd go about with a thunderous scowl on his usually sanguine face.

Now Eve recalls him saying over the phone, when he too was diagnosed with cancer, Eve's mum already suffering from the disease, 'I've something I must tell you when we meet, some business with your adoption...' But they never got around to discussing it, for her mother went downhill soon after and died within weeks, and her father never quite recovered from it. Then the accident happened and after that, Eve ignored all the mail that accumulated. She'd neither the heart nor the energy to look into and sort her parents' legal affairs while she was dealing with all the heartless paperwork arising from the death of her husband and child – her family's passing, so huge as to be incomprehensible, the end of her life as she knew it, reduced to a few emotionless sheets of paper. She'd ignored the many letters and calls from her parents' solicitor.

The applause of happy noise wafts on the sun-sizzled air, startling Eve from her musing. The fields explode with the joshing of children, the music of their voices.

'Ah, they're back.' Sunitha smiles.

The children sit in rows on mats on the floor of the dining room of the kitchen cottage, banana-leaf plates in front of them. The older kids on serving duty dish out pickle and chapatis, rice, sambar, rasam, curried bitter gourd and spiced potato, with *sheera*, semolina pudding studded with raisins and nuts, for afters.

The hall resounds with chatter and laughter. The women from the refuge drift in, babes on their hips, multi-hued saris and glass bangles reflecting light in kaleidoscopic radiance, anklets ringing a merry tune. They natter among themselves and peruse Eve shyly, blushing and turning away when she catches their eyes.

The children have no such qualms and bombard her with questions.

'Who are you?' they ask.

'She's Bindu's daughter,' Sunitha says, pride coating her voice.

'Bindu,' they breathe, voices awed. 'The lady after whom this orphanage is named?'

'The very one.'

Their eyes light up in wonder, even as they eat their food with merry gusto.

They smell of mud and innocence, gritty sweetness, these children who have no parents but are loved and looked after by a village of volunteers, Eve's mother's continuing legacy. Her mother who lived such a short life to the very fullest, in that time making a lasting impact.

After they've eaten, the children run among the fields playing hide-and-seek and catch like kids everywhere, their wild cries startling the crows chattering in the trees above them. They fly away in a fluster of wings, dark scribbles upon a white-gold canvas. Parrots screech in annoyed agitation, red beaks glinting, green feathers ruffled. Peacocks rival the children's noisy clamour as they scatter among the paddy, tails spread in rainbow-bright outrage.

The women gossip, sharing paan, babies clinging to them, watching Eve with wide, curious eyes when they think she's not looking.

The older girls cluster around Eve, admiring her hair, her clothes.

Festive scents waft from the kitchen cottage, sugar syrup clashing with sizzling garlic.

Sunitha, sitting amid a cluster of women shelling tamarind and weaving coconut fronds into mats, smiles at her.

The dog licks her feet in loving caress despite the obstruction of her shoes.

Eve thinks of her mother, growing up here, pounding spices in the shade of the guava and cashew trees. She throws her head to the heavens, twilight descending majestic over the fields, the sky orange and magenta, burnt sugar and crimson rose, the setting sun mellow honey, the evening air, flavoured with spiced fruit, fragranced with love and loss and nostalgia, rustling with whispers of her beloved lost, caressing her face.

Her heart feels full.

EPILOGUE
EVE

The line is crackly and plagued by static, but, nevertheless, Eve hears the barely suppressed excitement in Sue's voice: 'Your memoir has sold for six figures! And translation rights have sold in seven territories already and are being hotly contested elsewhere.'

'I...' Eve begins.

But Sue has more to say. 'And that's not all – your *mother's* memoir has gone to auction and is set to break all records!'

Eve had crafted the book over the past few months from the journals that Sunitha saved, adding explanatory notes to fill in the gaps.

'One publisher declared that it "chronicles the changing face of India pre-independence alongside an Indian woman's coming of age".' Sue's voice breathless with excitement. 'There's even talk of a movie deal!'

'Oh!' Eve is overwhelmed, one hand upon her heart, the receiver, sticky with sweat and wonder, in the other. 'Thank you, Sue.'

'Don't thank me. It's all down to you and your mother. Well done.'

From the fields, happy noise drifts on the sugary breeze. 'The children are coming. I must go.'

'You're still persisting with your stubborn idea of staying there then.' Sue affects a long-suffering sigh.

'I've a purpose here, Sue. I'm making a difference, continuing my mother's legacy. I lost one family but have, miraculously, found a new one. Where I had one child before, now I've several. The women at the refuge are my friends.'

'The women and children here are my family,' Sunitha had said simply, her eyes glowing with contentment, when she first gave Eve the tour. 'When I was a girl, I wanted a large family, more than anything. And now, thanks to your mother, I have one.'

Eve couldn't have put it better herself – it's exactly how she feels now, several months on. In the evenings after the children are in bed, she sits in the courtyard with the women, shadow-spattered dusk infused with cinnamon and chillies, spiced ginger and jaggery, Dishoom's head resting on Eve's lap, floppy ears and wet nose twitching as he snoozes. They burn eucalyptus to keep mosquitoes away, sip caramelised tea and snack on jalebis and nut brittle to sweeten the woes they share alongside paan and sisterhood. It is humbling and eye-opening, sharing confidences with these women who've been through so much. When Eve hears what some of them have endured, it dawns on her afresh how lucky she's been, how blessed. And yet, they are generous and open-hearted, they haven't lost their humanity despite having undergone inhuman suffering.

'Every experience teaches you something about yourself and the most difficult ones shape you. They brand you, burn you, but you come out of them changed for the better,' one of the women at the refuge had said the previous evening.

And Eve had thought of Joe and Izzy, her two loves, once her whole world. She would always miss them, always mourn them, but loving them has shown her how much love she has to give. Losing them was the worst ordeal of her life and she had thought her life was over – but here, she was wrong, as her daughter had pointed out, for she had more to give. Like these women, Eve has endured; not on the same scale, perhaps, but she's been branded by pain and loss and come through the stronger for it.

'Are you planning a visit home any time soon?' Sue is asking.

Home. England will always be her home, but Eve has realised that a person can have more than one home, family. 'Not in the near future. I'm in the midst of establishing refuges, orphanages, schools and hospitals in other villages with the proceeds from my birth father's bequest...' Eve is grateful for many things since coming to India, not least learning more about her birth father, a complicated man who ultimately did the right thing.

'I get it. You're doing vital work. But I miss you, you know.' Her brash friend suddenly soft, her voice tender.

'Come visit, Sue. Jenny and Maya are visiting when school breaks up. Come with them. You'll love it here, I promise.'

'It's one thing to trek across London, another to cross continents and oceans for an author!'

'Ah, but not just any author. Your favourite one.'

'Debatable.'

Eve hears the love in her friend's voice. 'You want to, really.'

'I'll think about it,' Sue says, but Eve can tell she's smiling.

'In any case,' Sue adds briskly, '*you* must plan a trip *here* next spring.'

'Oh?'

'Your memoir. The publisher says it's good to go, very little editing necessary. They've scheduled publication for the twentieth of March next year, the first day of spring. Put that in your diary.'

Oh. Eve is overcome, the hand not holding the phone upon her heart, for she's learned from Sunitha that the twentieth of March is Bindu's birthday. What a fitting tribute to her amazing mother this will be! 'I've one request.'

'Yes?'

'For the book jacket...' Eve shuts her eyes, imagining a world where Bindu is alive and well. She and Bindu cook side by side in Eve's home in England, where she once concocted her mother's recipes with her daughter and imagined the woman who gave birth to her cooking these recipes as a child on the hearth of a mud hut a world away. Samosas warm in the oven, tea, spiced with cinnamon, cardamom and crushed ginger, is stewing and the gulab jamuns they've made together have infused the house with their heady nectar aroma. Outside, daffodils grin sprightly yellow smiles, revelling in the gilded spring sunshine that carries the promise of warmth to come. 'Do you think the designer could depict that on the cover? And I'd like to call it *Cooking with the Mother I Never Knew.*'

A LETTER FROM RENITA

Dear reader,

I want to say a huge thank you for choosing to read *The Spice Maker's Secret*. If you did enjoy it, and want to keep up to date with all my latest releases, just sign up at the following link. Your email address will never be shared and you can unsubscribe at any time.

www.bookouture.com/renita-dsilva

I hope you loved *The Spice Maker's Secret* and if you did, I would be very grateful if you could write a review. I'd love to hear what you think and it makes such a difference helping new readers to discover one of my books for the first time.

I love hearing from my readers – you can get in touch through social media or my website.

Thanks,

Renita

facebook.com/RenitaDSilvaBooks
x.com/RenitaDSilva
instagram.com/RenitaDSilva

AUTHOR'S NOTE

This is a work of fiction set around and incorporating real events.

I have taken liberties with regards to the Indian setting, picking characteristics, such as food, vegetation and customs, from different parts of India to fashion my fictional villages and cities; the areas I have set them in may not necessarily have places, cuisine, flora, fauna and rituals like the ones I have described.

The verse from the Bible that Bindu remembers Sister Hilda quoting when she enters the landlord's mansion for the very first time is not quite word for word – I have employed artistic licence for the purposes of the story.

I apologise for any oversights or mistakes and hope they do not detract from your enjoyment of this book.

ACKNOWLEDGEMENTS

I would like to thank all the incredibly wonderful, efficient, brilliant and so very nice team at Bookouture for all you do for my books.

I am especially grateful to Maisie Lawrence – you are beyond amazing and I feel incredibly lucky and *so* privileged to have you as my editor. Thank you for your advice, kindness, patience and insight. You are the absolute best.

Huge thanks to Jenny Hutton, editor extraordinaire. I am so grateful to you for homing in on the story I want to tell. I cannot thank you enough.

Thank you, Jade Craddock, for the wonderfully thorough line edit. I'm so very grateful and lucky – you are amazing.

Thank you, Jacqui Lewis, for your eagle eye and wonderful suggestions during copy-edits for this book. Thank you, Jane Donovan, for proofreading this book.

A million thanks to Lorella Belli and all the team at Lorella Belli Literary Agency for your untiring efforts in making my books go places and for being all-round wonderful and brilliant.

Thank you to my lovely fellow Bookouture authors, especially Angie Marsons, Sharon Maas, Debbie Rix, June Considine (aka Laura Elliot), whose friendship I am grateful for and lucky to have.

A huge thank you to my mother, Perdita Hilda D'Silva, who reads every word I write; who is encouraging and supportive and fun; who answers any questions I might have on any topic – finding out the answer, if she doesn't know it, in record time – who listens patiently to my doubts and who reminds me, gently, when I cry that I will never finish the book: 'I've heard this same refrain several times before.'

I am immensely grateful to my long-suffering family for willingly sharing me with characters who live only in my head. Love always.

And last, but not least, thank you, reader, for choosing this book.

PUBLISHING TEAM

Turning a manuscript into a book requires the efforts of many people. The publishing team at Bookouture would like to acknowledge everyone who contributed to this publication.

Commercial
Lauren Morrissette
Jil Thielen
Imogen Allport

Data and analysis
Mark Alder
Mohamed Bussuri

Design
Jules Macadam

Editorial
Maisie Lawrence
Ria Clare

Copyeditor
Jacqui Lewis

Proofreader
Jane Donovan

Marketing
Alex Crow

Melanie Price
Occy Carr
Cíara Rosney

Operations and distribution
Marina Valles
Stephanie Straub

Production
Hannah Snetsinger
Mandy Kullar
Jen Shannon

Publicity
Kim Nash
Noelle Holten
Myrto Kalavrezou
Jess Readett
Sarah Hardy

Rights and contracts
Peta Nightingale
Richard King
Saidah Graham